ONE NICE DAY IN LOVELY BAY

POLLY BABBINGTON

POLLY BABBINGTON

AuthorPollyBabbington.com

Want more from Polly's world?

For sneak peeks into new settings, early chapters, downloadable Pretty Beach and Darling Island freebies and bits and bobs from Polly's writing days sign up for Babbington Letters.

© Copyright 2024 Polly Babbington

All rights reserved.

This book is a work of fiction. Names, characters, businesses, places, events, and incidents are either the products of the author's imagination or used in a fictitious manner. Any resemblance to actual persons, living or dead, or actual events is purely coincidental.

1

'All I want is one simple, easy, nice day. One nice day. That's it. Just one,' Cally de Pfeffer mumbled to herself. 'Really? Is one nice day just too much to ask?'

Going by the way her life had panned out so far, clearly, it was. In actual fact, she'd go for half a day. An hour would do.

She continued to talk to herself as - in her regular Cally uniform, she wore rain or shine, of thick tights, short skirt, white shirt with a ruffle and jumper - she sprayed cleaner onto the bathtub in her best friend's house with abandon. As she scrubbed the bath's sides with a cloth and chatted to herself, hot, miserable tears ran down her face. Wiping the plughole until it shone, she shook her head as she played out her grandma's funeral in her head. Truly awful. So *very* bad. None of it had been nice. Were funerals ever nice? Probably not. Her grandma's, though, had been particularly horrible, sparse, and sad. Grim, actually, and to cap off the grimness, she'd never felt more alone. Grim and alone. Pretty much summed up her life, really.

She stood up, analysed her work in the bathroom, grabbed a cloth, and rubbed the bath taps until they gleamed. She then did the same thing on the sink taps as she thought more about what had occurred at the funeral. She shook her head in bewilderment that neither her stepdad nor her half-brother David had even bothered to grace the occasion with their presence. Not that she'd wanted them to be there anyway, but somewhere in the back of her mind, she'd thought that they might have had the decency to turn up. No such luck in that department. Neither was particularly decent, so she shouldn't have been surprised when they hadn't shown their faces. It still stung, though, in a way. Anyone would have felt the same.

They had been there quickly enough, cap in hand, when Cally's grandma had been taken into a home and the house had been put up for sale. They'd also lined up with their hands out, palms up, when Cally's grandma had died and the finances were being sorted by the solicitor. Cally did a funny little sniffy snort at the notion that her half-brother David had thought that he was going to get his hands on some of their grandma's money. Little had David known that most of the money had been spent on a multitude of costs, mostly care and equipment.

There had been *some* money left, though it wasn't really much to speak of at all. Thankfully, it had been cleverly tied up in a trust. Cally's grandma might not have had the use of her legs at the end, but she'd still had her marbles, just about... and had been adamant about finding a way for Cally - and Cally *only* - to get what was left of her money. Cally and her grandma had thought they were pretty clever in tying up the money by squirrelling it away into a trust. What neither of them had seen coming was that David would contest everything and that it would get ugly.

Thank goodness they'd had the best legal advice and David hadn't stood a chance. Cally bit her lower lip and shook her head as she wondered how David had had the brass neck to try to get his hands on anything to do with their grandma. He'd never been interested in being part of the tiny family since the day he'd walked away when he was fifteen. He hadn't even stepped foot in his grandma's house, as far as Cally had worked out, for a good fourteen years but had been there quickly enough for a handout.

As she smeared her tears away with the cuff of her sleeve, she took a couple of disinfectant wipes from a bright yellow packet and began to work her way backwards on her hands and knees out of the bathroom. Scrubbing back and forth on the tiles, she tried to put what had happened with David behind her. He wasn't worth her tears and definitely shouldn't be given any of her headspace. Finishing with the wipes and pleased with the sparkly clean floor tiles, she then folded two white towels so perfectly that they didn't look real, placed them carefully on the heated towel rail, and closed the bathroom door. Her best friend Eloise had let Cally stay in her place for a month as she'd gallivanted around the Caribbean. As one did. Cally made sure that Eloise would be getting home to a spotless house.

As she cleaned, Cally couldn't stop thinking about the fact that David had had the audacity to ask for money when, all the while his grandma had been sick, he'd not even shown his face. He clearly had no qualms at all about what was right and wrong in the world. Cally had been the one there through it all. He'd not even darkened the door at any stage. She tried not to worry about it, but in the back of her mind, she kept thinking about all the sacrifices she'd made over the years to look after her grandma. All the times she'd had to turn down things she'd wanted to do. The many events she'd missed out on. To have him turn up and think he could have a slice of the tiny pie made her see red. Sometimes, she'd thought she would blow a gasket as what felt like literal red-hot steam hissed out of her nose and ears. To top it all, the saddest thing was that before Cally had cared for her grandma, she'd been David's and her mum's carer, too. Cally de Pfeffer had been a carer for most, if not *all*, of her life. At least one thing was clear: now the only thing she had left to care for was herself. First time ever.

Cally had spent too long feeling as if she'd held up the sky for everyone and everything: for her grandma, for finances, for her mum, for David, for anyone who cared to chime in, really. She'd kept the sky up with the best intentions because she'd loved her mum and her grandma and, for that matter, David, too, but she now realised that holding up the sky had been a long, hard slog of doing stuff for other people and totally forgetting about herself. Who'd been holding up her sky? Who'd washed and ironed her blouses for school? Who'd looked after her heart? Who'd scrubbed her toilet pan? Who'd cared about her infrastructure? Who'd plaited her hair when she'd not been able to reach the back? Who'd tucked her up in bed and read her a story at night? She winced in recognition of the answer. It was quite simple, really: no one at all.

She yanked another disinfectant wipe out of the packet and ran it across the top of the brilliant white bannister in Eloise's house and felt more than grateful that she had Eloise in her life. They'd met one summer strawberry picking at a farm to earn extra money and had been friends ever since. Eloise's life had taken a very different turn from Cally's, but their friendship had strangely stood the test of time. Eloise had been a steadfast support, always there with a cup of tea and a listening ear, ready to help Cally vent. Eloise was about the only person in Cally's life who knew a modicum of the truth.

Finishing cleaning all three upstairs bathrooms in Eloise's huge house, Cally grabbed the vacuum cleaner, plugged it into the socket on the landing, whipped off the long pole section and began to push the nozzle brush back and forth, going backwards down the stairs as she did so. With each push of the nozzle into the pure wool carpet, she went over the state of her life. By the time she got to the ninth step, she'd admitted to herself that unless something changed, and quickly, she was going to have to consider herself officially homeless. The tears continued to pour.

As the vacuum sucked and Cally pushed, she felt delirious about what she was going to do. The problem was that she'd taken her eye off the ball. When her grandma had finally been taken into a hospice and the house had been sold to pay for care, Cally had rented a tiny house on a seventies housing estate about forty-five-minutes or so on the train from a little coastal town called Lovely Bay where she worked in a pharmacy. She'd hated the house with its horrid cheap windows, kitchen with a hatch, dreadful excuse for a landlord, and naff plastic front door, but it had done the job and kept a roof over her head. As she'd focused on her grandma, who had got sicker and sicker but not quite sick enough, the rent on the little house had gone up month by month, the cost of living crisis had tightened its grip, and competition for rentals had become fiercer than fierce. She'd known that rental increases and the housing crisis were a thing and that she'd needed to do something about it, but between her grandma's final days, her shifts at the chemist, organising the funeral, her online job, and all the stuff she'd had to deal with at the solicitors, she'd simply lost track of time. That was a huge mistake.

As she'd realised that she was no longer going to be able to stay in the rental house and had looked around to find somewhere else, it had become a losing battle. One she now desperately needed to win. It was *terrifying*. Cally might have had to worry about a lot of things for the whole of her life, but concern about a roof over her head had never been one of them. That had changed. A new low.

By the time she'd made it to the bottom of the stairs, in her head, she'd been around and around in circles. The landlord had given her notice on the house because she'd simply not been able to stretch to his latest hike in the rent. She'd been turned down for every place she'd applied for, and when she'd been to the council in the hope of having a chat with someone who could help, she'd been told in no uncertain terms that she was barking up the wrong tree. There was a long line of people, some with babies, some who had arrived on boats, some with many more problems than her and she'd be right at the end of that. Get in line Cally de Pfeffer and wait your turn at the back. Just as you always have.

Sitting on the bottom step of the stairs, she pulled her phone out of her pocket and refreshed the page on the property site to see if anything new had appeared. Her heart jumped for a second as she saw a new listing. The house was the same as the one she was about to vacate, but with an even worse, tattier front door. She tapped excitedly and then felt her heart sink when she saw the price. No go there, then. She couldn't even afford to live on a horrible, dated social experiment estate from the seventies where no one really wanted to live. Grim.

Tapping onto one of the many Facebook property rental groups she belonged to, she trawled through despondently. About the only comfort she could take from it was the fact that she was definitely not alone in not having anywhere to live. There were so many posts from other people desperately looking for places to rent that it actually made her feel ever-so-slightly better. At least there were other people in the same boat. She scrolled back to the top and tapped the community page for Lovely Bay, the place she worked and wanted to live. She read down and let out a gigantic sigh. Not only were properties super expensive, there were hardly any available either. For a long, long time, she'd wanted to move to Lovely Bay, but as the months had marched on, the third smallest town in the country had become further and further out of her reach. In light of the ferocious competition to secure a house in Lovely, clearly she wasn't the only person who could see its merits.

After making herself a cup of tea in Eloise's kitchen, she decided to make a list in an attempt to get some clarity. By the end of the list, she wasn't sure whether she should feel better or worse. There were a few things on the positive list: she could look for another job now that she didn't have to fit things around caring for and visiting her grandma, she had a good little part-time job at a chemist in Lovely Bay and another online job working as a customer service chatbot responder for a retail company, she had a degree not that it meant much and she had support from Eloise. She had money in the trust she could dip into for absolute emergencies and she had a friend who always had her back. The negative list wasn't looking quite as rosy; she had no real opportunities for a career having missed that boat way back when she'd been in the midst of caring, she was a disaster at relationships, her family was non-existent and she only had a few weeks before she had to move out of the house she was renting and her horizon wasn't looking pretty at all.

Sighing almost constantly, she finished her tea, tucked the vacuum back in the cupboard under the stairs, and went around the house checking everything was shipshape. She made sure each window was locked, gave the marble kitchen worktop an extra polish, and moved the vase of faux flowers from the table in the sitting room to the hallway so that Eloise would be greeted by them when she walked in. Eloise wasn't back for a while but Cally had a lot on and wanted the house to be ready. After switching the alarm on, she listened by the front door and waited for it to stop beeping, checked on the app that it was set correctly, took a carton of Ribena out of her bag, stuck its straw in the top and headed for the train station as another fresh batch of tears pricked at the corner of her eyes.

Cally de Pfeffer needed one nice day in her life and it needed to happen very soon.

2

An hour or so later, after popping into the chemist in Lovely Bay where she worked, Cally had talked herself up. Someone needed to. She still had two weeks before she was homeless, so all was not lost. Even though she really did not like her plastic door rental on the seventies estate she was going to jolly well make the most of it. She'd decided that the merits of a good curry, the fire (albeit electric and bar) on, a bottle of wine, cosy slouchy socks, and a book would do her the *world* of good. She'd gone to the little shop in the middle of Lovely Bay, bought herself ingredients to make a curry, treated herself to a bottle of wine and a new book, and told herself not to worry too much and that *something* would come up. It had to. Homelessness wasn't for someone like her, was it?

With her shopping bag over her arm, as she was ambling along the High Street in the direction of the train station, she bumped into Millie, the woman who worked in the chocolate shop. Cally knew Millie via Birdie, her boss at the chemist.

Millie smiled and raised her eyebrows. 'Hey, our Cal. How are you? So sorry to hear about your grandma. Birdie told me everything that's been going on with you. Sounds tough. Hope you're okay.'

Cally felt pleased to have someone care, at the same time as not wanting to really talk about it. In an instant, she flicked a switch at the back of her throat to pop her voice up a level. At the same time, she widened her eyes just a little bit and blinked rapidly a few times. It was a little trick she'd learned at school when teachers had asked her how she was. In those days, she'd pretended she was fine. She'd not wanted to alert anyone about what she'd been dealing with at home. She'd not been okay in those days either. Not in any shape or form. Caring for a mother with mental health problems and a younger brother did that for a girl. She was, however, an absolute master of looking as if she was bobbing along nicely on the top of the water whilst, in actual fact, she was flapping at full speed underneath. 'I'm fine. Thanks for asking.' People were kind to ask, but in a way, she was over it.

'It must have been hard for you. How was the funeral? Bit of a silly question, but you know what I mean. Bad or much worse than bad?'

Cally contemplated for a moment. Millie didn't really want to hear the answer that Cally really wanted to give. People didn't want to know that the funeral had been grim and sparse and that no one had been there to have Cally's back. No change there, then. It was much easier to say that her grandma had had a nice send-off. People preferred to think that's how it had gone. No one wanted to get their head around sad, grim, miserable funerals with a few odd people here and there. Then there was how Cally felt about it: an odd mix of shame and embarrassment that the funeral had gone as it had. She lied through her teeth. 'Ahh, yes, it was fine as funerals go. Not too bad.'

Millie looked sympathetic. 'Yep. Not nice ever, in my opinion.'

'No.' Cally attempted to sound a lot brighter than she felt.

Truth be told, she'd come to terms with her grandma's passing a long time previously. Now, she wasn't deeply sad as such, more sliding slowly on from it, transitioning. She'd only really told the truth to Eloise that her grandma's passing had, in the end, been *mostly* a relief. Part of her was glad it was over. She needed to start being Cally and just Cally, not Carer Cally for the rest of her life.

'What have you been up to otherwise? Trying to get over it all? Birdie mentioned you've had a few problems with family stuff.' Millie rolled her eyes kindly. 'You can't make it up sometimes, can you?'

There was no way Cally was going to say that she'd spent the previous few weeks desperately searching for somewhere to live and that the way she was going, she would end up in the hotel on the side of the motorway near her rental house. Cally nodded. 'Yes. This and that. Keeping busy…'

'Birdie said you've been a bit down. Is there anything I can do to help at all?'

What would Millie say if Cally answered by asking if Millie could find her somewhere to live? 'Ahh, thanks for asking, but no, I'm fine. All good.'

'Have you had any luck finding anywhere to rent? Birdie said you'd come to a dead end.'

'I haven't, as of yet. I've had my fingers crossed that I'd find somewhere in Lovely, but it looks as if that's not going to happen. You know how tightly held it is. Plus, it's all about who you know.'

'Yeah. It's tough. Places hardly ever come up in Lovely, let alone at the moment.'

'Nope, and everyone wants to live here. The rental market is cutthroat.' Cally raised her eyebrows. 'I've wanted to live here for a long time. At least I work here, so I get some of the benefits. I was lucky to find a job with Birdie. She's been so good to me, too.'

Millie nodded in agreement. 'It's a great place to work, sure. Sorry to hear you haven't found anything yet. What are you going to do?'

Cally thought about the fact that she'd looked at rooms in some dreadful places. She felt embarrassed that she was even considering some areas. She told a little white lie which, although not wholly untrue, was definitely stretching the truth. 'Oh, it's fine. I can stay at my friend's house if the worst comes to the worst.' There was no way that Eloise would turn her away, but she didn't want to be the loner in someone's spare room who had outstayed their welcome. Plus, she'd always thought of herself as independent and able to look after herself.

'Ahh, you poor thing. Hopefully, something will come up.'

Cally felt herself gulp. She was dismissive and appeared not to be concerned. 'I'll be fine.'

Millie held her hand up. 'Hang on a sec. I'll get you something to cheer you up.'

A few minutes later, Millie handed over a small white box. 'A new recipe we're trying. They're not even on sale yet. Salted caramel truffles but with a sprinkle. A Lovely twist. I think you'll like them. They might cheer you up a bit. Chocolate has its very own healing properties.'

Cally smiled. She adored the chocolate from the chocolate shop. Not that she ever bought it for herself. It was way too much of a luxury, but Birdie always had a box of it on the go. 'Oh, wow, thank you so much. So kind of you.'

'You're welcome. Right, I'd better get on. I hope you're feeling brighter soon. Go easy on yourself.'

'Yes, thanks.' Cally held up her brown paper shopping bag. 'I've just treated myself to a bottle of wine for this evening and I'm going to make a curry, which will help. I need comfort food. The truffles will top it off nicely.'

'Sounds like just what you need. Have a nice evening. Stay warm.'

'Will do. See you later.'

~

About ten minutes later, Cally was sitting on a bench at a jetty beside the River Lovely, waiting for a riverboat to arrive. She chuckled to herself as she read the signs that use of the wharf was entirely at one's own risk and that tide times varied. French-speaking patrons were apparently welcome and passengers had to check the noticeboard for the Friday lunchtime timetable. Everyone in the know knew what that meant - one of the owners disappeared on Fridays to meet up with an old flame. She loved the funny little riverboat service, its staff and patrons.

She watched as the riverboat puttered along towards the jetty, rocking gently with the current. Slap bang in the middle of commuter time, the boat was packed with people on their way home from work. As it approached the wharf, strings of fairy lights twinkled against a clear, dark, early evening sky and started to unload passengers. She pulled her beanie closer around her ears, picked up her shopping bag, and shuffled over to the end of the queue of people waiting in line to get on.

Despite the chill in the air, the riverboat, doused in its little lights, looked cosy and inviting, and it made Cally smile. The tiny little cabin windows were steamed up and the name painted on the bow in an old-fashioned font glinted in the jetty lights. It was really cold but oh-so-pretty. Cally watched as it docked, and the ramp creaked under the footsteps of disembarking passengers. Like her, they were wrapped up in scarves and hats against the biting wind coming off the river, little puffs of vapour coming from their mouths as they hurried along.

A few minutes later, unable to find her usual spot downstairs at the back, she walked up the stairs in the middle of the boat, heaving the hefty bag full of shopping, and snagged the last seat on the top deck near the front. She settled onto the hard bench seat, grateful to have found a spot, popped her bulging shopping bag by her feet, and tucked her scarf in her coat, bracing against the chill river breeze. As the riverboat chugged away from the wharf, Cally lost herself in a world of her own for a bit and stared out over the inky dark waters of the river. The strings of fairy lights adorning the boat twinkled their reflection in the current, making the surface appear to shimmer and dance. As she watched the little lights sparkling, she pondered her increasingly frustrating and bordering on downright scary house-hunting situation.

She'd been scouring online property listings, Facebook groups, and estate agents' windows for months. Along with a multitude of other people, she'd traipsed from viewing to viewing around the area. At first, she'd thought that nothing had ticked any of her boxes, but now she couldn't give a hoot about ticking boxes. There was now only one box and it was a crucial one - a roof over her head. At the start of her hunting, she'd seen an affordable little terraced house not far away from the hospice her grandma had been in but had thought that it was just that little bit too far from the train station for her commute into Lovely. She'd not jumped on it right away, and it had been snapped up from under her nose by another prospective tenant who'd offered six months' rent in advance. It had been then that she'd suddenly realised that she was playing a game with not many winners.

Trying to quell a rising panic that she had nowhere to live, Cally exhaled heavily, her breath puffing out in a cloud in front of her. At the rate she was going, she would have to settle for a room in a shared house. The idea made Cally's chest tighten with stress, disappointment in herself, and annoyance about her situation. She didn't want to be in a shared house. She was too old and too set in her ways to be sharing a bathroom with twenty-year-olds and labelling her milk in the fridge.

'Next stop, Lovely Bay station!' she heard Colin, the boat pilot's scratchy voice crackle over the tannoy. Cally continued to stare at the twinkling lights reflecting on the rippling waters as the riverboat puttered onwards through the darkness with the looming Lovely lighthouse lit up in the distance. She tried to stay positive and cling to the idea that something would come up. She just had to persevere until the right place appeared. Getting down in the dumps and sinking into feeling sorry for herself wouldn't help anything. She straightened her shoulders and forced herself to take a few deep, calming breaths of the cool river air. All she could do was keep pushing forward.

As the riverboat approached Lovely Bay station, Cally gathered her things, preparing to disembark. She heaved the bulging shopping bag onto her lap, the weight of it digging into her thighs. Then, getting up and holding onto the railing, she stood at the top of the stairs, waiting for the person in front of her to get to the bottom. Just as she began to make her way down the stairs from the top deck, the bottom of the bag suddenly split open and her shopping flung itself this way and that.

Cally swore. 'What the heck?' she yelled as she watched her new paperback book, the chicken for her curry, a bottle of Ribena (not the supermarket version, the one with the actual gold top) and a pot of curry powder go tumbling down the timber steps.

Everything suddenly went in slow motion as she watched her bottle of wine plop down step by step and land at the bottom, still in one piece. Just like that, a man in tan chinos, a shirt with a crew-neck jumper over the top, a scarf, and boots who was sitting on a bench seat at the bottom of the stairs immediately sprang into action at the commotion. He picked up the bottle of wine and gathered the chicken from under the bench as Cally stepped down the stairs.

'That was something,' the man said as he lunged after the pot of curry powder, which was rolling its way across the deck.

Cally immediately took in his fancy accent and expensive-looking wool jumper as he scrambled to collect the fallen items. He was not too hard on the eye. 'Oh my goodness. Sorry! You don't have to do that. I'm so terribly sorry,' Cally fussed. She felt her cheeks flush with mortification as all eyes on the boat turned on her. She hurried down the bottom step, almost tripping over her own feet, and crouched down to scoop up the book before it got trodden on by disembarking passengers.

'Not a problem.'

The man's eyes. Brown, serious, clear. Just so very nice. The end. She snapped her head to bring her back to the situation. 'Nothing landed on you, did it?'

The man smiled, gathered up Cally's planner and a tin of tomatoes that had rolled under the bench seat, and started to hand things over. 'Nope, I'm still in one piece even though I just got rained on by...' He looked at the pot in his hand, 'A jar of curry powder. Not to worry. I've had worse things thrown at me, to be fair.' His accent was posh, his arms muscly. The legs were long. Chest, oh-so-wide. He handed more retrieved items back to Cally.

Cally gulped as she held her hand out and looked up. A literal movie star was standing in front of her. Everything about him, from the way his hair was cut to the jumper with the scarf, screamed wealth, confidence, and general all-around gorgeousness. So out of Cally de Pfeffer's league. So very, very nice. Cally had never felt more frumpy and self-conscious. The smell, yes, that too. Was it something citrusy mixed with vetiver or patchouli? Old money thrown in there with the citrus? She fussed with the packet of chicken. 'Sorry about that. I didn't think the bottom would fall out. Obviously.'

The man looked around as he gave Cally the items. 'Do you,

err, have another bag?' He patted the pockets of his chinos. 'I might have one.'

'Oh! No, you really don't have to do that...' she started, flustered. She pulled her handbag around to the front and pulled out a carrier bag that she'd folded origami-style into a triangle.

The man took the bag and raised his eyebrows, 'Nice. Organised and prepared. I like a bit of origami on a Waitrose bag.'

Ooh, he sounded kind and nice and confident and sort of casual, but not, all at the same time. Cally's legs did a very strange thing. Were they, in fact, going to give way just as the bag had? She felt as if they may stop working, no longer able to do their job of holding her up. She heard herself do an unfamiliar and strange giggle. 'Ha.'

Just about everyone who was standing by waiting to disembark watched as Cally's face burned even hotter with humiliation. She felt as if even the ends of her hair were flushing. The man flicked open the plastic carrier bag, and she quickly shoved the chicken, spices, book, and planner into it.

Then, as if by magic or some sort of emotional tidal wave, in an instant, she felt overwhelmed. As if the bag had tipped her over an emotional precipice she hadn't realised she'd been standing right on the edge of. The man was kind and bothered; he had noticed her and was being nice and it threw her exponentially. No one ever, ever, ever really noticed Cally de Pfeffer. It was as if she was, sometimes, invisible. Suddenly, she felt as if she was going to burst into tears. All she wanted was one nice day and to stop having to hold up the sky. She couldn't even do a bit of shopping without it turning into a disaster. She bit her lip, trying not to cry as frustration and embarrassment welled up inside her. She'd been pathetically excited to have a homemade curry for one with a new book and the pitiful contents of her evening curry had now been scattered over the floor of the riverboat. The bag's bottom giving way felt as if it represented her life.

Cally fiddled and fussed with the bag and willed the sting of tears pricking her eyes to go away, but they were having none of it. Her emotional reserves were drained and a little incident like a ripped bag felt like the last straw. The bag had sat on top of a huge pile of worries about money, exhausting grief, concerns about finding somewhere to live, and fears about her uncertain future in general. She took a shuddering breath, chest tight, as she fought to maintain her composure. *Do not cry on the riverboat*, she said in her head. *Do not cry.*

'You okay?' the unfairly handsome man asked. Had he picked up on the emotional tidal wave that had swamped her?

Cally wanted to scream to him, to the whole boat, to the entirety of Lovely Bay, to the whole of England itself, that no, no, no, she was not okay. Not at all. She wasn't okay and it wasn't fair. Instead, she mustered up a tight smile and gave a little, self-deprecating shrug just as she always did. 'Yeah, I'm fine. Just been one of those days, you know how it is.'

As she looked up into the man's brown eyes, she got another whiff of something very nice, very expensive, and *very* out of her league. She realised that this man really wouldn't know how it was for her. There was no way someone like him would have even half a clue about her struggles. She forced a brighter, more nonchalant expression. 'Thanks again for your help, really appreciate it.'

'No worries.' The man sat back down on the bench. 'I hope you get home in one piece.'

Cally nodded and shuffled along with the other disembarking passengers and stuffed the broken paper bag into the carrier bag. As she walked in the direction of Lovely Bay train station, she took a breath in and tried to regain her composure. She blinked a few times to dispel the prickling tears as she took a few more deep, grounding breaths. A little voice in her head chastised her for being so overly sensitive and told her to get a grip. But she couldn't seem to shake the overwhelming feeling that her life was slowly unravelling around her. She didn't really want to know what would make itself known next. Rock bottom felt so very close.

3

As Cally got to the station, she followed the other commuters onto the platform and waited.

She took a few moments to collect herself and took a couple of deep, steadying breaths of the icy cold evening air. She whipped a carton of emergency blackcurrant out of her handbag, popped in the straw, and attempted to will away the lingering sting of the escapade on the boat. She replayed the bottom of her bag falling away on the stairs. At least the wine was still in one piece: that breaking would have tipped her ever further over the imaginary emotional edge. Just as she pulled the scrunched-up paper bag out of the carrier bag and put it in the bin, the stationmaster's door opened, and Nancy, the woman who ran the station who Cally had got to know through the chemist and her commute, strolled out.

Cally smiled at Nancy and raised her eyebrows in greeting. They knew each other in passing around Lovely Bay and sometimes found each other at the same events, especially the drinks at Lovely Bay's lighthouse. Nancy was a character Cally had enjoyed getting to know.

'Evening, our Cally! How are you?' Nancy called out with a

friendly wave as she put the hood of her Lovely wax coat with its striped hood up over her railway uniform and winced at the cold.

Cally mustered up a smile and tried to sound a whole lot brighter than she felt. She switched her "I'm okay" voice on. 'Good, thanks. Nice night for it. Cold but clear.'

Nancy chuckled. 'Well, it's not tipping it down, at least. No umbrella needed for the walk to the boat this evening.'

'There is that. Good point.'

'Same old Lovely. Four seasons in one day. What have you been up to? Any luck yet with your house hunting? Found yourself a little place?'

Cally sighed, her shoulders sagged. 'No, not yet. Starting to wonder if I'm ever going to find anything. At the beginning, I was being too picky. Now I'm bordering on desperate.' Cally smiled, determined not to let on how anxious she actually was, show in her voice.

Nancy looked sympathetic and nodded along as Cally explained how the cost-of-living crisis was cutting into real, daily lives like hers. She rolled her eyes as she chatted about the unaffordable prices and seemingly endless viewings she'd attended, only to be turned away often before she'd even gone in.

Nancy sighed. 'Yup, it's a right nightmare trying to find somewhere decent these days, isn't it? Prices have gone daft and there's such a lot of competition. You're not being too picky at all. There's some right old rubbish out there.'

'Tell me about it.'

'You'll find something. The perfect place is out there, just you wait and see. Might take a bit of time, but it'll happen.'

Cally wasn't quite as sure. She'd more or less resigned herself to the fact that she was going to have to rent a room in a shared house. Her grandma had always called them "bedsits". That didn't sound very pleasant to her. 'There's nothing. If I don't find something soon, I'm going to end up in some dodgy rental or piling in with housemates.' She rolled her eyes. 'At my age. Who would have thought?'

'No, no. I'm sure you'll come across something. It works like that.'

Despite her despondency, Cally felt a tiny blossom of hope at Nancy's words. 'Thanks, Nance. There's no way I'm going to be in Lovely Bay, though, as I'd hoped. For a start, there isn't anything, and even if there was, I wouldn't be able to stretch to it.'

Nancy narrowed her eyes. 'Have you put the word out?'

'I've constantly looked at the Facebook page, and I've spoken to Ella, but she literally has nothing on her books. She said it's bad enough normally but everyone is sitting tight at the moment because of what's going on with house prices and the way of the world.'

Nancy frowned. 'I didn't mean like that.'

'What did you mean? Sorry?'

'Basically, I mean, have you asked Birdie to get involved?'

'No, not really. She's been really busy with the new chemist she's opening and she's been away on a pharmacist's course.' Cally wrinkled her nose in confusion. 'She wouldn't know about rent and stuff, would she?'

'Is the sky blue?'

Cally chuckled. 'Good point, actually. She knows everything. Why am I even saying that?'

'She does, along with someone else I might just happen to know.'

'Who?'

'You're looking at her.'

'Ha!'

'I'll get on it. We'll find you somewhere.'

Cally shook her head. 'But there's nowhere in Lovely Bay. There is nothing, and trust me, I have looked and looked. Not a single thing. I'd settle for a shed if there was one. Or a caravan if it was located in Lovely.'

'There's nowhere that you can *see*. That doesn't mean anything at all. Leave it with me.'

Cally rolled her eyes inside. Nancy was nice enough, but she didn't understand. Nancy was a true blue, born and bred Lovely, and Cally had clocked that what came with that was a sort of ignorant entitlement about the world. Nancy lived in a cottage just behind one of the Lovely Bay greens, had a stable job at the station, and had lived in Lovely Bay all her life. No seventies housing estates with plastic doors for our Nancy. No caring role since the day dot.

'Thanks, Nance. That would be great.' Cally tried to keep an open mind, but she was sure Nancy would come to a dead end just as she had.

Nancy, however, sounded very sure of herself. 'Don't worry. I'm on it.'

'It's just so expensive. I'm not sure even Birdie could suss out a place for me,' Cally laughed. 'Unless she can wave some sort of property wand.'

Nancy wasn't having any of it. 'Ah, don't be daft. You never know what Birdie can pull off with her connections. Our Birdie might surprise you yet.'

Cally shrugged, not wanting to get her hopes up. The previous few months of fruitless flat-hunting, her grandma's funeral, the train wreck of her finances and her non-existent family had really taken their toll. 'If you say so. I'd give my right arm for a tent in Lovely Bay at the moment, but I'm not holding my breath, you know? It seems like a pipe dream at this point.'

'Keep your chin up. Birdie's sorted out bigger pickles than this before. Plus, she likes you, which always works in this town.'

Cally laughed. 'I should be grateful for that, actually. I know what she's like when she doesn't like someone. I've seen it in action at the back of the chemist. The woman is brutal. It's not pretty.'

As a whistle from the other side announced the next train's arrival, Nancy gave Cally's arm a squeeze. 'Look, sorry I've got to dash, but I'm on the case, don't you worry! I'll drop Birdie a word tonight. You just sit tight. I'll sort it.'

Cally smiled at Nancy's optimism, even if it felt totally and utterly misplaced. 'Thanks.'

Nancy looked at her watch. 'Leave it with me. Sorry, I've got to rush. I'm opening the lighthouse. I'll put the feelers out.'

'Yeah, right, okay, thanks.'

'See you later.'

'See you.'

Cally watched Nancy go and shook her head. Nancy was in a dream world – a Lovely Bay dream world where life was simple and everybody knew your name. In Nancy's world, people were real walking, talking versions of the fake Insta lives existing on the screen of Cally's phone – winning at life and oh-so-blessed. The difference in Lovely Bay was that it wasn't fake. Cally's world, however, wasn't quite like that. Cally was in no way, shape, or form hashtag blessed. She felt as if she had so many boxes to tick in life. There were that many boxes that she didn't even know what they were. There was no way she'd be able to afford anything in Lovely Bay. She'd be lucky if she could secure a grotty high-rise in a satellite town the way she was going.

'Lovely Bay, here I don't come,' Cally muttered under her breath.

As she turned to look at the tracks and waited for the train, she closed her eyes and nodded. She hoped that Nancy's optimism was correct, but she didn't really think so. Was Nancy going to conjure up a place out of nowhere? As Cally's train pulled into the station and she got on, she felt more and more despondent by the second. She felt as if she was being attacked every which way she turned. Grandma dying and grief? Slapping her hard every single day. Given notice by peeping Tom-style landlord? Email in her inbox. Concerned about the future? Every few minutes or so. Verging on homeless? The struggle was real.

Cally tutted and sighed. She could really use a spot of good fortune in her life. All she wanted was one nice day. She wasn't going to hold her breath.

4

A freezing cold, bitterly bright Monday morning greeted Cally the following week as she arrived in Lovely Bay early on her way to a shift at the chemist. Strolling over St. Lovely green on her way to the shop, crisp air bit at her cheeks and took up residence on the end of her nose. The crunch of frost under her feet chilled and she could feel cold sea air through her thermal-lined tights. She stopped on a bench, the cold feeling as if it was seeping through her coat as she sat down and leant on the back. She gazed out at the sparkles on the frosty lawn, each little blade of grass coated in a sheath of tiny icy twinkles and took a blackcurrant carton out of her bag. For a moment, she just sat, staring up at the lighthouse towering over the town and listened to the distant sound of seagulls. She wrinkled up her nose, tipped back her head, and inhaled the freezing salty tang of the sea, the scent of cold earth and frosty leaves in the air.

Little plumes of smoke came out of her mouth, and she rubbed her hands up and down her legs, wondering if the forecasted rain was going to come in by the end of the day. If so, by the look of the temperature, it was going to most probably turn into sleet for her journey home. Taking out her phone, she refreshed the estate agent site she visited hourly and was pleased to see a new listing for a part-furnished place not far from the estate she'd lived on for the previous few months. What was even better was that she could afford the rent. The fact that the listing opened with a picture of the garden fence was suspicious. She tapped and waited as the post loaded in a new window and felt her heart sink like a stone. As she took in the images, she swiped right anyway just to make herself feel a little bit more despondent. Then she raised her eyebrows and shook her head in disgust. Rather than being affordable, the rent appeared astronomical for what it represented. The pictures were not pretty: a horrid grey metal frame bed from the eighties with a burgundy satin bedspread shoved under the eaves, next to it an oversized, no-longer cream, grubby leather armchair, and brown filthy once-fluffy carpet topped with a pink stained rug. There were no words for the plastic gold fan suspended above the sofa. It got worse: a brown toilet with no lid next to a deep red wall, a bedside table as a vanity unit beside a sink with a forlorn bottle of economy bleach balanced by the tap, a shower outside. A fridge over a window, a microwave on the floor. Dire straits.

Cally shook her head and closed her eyes for a second. One nice day was all she wanted. A decent roof over her head might be good, too. An indoor shower wouldn't go amiss. She read through the accompanying copy a little bit bewildered at the front of the person who had written the blurb.

Em Robinson Estates are DELIGHTED to offer this cosy self-contained studio apartment that has everything you need. Are you looking for somewhere away from the hustle and bustle of everyday life, with jaw-dropping views of fields? This property would make an ideal base for any working professional. Within driving distance of the train station and the best country pubs, you'll be spoilt for choice, and with your utilities included in the rental price, you're onto a winner! Look no further. Simply bring your suitcase. Situated within a traditional farm building, with parking and outside space to relax after a hard day's work. Be quick! This one won't last long.

Cally didn't know whether to laugh or cry. It was one of the worst places she'd seen and right out in the sticks, nowhere near Lovely Bay. Its price made it all the more evident that her chances of snagging a place in Lovely or even a train ride away from it were getting slimmer by the day. Closing her phone, she got up from the bench and started to make her way to work at the chemist. She may have to ditch her job and move away from the area altogether. The thing was that Cally de Pfeffer had never lived anywhere else. She'd lived in the same area for her whole life. A forty-five-minute ride up the train line from Lovely in an area she no longer wanted to be. Granted, where she'd lived wasn't anything like Lovely, but it had done the job. She'd not even been out of the county much. She'd been to London once on a school trip but hadn't liked it at all and so had stayed on the coach.

What had happened to her life? She looked around. This panic-filled, terrified feeling had never been part of the plan. Hang on a sec. What had the plan been again? It felt really as if there'd never even been a plan. Constant caring had put paid to plans. To be frank, nothing had worked out in her life. In Cally's world, there were no happy ever afters. No little house with a couple of chimney stacks, no fancy hot yoga classes, no super-duper career, no cosy bedrooms and marble kitchen islands, not even a sniff of a few sweet little cherubs tucked up in bed in nice pyjamas, no partner, no range cooker or coffee machines. No Instagram posts and hashtags that she was living the dream. None of it. Nada. There was no dream. Seventy-three Facebook friends, most of whom weren't actually her friends at all. None of them had turned up at the funeral.

As she strolled along the High Street, she smiled at the place. At least Lovely Bay always delivered even when it was freezing cold and looking as if it was about to rain. The light changed, things seemed to glow and the air was still and somehow pretty. She was grateful that her place of work was nice. The little things and all that. The woman from The Drunken Sailor pub smiled as she opened the pub door and Clive, who worked on the riverboats, waved as he hustled along the pavement. Everywhere Cally looked, people were pottering along in the famous Lovely coats – a navy-blue wax coat with a stripy hood only worn and sold to those known as "Lovelies". The way Cally de Pfeffer was going, she was never ever going to be a Lovely and had a fat chance of getting one of the elusive coats.

She stopped by the window of the hardware store and peered in for a minute, then continued along the pavement, turned left down the alley between the shops, and made her way to the back of the chemist building. Putting her hand over the gate, she pulled back the bolt, shoved the gate with her shoulder, and turned left. Despite the bitterly cold weather, the windows were ajar and Cally could hear the Shipping Forecast blasting from the storage room. Birdie, the owner and pharmacist, was perpetually accompanied by the Shipping Forecast either by way of it playing from her phone attached to her shoulder, on a speaker in the back room of the pharmacy preparation area, or in the kitchen of the deli she also owned just down the street. *On behalf of the Maritime and Coastguard agency. There are warnings of gales in Viking, Dogger, Fisher, Trafalgar, Hebrides, and Faeroes.*

Cally pulled her beanie, with its huge bobble on the top, off as she turned the door handle, yanked her white-blonde hair out of its scrunchie, ruffled it a bit, scooped it all back on top of her head in a bun, and refixed the scrunchie. Unwinding her scarf as she walked in, Birdie poked her head around the doorframe of the dispensary. 'Morning. Cold enough out there for you? Nippy isn't the word. Hope the weather turns soon. This should be the last of it. How are we?'

Cally pretended to be happy and bright. She flicked the voice switch, did the thing with her eyes and turned her head. 'Good thanks! How are you? Yep, it's certainly cold out there and I thought we'd seen the back of it.'

'Yes, get in here in the warm. I'm fine, thanks, good actually.'

Cally nodded and attempted to look happy. 'Great. Did the orders come in okay? How did you find the cold this morning on your joints?'

Birdie stayed where she was and ignored Cally's question about the orders and her joints. 'I'm fine, but I've heard you're not.'

Cally frowned. 'Pardon?'

'Our Nancy. She said she bumped into you at the station.'

'Ahh, yes,' Cally said with an awkward chuckle. 'We did have a bit of a chat at the station the other night.'

Birdie nodded knowingly. She narrowed her lower eyelids. 'Indeed and from what I heard, things aren't going too well on the house-hunting front, eh? Why didn't you say?'

Cally knew exactly why; she was embarrassed and didn't want anything to jeopardise her job in Lovely Bay. With her current financial status that was the last thing she needed. She scrambled to make up an excuse and batted her hand in front of her. She switched the voice up a notch. 'I didn't think it would get to this, to be quite honest. Anyway, all good, it'll be fine.' She did *not* think it would be fine. She was beginning to panic.

'You haven't found anything?'

Cally sighed heavily. 'You can say that again. It's a nightmare out there at the moment. Prices have gone nuts unless you want to live in a shoebox or some manky grotty high-rise. It's all good, though. I'll be fine.'

Birdie did a little wincing movement with her jaw. 'Right, so what are you going to do?'

Cally had no idea, but she pretended she was all over it. She beamed. 'I don't know. It's not a problem. I'll get a house share or something.'

'Our Nancy mentioned you were dead set on finding something in Lovely Bay?' Birdie probed.

Cally rolled her eyes a touch. 'Who wouldn't be? I would give my right arm to live here, but with the prices, it's totally out of my budget at the moment.'

Birdie tutted sympathetically. 'Well, Lovely's not a cheap area to buy or rent these days, that's for sure. Still, don't lose hope just yet.'

Cally raised a sceptical eyebrow. Just as Nancy's had, Birdie's words irritated her a bit. Neither of them knew the ferocious and debilitating state of the rental market and what it was like not to live in Lovely Bay. Both of them were fully initiated Lovelies. They both took it for granted with its beach, fabulous little speakeasies that served chowder in sourdough bowls, the Lovely coats, the gorgeous old pub, the lighthouse and the chocolate shop. Cally felt envious about how Lovelies took the amazing things about living in Lovely as a given. She wasn't going to let on about all that, though. No need to sound bitter. She continued to shrug it off. 'I know you're good, but I don't even think *you* can solve this one.'

Birdie tapped the side of her nose. 'Now, that's where you just don't know. I am a woman of many means and I love to solve a problem. You know that from working in the back here with me. How many times have I rustled up things out of thin air?'

Cally laughed. 'Are you going to pull a little cottage out of a hat for me? If you are, can I have one over Nancy's way, please?' Cally pointed to the huge pile of cardboard boxes waiting to be opened and sorted. 'Or how about pulling a nice warm flat over on the harbour side from one of those boxes there? Or the lighthouse. Mmm, one of those little places in that strip at the bottom there…'

'Never underestimate the power of my contacts and local knowhow,' Birdie cackled with a conspiratorial wink. 'I might see if I can dig up something that's flying under the radar.'

'I wish and live in hope. There's just nothing much around, though. I've had my hopes up too many times already.' Cally didn't say that in her lunch break, she was going to book a fully refundable room at the First Lodge Hotel at the petrol station near the motorway not far from where she got off the train.

Birdie held up a hand to halt Cally's protests. 'Just you wait and see before you go writing anything off. I know every Lovely known to man around these parts. We'll find you a little place not on the open market if you catch my drift.'

Cally's eyes widened, she chuckled and played along. 'You're full of surprises. I like the sound of that. Do you mean like some sneaky little deal under the table before it gets advertised? You are a dark horse.'

'Call it what you like, our Cally. Let me tell you: when you're in charge of the drug supply in the third smallest town in the country, you get to call in a few favours. Ask me how I know.'

'Ha! You sound like a dealer.'

'I call it networking and using my knack for opportunities.'

'You're too funny.'

'I'll have a poke around before you give up the Lovely Bay dream altogether. In fact, I actually have somewhere in mind if the worst comes to the worst.'

Little did Birdie know that the worst had come to the worst in Cally's world. It had a name: homeless. Cally did, however, feel a flicker of hope. She'd seen how Birdie operated and how she seemed to pull invisible Lovely strings and come up with things thought otherwise impossible. 'You know what, Birdie? Why not? If anyone can pull off a miracle, it's you. I'm officially leaving it in your capable hands.' Cally joked. There was no way she was leaving it in anyone's hands. She had to find a solution and fast.

Birdie clapped her hands together decisively. 'Leave it with me, our Cally. Your luck is about to change.'

Cally pulled one of the huge cardboard boxes over towards her, flapped the top open, and dived in. With the Shipping Forecast in her ear, she muttered to herself. 'I'm coming for you, Lovely Bay. Just you wait and see.'

But really, inside, she knew that there was a fat chance of that. The reality of having nowhere to live loomed. Life was not good.

5

Cally stood at the traffic lights as rain more or less fell down from the sky and thumped on top of her umbrella. She tutted as a woman with a personalised number plate in a grey BMW left it way too late to stop, skidded and slid all over the show and only just missed hitting the crossing bollard. Cally shuddered. It was so grim and cold that the automatic headlights on the cars all around her had come on, casting a weird glow on the wet streets as rain and a little helping of fog swirled around the beams. She huddled under her umbrella and frowned at the deserted Lovely Bay street. It wasn't very often that Lovelies were put off by the weather. They were used to experiencing many different seasons in a day, but there weren't many people around at all. The only souls out braving the rain were a few people standing under the awning of the deli, a man with an oversized umbrella, and a woman in black clothes and a raincoat with her hood up.

As she hustled along, keeping her umbrella as low as she could, she watched as long pools of water gathered in the middle of a pedestrian walkway and a plethora of circles spread out towards the edges. Streams of rain poured down from the gutters, splattering onto the pavement and rain gushed along the verges to her right. A white van with blue writing whooshed into the gutter, completely covering a woman right in front of her in a shower of water. Not very Lovely at all. Meanwhile, a man at the hardware store hurried to take the baskets back inside out of the pouring rain. Streams of water flowed down the side of a building with bottle-green subway tiles and driving rain somehow found its way under Cally's umbrella as she hurried along. She was very pleased she had worn her wellies.

At the next pedestrian crossing, a fancy white Tesla didn't stop as it reached the lights and sailed right on by through a red light. Cally tutted and rolled her eyes and a woman who was standing beside her without an umbrella screwed up her face. 'It's awful, isn't it? What a day!' She gestured up to the clouds and into the far distance. 'Look at that coming over the sea.'

'I know. It's raining cats and dogs.'

Once Cally had crossed the road, she made her way to the jetty to catch the riverboat and inched her way forward in a crowd of people who were shuffling together to get under the shelter. She watched a woman with an inside-out umbrella struggle in the wind, and just as she was peering out to see the whereabouts of the boat, Nina, someone she knew from working in the chemist, hurried up and nudged herself under the shelter.

Nina fussed with her umbrella and beamed. 'Oh, hey, our Cally! How are you?'

'Good. Not too wet, thankfully.'

'What's with this weather? We've had it all today.'

'I know!'

'I was just thinking about you, funnily enough.'

'All good, I hope.' Cally joked.

'Of course.'

'How are you feeling now?' Nina asked.

Cally assumed Nina was referring to Cally's grandma's funeral and recent family dramas. The switch swiftly hit its position. 'Ahh, you know. I've been better but mostly I'm fine.'

'At least it's all over, I suppose.'

'Yeah...'

'It will get easier.'

'Yes, people have said...'

'I mentioned to Birdie when I was in the chemist before. I must have *just* missed you. Not sure if you're interested or not, but I have a job up at Lovely Manor. I need someone to help out. Birdie said you might be interested now you've got, well, a bit more time on your hands. She said you were on the lookout for more work. Obviously, say no if you'd rather not but I thought I would mention it.'

Cally smiled and jumped at the chance. She already knew she liked the way Nina operated. They'd worked well together sorting orders in the back of the pharmacy quite a few times. Nina just got on with things, put her head down, and didn't make a huge amount of fuss. They also clicked and had chatted about all sorts of things. Cally just felt nice around Nina, really. 'Love to. When do you need someone? I have my online stuff for the call centre, too, so as long as it fits in with that. That's normally a really early start, though, so it fits in well with other things.'

Nina pulled out her phone. 'I'll message you the dates. It's a massive job and what with Faye and everything. I'm surprised I got it, but I did.'

Cally smiled. 'Yeah, I'd love to help out. Thanks for asking.'

'Only if you're sure. Don't feel as if you have to.'

'I'd love to, honestly. Just let me know when you need me and I'll make sure I'm available.'

Nina nodded enthusiastically. 'Birdie said you'd say that. Brilliant, that's a weight off my mind. I was stressing about finding someone reliable on such short notice. To be quite honest, I didn't even think I would get the job, which is why I hadn't sorted anything out. I'm normally much more organised. I thought they would go for someone fancy, but there you go.'

'They must have heard about your reputation.'

Nina glanced around at the dreary, rain-lashed jetty with a grimace. 'I was hoping to have someone lined up to give me a hand so I could get it done quickly.'

'You're looking at her.'

'Great. I'll text you all the details. All we need now is for the weather to improve. I'll be counting down the days until I can ditch these woollies and defrost my bones properly!'

'Same here,' Cally said as the riverboat emerged through the rain-speckled water. 'Looks like the boat's here, thank goodness. I feel as if I'll be soaked to the skin by the time I eventually get home. It doesn't seem as if it's going to let up.'

As they edged forward in the queue, Nina filled Cally in on the finer details of the Lovely Manor job as they dodged the rain. 'So, it's just helping me out with the decluttering and sorting that kind of thing. The odd bit of cleaning too, if and when. But there are cleaners booked, but for some things, it's easier just to do it yourself. Nothing too taxing.'

'I'm well up for it,' Cally replied. She didn't quite relish the idea of cleaning but was already envisioning her bank balance looking a bit healthier, so she kept that quiet. 'Pop me down for as many hours as you need, my diary's pretty free and empty at the moment apart from the chemist and the customer service portal is out of hours anyway...' She trailed off, not wanting to delve into the topic of her grandma. She'd had enough sympathy on that.

'Will do.'

As the boat chugged upstream, Cally felt like one of the clouds residing full-time over her head had lifted. Getting some work for Nina's company, A Lovely Organised Life, would see her through until she got herself more together. Her money worries could take a back seat, and maybe sorting through someone else's old junk would take her mind off things. As she looked out at the thick grey clouds and rain, she hoped that she'd find somewhere to live. Then, she'd be able to get her life back together again.

6

Push had come to shove and Cally had had to make emergency plans about her situation. Her heart sank as she walked into the car park of the hotel not far from the housing estate where her rental house was situated. Even from the outside, it looked like an absolute dive – a rundown building squatting miserably beside the constant roar of traffic from a nearby motorway. Litter was strewn across the tarmac, the few vehicles present were rust buckets, and a tattered 'Vacancies' sign twisted forlornly in the breeze. Cally squinted at the odd shapes in the car park and realised they were potholes. A dirty, great cymbal of doom clanged above her head. Things were not great. This was definitely rock bottom in Cally de Pfeffer's life.

Steeling herself, she gripped the handle of her bag and headed for the lobby. As she stepped up two horrid, long, wide, dirty, tiled steps, grubby automatic glass doors streaked with grime, and goodness knows what, creaked open. The doors scraped over a dirty, black plastic-backed mat which was skew-whiff on the far side. Cally felt her nostrils go wide and her eyes close for a second as she took in the entrance area. The interior was even worse than the car park – dingy carpets with a plethora of stains, once white, now marked grimy walls, and an overwhelming stench of stale air topped with a faint whiff of dampness. Trying to keep an open mind despite the dingy surroundings, Cally took an emergency carton of blackcurrant out of her bag, pierced the top with the straw, sucked and forged on.

A miserable-looking teenager behind the counter barely looked up from his mobile as she approached. 'Alright?' he just about grunted. He looked back down right away clearly in no way interested in Cally's answer. He continued tapping away at his screen, chewing loudly and shovelling food into his mouth from a plastic noodle container.

Cally looked at her phone and then up again as she approached the desk. 'I've got a viewing, ' she said hesitantly. 'For the, err, room with cooking facilities? The studio apartment?'

The teenager flicked his eyes towards Cally and jerked his thumb towards a lift area and dimly lit corridor. 'Yeah, go ahead. Last door on the left. It's open. Cleaners are in that corridor.' His disinterested tone said it all, really. What had happened to her life?

'What, just down there?' Cally pointed to the dingy-looking corridor.

With an exaggerated sigh, the teenager dragged his gaze away from his phone to meet hers. He looked her up and down dismissively. 'Yeah. Anything else?'

Cally felt her cheeks flush. 'Sorry. The message said to check in at reception.'

'Did it?' The teenager looked Cally up and down again.

She bristled at his condescending attitude. 'Is there a problem?'

'As I said, down there, follow your nose.'

Cally swallowed as she made her way down the gloomy hallway, the smell of cheap, artificial air freshener making her eyes water, her battered self-esteem felt worse than it *ever* had. The place was grimmer than she could have imagined in her worst nightmares. She'd clearly lived a sheltered life. The hotel, if it could be referred to as such, was *diabolical*.

She shimmied around a dirty cleaning trolley and made her way to the end, where a door was propped open by a gigantic pile of grey-white sheets. Cally wasn't sure what the smell was as she got close. She did know it made her want to heave. Walking in, she swallowed and then pulled her sleeve over her hand and cuffed her hand over her mouth and nose.

The "studio apartment" was even worse than what she'd seen out the front. It was barely bigger than the bed, a single window looked out over the petrol station's rubbish area and a long line of HGVs snaked away into the car park at the back. Out the window, there was a grotty-looking area with corrugated, mouldy green roofing and the delights of the motorway just beyond.

Pushing the door to the bathroom open with her foot, Cally recoiled at the plastic, mould-speckled suite. The toilet lid and seat were up, the shower area looked passable and smelt faintly of bleach. Coming back into the room again, she stared ahead, shaking her head. The double bed was tightly made with a cheap striped red and gold runner tucked in along the bottom. The runner matched the limp curtains at the windows. A small melamine built-in desk had a bolted-down lamp and a flat-screen TV on a clamp crowded from the top of the wall. As Cally stood gawping, the hiss of lorries thundering past seemed to make the entire window shake. All of it had a sordid and depressing feel, as if she'd reached the pits of life. She tried not to let self-pity swamp her as she was overwhelmed with disappointment. Her feet stuck on the grimy stained carpet as she shimmied around the bed. Humiliation welled up inside her and she blinked back tears. She'd been reduced to a motel beside a motorway with lorries zooming by the window and lamps bolted to desks.

She felt so wildly desperate that she found herself laughing. Stepping back over the pile of soiled laundry, the laugh didn't last long. She swallowed and stomped along the corridor and made her way out to the lobby area. She'd rather live in a shed or swallow her pride and move in with Eloise for a bit than be anywhere near the hotel. It was more than terrible. She tossed her hair back in an attempt to be defiant, which was ridiculous because no one cared in the slightest anyway. One thing was for certain – she'd never set foot in the place again, not if it was the last place on earth.

As she marched back down the stained hallway, past the vile teenager, and out into the fresh air, she couldn't believe a place like it was only a forty-five-minute train ride away from somewhere like Lovely Bay. It was like chalk and cheese. As she walked away, her mind swirled about what she was going to do. She didn't have a clue, but she did know that she deserved better than a cheap, nasty, putrid hotel. Didn't she?

She did have a semblance of self-respect to cling to, at least. She vowed to dust herself off and get back on the horse. She may have hit rock bottom, but that meant that there was only one way to go – up. Wasn't there?

7

The next morning, Cally made her way to work at the chemist, her mind still replaying her conversation with Birdie a couple of days before. She felt a glimmer of hope, but honestly, not a lot. Finding an affordable place in Lovely Bay was unlikely even for the Birdies of the world. Birdie was good but not that good. A miracle worker, she was not. Cally pinning her hope on something that most likely wasn't going to happen wasn't up there with one of her better ideas.

As she entered through the back gate of the row of buildings that housed the chemist, she heard Birdie's voice drifting out from the storage room, punctuated by the familiar tones of the Shipping Forecast. Cally smiled as she unwound her scarf, ruffled her white-blonde hair free of her beanie, scooped it up behind her, and fastened it with a clip.

'Morning! If it isn't my favourite house hunter!' Birdie laughed as she poked her head around the doorframe. 'Just the person I wanted to see. How are you?'

Cally raised an eyebrow. She didn't even want to talk about house hunting after the debacle at the hotel. In fact, she wasn't in the mood to joke about it. However, it wasn't Birdie's fault, nor was Birdie going to know how down in the dumps she was, so she switched her happy voice on and joined in the banter. 'Morning! Do I detect a scheme brewing?'

Birdie cackled. 'You could say that! Come through to the dispensary. I've got something special to show you.'

Cally followed and then stood with her eyebrows raised as Birdie leant against the counter with her arms folded, looking a little bit smug. Cally turned her head to the side. 'Right then, don't keep me in suspense. What's this all about?'

Birdie looked like the cat who'd got the cream. 'Well, as I mentioned, I've been putting some feelers out regarding your housing predicament and I might just have stumbled across something rather interesting that could be right up your alley...'

Cally felt a bit put out that Birdie was joking around. Having a roof over her head was not a joking matter as far as she was concerned. She kept her thoughts to herself and a smile on her face. 'You just stumbled across a little flat or house, did you?'

Birdie paused for a second. 'How do you fancy taking a little look at a cosy one-bedroom flat right here in the heart of Lovely Bay itself? Rent controlled and everything, just for you!'

Cally was over the joke. A one-bedroom flat would suit her down to the ground until she got herself on her feet again. She tried not to let her irritation show in her voice. 'Sounds nice.'

Birdie cackled. 'And it has views. I don't think you can beat it. You can see the lighthouse and the bay.'

'Yep, very funny. There's just nowhere like that available around here, I've looked everywhere a million times over. I'm over it, to be frank.'

Birdie shook her head. 'Ah, but that's where you're wrong.' She mimicked estate agent speak. 'This one's so under the radar, it's practically invisible to the naked eye. A proper hidden gem, just waiting for the right tenant to snap it up.'

'Right...'

Birdie continued in the same voice as if she was reading

estate agent's particulars. 'Sweeping rooftop views of Lovely with the riverboat a hop, skip and a jump away. One bedroom, a sitting room and kitchen area, ample storage, bathroom with tub. Reasonable rent and good landlord with all utilities included.'

Cally couldn't tell what Birdie was up to. 'Go on. How do you know about this? Who is it?'

Birdie winked. 'Someone I know very well.'

Cally wasn't sure what to think. 'Who? It's just, I couldn't bear to get my hopes up only to be turned down again...'

Birdie leaned in. 'I know her very well. Very well, indeed. She's nice.'

Cally was losing patience. She made as if to turn away. 'Oh well, I hope this person puts it up for rent soon so I can go and have a look.'

Birdie laughed, 'I know her well because it's me! I own the blooming place myself!'

Cally frowned and wrinkled her nose in confusion. 'What? Where?'

'It's a little hidey-hole right above the deli. You're aware I own the deli, too. When I say above, I mean up the top there. Been empty for donkey's years since my dear old aunt passed on.' Birdie made the sign of the cross. 'God rest her soul.'

Cally could scarcely believe what she was hearing. It seemed too good to be true. She narrowed her eyes. 'Sorry, are you being serious?'

'I am indeed.' Birdie cackled. 'The only minor catch is, you have to take the stairs through the back to get up there. No bohemian open-plan loft situation, I'm afraid. But it's fully self-contained and it does have a bed, I think, if I remember rightly and there's loads of furniture and stuff. I've not been up there for years. When I say years, I mean like twenty years. That's not true. I have been up there but just to shove in clutter and junk that I should have dealt with and check on the pipes. It's my dirty little secret.'

Cally nodded enthusiastically, her mind spinning. 'Sorry, are you kidding?'

Birdie frowned. 'No, why would I be kidding? I said I'd find a solution and I have. Did you underestimate me, our Cally?'

Cally clapped her hands together. 'Oh my goodness. I'll take it! I'll take it right now! When can I see this magical flat of yours?'

Birdie flipped the wallet flap over on her phone and checked the time. 'Why don't we make a coffee and pop across there now?'

Cally nodded. She hadn't had such a good proposition in her life. 'That would be great.'

As Birdie busied herself filling the kettle and gathering a couple of travel mugs, Cally felt almost sick with anticipation. Could this be the answer to her housing prayers? A cosy flat, right in the heart of Lovely, within her meagre budget? She wasn't quite sure whether or not to believe Birdie.

Birdie chatted away as she pressed a button on a small coffee grinder, waited for it to do its thing, and then spooned coffee grounds into a cafetière. 'I must warn you, it's been acting as a bit of a storage room for my shop inventory overflow and, well, just about everything, really. Boxes of holiday decorations, out-of-season bits and bobs. You can hardly move around up there at the moment. I was joking when I said I hadn't been up there for twenty years. I have just to shove things in and, as I said, to check on the pipes. Trust me, no one wants frozen pipes up there.'

Cally barely heard anything. She was too caught up imagining herself settling into a flat in Lovely Bay. Her mind was full-on spinning. Somewhere she could heal from the heartache of the past year surrounded by Lovelies. She certainly didn't care about a bit of clutter. Anything had to be better than what she'd seen at the motorway services hotel. She'd live in a cupboard under the stairs if it meant that she could live in Lovely. Potter had nothing on her. 'I'm not bothered,' Cally said brightly as she took one of the mugs from beside the cafetière. 'I'd live in a postage stamp if I had to at this point.'

'Well, it's a smidge bigger than that, at least. But I must emphasise it needs a proper going-over. My aunt was a bit of a hoarder, God rest her soul. Never could bring myself to clear it out after she passed, so everything's just sat there doing nothing. Then stuff has been loaded in there willy-nilly. I'll get a skip delivered in the lane there.'

'I don't care about clearing it out.'

Birdie took a tub of chocolate truffles out of the cupboard, took off the lid, and offered it to Cally. 'Let's have a little sustenance before our adventure, eh?'

'Early morning and we're already having chocolate?'

'Ah, go on. Chocolate's good for the soul. Especially when mixed with a little caffeine! You're going to need it to get up the stairs. When I say it's been shut up a while, I *do* mean it. The access is a bit unorthodox, it's tricky getting up there.'

Cally frowned a bit. 'Unorthodox how?'

'The stairs. Calling them steep is putting it kindly. More like a boxed-in ladder going up to a small landing, if I'm honest. Not exactly to building code, as they say. That's why I've never rented it out. I had someone around to have a look at it and it was such a palaver to get it up to scratch, to be able to legally rent it that I just let it sit there empty. The bannister was so many centimetres too low blah, blah, blah. It was more trouble than it was worth.'

Cally really didn't care. Breaking her neck had to be better than living in a hotel.

Birdie shook her head back and forth. 'I won't lie, it's a project. You'd be doing me a favour taking it on, truly.'

Cally could handle a few quirks. As far as she was concerned, if it was in Lovely it was a palace. If she could afford it, she'd be laughing. 'Well, I'm certainly not scared of a little hard work.'

'Shall we embark on our grand tour, then? Don't get your hopes up but it is a little flat in Lovely…'

'Lead the way. I'm ready for anything.'

8

After bundling into their coats, Cally and Birdie went out through the back door of the chemist, headed down a narrow brick-sided alley, and turned to walk along the cobbled back access lane to the deli's rear entrance. Birdie fiddled with a keypad and waited until a gate to the deli's yard yielded with a creak. The smell of chowder hit them as they walked through the back entrance and stopped for a bit to speak with Alice, the deli's manager. Cally looked through into the kitchen as Birdie and Alice chatted about a delivery of sourdough and how much room there was in the freezer. The kitchen was small, extremely tidy, organised, and full to capacity. Huge vintage stockpots sat on top of a commercial hob. The whole place smelt amazing, a mix of seafood, fresh herbs, and comfort. Cally had heard so much about Birdie's grandmother's chowder recipe with its secret ingredient and had tasted it a few times, but in the back of the deli, it smelt even better. She hoped the flat was as nice as the kitchen and its smells.

As Alice and Birdie chatted, Cally stepped to the side and peered into a room in the middle where the deli's speakeasies were held. She crossed her fingers that the flat upstairs would be even half as good. Her eyes flicked around at rustic wooden bistro tables and mismatched chairs, piles of books here and there, and a floor-to-ceiling French paned window in the middle of the far wall. Numerous shelves were packed with herbs and spices, homemade jams, chutneys, and other delicacies, all of them in little jars, their labels handwritten. Slotted between the jars, old photographs of Lovely Bay in frames were dotted about randomly. On top of a fireplace, lanterns with candles were waiting to be lit. Cally swallowed and closed her eyes briefly. It was another world to that of the roadside hotel with the sulky teenager and hideous smell.

Once Birdie had finished up with Alice, Cally followed her to a small room opposite the speakeasy room. Similar in style, but smaller it also had a fireplace and stripped timber floors. The walls were lined with industrial metal shelves and crates meticulously organised with supplies for the deli. A staircase ran down the right-hand side. A few seconds later, they were on the first floor, the stairs turned, passed a French window overlooking the bay and then as they turned again the stairs became much steeper.

Birdie pointed up to the landing above them. 'Watch your step here. Make sure you hold on to the bannister.'

Cally gulped, eyeing the steep, narrow steps warily. 'Blimey, you weren't joking about the climb.'

Birdie chuckled. 'Wait 'til you see the view from the top. It will be worth it, promise. My aunt was the last one to properly live here, the batty old bird. God rest her soul. Loved her eccentricities, though she was not quite right up top, you know? She insisted on living here nearly until the end. Goodness knows how she made it up here but she did. The place has been shut up more or less since she passed on. She went into a home before she passed away and never came back.'

As they got to the top, Birdie wasn't wrong about the steepness. Cally's heart was hammering in her chest as they arrived at a small top-floor landing with off-white yellowing walls, stripped floorboards, an old rug, and a tall built-in bookshelf on the left filled to the brim with various books. She spiralled around to look at where they'd come from and a window opposite where dusty full-length curtains on either side let in soft natural light, and a small wonky chandelier hung from the ceiling.

Turning back towards the bookshelf, Cally peered at an extensive collection of dusty books piled onto wooden shelves in a variety of colours and sizes. Magazines and books were stacked vertically and horizontally to maximise space. She ran her fingers along the spines, thinking that they could use a good sort and tidy up.

Birdie nodded. 'Aunty Ling-Ling loved nothing more than getting lost in a good book, as you can see.'

'Amazing. I bet there are some good ones there.'

Birdie fiddled with a huge doorknob. 'Watch your step. It's a bit of a squeeze. I hope you'll think it's worth it.'

Birdie pushed the door open and they stepped inside the flat. Cally's eyes widened as she took in the sight before her. Dust bunnies danced in the air of a main room, which was bathed in soft light filtering through a large window framed by bamboo blinds and heavy old beige velvet curtains. Wooden floors creaked underneath their feet as they squeezed through stacks of white cardboard filing boxes, plastic crates, and various junk piled everywhere. The flat was larger than Cally had expected, with a small balcony off the sitting room area, but the bones of the place were nearly lost beneath a jumble of cardboard boxes, dusty sheets over furniture, and bric-a-brac. A vague smell of disuse hung in the air.

Cally couldn't believe how nice it was. 'Oh,' Cally breathed, 'it's lovely. You're not a very good estate agent. You totally undersold the place.'

Birdie chuckled. 'It's a bit rough around the edges, but it's got potential. Gosh, no one has been up here for ages.'

Standing at the front window, Cally traced a clear spot in the dusty glass. The view wasn't half bad. A jumble of Lovely Bay's rooftops went down to the sea in the distance and the lighthouse towered above the whole scene. She could see Lovely Bay train station and the railway line stretching off into the distance. 'I love it already.'

'Don't speak too soon. But basically, there are no leaks, no vermin, or other nasties to worry about. It's warm, has all the utilities and you can hop onto the deli's WIFI. Just needs your own stamp on it.'

Birdie led Cally through to a kitchen, where one lone strip of base units held a white porcelain sink, cooker, and fridge from what looked like the eighties and a run of three double cabinets above. Every surface was crowded with stacks of cardboard boxes, plastic crates, and bulging bin bags. A faint sheen of dust coated everything, and motes danced in watery sunbeams coming from a skylight above.

Birdie jerked her thumb upwards. 'Focus on those high ceilings, the character. Not all this rubbish cluttering it up.' She gave a nearby box a kick, sending up a puff of dust. Cally smothered a sneeze into her elbow.

Picking her way carefully through the tripping hazards, Cally made a circuit around the space. Despite the neglect, she could see the promise – worn hardwood floors, tall skirting boards, a beautiful old sash window, and outdated floral wallpaper. Even a tiny, old-fashioned fireplace tiled in sage green, acting as an impromptu shelf for a teetering pile of old magazines, had some potential.

Birdie gestured across the room. 'Through that door is the bedroom. Small, but it's got two windows for a nice cross breeze. And its own fireplace, hidden by loads of junk.'

As Cally continued to walk around in between the boxes and

clutter, her mind raced with possibilities. She envisioned herself curled up on a cosy armchair, lost in a book. Safe, not having to worry. No one to hold the sky up for.

Birdie stood at the doorway, smiling. 'The wheels in your head are practically smoking. It really is nice up here, isn't it?'

'It is.'

In the bedroom, weak sunlight landed on a wrought-iron bed frame buried beneath boxes. Cally perched gingerly on the edge, the metal creaking, and looked around as Birdie fiddled with a blind at the window. A small antique lamp with a fringed shade sat on a pile of books on the bedside table and built-in wardrobes on the left were spilling with old clothes and boxes.

Birdie looked up to a corner of the bedroom where wallpaper peeled away from the top of the coving. 'You can do whatever you like with it. Paint it bright pink for all I care.'

'Really?'

'Yup. Well, no, maybe not bright pink, but yeah, the whole place needs an overhaul. I have loads of paint and stuff in the basement under the shop, so if you use that, it would be all in keeping, as it were. But, yeah, do whatever you like.'

Cally felt as if she was going to burst into tears. 'It's perfect, Birdie. Absolutely perfect.'

Birdie barked a laugh. 'Perfect might be overstating things a tad. But it's got potential in spades. Just like a certain strong woman, I know.' She winked, bumping Cally's hip and laughing.

Cally turned, beaming. 'I can already picture it – a cosy reading nook by that window, twinkle lights strung across the kitchen. Lamps by the dozen. Oh and that balcony.'

'I might have to join you.'

Cally's eyes shone. 'Thanks. Like so much.'

'You're welcome.'

About half an hour later, they made their way down the precarious stairs. Cally couldn't quite compute how generous Birdie was. After months of false starts and so many disappointments, it seemed Cally's luckless house hunt was finally, finally, at an end. With Birdie's secret flat having fallen straight into her lap, she was going to be able to breathe for a bit. She gave Birdie an impulsive hug. She felt nauseously grateful. 'You are quite literally a life-saver.'

'Ahh, less of that. It's the least I could do after all you've been through lately. I saw how hard you were working and all that caring you were doing. The flat is yours for as long as you need it, you hear?'

'I'm so grateful. I can't believe you've solved my problem and I'm going to be in Lovely full-time.'

'Like I said, never underestimate my connections.'

'I won't ever again.'

9

Cally had spent the rest of the day sorting orders with Birdie. As she'd slit open cardboard boxes and organised, she'd constantly played a reel about renting the flat over and over in her head. She kept imagining letting herself in at the bottom, climbing up the stairs, going past the shelving full of books on the landing, closing the door, and then sitting rugged up by the balcony door, looking out over the rooftops of Lovely Bay. A glass of wine, cosy pyjamas, perhaps a good book, and staring in the direction of the lighthouse. There was not a single person in the daydream that she had to care or do things for. She would only have to care for herself. Yes, and yes again.

In her head, she'd already decorated the flat six times over. Her mind displayed the flat with all the junk long gone, strings of little lights everywhere, the floor stripped and covered in a lovely rug, pots of herbs on the balcony and the bathroom no longer painted in avocado green. As she'd finished the drugs order and daydreamed, she flattened the cardboard carton outers and took them out to the recycling area. She imagined herself making a nice dinner for one as she pottered around with a cosy little playlist on. The horrid old actual kitchen wasn't quite part of the dream scenario, but she'd make do with it. The strip of past-their-best kitchen cabinets wasn't anything a bit of thought and elbow grease couldn't improve. She imagined the sitting room with a little side table, a nice candle, and a stack of books. A desk, yes, there would be a desk for her laptop and computer and lamps would be on that, too. There would be gingham bed linen in a lemony beige, piles and piles of cushions and pillows, and scalloped wicker. Oh yes, plenty of scalloped wicker.

Once she'd finished her shift and had said goodbye to Birdie, she could barely stop herself from skipping down the road on the way to the train station. She was going to be saying goodbye to the horrid house with the beady-eyed, bald, short little landlord who had always made excuses to come around and peep at her. Yuck. She wouldn't be sad to see the back of him. No, rather than have to worry if and when he might knock on the door, she would be high above Lovely with no one checking up on her at all. To top it off, Birdie's proposed rent was considerably less than what she was currently paying and it included the electricity and water chucked in for nothing. Happy, happy, *happy* days.

As she made her way to Lovely Bay train station, she strolled along going over the flat again and again in her head. She went past Lovely Bay House with its blue 1920s front door with a huge brass knob in the middle and smiled. She was going to be a real living part of the Lovely community. She was a little bit dumbstruck. To the right of the blue door, a cheery yellow bench sat next to a couple of big white pots. She loved the houses of Lovely Bay, and it was one of the reasons she'd always fancied living there. With what had happened that day and Birdie's kindness, it was actually going to happen for real. Hoo-blooming-ray. She'd always lived not too far away from Lovely and in the same county but never quite near enough. That was changing.

Buoyed by her news, she slipped her phone out of her pocket and phoned Eloise, who had extended her stay in the Caribbean for a bit.

'Hey. How are you?' Eloise asked as she picked up on the first ring.

'Good. I'm just checking in to see if you're all set to come home. The house is good and the alarm is on. I'm going to pop in tomorrow with some milk and eggs for when you get in so you can make a cup of tea as soon as you walk in.'

'Ahh, thank you so much. Thanks for caring, Cal. You didn't have to.'

Cally always cared. She'd had to. It was deep down in her DNA. She switched on the same little 'I'm okay' voice in the back of her throat that she always used to make sure people weren't concerned about her. 'Don't be silly. How are the delights of the Caribbean?'

Eloise sounded relaxed and happy. 'Warm, sunny and lovely.'

'Ahh. I bet you don't want to come home. It's not warm and sunny here! The total opposite, in fact.'

'Actually, I'm ready to get back now. You know when you get that feeling when you've been on holiday?'

Cally didn't know. She'd give her right arm to be away and to have the feeling that she wanted to come home. She'd love a holiday anytime soon and an actual home of her own, too. 'Hmm.'

'How are things with you? How was that hotel you went to look at? Not that I'm letting you stay there.'

Cally groaned. 'Dreadful. Much, much worse than I thought. You don't even want to know how bad. Trust me, I won't be staying there.'

'Right, so you're staying at mine for a bit,' Eloise commanded.

'I won't need to.'

'What? Why not?'

'I've actually found somewhere.'

'Wow, great. Oh, that is good news. Where?'

Cally still couldn't quite believe it herself. She had to pinch herself that it was true. 'Via Birdie. It's a little flat over the deli you know the one just along the street from the chemist. It's a tip at the moment, but yeah, I'm moving in. I've just been to have a look at it today and it's locked in. Utilities included. I won't even have to bother with all that rigmarole.'

Eloise's voice was full of excitement. She practically yelled into the phone. 'That's such wonderful news! I'm over the moon for you. Where exactly is this little flat hiding?'

Cally couldn't keep the grin out of her voice. 'As I said over the deli. You know the shops there in Lovely Bay. Apparently, it's been sitting empty for donkey's years. An old aunt of Birdie's, one of the Lings, lived up there back in the day, but no one's really been up there for years. The access is terrible, so it's not really legal to rent it officially, so she just left it. There is a *lot* of dust and loads of sorting out to do. Birdie's going to order a skip.'

Eloise sounded delighted. 'You mean you're going to be living smack dab in the heart of Lovely Bay itself?'

Cally chuckled. It sounded good when Eloise said it like that. She had to stop herself from jigging a happy dance down the street. 'I know! I'd just about given up any hope of finding anywhere halfway decent to live and then she goes and pulls this utterly crackers but brilliant little hidey-hole out of the hat. I'm telling you, it's really nice and quiet and just perfect for me, really.'

'Those buildings are to die for. I can just picture it now – very vintage and quaint, and yes, so you. That sounds right up your street. I can see you up there all cosy. It has to beat that housing estate...'

Eloise just got it. Cally was grateful for that. 'I don't care if it's straight out of the nineties, to be quite honest. I've been desperate, as you well know.'

'You've always had an eye for charming bits and bobs. You'll make it so nice. And you just have yourself to worry about. Oh, and me when I come for a sleepover.'

Cally laughed. 'It's basically a time warp up there. I saw woodchip wallpaper and there is avocado paint in the bathroom. But I absolutely love it already, it's got so much potential to make my own. Sorry, I'm getting ahead of myself. I'm only renting, but you know, after the last few years and all that.'

'I'm dead chuffed for you. You deserve this chance more than anyone after all the rotten luck you've had with house-hunting, not to mention what went on before that with that pathetic excuse for a brother of yours.'

'Don't even mention him.' Cally said flatly.

'Nope. Lovely Bay is finally going to be your home, just like you wanted.'

Cally sighed scarcely able to believe her luck. 'I know, I can barely believe it's real myself. No more having to trek up and down on the train either. That creepy landlord at the house is on borrowed time, too.'

'You've certainly earned it. So, when do you get to move all your worldly bits and bobs in, then? I'll help. Many hands make light work and all that.'

Cally felt a rush of gratitude for Eloise, so much so that she felt her eyes prickling. 'It's hardly a big move. I got rid of most of Grandma's stuff when she got really sick if you remember rightly. The place is in a bit of a state at the moment – it needs a jolly good clear out and a lick of paint before I can properly nest in and make it homely. I don't really care, though.'

'We'll have you sorted right out in a jiffy. Ooh, I can't wait to come round and have a good old nose.'

Cally felt a lump rise in her throat at Eloise's words. After endless years of disappointments, knockbacks and false starts, she was going to get a fresh beginning somewhat. 'I'm completely over the moon. This time last week, I was staring down the barrel of some grim grotty high-rise somewhere far away from here.'

'As if I would have let that happen! You would have been moving in with me.'

'Thank you, Els.'

'Don't be silly.'

As the chat wrapped up and Cally slipped her phone back into her pocket with a massive grin, she gazed around at the street and nodded. She was not only going to be okay but she would be living in Lovely Bay with its pretty pastel-painted cottages with their climbing roses, sweet bunting flapping around, and the joys of the gorgeous shops all along the High Street. All of it was going to be hers to enjoy each day just by simply walking out her front door.

For so long, she'd been the one enviously passing through Lovely on the train, watching wistfully as it went past the back of beautiful old houses and chugged along by the river. She'd done many a walk over the greens, hoping for one of the little cottages, and had stood peering up at the lighthouse in wonder. Now, she was going to be a part of it rather than an observer on the outside always looking in. No more fleeting glimpses and pretending that because she worked there she was in. Maybe she'd start to get in the queue for a Lovely coat.

As she got to the train station, she tapped her card on the machine and stood waiting and looked over at the moveable platform on the other side. As a train slid away from the opposite platform, she peered around the pretty Victorian station. To her right, an old brick station house with lovely fretwork, two huge chimneys, and old advertising signs from years gone by faded and weathered at the top. Her eyes flicked around the platform where Lovelies, many of them dressed in the locally worn blue wax coat with its striped hood, waited for trains as pretty bunting fluttered around the platform signs for Lovely Bay. Cally squeezed her lips and nodded at the same time. Time for newer, better things. Time to actually call Lovely home. It had been a very long time coming.

10

Cally finished wrapping a mug in protective bubble wrap and lodged it carefully in a cardboard box. She'd packed up most of the kitchen in the rental house apart from a few things, the kettle and toaster. When she'd moved into the house just after her grandma's place had sold to release some of the equity so that she could go into full-time care, Cally had got rid of most of her stuff. She'd wanted to declutter and had at that time assumed her grandma's time was limited and that she would soon be gone. It hadn't happened that way and her grandma had defied the odds and clung on. At some points, Cally had wished she'd not been quite as ruthless with getting rid of things. On top of that, as the rent had gone up and her grandma's care costs had increased, she'd not had spare cash for anything to make the house feel like a home. Which meant she had little to pack. Silver linings and all that.

After taping up the box, she flicked on the kettle and busied herself with making a cup of tea. She then cradled the mug close to her chest, stood by the kitchen window, and gazed out at the tiny, tatty garden that had been her little pocket of nature for the past few years. The unkempt lawn was scattered with frost-encrusted leaves, the flowerbeds a post-winter mess, the forlorn washing line a bit rusty and askew.

Cally shivered as an icy gust of wind rattled the pane. The draughty little house felt as if the cold seeped in through the cracks. As she stood and sipped her tea, she couldn't wait to see the back of the place. Sometimes, she'd felt as if it was a bit of a prison as she'd juggled working in the chemist, her grandma's care, and logging on to the chatbot to solve people's problems with their deliveries of trousers that had cost them five hundred pounds. It had served its purpose, providing a roof over her head, but it was time to move on with her life. Hopefully, to bigger and brighter things. She was one step closer to making her Lovely Bay dreams a reality at last. The sooner she could bid farewell to this chapter, the sooner she could put all the horrible things that had gone with it in the past.

As Cally moved through the house, packing up the last of her belongings, as she closed each box, she felt a strange but not unwelcome feeling of closure. Each item she wrapped and placed in a box felt as if she was tucking up an old life ready to embark on a new one. She made her way into the cramped sitting room, where a bare bulb hung from the ceiling. Worn furnishings were at the fore and a saggy-in-the-middle sofa was faded and threadbare. A rickety bookshelf leaned against one wall where she'd placed a few books. As she packed away the books, she couldn't remember the last time she had actually sat down for a long stint and totally got lost in a book without any worries. Her life had been consumed by work and worry about her grandma and what had gone on with David and her stepdad for so long there had been little room for anything else. That had changed.

With the move to the flat in Lovely, the drop in the rental amount, no more train fares, and the lack of worry about her grandma's care, she suddenly realised that she felt lighter than she had possibly ever felt. She let her mind wander as she packed up her few remaining things and pictured herself curled up in a cosy armchair in her new flat, with a mug of steaming blackcurrant.

She skipped over the part where the flat was filled with clutter and dust and imagined stripping away the faded wallpaper and painting the walls. She could almost feel a lovely old rug under her feet and smell the salty sea air wafting through the balcony doors. And then there was the tiny kitchen, with its old-fashioned stove and worktops. Cally couldn't wait to get stuck into that. She'd already thought about paint and ordered vinyl adhesive for the worktops and new stick-on tiles. The bathroom, in particular, had seen better days but she couldn't care less, and more, she was up for the challenge. She had never been afraid of hard work, and the thought of putting her own stamp on a space in Lovely Bay filled her with happiness.

Just as she was going up to finish removing her stuff from the bathroom she got a text from Nina.

Nina: *Hey, just confirming tomorrow at Lovely Manor.*

Cally: *Yes, looking forward to it. See you there.*

Nina: *I can pick you up if you like.*

There was no way Cally was having Nina drive over her way. For a start, it was too far, and she was ashamed of the tatty little place. She'd get the train and then walk up to Lovely Manor.

Cally: *I'm fine, thanks.*

Nina: *No worries, just thought I'd offer. What time do you think you'll arrive?*

Cally: *I'll get the 8:01 train, so should be there by quarter to and then ten or so minutes from there.*

Nina: *Perfect. Let me know if you want me to swing by the station after I drop off Faye.*

Cally: *No need. Is there anything specific I need to bring or wear?*

Nina: *Just your lovely self! If you have a white shirt that would be great. I normally wear a white shirt and black trousers to look a bit professional. Oh, and comfortable shoes - you'll be on your feet a lot.*

Cally: *Got it.*

Nina: *See you bright and early then!*

Cally: *Can't wait! Thanks again for this.*

Nina: *Don't mention it, I'm just chuffed to have you on board. Get a good night's rest, tomorrow's going to be a busy one!*

Cally: *Will do.*

Cally smiled as she slipped her phone back into her pocket. It felt good to have something positive to look forward to, especially with all the upheaval of the move. She spoke aloud to no one in particular. 'Lovely Bay, here I come. Hope you're ready for me.' Little did she know, Lovely was most definitely ready to work its magic on her.

11

The next day, Cally nodded and waved hello to Nancy as she walked out of Lovely Bay train station, turned in the opposite direction of the riverboat and jetty and made her way down the road heading for Lovely Manor. As she strolled past St Lovely church with its beautiful blue nave door, she stopped for a second, untucked her scarf from the collar of her jacket, and gazed up at the tall church spire towering into a deep blue sky. The sky was a beautiful, clear blue, the wind biting, as a crisp day dawned around her in Lovely Bay. Despite the cold, Cally was warm from the overly heated train carriage; she flapped her hand a bit in front of her face and unzipped the front of her coat.

She stopped and looked at the old-fashioned sign for St Lovely church.

Join us this Sunday at St Lovely.
Lovely Bay's prettiest little church sitting right by the River Lovely.
8 am Traditional, 10 am Contemporary, and 5 pm Youth and Young Adults.

Cally did a funny sort of puffy snort at 'Youth and Young Adults'. Those were actually a thing, were they? She felt as if she'd missed out on that stage of her life. As she walked along, doing the kind of therapy that was accessible to her – walking in the fresh air –she thought about how Eloise had asked not long after the funeral if there was a possibility that Cally was burnt out. Cally had remained quiet and hadn't said much at all. Eloise, bless her, had no idea. Yes, she probably *was* burnt out. More than likely, actually. After years of caring for everyone else, she had never really been a child and was sick to the back teeth of looking after people. She was burnt out in more ways than one. But her circumstances meant that she didn't have the luxury to burn out. There would be no retreats or digital detoxes for her. The only way for Cally to keep her head above water was to continue working two or three jobs whilst looking for another and start to build a life and secure future, burnt out or not.

Strolling along taking in the sights of Lovely Bay as the River Lovely snaked away to the east and with plenty of time on her hands, she sat on a wall for a minute, swung her bag around to the front, and grabbed the small flask of hot blackcurrant she'd made before she'd left home. Flipping the lid on the top, little plumes of steam twirled up into the sky as she took a sip. After a few minutes of taking in the early morning view, with her bottom going cold on the wall, she got up and strolled along with the blackcurrant, thinking about what she was going to do with her life. At least she now had an interim solution to where she was going to live. She hadn't wanted to gush too much at Birdie's place, but she'd loved it on sight. It was in a time warp admittedly, tatty yes, and packed to the rafters for sure, but she couldn't stop thinking about the fact that she was going to have somewhere in Lovely Bay to call her own. Not only that but she would also be tucked up on the second floor, private, quiet and alone. With its heavy old door and little staircase, it felt safe and secure, almost as if it had been made for her. She could but wait and see.

As she strolled along with her hands around her blackcurrant, lost in thought, crisp, cool air filled her lungs and sunlight glinted off frost-kissed shell-shaped roof tiles. A few hardy sparrows chirped from tree branches, and a woman rugged up in a coat and scarf smiled as she walked past with a Labrador.

Cally side-eyed when she actually heard herself humming as she ambled along. Birdie's solution to her problem had lifted a huge weight from her shoulders. She felt as if just solving her living arrangement problem had unshackled her somehow. The two gigantic boulders that had been living on her shoulders ever since she'd received the tenancy notice had fallen off and rolled away down the road on their merry way. Everything about her and her surroundings, even the way her hot blackcurrant tasted, seemed to feel better now that she had eradicated the problem of a roof over her head.

Being in Birdie's flat would give her time to work out what she was going to do with herself, save up some money, maybe look around at doing a course, and just settle down and see how life ebbed and flowed for a bit. After being a carer for so long and having had to put so much on hold, she felt as if she had loads she wanted to do with her life, but she wasn't sure what. Silly little inconsequential things that would be *just* for her. No beeping of machines telling her to administer some kind of medicine, no pushing of wheelchairs, no liquidising meals, no hoisting over beds, no rushing to get stuff done to make sure someone else was alright. Not that she was bitter or had begrudged any of it. Oh alright then, just a bit, but she was ready to just be Cally, not do stuff for anybody else.

Living over the deli in Birdie's place was going to help her facilitate doing just that. In the short amount of time since she'd locked in the flat, she'd kept imagining silly little things and how they were going to up the ante in her life: a cosy sofa with a throw, Lovely chowder bubbling in a pan, pot plants in hanging wicker baskets, long, deep baths with her book, tealights all over the place, thick snuggly socks, mugs of hot blackcurrant made just for her and nobody else. Herbs on windowsills, piles and piles of books, an afternoon of baking, candles by the fire. The joys of warmer weather. A day on the beach. All of it to let Cally de Pfeffer just be Cally for a while. All of it to bring her back to life.

She daydreamed, smiled, and sipped on the piping hot blackcurrant as she walked past a house with smoke coming out of its chimney and a front glass verandah conservatory with a little cat in the window. She thought about how she was going to get the flat spick and span, move in and just take a breather for a bit. As she pondered further, she thought that rather than race on with doing this and that, she might, in fact, not do much at all. She would maybe simply hibernate with this new thing she had accompanying her, her *actual* life.

Strolling along the picturesque Lovely road, preoccupied with thoughts of the flat and what she was going to do with it, she lost all awareness for a bit. Until she was suddenly jolted back to reality as a loose cobblestone in the pavement, hidden beneath a dusting of frost, caught the toe of her boot. She swore, stumbled forward with a gasp, just about managed to keep her flask upright, but then slipped again. As she attempted to regain her balance and tried to keep the blackcurrant from falling, her arms pinwheeled comically, and the flask of blackcurrant slipped from her grasp. Time seemed to slow down as she watched as the flask tumbled end over end, its contents sloshing out in a steaming arc. Before she could even think to try and catch it, she slipped again and felt her feet fly out from under her. Not good. Landing with a heavy thud on her left hip, the impact knocked the wind from her in a whoosh. Pain radiated down her leg and up her back, and as she pressed her hands into the frosty pavement, she could feel the cold, damp on her palms. Was someone having a chuckle with her? She'd just been thinking about how her life was on the upturn now she was face down on the pavement. To add insult to the hip injury, the flask cup had upended its contents squarely onto Cally's front. Her once-pristine white shirt was now the proud owner of a dirty, great purple-red stain. Cally added quite a few blue swear words to a yelp of dismay as the liquid seeped through to her bra, and she felt it on her skin. *Fabulous. Or not.*

She sat there for a long moment, stunned and winded, blinking down at the mess in disbelief. Of all the days to fall flat on her face. She gingerly reached up to pluck at the sodden fabric of her blouse, wrinkled her nose at the smell of spilled blackcurrant and tutted.

A car passed by, and Cally glanced up to see a teenager gaping at her from a back passenger window. Heat bloomed in her cheeks as she realised she was still slap-bang in the middle of the pavement. With a groan, she heaved herself to her feet, wincing as her hip protested. A twinge in her ankle made her pause, and she tentatively rotated it, testing to see if she'd be able to put her weight on it. It was fine; she was okay, but her shirt was not. Rueing the fact that she'd said no to the lift from Nina, she brushed down her top, secured the lid on her cup, and picked up her bag. As Cally de Pfeffer always did, she soldiered on.

She looked down at herself, taking stock of the damage. Her thermal tights had a small, not really noticeable hole in the knee, her boots were a bit muddy where she'd slipped into the verge, and her top was clinging to her skin. So much for her once-crisp shirt she'd taken so much care to iron the night before. It was now a crumpled, blackcurrant-stained mess. Even her scarf hadn't escaped unscathed, the chunky knit now marred with splatters of red.

Tutting and sighing, she checked the time on her phone and decided she had little choice but to keep heading towards

Lovely Manor. With her hip feeling sore and her shirt clinging to her, she picked up her pace a little bit and continued on her way. Best laid plans.

About five or so minutes away from the manor, she felt her phone buzz in her pocket. Frowning, she fished it out and glanced at the screen to see Nina's name flashing up at her. *Now what?* Cally swiped to open the message.

Nina: *Hey. Morning. I'm so sorry, but I'm going to be a bit delayed. Faye was up all night with a stomach bug and I've been dealing with the fallout.*

Cally digested the text: if Nina was delayed, that meant she'd be tackling the initial stages of the decluttering project on her own when she really had no idea what she was doing.

Cally: *Oh no, poor Faye! Is she OK? Don't worry about me.*

She hit send and waited. She wasn't enamoured by the thought of going into Lovely Manor on her own if she could help it. A moment later, her phone buzzed again.

Nina: *She's a bit better now, just exhausted. I'll be there as soon as I can! If you wouldn't mind going in and introducing yourself.*

Cally: *No worries.*

Nina: *I'm already in the car, but I've got to sit through those lights by the roadworks. Robby's on dad duty...*

Cally: *OK. I'm not far away. See you there.*

Nina: *Thanks, Cal. I knew you wouldn't mind. I'll be there as soon as humanly possible. See you soon.*

Cally slipped her phone back into her pocket and took a deep breath. Just her luck. She was going to turn up not having a clue what she was doing with a dirty great stain on her shirt to boot and would know nothing. Village idiot of the third smallest town in the country sprang to mind.

She sighed out through her nose, stomped up the road and set her mouth in a straight, determined line. *Hello, new life. Blackcurrant stain and all.*

12

As she rounded the corner, Lovely Manor came into view. Cally gulped and raised her eyebrows. She looked down at her shirt and then up again as the manor house loomed in the distance. Oh, the irony. Here she was, about to turn up for work with no idea what she was doing, looking like something the cat had dragged in and having to wing it all the way.

Finally getting to a pair of huge black gates, she realised that Nina hadn't actually given her any instructions about how to get in. She winced and wondered what to do. She considered just waiting for Nina and seeing what happened from there. At the end of the day, Nina was the one who was late. Presuming that wouldn't go down very well with Nina, or Birdie for that matter, she strode up to the intercom system set into a stone pillar beside the gate. A sleek brass panel gleamed and a row of buttons and a small speaker ran along the top. Cally scanned the names listed alongside each button, searching for anything she recognised or a clue about where she was meant to be working.

She leaned in closer to examine the panel. A few of the buttons were worn and faded, the lettering barely legible in places. She took in the names here and there and ascertained that the surname of whoever owned the place was Henry-Hicks. She squinted, trying to make out the tiny text, and wondered which one was relevant to her. With a bit of a sigh, she pressed the button labelled "Main House," hoping that someone would be able to direct her to where she needed to be. A harsh buzzing sound emanated from the speaker, making her jump back in surprise. She waited, frowned, wondered what to do, heard nothing, and frowned again. Thinking she did not have much to lose, she pressed the button again, holding it down for a bit longer. The buzzing echoed in the morning air, but there was radio silence and no one answered. Just as she was about to try a third time, the intercom crackled to life so loudly that she nearly dropped her empty flask. A tinny, distorted, but very well-to-do voice emerged from the speaker.

'Yes? What? Who is it?' The hoity-toity voice sounded harried and impatient. Cally had to strain to make out the words.

Cally leaned in close to the panel and spoke loudly and clearly. 'Hi, um, it's Cally? I'm here from A Lovely Organised Life.'

'A what?'

'A Lovely Organised Life.' Cally repeated.

There was a long pause and then the voice came again, sounding slightly less irritated but just as posh. 'Cally, you said? From the agency? Another cleaner?'

Cally shook her head and then realised the person on the other end couldn't see her. She decided to just say yes so that the gate was opened and then she'd clear it up when she got to the house. 'Yes, that's right.'

Another crackle of static. 'Right, well, you'd better come on up then. Doreen should be here to answer the buzzer. Take the path to the left once you're at the top of the drive, it'll bring you around to the service entrance.'

Before Cally could respond, a loud buzzer sounded and the

gates began to slowly swing inward. She jumped back, startled by the sudden movement, then hurried to slip through the opening before they could close again. Once through the gates, she realised the magnitude of the house. Wow. With a bit of a sinking feeling, she realised that she'd made a mistake in saying no to Nina giving her a lift. The driveway was much longer than she'd anticipated. As the heavy wrought-iron gates clanged shut behind her, she was struck by the grandeur of Lovely Manor. The whole estate stretched out before her, its immaculately manicured lawns and pruned hedges a far cry from the grim, seventies housing estate she'd just left.

The gravel pathway to the side of the drive crunched beneath her feet as she made her way towards the main house. With its beautiful old brickwork, soaring windows, graceful lines, and symmetry, Cally shook her head – how the other half lived. She stared around the gardens as she walked: sculpted topiaries here, huge trees there. Frost-tipped ivy climbed a walled garden area, statues and fountains sat near a pond – Mr Darcy land. Cally tried and failed to swallow what was purely and simply envy. What would it be like to live in a place like it? She thought about her own circumstances and couldn't quite compute the two.

Lost in thought, she almost didn't notice a man standing near one of the sculpted hedges. In a thick green fleece and cap, he had a pair of pruning shears in gloved hands. He regarded her with a quizzical expression, his weathered face creasing into a frown. 'Morning. Long walk up there on a morning like this.' He nodded in the direction of the main house.

'Ahh, yes, longer than it looks from the road.'

The gardener smiled. 'New from the agency, are you?' He gestured towards the house with his shears, the blades glinting in the sunlight. 'You'll want to head round the back to the service entrance. I think Doreen's dealing with all that this week.'

Cally went to explain that she wasn't from the agency but decided he didn't really need to know. She would just walk up to the house and see what happened from there. She thanked him and set off in the direction he'd indicated. With the last part of the driveway to go, she was wondering where the service entrance might be and when Nina was going to turn up when the sound of tyres crunching on the gravel behind her made her pause and step further to the left. She turned, expecting to see a delivery van or perhaps another member of the manor's staff arriving for the day. Instead, she saw a sleek, black BMW. She pulled out her phone to check for a message from Nina as she waited for it to pass, but instead of going right on by, the car slowed to a stop beside her and she heard the window on the passenger's side slide down. Looking up from her phone, she squinted and frowned in the direction of the window and into the car.

'Hello again.'

Cally frowned and then, in an instant, recognised the driver. The man from the boat. Her stomach fluttered, followed by her heart. **** he was handsome. There was a wobble in her legs. She suddenly felt really small and insignificant standing on the driveway with the large blackcurrant stain on her blouse. 'Morning.'

He leaned over the centre console. 'Morning! I thought it was you. The woman who showered me in chicken and curry powder, right? From the riverboat.'

At least she'd been remembered. Cally was fairly pleased with that. 'Yep. Hi.'

The man indicated in the direction of Cally's shirt. 'So, last time it was chicken, this time it's?'

Cally frowned. 'Sorry?'

He pointed to Cally's shirt again. 'I'm presuming that's not a fashion statement.'

Cally shook her head. 'Ahh. No.'

'What happened? Rough morning?'

Cally rolled her eyes. 'I took a bit of a tumble on the frost just outside the church there. I had a bit of a run-in with a loose cobblestone, or at least that's what I think it was.'

He chuckled. 'Happens to the best of us. I once lost an entire mug of tea to a particularly vicious pothole on the road to the manor.'

'Well, I suppose I should count myself lucky that it was just a bit of blackcurrant and not something more sinister,' Cally joked, glancing down at the stain on her blouse.

His eyebrows rose. 'Blackcurrant, eh? Not coffee or tea like us mere mortals?'

Cally felt her cheeks flush. She wasn't going to stand there and tell him that she was addicted to blackcurrant and carried a carton of it with her at all times. She joked. 'What can I say? I like to mix things up a bit. Keeps life interesting.'

'I'll say,' the handsome man in the car laughed, shaking his head. 'Hang on, come to think of it, I recall a bottle of blackcurrant rolling in my direction on the boat.'

Cally's stomach did a little flip. He was *absolutely* gorgeous. Shame he was clearly *way* out of her league. She heard herself doing a strange little giggle and bantered back as quick as a flash. 'You're not wrong.'

'Right, so you drink blackcurrant on cold, frosty mornings and douse yourself in it for fun?'

'It was hot blackcurrant actually.'

'Different.'

'That's me, always keeping everyone on their toes.'

He leant his elbow on the console and beamed. 'Sounds like you certainly do that from what I've seen so far. Anyway, I'm Logan. And you are? Or should I just call you Blackcurrant? Has a ring to it.'

Cally's eyes widened. 'I've been called worse.'

'I bet you have if you go around throwing chicken and curry powder at people at regular intervals.'

Cally groaned. 'I'm never going to live that down, am I?'

'Not a chance, Blackcurrant. That's the kind of first impression that sticks with a person.'

'Cally.'

'Nice. Short for anything?'

Cally hadn't been asked that for a very long time. She hesitated for a second. 'Claudette.'

'Mmm. I'm Logan. Plain old Logan.'

'Nice to meet you.'

Logan glanced towards the house as if suddenly remembering where they were. 'So, what brings you to Lovely Manor anyway, Blackcurrant, I mean Cally?'

'I'm actually helping someone. Nina, from A Lovely Organised Life. Do you know her?'

Logan shook his head. 'No, no.' He contemplated for a second. 'I'm not here all the time so I don't know what's what. My mum lives here. It's complicated.'

'Oh, right.'

Logan raised his eyebrows. 'So, what does that involve?'

'It's a decluttering business.'

'Got you. Must be in the new wing.'

'The new wing?'

'Yep. It'll make sense when you get there. Sorry, so where is this Nina, then?'

'Oh, she's late.' Cally heard herself rambling a little bit. 'I like to walk, especially in the mornings, and yeah, I came on the train. To be honest, I didn't realise how far it was, but I always leave myself enough time.'

'Makes sense. Right, well, I'll leave you to it. You'll be dealing with Doreen, I assume. She's the housekeeper up at the manor. Runs a tight ship.'

'I'm not sure. It's all in Nina's hands.' Cally hitched her bag higher on her shoulder and gestured towards the house. 'Well, I suppose I'd better get a move on.'

'Do you want to hop in?'

Cally swished her hand in front of her and shook her head. 'No, no, thanks, I'm fine. Thanks for the offer.'

'Anytime, Blackcurrant. Nice to bump into you again.'

'Yep.'

Logan gave a jaunty little salute before pulling away. Cally watched the car cruise over the gravel and quickly disappear down the long, winding drive. Well, Lovely Manor was looking up. Its residents weren't too shoddy, that was one thing for certain. Cally de Pfeffer could work with that. It had to be better than the online customer service portal any day of the week.

13

Once Logan's car had disappeared, Cally looked up at the huge house as her boots crunched on the gravel. Part of her couldn't believe the imposing property was actually someone's home that needed decluttering. To her, it was almost unbelievable that someone actually lived there, let alone found the time to junk it up. In Cally's world, Lovely Manor had stepped right out of a BBC drama, and it certainly didn't have humble things such as clutter anywhere near it.

Cally shook her head. Any moment now, a Jane Austen heroine would run across the lawn in a bonnet. A man in a wet white shirt would emerge from a murky pond. For a bit, she just stood and looked at the vast lawns. Her eyes settled on a little timber sign pointing to a kitchen garden. Cally shook her head again - this was the sort of place that had gardens with names. She chuckled to herself; here she was, thinking about buying a few pots of herbs from the garden centre for the little balcony she'd be renting from Birdie. This place, on the other hand, had named gardens. How the other half lived.

Cally shivered as a gust of icy wind whipped across the

manor grounds, the chill blasting against her still damp blackcurrant-stained blouse. She burrowed her chin deeper into her scarf and stomped her feet on the ground. Looking up, she took everything in: the huge trees in the blue sky, the frost clinging to the stretching-away lawns, glints from the pond, tall windows sparkling with frost. Checking the time on her phone and not seeing a message regarding Nina's whereabouts, she raised her eyebrows towards the heavy timber door where a wicker wreath hung from a polished brass knocker. And this was the service entrance. It certainly wasn't a plastic (with additional mouldy bits around the window) door to a social experiment that had dismally failed not long after it had been built.

Taking a few steps up to the door, Cally raised her hand to push the buzzer on a panel on the left-hand side. Just as she was about to push the button, her phone pinged. Fumbling in her pocket, her fingers stiff from the cold, she pulled her phone out to see Nina's name flashing on the screen and quickly swiped to answer. Thinking that Nina would be calling to tell her she was stuck in traffic, she eyerolled. Great, she was going to have to blag her way in and pretend she knew what she was doing. Talk about jumping in at the deep end.

'Hi.' Her voice sounded oddly loud in the stillness of the grounds.

Nina sounded harassed. 'All good. Sorry about this. Look, I'm just pulling up to the main gate now. I'm never late. So sorry. Where are you?'

'I was just about to knock on the door. It took me longer than I thought because I didn't realise the driveway was a good ten-minute walk from the gate.'

'Where?'

'At the service entrance,' Cally replied, glancing around at the manor. 'This place is massive, Neens. I feel like I've stepped into a period drama.'

Nina laughed. 'Wait until you see the inside. It's like a museum or a national library or both. Anyway, stay put. I'll be there in a jiffy.'

Cally felt more than relieved that she wasn't going to have to go in on her own. 'Okay, see you in a bit.'

A few minutes later, she heard the crunch of tyres on gravel just before she saw Nina's car go down the side of the kitchen garden and park just in front of what looked to Cally like stables. Cally walked around the kitchen garden and stood waiting for Nina to get out of her car.

Nina hopped out, her cheeks flushed. 'Sorry! What a nightmare. How are you?'

'Good. Not a problem.'

Nina frowned at the Ribena stain. 'Oh, what happened to you?'

Cally rolled her eyes. 'I took a bit of a tumble.'

'Yikes.'

Cally pointed to her knee and the hole in her tights and patted her hips. 'I slipped on a frosty bit over by the church. You know where the cobbled pavements are there?'

'Ahh, yes. I only thought that the other day when I had the pram with Faye. It's really slippery there. Someone should do something about it. It's a death trap.'

Cally nodded. 'Yep. It was right there. Those old cobbled pavements get mossy and then what with the frost on top of them, I went flying. I wasn't looking where I was going properly...'

'Oh well. At least you're in one piece.'

'I'll live.'

Nina gestured towards the house. 'Well, here we are. Fancy, eh? Are you ready?'

Cally laughed. 'It's a bit surreal. Like something out of a fairytale.'

Nina lowered her voice. 'We're in the other wing in the newer section. There's a lot of work to do.'

'Really?' Cally flicked her hand around at the manor house. 'It doesn't, umm, look like the sort of place that has clutter.'

'Oh, yes.' Nina also waved her hand around. 'This place takes it to whole new levels. We're not in the old stately home bit. There's a different wing and it's *full* of clutter. Lots to get our teeth stuck into.'

'Oh, right, okay.'

'And trust me, everyone has clutter.' Nina stated.

'Actually, not me. I got rid of most of my stuff when my grandma went into the hospice.'

'Yep, makes sense. That's when a lot of people declutter when they move house or, you know, have a stressful thing happen like you did.'

Cally swiftly moved the conversation away from her troubles. She lifted her chin to look up at the chimneys. 'It's such a lovely old place. I can't believe there's a mess behind this beautiful exterior.'

'This is the old part of the manor, but the newer wing is where they actually live. Though that's still as big as this. There's a heap of stuff to get on with,' Nina said with a chuckle.

'Show me the way.'

Nina laughed as she clicked the boot and waited for it to open. She started to load bags out onto the ground. Cally grabbed a couple and swung them over her shoulders. Nina held up a big stack of folded, empty storage bags. 'Be prepared to get your decluttering hat on.'

Cally puffed out air and watched as little plumes of smoke rose. 'At least we'll be warm in there, or at least I hope we will be. I can't feel my toes anymore. What's happened to the spring weather?'

'I know, it's so cold again. Rightio, let's do this.'

'Yup, let's get stuck in.'

∼

After going in the service entrance, the housekeeper, Doreen led Cally and Nina through the old manor house. They followed her through dark corridors and across rooms with vast ceilings and long tables. Cally hid a shiver as they walked through an entrance hall. Their footsteps echoed on a beautifully laid herringbone floor. Trying to keep her chin from dropping at the size of the place, she inhaled the scent of lemon polish, a faint whiff of mustiness commensurate with the house's age and a little bit of dampness. The damp smelt similar to the smell in the flat. That was where the similarities ended.

Doreen pushed open a huge, heavy door, and they passed through a long hallway where heavy velvet drapes framed the windows. Mildly scary faces in paintings looked down on them and seemed to watch them as they passed. Doreen paused at a large wooden door at the end of the corridor, fiddled to open it and then they crossed a huge room with a fireplace as big as Cally's rental house. Then after what felt like a labyrinth of narrower, shorter corridors, they arrived at a huge old kitchen with flagstone floors. The kitchen was vast and dominated by a colossal navy blue double-width Aga running along the back wall. Cally felt herself sag a little bit at the warmth radiating around the room. The Aga's polished lids gleamed from overhead lights and a table that could seat at least twelve displayed a huge bouquet of flowers in the centre.

Doreen chatted as she gesticulated for Cally and Nina to sit down and moved with ease around the kitchen. She filled a kettle with water from an old-fashioned brass tap that made a gurgling noise as it turned, placed it on the Aga, and gathered mugs, a box of tea bags, and a small jug of milk. Cally sat there, taking it all in, feeling as if she'd been dropped into another world. As the water came to a boil, Doreen put a plate of scones on the table and waved out the window to someone going into the stables. Cally looked around at the high ceilings and row upon row of copper pots and pans hanging from a wrought iron rack above the island. 'It feels like stepping back in time.'

Doreen chuckled as she poured boiling water into the teapot, the steam swirling up into the air. 'Yes, it does have that effect on people. The family has tried to keep this side of the house as original as possible. This Aga has been here a lot longer than I have, and I've been around quite a while.'

Nina laughed. 'Cally said she felt as if she was in a period drama when we arrived. I do, too. I just need the costume and someone to dress me before I am presented with afternoon tea.'

Doreen stirred the teapot. 'Well, we've had shoots, movies, and all sorts here over the years. Let me tell you I've seen it all. We've got one coming up soon.'

Cally frowned. 'It must be a bit surreal, having film crews in and out.'

'Oh, it is. When they're here, I'm making twenty cups of tea at a time. It's good for the house, keeps it alive. We've had some lovely actors and actresses grace this kitchen and some not-so-lovely ones.'

Nina chuckled. 'Ooh, gossip. You'll have to sell your story to the Mail.'

Doreen raised her eyebrows. 'I wouldn't dare.' She handed Cally a mug of tea. 'Here you go. That should warm you up. So much for Spring, eh? What's happened to the weather again? I thought we'd seen the back of it and here we are again freezing this morning. At least the pipes have stood up to it this year. Last year, it was a right old two and eight.'

Cally put her hands around the mug and took a sip. 'Yes, it's meant to start improving next week. Bring on the daffodils and sunshine; that's all I can say.'

'I hope so,' Nina said as Doreen passed her the plate of scones. 'I need warm days on the beach.'

Doreen chuckled. 'You and me both.'

As they sat sipping their tea, Cally couldn't quite believe where she was. She imagined the kitchen bustling with servants long before, the air filled with clattering dishes and people busying around.

Doreen sat down. 'So the pair of you have got your work cut out for you, then.'

Cally kept quiet as Nina replied, 'We have.'

Doreen tutted. 'It's taken long enough and there was no way I was putting my hand up for that job over there.'

'It's a big one.'

'It'll be interesting to see what you find and what she'll part with.' Doreen pursed her lips and raised her eyebrows. 'The things she shoves in those cupboards and she thinks no one knows.'

Nina nodded. Cally clocked that Nina was being careful about what she said. 'I think I saw some of that when I came to quote for the job.'

'Said she wanted someone local which I was pleased about,' Doreen noted.

Nina leant forward. 'So, who actually lives here nowadays?'

Doreen nodded. 'Well, you met the lady of the house, Cecilia Henry-Hicks, and then Reginald. Never call him Reg, not that you'll ever see him anyway – he's mostly in the place in Knightsbridge. Then, the boys Alastair and Jasper. Then we have Reg's sister over at one of the cottages and various others who are in and out – Logan's here at the moment. It's not a quiet place. Then the staff...'

'And what do you do?' Nina asked.

'I'm the housekeeper for the manor itself.' Doreen waved her hand around. 'I don't get involved over there much these days. Cecilia is funny about it. She has her own set of rules and suchlike. I'm an expert in the old house and I keep myself out of the way. I organise everyone.'

'Right.'

'So, how long do you think you'll be here?' Doreen asked. 'There's a lot to fill your time over there. Cecilia likes her things, shall we say.' She rolled her eyes. 'Trust me, I take most of the Amazon orders in.'

Nina was being diplomatic. 'It's a big job. I left it open.'

Doreen pushed her chair out and picked up her mug. 'Right, well, I'd better let you get on. I'll take you over there so you know the way. You can actually park around there tomorrow. It might make it easier for you.'

The newer wing still felt old to Cally. Let's be frank, it wasn't in the league of an estate of shoebox houses where every thirty or so were centred around a concrete square. In contrast to the main house, the adjacent wing looked to Cally to have been built in the twenties. A gust of deliciously warm, heated air rushed to greet them as Doreen pushed open a side door and led them through a sitting room to a main hallway. Cally stopped herself from gaping. It was different to the manor and felt as if opulence was suffocating her: beautiful light fittings, heavy furniture, thick made-to-measure floor-to-ceiling curtains, big luxurious rugs. Cally felt as if she'd just jumped into the pages of Country Life magazine. She kept quiet as she soaked everything in and trailed along behind Nina, lugging one of Nina's heavy bags.

Doreen took them through further rooms of equal elegance to a small side room with a large armchair, a row of cupboards along a wall, and a long, wide desk flanked on either side by a pair of huge lamps. 'Cecilia said to pop you in here as your base. You can put all your stuff in here and not worry about it getting in anyone's way.' She chuckled. 'You can escape if you need to, too.'

Nina dumped her bags on the floor. 'Thanks for the tea, Doreen.'

Doreen smiled. 'No worries. Will you be wanting lunch? It's soup for the staff today. Pea and ham.'

Nina smiled. 'Works for me.' She looked at Cally with raised eyebrows. 'You?'

'Yes, please, that would be great,' Cally replied.

'Okay. It'll be a late one today because the gardeners are over on the other side. Will that work for you?'

Cally wasn't going to turn down a free lunch in a manor house, whatever time of day it was. 'Yes, thank you.'

Doreen nodded. 'Just make your way back over to the kitchen at about two-ish. It'll be nice to have you.'

Cally watched Doreen walk down the corridor and then turned to look at the bag and equipment Nina had put on the floor. Nina took charge and pulled out an iPad that she tapped and handed to Cally. 'That's my plan. If you're okay with it, you're starting in the third office, which is an annexe off the dining room. Yes, there are two other main offices. Trust me, all of them need help.'

Cally read down the list. Nina was no amateur. She immediately relaxed as she saw that Nina was all over it. Cally had been assigned jobs with estimated timeframes, taking into account when she was working for Birdie for the whole week. A few minutes later, she was standing with her hands on her hips beside Nina, assaulted by the organised chaos of the third office. What greeted them was a kaleidoscope of colours and textures, stacks of boxes filled with various knick-knacks, piles of old newspapers, and rows of books and magazines stacked waist-high. Piles of old manila folders swamped a cluttered desk, along with two old computers, too many lamps, baskets of stationary, planners, hand creams, all sorts in a jumbled mess.

Cally raised her eyebrows. 'Wow.'

'I know.'

Cally joked and lowered her voice, 'Are we calling this an annexe?'

Nina whispered, 'It's bigger than my sitting room.'

Cally chuckled. 'At least you have one.'

Nina pointed to overflowing bookcases and piles of books. 'As I noted, the first job of the day is to get that lot in order. Cecilia wants to be able to work here.' Nina paused for a minute and looked at the iPad. 'So, pull everything off those shelves. Anything you think needs to be dumped pop in boxes, which I'll get from the car in a minute.' Nina gestured to the boxes of clutter and the shelves. 'She said she wants most of the knick-knacks packed away.' Nina pointed to the books blocking the French doors to the garden. 'Those will go on the shelves once you've cleared everything off and started again, and then at least there will be room to move in here.'

'Rightio.'

'Easy enough?' Nina chuckled. 'At least we're not sorting drugs in the back of the chemist accompanied by the Shipping Forecast.'

Cally nodded and tapped her phone. 'I can pop the Shipping Forecast on if you like.'

Nina rolled her eyes. 'God, no. Okay, I'll love you and leave you. I'm starting on the guest bedroom or at least one of them. You'll be okay in here on your own?'

'Absolutely. Don't worry about me.'

'That is why I wanted you to work with me on this.' Nina nodded. 'You get it, and you don't need hand-holding.' Nina shook her head. 'Nothing worse than having to babysit someone who is *supposed* to be working for you. They let you down and don't put in their pound of flesh but bite your hand off quickly enough for a pay rise which is why I am so very glad I have you to help because I know you *want* to work with me.'

Cally raised her eyebrows. She was surprised to hear the business side of Nina. 'I like you, Boss Neens.

'Ha. Don't mess with me, our Cally. I'm learning quickly to take no prisoners in business. Slackers get the push.'

'I won't.' Cally gestured at the room. 'Actually, I can't wait to get stuck in.'

14

About three hours later, Cally was covered in dust. She'd lugged everything from the bookshelves to the other side of the room and had piles of things everywhere with one small channel on the carpet left for her to shimmy through. She'd made the mistake of using one of the feather dusters Nina had brought in to dislodge the dust. She'd fluffed the brush in the direction of the shelves and it had thrown clouds of dust up into the air, most of which had then landed all over her. There was dust in her hair and up her nose. It added to the attractive look she was going for with the blackcurrant stain on her shirt.

On her hands and knees with her head in a cupboard, she stopped as she heard a door open and voices come into the dining room next to the third office. Crawling backwards out of the cupboard, she listened to the decidedly nice received-pronunciation-pretending-they were-normal voices rattling onto each other.

'Yeah, yeah, whatever. You just swan off to Mustique like you always do. Leave other people to hold the fort. We get it.'

'Rich to you! The person who had more holidays last year than any of us, and yes, it was noted.'

'What is that supposed to mean?'

'White powder pretty much sums it up.'

Another voice interjected. 'Don't you two start. We're meant to be having a nice early lunch.'

The first voice continued. 'So, have you booked the flights?'

'I have. I mean, look at the weather. Loads of us are going. It's only a couple of weeks.'

'Does Daddy know?'

There was a guffaw. 'No. *As if.* He won't even notice.'

'He's just paying for it,' the first voice stated.

'Sorry, when was the last time you paid for anything? Don't start getting nit-picky because you have to stay here and have meetings with the accountants. Daddy asked you to do that, and you said yes. You were sucking up to him at the time so that you could go to France.'

'I know. I just wanted to go skiing and have a bit of time off.'

'Time off! From what precisely?'

'Whatever. Logan, you could have the meeting with the accountants, couldn't you? Problem solved.'

Cally heard the third voice, Logan. Mmm. She shook her head. Logan from the boat and the car on the drive, was it? It sounded like him. She strained to work out if it was the same voice. She assumed there wouldn't be more than one Logan. 'No can do. I am not first-line blood.'

Cally continued to earwig, feeling as if she was being exposed to life on another planet with the hoity-toity talk of Mustique, holidays, and accountants. She crawled over, knelt on the floor, pressed her ear against the door, and listened. She wondered if she'd stumbled into a parallel universe. The posh accents and entitled attitudes of the voices on the other side of the door were in stark contrast to her own reality. She felt as if she counted every penny every day. No trips to Mustique for her. She'd literally, a few days before, encountered the real threat of homelessness, which had been looming over her for weeks, and here were these voices complaining about their hard-done-by lives. To be fair, it was only the first two who were complaining.

'I just don't see why I have to be the one to deal with all this tedious financial stuff,' the first voice whined, the petulance in its tone making Cally roll her eyes. 'It's not like I'm equipped to handle these sorts of things. That's what accountants are for, isn't it? Just pay someone already. Remember how bad I was at school? The only reason I didn't get thrown out was because of the family name.'

'Oh, do quit your moaning,' the second voice chimed in, sounding exasperated. 'It's not like you've got anything better to do. Unless you consider getting sloshed on Daddy's money a valuable use of your time.'

Cally stifled a snort. She'd never met these people, maybe she had Logan, the third voice, but she could picture them perfectly – all wealthy clothes and old money style, with not a worry about where their next meal was coming from. No trips to First Lodge Hotel to check out dodgy rooms for them. No clearing out someone else's clutter. Grrr.

'Now, now, let's not start throwing stones,' Logan interjected. 'We all have our crosses to bear. AJ, I know it's a pain, but you did agree to handle the accounts this quarter. It's only fair.'

Cally shook her head in disbelief. *Crosses to bear? These people wouldn't know hardship if it bit them on the nose.* The bathroom in the motorway hotel flashed into her mind. She thought about the constant worry about making rent, having to work on the customer service chatbot and her grandma's care costs. The pure and utter fear when she'd been given notice and she'd thought she would end up on the street. How she'd basically had to take charity from Birdie.

'Fine, fine,' the first one grumbled. 'But I expect a good holiday for my troubles. And no, I do not call a week in the New York apartment a holiday. Oh, and let me tell you now, I am not getting involved in the charity event for Lovely. No way.'

Cally had to physically restrain herself from banging her head against the door. The sheer audacity of these people was astounding. Holiday? She'd be lucky if she could afford a National Express ride to Cornwall.

'Speaking of the event,' the second voice piped up, 'Mummy's been pestering me about the guest list for weeks now.'

'Can't we just skip it? It's always such a bore. The same stuffy old codgers droning on about their investments, holiday homes, and tax evasion in the Channel Islands. I'd rather watch paint dry. Just get Daddy to shove a load of money to a few charities and be done with it.'

Cally bit her lip. Poor little rich boy, forced to endure the tedium of his family's lavish soirées. What she wouldn't give for a taste of that lifestyle, even just for a day. One nice day.

As the conversation turned to the merits of various ski resorts and the best places to find truffles in the off-season, Cally felt her initial amusement give way to full-on bitterness. Her whole being slowly turned green. These people had no idea how lucky they were or how privileged their lives were compared to the vast majority of the population. It made her sick.

She thought about her own dire straits, the constant stress and uncertainty, and how she'd had to struggle to do her degree through the Open University. The cold, damp house she'd rented with its leaky taps and dodgy electric heating. She gritted her teeth together. *So not fair. ****wits.*

These people had everything handed to them on a literal silver platter while she had to fight for stability and security. They didn't have a clue. Cally surprised herself with her feelings as she sat crouched by the door and felt resentment bubble up inside her. She hadn't realised how cynical she was until she heard the entitlement playing out on the other side of the door.

It was so unlike her to be bitter and twisted, at least not on the outside. Normally, she masked it well. Usually, she just got on with things, but the whiny voices and talk made her seethe.

Deciding that she didn't have time to listen to pouty rich people whose main concern was where to go skiing, she got up. With a deep breath, she then blew out slowly through her mouth, brushed the dust and cobwebs from her clothes, and looked at the shelves in front of her and the task at hand. She was at Lovely Manor to do a job, not to judge. She flicked the duster over the shelves again and clouds of dust instantly filled the room. She coughed and sputtered a bit, plugged in the vacuum, and started to suck up the dust from the shelves. As she got on with it, she put the conversation on the other side of the door out of her mind and put her head down. She had a living to earn, and she wasn't about to let the pathetic complaining of a bunch of spoiled rich kids annoy her any more than it already had.

As she turned back to the bookshelves, though, she couldn't shake the conversation and went over it in her head. What a load of grown-up brats. She might have come from the other side of the fence, but at least she knew the value of an honest day's work, of earning her keep and making her own way in the world. Daddy's money? Really?

Once Cally had finished vacuuming up years of dust, she was entirely focused on her task and put the toffs out of her head. There was not enough brain space for them in her world. She methodically loaded books onto the top shelf of the towering bookcase, trying to ignore the chat emanating from the next room. With the vacuum cleaner now off, she again tuned into the conversation.

'I must get Doreen to pass this lunch recipe to the London staff. She's truly outdone herself this time,' one of the voices exclaimed.

Cally rolled her eyes, tutted, shook her head, and muttered

to herself, 'Must be nice, having someone to cater to your every whim and fancy.'

She stretched up on her tiptoes to wedge another heavy book back into place. She was cracking on at a good pace, and despite her insight into the world of privately educated whiners, she was quite enjoying herself. There was something very therapeutic about clearing and tidying someone else's junk. She reached up again with a book. The top two shelves were nearly full, a load of old leather-bound volumes teetering as she tried to squeeze in just one more. 'Get in there,' she said to a book and wobbled as she pushed it in.

As she banged it into place, she suddenly felt the shelf give way beneath her hands. There was a sickening crack. Cally's eyes widened in horror as the books began to tumble off the shelf, onto the floor, her feet, and onto the shelves below – a deluge of books dropped down in one fell swoop. She let out a yelp of pain as one particularly weighty volume landed squarely on her outstretched hand, the edges of the binding digging into her skin.

'Ow!' She stumbled backwards and twisted her ankle in a vain attempt to avoid the avalanche of literature. But it was too late. To her absolute horror, as she peered up, she could see that it looked as if the entire bookcase might come down. It swayed ominously; she dodged to the left and then watched as it tipped forward with a deafening crash, a couple of books landing on her feet.

Her feet were buried beneath a mountain of dusty old posh people's books, her hand throbbed and she swore repeatedly. For a long moment, she just stayed where she was, looking at the chaos around her, mortified. Her mind raced as she tried to figure out how on earth she was going to explain the disaster to Nina. She thought about how much it was going to cost to repair. She tried not to cry. Pulling her foot out from under the books, she plonked down on the floor and rubbed her ankle.

Suddenly, the door to the room burst open, revealing the concerned face of none other than the man from the boat and the driveway, Logan. 'Oh, it's you! What the hell? Blackcurrant! What in the world have you done?' His eyes widened as he took in the scene: the broken bookcase, the books scattered all over the place, the piles of clutter and junk. 'Are you okay? You don't look okay. What happened here?'

Cally felt her cheeks flame with embarrassment as she struggled to stand up, wincing as her bruised hand throbbed in protest. 'Sorry! I'm fine. Just had a bit of an accident with the bookcase, that's all. I'm terribly sorry, I'll clean it up straight away.'

Logan was already striding across the room, he knelt down beside her. 'Don't be ridiculous. You're hurt. Let me have a look at that hand and your foot. Is that okay?'

Cally gulped. He smelled more than fabulous – like so, *so* nice. Stuff the hand. She was acutely aware of his proximity as he squinted and touched her arm. She went to argue, to insist that she was perfectly capable of taking care of herself. But she crumbled so very quickly and found herself nodding mutely. She'd just wallow in it for a minute. Smell him. 'I'm fine.'

Logan squinted at Cally's foot. 'Sure?'

Cally rubbed her hand. 'Just a bit shocked. It all happened so quickly.'

'Hmm, it doesn't look like anything's broken, not that I have a clue what I'm talking about. But we should get some ice on it, just to be safe. Come on, let's get you sorted out.'

Logan helped Cally to her feet, steadying her as she swayed slightly. 'Lean on me.'

There was no way Cally was going to say no to leaning on Logan. He slipped an arm around her waist to support her weight. It felt so nice. He was huge. She fizzed. 'Thanks.'

Logan pointed to the chair by the desk. 'Actually, you sit there. I'll be back with some ice.'

As Cally sat looking at the mess in the room, she shook her head at what had happened – so much for wanting one nice day. Her day was going from bad to worse. Though being tended to by a fancy-pants man in a manor house wasn't too shabby. She felt something she couldn't quite put her finger on. As if, despite their vastly different backgrounds and circumstances, she and Logan had somehow been meant to cross paths. She shook her head. *Ridiculous.* She must be concussed or something. Men like Logan did not cross paths with someone like her. And anyway, she had much more pressing matters to worry about like the mountain of mess around her than whether or not fate had made her come across Logan. It was a nice notion, though. Exceedingly nice.

When Logan came back from wherever he'd been, he had a tea towel and a bag of frozen peas in his hand. He knelt down beside Cally and placed the tea towel-wrapped bag of frozen peas on her ankle. 'That should help with the swelling if there is any.'

Cally nodded, a bit embarrassed by the fuss. 'Thank you, really. But I'm sure it's nothing serious. Just a bit of a shock, that's all.'

Logan raised an eyebrow. 'Well, I'm no doctor, but I think it's safe to say that having a bookcase fall on you qualifies as more than "just a bit of a shock". You're lucky it wasn't worse.'

Cally grimaced as she surveyed the chaos in the room. Books were strewn everywhere, pages crumpled and spines bent. The once-tidy piles of clutter she'd been sorting through were now scattered haphazardly across the floor, a chair was on its side. It was going to take ages to clean up the mess. 'I don't know what happened. One minute I was shelving books, and the next...' She trailed off, shaking her head.

'Don't worry about it. Accidents happen. The important thing is that you're not seriously hurt.'

Cally gestured to her dishevelled appearance. 'This is my

second accident of the day. I must look like I've been dragged through a hedge backwards. Twice.'

'You don't look bad to me.' Logan smiled as he shifted the bag of peas slightly. Cally felt a fluttering sensation in her stomach that had nothing to do with what she was feeling in her ankle. It moved lower and tingled. To be frank, she'd feign more injuries if it meant Logan might touch her elsewhere. She'd give anywhere a go. Mentally scolding herself, she tried to focus. 'I should really get started on cleaning this up,' she said, making to stand.

Logan placed a hand on her shoulder and gently pushed her back down into the chair. 'Whoa, not so fast. Give yourself a chance to catch your breath, at least. I'll stand the bookshelf back up and clear up these broken bits.'

'I just need to get on.'

'So, how did you end up working up here, anyway?'

Cally latched onto the topic. 'Oh, it's a long story. I'm new to Lovely Bay. I was struggling to find a place to live and Birdie, you know, from the chemist, she sort of took me under her wing. I work there. She offered me a flat above the shop, well not that shop, one of her other shops, she has loads and she also put me in touch with Nina about some work. I already knew Nina through the chemist, too. That's the short version anyway. Nina and I have worked together for Birdie a few times. She's an organising genius.' Cally heard herself rambling.

'Glad you found your way to Lovely Bay.'

Cally swallowed. She wasn't sure what to think apart from the fact that she was having a very nice time talking to Logan. She might have to start pulling bookcases down on herself more often. 'Me too.'

Logan smiled, giving her ankle a gentle pat before standing up. 'Right. I'll give you a hand.'

Cally protested. 'No, no. I really don't want you to help.'

'You *really* don't?' Logan mimicked her. 'If you think I'm

going to let you clean up this mess all by yourself you've got another thing coming,' Logan said as he began to gather armfuls of books, stacking them on the desk. He then lifted the bookcase as if it weighed nothing, put it back into place, took the broken shelf and propped it against the desk.

Cally stood up gingerly, testing her weight on her ankle. It twinged a bit, but overall, it was fine. She thought about pretending it was really bad so that he would stroke it but she resisted. Satisfied that she wasn't going to keel over, she bent down and started collecting scattered papers. She couldn't stop looking at Logan or smelling him. *Stop it,* she admonished herself. *You're being ridiculous. He's just being nice, helping you out.*

About five minutes later, most of the stuff that had toppled was off the floor and on the desk. Cally smiled. 'Honestly, I'm good from here.'

'If you're sure.'

'Yep. I'd rather just get on with it myself, if you don't mind.'

'Oh, right, okay then.' Logan nodded, running a hand through his hair. 'Of course. I should probably go.' He trailed off, gesturing vaguely towards the door.

'Yes, you should... I mean, I should get on.' Cally stammered, feeling like a tongue-tied schoolgirl.

'Take care of that ankle, Blackcurrant.'

'Will do.'

'Right, okay. Well, see you whenever, then.' Logan's smile widened, his eyes crinkling at the corners. 'I'll look forward to it.'

'Yes, thanks for helping and for the peas.'

'Not a problem.'

After Logan left, Cally couldn't stop thinking about him. Her thoughts raced and her mind reeled. He was a bit posh, unfairly attractive, and polished on the outside, but with an undercurrent of something. What even was it? Authenticity maybe? Genuine. He seemed kind. She wasn't sure. She *was* sure about how much she liked his bones. It all felt a bit much to take in. Cally felt like she'd just stepped off a roller coaster. Her stomach did somersaults. There'd been a zap, or a zip, or a charge between her and Logan as far as she was concerned or maybe she'd totally imagined it.

She shook her head. She was getting ahead of herself, letting her imagination run away with her. The smell, though. Logan was just being kind, doing the decent thing by helping her out. A shelf had fallen on her; it wasn't as if he was going to stand around and do nothing. As she sat surrounded by the musty smell of old books, she turned her head to the side. At least her existence was no longer quite as dull. If the day was any indication to go by, her life might get a little bit more interesting from here on out. If it involved this Logan fellow she wouldn't mind in the least. Not at all. What other item of furniture could she pull down on top of herself?

15

It was a couple of days later. With a carton of blackcurrant in her hand, Cally heaved herself up the steep stairs to the flat over the deli. She was there to get a head start on moving the clutter and doing some basic cleaning before she moved in. As she stepped into the small flat, she felt as though she had been transported back in time. The décor, to her eyes, was an odd explosion of murky colours, wood chip and bright patterns that jumped out at her from every surface. One of the walls was covered in a bold, geometric wallpaper featuring various dirty shades of orange, brown, and yellow. It had the effect of making the eyes feel as if they were bulging and sort of pulsating with energy. It wasn't groovy. The rug beneath her feet was a deep shag in a dirty off-white. The thought of what might be lurking in it wasn't very pleasant.

Cally slowly moved through the space, not sure what to think. At the end of the day, a flat in Lovely was a flat in Lovely. She was never going to be ungrateful and spoilt princess-y but some things would be making a very fast exit stage left to the skip or the charity shop: a large, circular star mirror with a chunky, wooden frame and a low-slung chair upholstered in a once-bright orange fabric that dominated a far wall would be first to go. The chair, flanked by two strange little oval-shaped side tables, looked as if it'd been plucked straight from a retro catalogue. All of it was dirty and worn with age and not in a good way.

As she ran her fingertips along a windowsill, she smiled at the kitschiness of it all. The furniture was a mishmash of styles and colours, the flat itself built in 1909, and the clutter and junk were next level. She could see though, that with a bit of work and given a good clear-out, it could be nice – like, really nice.

There was loads and loads of dust. Every single surface was thick with it and there was definitely a musty smell in the air. Not even in the same league as the hotel, though, so Cally was grateful for small mercies. It was clear that for a long time, the flat had been used primarily for storage, with boxes and crates piled high in every corner. She recognised some of the labels on the boxes as products from the deli downstairs and realised that the space must have been used as an overflow stockroom for both the chemist and the deli.

Despite the clutter and the dated décor, however, Cally wanted to fist pump and felt the possibility of the flat bubbling up inside her. She was going to get a little slice of Lovely Bay. Hooray. It was a start. It sure beat a transport hotel on the side of a motorway. She felt as if she didn't want to let herself get too excited. As if she hadn't yet found the elephant in the room.

Lost in thought as she squeezed around the clutter, Cally pulled back the blind on the balcony doors and shook her head at the view. The shell-tiled rooftops of Lovely stretched away, the iconic lighthouse stood tall and proud, its whitewashed walls gleamed in the sunlight, and all around her, Lovely Bay bustled and did its thing. Somehow, she liked it in the quaint little flat. She liked it a lot. In a funny little odd way, she felt as if it was where she was meant to be – tucked up away from it all and safe. At last.

Her phone rang from her bag. She shimmied around a large stack of cardboard boxes, took her phone out and pressed to answer Eloise.

'Hey.'

'Hi, what's happening with you?'

'You'll never guess where I am right now.'

'No idea.'

'I'm in the new flat scoping it out before I start the initial clear up.'

'Exciting! How is it?'

Cally lowered her voice. 'It's not exactly a dream flat – more like a time capsule – but it's a start. We're talking avocado paint and you should see the shaggy rug. I think it could grow its own mushrooms. I know I'm only renting it, but I don't know, it feels good to have secured my own place here. I feel like it's given me a bit of breathing space; at least, I hope so. There's so much I want to do once I settle down.'

'Yeah, it's a start for sure – a start in the third smallest town in the country. I'm so blimming well proud of you, Cal. You're doing well.'

'Don't be ridiculous! What are you proud of exactly?'

'You've worked so hard for so long looking after your grandma and all that. You deserve a bit of luck. Even if it does come with a side of avocado-coloured walls and shag carpeting.'

Cally chuckled and ran her foot over the shaggy pile of the rug. 'It's not too bad. It's got character, you know? You should see the view from up here. It's like something out of a painting. Anyway, the rug will be toast very shortly.'

'You'll have to give me the grand tour soon. I want to see every inch of it. And then we're going out to celebrate. Drink in the pub, I might even crack out a bit of dancing.'

'Not sure I can cope with any of your moves.'

'I'll bring the moves, don't you worry. I know how you love them.'

'Ha.'

'Right, well I'd better go. I'm running late for work. I was just checking in to see if you're okay.'

'Yep, I'm fine.'

'See you later.'

It was a few hours later. Cally laughed to herself as she balanced a huge file box in her arms, which contained some kind of pharmaceutical drug forms, and made the awkward trip down to the first floor of the building. She had been up and down the stairs multiple times with so many filing boxes she'd lost count. She'd placed them in the room over the back where Birdie had instructed her to and felt as if they were multiplying in front of her eyes.

After many trips up and down, most of the boxes had been cleared from the sitting room, though she still had a long way to go. Heaving herself back up the staircase, holding onto the old, worn, timber handrail, she reached the top and walked back in. Now free of boxes, she was able to see most of the sitting room area. There was a once half hidden small fireplace with a tiny old-fashioned wood burner tucked into the bricks. Loads of ash, soot, and what appeared to be fifty years' worth of dust and debris from the chimney covered the floor and the top of the wood burner. Despite the dust, Cally clapped her hands together. Now she was able to properly see the fireplace and wood burner, she was more than happy.

Her heart skipped a beat at the wood burner. Crouching down to get a closer look, she ran her fingertips along the cast-iron surface and smiled. The metal was rough with rust and grime, but she could see the potential hidden beneath the layers of neglect. With a little elbow grease and some TLC, she was sure she could bring it back to life. She'd always dreamed of having a cosy little fireplace, a place to curl up with a book and a mug of tea on chilly evenings, but it had always been a bit of a pipe dream. The fact that this little flat had one, felt like a small miracle. In the housing estate house, which had been freezing in the winter, there'd been an old electric bar heater stuck in the middle of the room that didn't do much at all. She was now a million miles from the horrid, depressing hole.

As she lugged over another heavy file box from the dining area, then pushed it with her foot over to the door and then carried it down the narrow staircase, she chuckled at the absurdity of her situation. Here she was, a grown woman, playing a real-life game of Tetris with decades' worth of dusty old papers and knick-knacks. The worn, wooden steps creaked and groaned beneath her feet, as if protesting at the added weight of the box.

Back up on the second floor, she stood in the doorway and shook her head at the sheer amount of stuff that had accumulated in the tiny flat over the years. It was as if she was on some sort of archaeological dig, each layer of filing boxes revealing both more clutter and another little interesting feature of the flat at the same time.

A good few hours went by, and she spent most of the time lugging things down the stairs, clearing away clutter, sorting through piles of old papers, and packing away knick-knacks. As the flat began to empty out, the better and better it got. She felt as if someone might be playing a trick on her. At any minute, she would be brought back to reality and faced with the prospect of stopping in the hotel until she found a solution. Somehow, though, it was really happening. She was going to be okay.

Finally, with the bulk of the main clutter cleared away and beginning to see the wood for the trees, Cally tried to decide what needed doing first. The real challenge she was finding as she shoved boxes around and moved things was that everything was coated in a really vile layer of dust and grime. She rummaged through the cleaning supplies she'd brought with her, then went down to find the vacuum Birdie had told her about. Once she'd located it and lugged it up the stairs, she plugged it in and wiggled the nozzle around. She spoke to herself and laughed. 'Let's get to work, shall we?'

As she went back and forth, clouds of dust, worse than had been at the manor, billowed up around her, making her cough and sneeze as she worked. But as she started to make a dent in it, a transformation took place before her eyes. The flat seemed to come alive, shedding years of neglect as the vacuum sucked up the dust. With the shag rug gone, the floorboards were a faded honey-coloured wood, worn smooth with age and character. Worked for her.

The hours ticked by, and as Cally got stuck in, she got lost in it all. After more vacuuming, sorting and cleaning, the flat was now largely empty, with only a few pieces of furniture remaining – a small dining table, a couple of chairs, and the old wood burner in the corner. But it felt different and full of promise. She'd been very lucky to have Birdie on her side and Birdie providing the skip had helped enormously. Maybe with a bit of luck, more good things were coming her way.

Just as she was thinking about a cup of tea, she heard someone coming up the stairs. With the Shipping Forecast reaching her ears, she knew it was Birdie. She stuck her head out onto the landing to see Birdie huffing and puffing and with very wide eyes.

'I'd forgotten how steep these things are!'

'Tell me about it. I must have been up and down a few hundred times. Or at least my legs feel as if it's that many.'

Birdie puffed out a whoosh of air. 'Phew. How have you got on?'

Cally turned around and Birdie followed her in. 'Not too bad. It's slowly getting there.'

Birdie stepped in and turned in a slow circle. 'Well, would you look at that! I hardly recognise the place! You've done an incredible job. You must have been going some. Have you done this all on your own?'

'Yup. I suppose I have been cracking on. I wanted to break the back of it.'

'You've certainly done that. Wow! Good work. It's actually nice up here. I remember I used to love it and the view. Those were the days.'

Cally gestured around. 'It feels much bigger now.'

'It was so junked up. It's amazing what a little bit of elbow grease and a lot of love can do. This old place needed someone to come along and bring it back to life. Thanks. It looks great already.'

'Don't thank me. I can't thank *you* enough, Birdie,' Cally said, her voice thick with feeling. 'I really was in a bit of a stitch before.'

Birdie smiled. 'You're welcome. Do whatever you want and stay for as long as you want.'

'Thanks. I'm so grateful.'

Birdie jerked her thumb downwards. 'There is leftover paint from the deli renovation down there. Might be a good idea to, err, give it a bit of a freshen-up if you fancy it.' Birdie ran her finger over the mantelpiece. 'Who had the bright idea of painting this brown? Must have been my aunt back in the day. Funny fashion, wasn't it? All browns and oranges?'

'Yeah, and the big orange and yellow flowers everywhere.'

Birdie pointed around. 'Lots of old relics.'

'I thought that.'

As they stood there for a second, surveying the tidied-out flat, Birdie took a few steps closer to the balcony. 'I see you've discovered the balcony. It's quite a view, isn't it?'

Cally shook her head. 'I can't believe I get to wake up to it every day.'

Birdie chuckled. 'Not a bad start to a day.'

Cally nodded. 'I think I could get used to sipping my morning coffee out there, watching the town come to life. Especially once the weather warms right up. I reckon it'll be gorgeous.'

Birdie's eyes twinkled. 'Or blackcurrant in your case. You'll have a front-row seat to all the action from up here. I might have to get you to start a log or a vlog, ha. You can help keep me up to date with what goes on. I don't know why I've never thought about putting a camera up here before.'

Cally laughed. 'You're funny.'

'Oh, you're in for a treat,' Birdie gushed. 'Lovely Bay comes alive in the summer months. Were you here for Chowder weekend last year?'

Cally raised an eyebrow. 'No. Chowder weekend? You're joking.'

Birdie shook her head, grinning. 'As if I would joke about a thing like that. The whole town turns out for it or goes under for it, should I say. There are speakeasies everywhere. It's a sight to behold.'

'This town is full of surprises.'

'That it is,' Birdie agreed. 'And now you're a proper part of it.'

'Thanks again.'

Birdie waved off Cally's gratitude with a flap of her hand. 'Nonsense. You've already thanked me plenty. Now it's time to focus on making this little nest your own. Starting with a good coat of paint, I reckon. Can't have you living in a time capsule, now can we?'

'Definitely not. I think a fresh start and fresh walls…'

Cally loved the idea of a fresh start and fresh paint. She'd had a gutful of life's not-so-nice starts. She thought back to all the heartache and the struggle just before her grandma had passed away. When she was young and her mum's illness had finally got the better of her. The long hours at the hospice, the endless shifts at the dead-end customer support chat job. It had felt like a never-ending uphill climb. She'd always felt as if she was trying to keep her head above water. Something had changed. She was still sad and sort of weary, but she felt as if she could now get on with things instead of living in constant limbo. Maybe she'd be able to just drift for a bit rather than having to flap like crazy to keep herself afloat. She'd have to wait and see. She wondered if the flat would give her that. Lovely knew what was coming. It was getting ready for the ride.

16

It was Cally's last morning in the rental house. She couldn't quite wait to see the back of it. She stripped the bed, took the sheets downstairs, and put them in the last box. She'd rented the place in a semi-furnished condition because she'd not been sure what was going to happen with the finances related to the sale of her grandma's house at that stage. In actual fact, her grandma had ended up being in the hospice a lot longer than anyone had predicted – which had meant that Cally had stayed in the house and had kept extending the lease.

Then things had become traumatic; the family stuff imploded, and she'd stayed put for longer than she'd initially intended. Now, it was the day to leave. It hadn't come quickly enough. She was not, in any shape or form, sad to see the back of the grim, depressing place. With its grotty little porch that had been neglected for years, the awful cramped galley kitchen with the hatch into a tiny living room with its drab brown carpet, and the dismal little downstairs separate W.C. Cally had never viewed the place as home, just as a depressing interim in her life. She wanted to slam a lid on the interim and jog right on.

Now, with hardly any belongings and not much money, she couldn't wait to put it behind her. She wanted to shut the door, move on, and get away from it as quickly as she could. As she walked down the path to the bleak parking bays, where woe betide you if you parked in the wrong one, she didn't even turn around to look back. Forwards and away from it was looking a whole lot more attractive. Best left as far behind as possible. Onwards and upwards to life in Lovely Bay. If she could help it, she'd never set foot on the estate ever again.

Nearly an hour later, she was so happy to be moving into the new flat she was practically skipping down Lovely's main street. There was such a bounce in her step she was more or less bobbing along on her own little tide for one. She smiled and stopped to chat with one of the pensioners who was a regular at the chemist and peered into the chocolate shop for a bit at the truffles and bonbons. She couldn't quite believe that she was actually going to be living in Lovely. She'd been dreaming about it for a very long time. She was so ready to actually live, not just work, in its quaint charm and friendly community. When she'd first arrived at the chemist for a shift back in the day, she'd often thought about what it would be like to just stroll along through the back streets to work and not have to commute in on the train. Now, she would be doing that for real.

She turned down the narrow brick alley between the shops and made her way into the deli building. Once up the narrow creaking staircase, she could hear the sounds of the shop below, but the flat felt like a little oasis above the hustle and bustle. It was now bare and nearly empty and not exactly gorgeous, but it was a blank canvas and no longer brimming with dust. She still had a way to go; the floors were scuffed and worn, the windows still waiting to be cleaned and grimy with years of neglect, but to Cally, it felt just right. The kitchen was outdated and in need of a good scrubbing, the bedroom wasn't large but now clear of junk and with its slanted ceiling, it had a cosy, cocoon-like feel.

The bathroom had seen better days and the mix of orange flower wallpaper and green walls were still in situ, but it was all a whole lot better than what had been on her plate.

She stood by the balcony door, looking and thinking and wondered how she was going to get on. With the flat as her jumping off point, she could now start thinking properly about what she was going to do with her life. She was no spring chicken with not many prospects, but at least she could breathe. She had a job in the back of a chemist and a chatbot as a work colleague, but she was now free of responsibility. It felt like an odd mix of exhilarating release and some sort of grieving of a situation she'd had no control over whatsoever.

She thought about all the things she'd wanted to do with her life but felt a little bit as if that ship had sailed. Had it? Could she still hop back on the ship and have a go? She wanted to go on holiday like normal people did, maybe meet someone nice, settle down perhaps, and have a little family. Learn to play chess, go to a class of some sort, take in a show, do things, not worry. Spend money on nice things, educate herself, and not have to care.

Just as Cally was thinking about how she would tackle the flat and how the delivery men would get her new mattress up the stairs, she heard a sound on the landing. She walked over and opened the front door to see Eloise with her one hand on her hip, a very large fern houseplant in the other and a lot of huffing and puffing.

'Blimey, Cal. You said it was steep and I thought you might be exaggerating! You won't need to join a gym going up and down these every day!'

'I know! I did tell you.'

Eloise looked at the bookshelf on the landing and the jumble of books and then turned back to the window overlooking the staircase. 'This is much better than I thought it was going to be. You clearly undersold it somewhat.'

'Did I?'

'Err, just a bit. It's a bit steep, but so far, it's much better than I had expected and I'm not even inside yet.' Eloise nodded. 'I mean the bannister alone and that window. Gorgeous. They don't make them like that these days.'

'Apparently not up to current day building standards.'

Eloise tutted. 'Right you are.'

'Come on in.'

Eloise passed over the house plant. 'Congratulations. I bought you a new friend.'

Cally took the fern and smiled. 'Thank you. You didn't need to. Let's see if I can keep it alive. I'll keep my fingers crossed.'

Eloise rummaged in her bag and pulled out a pair of bright yellow rubber gloves. 'I'm well prepared for you to put me to work today.'

'You should be. I think I'm going to need many pairs of hands when the mattress arrives. I just cannot see how they're going to get a mattress up these stairs. We got the other one down and in the skip, so it can be done. It's just that I ordered a deep one, and I think it will be bulky. I didn't think it through properly.'

'Leave that to them, I reckon. That's what they get paid for.' Eloise said as she stepped into the flat further. She walked over towards the fireplace and shook her head. 'It's much nicer than you made out. I had visions of a different version of the house you just left.'

'God no. Don't even remind me of that dreadful hole of a place. What do you think, then?'

'Nice.' Eloise looked at the fireplace and around the sitting room. 'Ooh, the floors will come up well. I love it. It's going to be gorgeous.'

Cally smiled. 'I hope so.'

Eloise walked over to the window. 'Look at this window and balcony. Love the view of the rooftops and the church spire in the distance, ooh and the lighthouse. You'll get such lovely light in here, Cal.'

Cally took in the patchwork of shell tiles and chimney pots stretching away from them. 'You're right. I hadn't thought about the light. It was quite dark in here before because of all the junk but yeah, the light is nice.'

Eloise went into the kitchen and opened one of the cupboards. 'Ouch, needs work. These have potential, though. A fresh coat of paint, maybe some new hardware, and they'll be as good as new.'

Cally leaned against the doorframe. 'I've ordered that vinyl stuff for the worktop and some white stick-on tiles for the backsplash. I'll just see how I go.'

Eloise pointed to the far side of the kitchen. 'Paint that open shelving and display some pretty dishes and cookbooks. Yes, it'll be nice.'

They moved into the bedroom, with its sloped ceiling and gorgeous old sash windows. Eloise nodded. 'Yep, love this too. You've come up trumps here. You could do a sort of shabby chic, romantic vibe with lots of soft bits and bobs and muted colours. Loads of pillows and blankets. I'm coming for a sleepover.'

'Ha, I need a mattress first. Right, I'll put the kettle on, and we'll get stuck in.'

'Yep, I'll start a Pinterest board. I'm so excited to see this place come together, Cal. You're going to make it into something really special. This is your time at last. After everything you've been through…'

Cally smiled. She hoped Eloise was right and that the flat was the start of good things to come. It was and things were going to get a lot, lot brighter.

17

A few weeks or so later, Cally had been to the dentist back in the area where she'd lived with her grandma. After she'd left the dentist and was exponentially happy not to have had anything done, she popped into a Red Cross shop next door. After a bit of a mooch, she'd made her way to have a look at the home bits. Now that she had a home that she actually liked living in, she was quite enjoying shopping for it. Right in the corner next to the cookery books, she came across a vintage standard lamp with a lovely old timber stand, huge white silk shade, and tassels all along its bottom. Right away, Cally loved its gorgeous shape and oversized shade. She ummed and ahhed for a bit and wondered how it would look in the flat. She'd pulled it out of the corner, had a look at the price tag, did a little happy dance, tried to picture it just behind the sofa and before she could deliberate too much, had taken it to the counter and tapped her card.

That was all very well; it was most definitely a very nice lamp. The problem was walking to the train station with a standard lamp bigger than her that had proved to be a bit of a challenge. On the train, it had sat beside her; she may have chatted to it, and after arriving at Lovely Bay station, she'd chuckled to herself as she'd lugged it up and over the station stairs. As she rushed down to catch the riverboat with the standard lamp and its shade precariously perched in her right hand, the tassels at the bottom flapped around in the breeze coming off the river. Cally could just about keep herself upright and in one piece as she struggled along with the awkward shape beside her.

With the boat already at the jetty, she attempted to run but did more of a strange half-run, half-walk, and clambered on, trying to lift the lamp up the ramp.

'Bonjour.' Clive called out in a very strange faux French accent, as he rushed up to assist. Clive was known in Lovely to adore France and the French way of life. Lovelies played along with it.

Cally followed suit. 'Bonjour.'

'What are we travelling with today, our Cally? I've seen many a passenger on this here river, but there's always a first in my job and today is one of those days. You have a new friend, do you?'

Cally tried to balance the lamp as Clive offered a hand. She laughed at the absurdity of the situation, lugging a standard lamp onto a riverboat. 'I couldn't pass it up. It was such a bargain. I've been to the dentist and came home with this about my person. I'm not sure what I was thinking. It's been quite the journey.'

Clive wedged a buoy on top of the lamp's timber base to secure it against the side of the boat but still close enough for Cally to keep hold of it. 'I bet you had some funny looks. I've seen stranger things, believe it or not. How have you been?'

Cally settled back against the bench seat and kept a grip on the lamp. 'I've been good, thanks. Just trying to settle into the new flat over the deli.'

Clive raised an eyebrow. 'Ah, yep, I heard you were in there. Nice. I hear it's got quite a bit of character.'

Cally was taken aback that Clive already knew where she was living, but she didn't let it show on her face. 'It has.'

Clive seemed to read her thoughts. 'Birdie mentioned it the other day when she was on board.'

'Yep. She's been such a great help with everything.'

Clive smiled. 'She's a good one. So, how are you finding the flat? Must be quite a change from where you were before.'

'It's definitely different,' Cally admitted. 'In a good way, and I love it. It's just a short walk to the chemist, so my commute is practically non-existent now.'

'Sounds like you're settling in well.'

Cally nodded and wiggled the lamp. 'Absolutely. I now have a friend to move in with me. It was a bit of a struggle to get it home, but I couldn't resist.'

'I can see why. Well, if you need any help, just let me know. I'm always happy to lend a hand.'

'Thanks, Clive. I'll keep it in mind.'

Cally sat back as Clive dealt with another passenger. As the boat pulled away, luckily, the river was smooth. The boat rocked gently as water lapped against the sides. Cally thought about the flat, painting the walls, adding some of her own touches, and how she loved the feeling of putting down a few roots in Lovely Bay.

A while later, as the boat approached Cally's stop, Clive expertly manoeuvred it into place and turned to Cally. 'Here we are. Need a hand with that lamp?'

Cally nodded. 'Yes, please. If you can just give me a hand to get off, that would be great.'

Clive picked the lamp up as if it weighed nothing, carefully lifted it over the ramp, and carried it onto the jetty. 'Thanks, Clive. I really appreciate it.'

'Anytime, our Cally. Take care now. Au revoir.'

'You too.'

As Cally walked in the direction of the deli, balancing the

ONE NICE DAY IN LOVELY BAY

lamp, she smiled as Lovely Bay bustled with people here, there, and everywhere. For the first time in a long while, she felt as if she had a home as she made her way along past the lighthouse. At the little row of lighthouse cottages just past it, she bumped into Nancy, in her work uniform, with her blue wax Lovely coat over her shoulders, hustling along on her way to the station.

Nancy made a funny face and chuckled as she approached. 'What have we there, then? A new purchase for the flat, by the looks of it. Nice.'

'I thought it would look lovely by the sofa. It's just right for the evenings.'

'Wow, that's gorgeous. Where did you find that? Some fancy antiques shop by the looks of it.'

'Pah! I wish. In the Red Cross shop next to where I go to the dentist.'

'Got to love a bit of charity shop hunting.'

Cally smiled to herself. It was about the only sort of shopping she did. 'Indeed. Off to work?'

Nancy flicked her Apple Watch towards her to check the time. 'I am, and if I don't get a move on, I'll be late. I'm on until later this evening because Sam's called in sick.'

'Oh, that's a shame.'

'Yep, no rest for the wicked. See you later, our Cally. Have fun with your lamp.'

'Will do,' Cally replied as she hoisted the lamp up again and the little tassels on the oversized shade swung around all over the place.

Nancy called out as she walked away. 'Oh, yes, I nearly forgot. There's a Lovely batch in the chocolate shop. Pop in there on your way past.'

Cally frowned and turned around. 'Lovely batch?'

'Just for us lucky lot who live here. Go in and get a coffee, and you'll get some. Free for Lovelies.'

'Oh, okay, right. Thanks for the heads-up.'

'Now you reside here and all that. Keep it under your hat. You will not want to miss out. I've just been in there.' Nancy patted her stomach. 'Meaning I will need to go up and down the station stairs many times this evening! See you later.'

As Cally walked away, she nodded to herself. It was nice to know people in Lovely Bay. Lovelies had always been nice to her when she'd worked in the chemist, but now she'd moved into the flat, there'd been a subtle shift in how people treated her. It was as if she was a bit more one of their own rather than just someone who worked in the town. She liked how it made her feel.

After navigating her way up the High Street with the lamp and struggling to walk without angling her body strangely, she checked her watch to see if she had time before her customer service shift started to go into the chocolate shop. With just enough time, she kept hold of the lamp and pushed open the door. A bell jingled as she stepped inside, and the scent of rich, sweet cocoa enveloped her. She angled the lamp to the side and squeezed it under the door. The shop was busy and easy on the eye, with stripped wooden floors and shelves lined with all manner of chocolate delights. In glass cases edged with brass, truffles, bars of artisanal chocolate, and huge slabs ready to be broken up were stacked in neat rows. All of it made her mouth water and not just the chocolate.

Millie, in a dark apron, looked up from behind the counter as Cally stood squinting in at the slabs of chocolate. Millie chuckled and widened her eyes at the lamp. 'What's this you've got with you today?'

Cally grinned. 'My new friend.'

Millie came out from behind the counter, wiping her hands on her apron, and touched one of the tassels on the lamp. 'Ooh, nice.'

'I went to the dentist and came back with this. As you do.'

'The best finds are always the unexpected ones.' Millie

lowered her voice. 'Take a pew in the corner there. We've been experimenting with some new flavour combinations. Today's ganache is infused with fresh orange zest plus a shell of 70% cacao chocolate.'

'Yes, I've heard. I just bumped into Nancy. Sounds good to me.'

Millie gestured to a row of plump, dark truffles dusted with cocoa powder sitting on the far side near the coffee machine. 'Yep. I'll bring some over just after I finish this order.' Millie pointed to a large white box with a huge pile of assorted truffles in the centre.

Cally nodded to the box. 'Looks like someone's got a treat today.'

Millie nodded. 'Yes, it's an order for the manor.'

'The manor?' Cally asked.

'Yep, up at Lovely Manor. There's a crew up there doing a day shoot, and they requested a special afternoon tea from the chocolate shop. Truffles are on the list for the celebrity, not that I'm sure who that is. Someone from the BBC, I think.'

'Nice,' Cally answered.

'You've been working up there with our Nina, haven't you?' Millie asked.

'Yes, I have.'

'How is it?'

'Like working in an episode of Bridgerton. I can't believe how massive it is.'

'Yeah, it's quite something. I used to work up there when I was a teenager, back in the day when they had a lot of staff and all that.'

'Right, so you know all about it.'

'I do. The family was much bigger then. When the old folk died, there were a lot of financial problems. They sold off another big house they had in Scotland, or so the story goes.' Millie explained.

'Interesting.'

'There's quite a story with the family. There was an American wife and all sorts. Google them if you like history.'

'I might.' Cally looked at the huge boxed truffle order and wondered how much it would've cost. She pondered what life might be like to be living it up in the manor and having afternoon tea courtesy of the chocolate shop. She'd thought she was fancy when she treated herself to a tiny little box of three truffles. This was on another level.

About ten minutes later, Cally was sitting breathing in the heady scent of chocolate and citrus. She popped a chocolate into her mouth and raised her eyebrows. 'Oh, my goodness.' Her eyes fluttered closed in bliss.

Millie beamed from the counter. 'We've been tinkering with the recipe for weeks, trying to get the proportions just right. Looks like we've finally nailed it.'

Cally nodded. 'You definitely have. These are *dangerous*. I could eat the whole tray in one sitting.'

'I won't tell if you won't. Life's too short not to indulge in a little chocolate now and then, I always say, which is lucky if you work here.'

'I don't know how you do it. Every time I come in here, you've got something new and delicious to try.'

As Cally settled into the corner, she cradled a steaming mug of coffee and laughed at herself sitting with the gigantic secondhand lamp for company. She'd moved a chair out of the way so that the lamp was sitting opposite her and it appeared as if it was at the table for a coffee, too.

Just as she was about to take another sip of her coffee, the bell above the shop door jingled. Cally glanced up. Her heart skipped a beat when she saw who had just walked in. Logan Henry-Hicks. He was nicer than chocolate, that was for sure. He walked straight past her and the lamp, scanned the display cases and looked over the counter at Millie.

'Hey. I'm here to pick up an order for the manor. A rather large one, if I'm not mistaken. It's for Doreen, but she had a bit of a funny turn, so I'm collecting it. I've been told not to hang around.'

Millie picked up the enormous white box she had just finished packing. 'All ready for you.'

Logan took the box from her. He held it up as if assessing the weight. 'Goodness, this is enough chocolate to feed an army.'

'Well, from what I hear, you've got quite the guest list up at the manor today. A celebrity, no less and half of the Beeb. Doreen said to make sure it pleased. I followed instructions.'

Logan shook his head. 'I hope there are leftovers.'

Millie smiled. 'You'll be lucky. I'll email the invoice to Doreen shortly.'

'Thanks.'

As Logan turned to leave, he stepped around the counter, took in the huge lamp, then frowned and then looked straight at Cally.

'Oh, hi. You again.'

'Hello.'

Logan's eyes narrowed at the lamp. 'Err, is that yours?'

'It is, yes.'

'Chocolate with a lamp?'

'Ha.'

Logan's eyebrows shot up. 'Unusual choice in companion, but each to their own.' Logan joked.

Cally laughed. 'What can I say? I have a thing for lighting fixtures. They speak to me on a deep, personal level.'

Logan didn't move to leave as he stood with the huge bow-topped box in his arms. 'So much so that you bring them out with you when you go out for coffee?'

'My lamp and I are a package deal. If you get on its bad side, there will be consequences. Death by standard lamp.' Cally joked.

Logan laughed. Cally's heart skipped a beat. 'What's the story behind this, then?'

'A thrilling saga,' Cally said, putting on a dramatic voice. 'Not really. I found it in the back of a shop. It's been a bit of a journey trying to get it home on the train and then the boat.'

'It's not every day you find a lamp that speaks to your soul.'

Cally giggled. There was just something about Logan. 'I guess not.'

Logan tapped the box of chocolates. 'Right, well, I had better be off.'

'Duty calls, right?'

'It does. See you, Blackcurrant. Nice to bump into you again.'

'See you.'

Cally watched Logan go. The bell jingled behind him as the door closed. She pretended to turn back to her coffee and her lamp, but flicked her eyes out the window and watched as he strode off down the street. She craned a little bit to see him pop the truffle box in the front seat of his car – the same one she'd seen him in before. He got in the passenger seat, indicated and drove off. She swooned inside. She knew one person she wouldn't mind sharing a Lovely Bay chocolate shop chocolate with. It wasn't Birdie.

18

Cally and Nina had just finished at Lovely Manor and were standing by the back of Nina's car chatting. The manor job had turned out to be much more extensive than Nina had originally quoted for and new rooms full of clutter and extra additions to the job had come to light every day. Cally had joined Nina on the days she hadn't been in the chemist or working on her customer service job. Nina's phone pinged. She looked down and checked it as Cally popped a few bags in the boot. Nina looked up from her phone.

'Ooh, that was a message from our Nancy. What are you up to later?'

Cally wasn't up to anything. She had the flat earmarked for a bottle of wine and a book. She'd settled into the flat nicely and it had been a long week. There was no way she was committing to anything. 'Not sure. Why?'

'Speakeasy tonight. Our Nance just snagged a couple more tickets because someone is sick. She asked if you and I wanted to come. Fancy it?'

Cally loved the famous Lovely speakeasies. It was an odd little Lovely tradition that took place all over the town. Spaces were very limited and only mostly available to people who resided in Lovely. It was all very clandestine; there was a secret Facebook community, passwords, a private WhatsApp group, and all sorts. Cally had heard lots of snippets here and there about it whilst working in the chemist. She actually didn't fancy going out but had gleaned that you only turned down an invite to a speakeasy once. 'Yep, love to.'

'Okay, I'll text her back to say it's a yes from you.'

'And you?'

'Yeah, I just need to check to make sure Robby will be home in time for Faye, but yes, I'm so in if he is. I need a night out. Plus, there's no way I'm saying no. You don't get asked twice.'

'Where is it?'

Nina wrinkled her nose. 'No idea. We don't get to know that, remember?'

Cally didn't really know how serious the secrecy thing was. She wasn't totally sure how it worked. She'd always been too scared to ask. 'Ha. Yep, sorry. I'm not really au fait with it.'

'Me either. I love it, though. It's so *weird*. I do know that we should be very honoured.' Nina laughed. 'I remember my first one…'

'Birdie was telling me the other day that there are rumours that you're going to start one over on the harbour side.'

Nina chuckled. 'They are just that – rumours. I don't have time to start one.'

Cally knew that Nina was also a relative newcomer to Lovely Bay. She had started off house-sitting at a local property and then had eventually moved down from London. She'd started to make chowders that had begun to get a bit of their own reputation. 'I'm first in line if you do one.'

'I'll make a note of that. Maybe I'll bring you a portion so you can have a try. I have some in the freezer. I'm always tweaking it. Robby says I'm obsessed.'

'Ooh, yes please. Wouldn't say no.'

ONE NICE DAY IN LOVELY BAY

As they continued to chat about chowder and the evening by the boot of Nina's car, the afternoon sun cast a glow over Lovely Manor behind them. Cally looked around at the house, standing tall and looming large. She turned the other way and took in the meticulously manicured gardens and driveway that stretched out before them. Compared to where she was in life, the manor and its goings-on were like something from a dream. She gestured in the direction of the house. 'Look at that sun this afternoon. It's really something here, isn't it? I don't think I'll ever get used to working in a place like this. I'm still expecting Mr Darcy to walk around the corner every two seconds.'

Nina smiled as she hefted a large box into the boot of the car. 'I know what you mean. Yep, as we said before, it's like something out of a Jane Austen novel. All grand staircases and sumptuous drawing rooms. What a job, eh? I think this is one of my better jobs. It's never going to end by the looks of it.'

Cally grinned as an image of herself sweeping through the halls of the manor house in a flowing gown popped into her head. 'Can you imagine living in a place like this? Waking up every morning to these grounds and this house. Having staff to cater to your every whim. How the other half live. Wafting around doing not much. Can't be bad.'

Nina did a funny little snort and shook her head. 'It sounds good, but I think I'd go mad with boredom. Give me a cosy little house and a garden to putter around in, any day.'

Cally laughed. Nina was down-to-earth, no-nonsense, and easy to please. It was why they got on well. As they finished loading the last of the bags and boxes into the car, Cally felt grateful that Nina had offered her the decluttering work. Not only had it meant that she'd had a bit of spare cash for the flat, it had come with other benefits and it had been strangely calming, clearing out someone else's junk. As she'd cleared and organised, she'd felt a real satisfaction of a job well done. Not that organising for a living was one of her career goals, but she'd most definitely had worse jobs to get by.

As if Nina had read her thoughts, Nina thanked her. 'Thanks for today. We've really broken the back of it now. Slow going, though, this one. It's been good to have you. We work well together…'

Cally waved away the compliment. 'Oh, don't be silly. Thank you. It's been great.'

As they got in the car, Cally pulled her seatbelt over and pushed it into the buckle. Nina pressed a button to start the engine and started to slowly pull out of the stable area. They drove onto the manor's long, winding driveway, the gravel crunching beneath the tyres, and Cally's mind flicked back to the speakeasy. 'So, what do you think the speakeasy will be like tonight? I've heard loads about the one near The Summer Hotel. I don't suppose it's that one, is it?'

Nina grinned. 'No idea. That's part of the attraction. Our Nancy knows which one it is. She knows everything about Lovely having been born here. But let's just say that if it's the one I think it might be, you're in for a treat.'

'Do we really have to give a password?'

'We do.'

'What is it?'

Nina rolled her eyes. 'You don't get it until just before.'

Cally giggled. 'Ha, seriously?'

'Yeah, I know.'

'Too funny. It's so Lovely, isn't it?'

'Yup. I have to say I thought it was all a bit ridiculous when I first moved here. Now, I'm totally sold. I'm right into it. I love all the little traditions. It's sort of what makes living here.'

'I know. I noticed it when I started working at the chemist.'

As they approached the halfway point in the drive, the manor's wrought-iron gates came into view and they could see another car approaching. Nina continued on, realised that she was going to have to give way, and stopped as the other car got closer. The man driving waved her forward, put his hand over the passenger seat, turned to look behind, and reversed to a passing spot.

Cally realised it was Logan driving the car. The same Logan from the boat and the one who had rescued her from the piles of books and fallen shelving unit. The one who did strange things to her head. Nina inched forward, stopped as she reached the driver's window of the other car, pressed the button on her door, and opened her window. Logan smiled. He was not ugly. Cally gulped. She felt a funny feeling in her stomach. What even was it? Was her stomach fluttering? She squeezed her eyes together and shook her head quickly. Of course, it wasn't. Was it? It absolutely was. To be fair, it wasn't just her stomach that was fluttering. Her whole being was. Logan pushed her buttons and then some. Striking was the word. Chiselled jawline, check, eyelashes check, friendly, that too. Unfairly, stupidly handsome. Gorgeous.

'Hey, Logan, how are you?' Nina asked. 'What are you up to?'

Logan smiled. 'Hi. Not a lot. How are you? All done for the day?' He flicked his eyes over to Cally.

Cally felt her cheeks flush. Her stomach moved from fluttering to churning. What in the world? Strange things were happening to our Cally. She could feel her heart pounding in her chest. She was uncharacteristically flustered. What in the name of goodness? She silently cursed herself. How ridiculous. Logan wouldn't even give her the time of day, let alone look at her twice. He probably had some fabulously maintained toff at home in a nice little, or actually, very large manor house of their own. They would most definitely be hashtag blessed.

Nina nodded. 'Yeah, we just finished up for the day in the new wing. There's still lots to do.'

'Bigger job than you thought?'

'For sure. Cally here has been an absolute life saver.'

Cally was only half listening. She may have been imagining things about Logan – the wideness of his shoulders. Something about him made her feel odd. Nicely odd.

Logan laughed. 'Is that so?'

Cally quickly tore herself away from the thoughts of the chest and back to the conversation. She bantered. 'I don't know about that. Not many people call me a life saver.'

Logan chuckled. 'No? What do they call you then? Blackcurrant?'

It wasn't just Cally's stomach that was churning, her heart joined it. She couldn't think quickly enough to respond. 'Ha.'

Nina flicked her eyes upwards, nudged Cally, and addressed Logan. 'Blackcurrant?'

Logan laughed. 'Private joke.'

Nina joined in with the quick banter. 'Don't let her fool you. She's got a heart of gold and a backbone of steel this one. I wouldn't be messing with her.'

Logan played along. 'I'll have to keep that in mind for the next time she chucks a few raw chicken breasts at me.'

Cally swallowed. Was she imagining that the air between them was electrically charged? Was he, in fact, flirting? She really, *really* hoped so. Her mind went completely blank for a second and all she could do was stare at Logan.

Nina jumped in. 'Chicken breasts? What am I missing?'

Logan chuckled. His eyes crinkled. Cally imagined the chest again. In her bed. Her heart progressed from flips and churns to somersaults. 'I err...' She felt her cheeks flush at the memory of the riverboat when the bottom of her bag had given way. She recalled watching everything tumbling onto the deck. She remembered Logan helping her gather things. She'd been so flustered and so down about her housing situation, the bag situation had tipped over an emotional edge. At least she was now feeling a lot more together. Her mind seemed to pause in a strange limbo where all she could see was Logan. She felt as if she'd lost the ability to connect her brain with her mouth. She stared at him as her tongue felt as if it was glued to the roof of her mouth and her thoughts were a jumbled mess.

Logan continued. 'It's quite the story. Picture this: the riverboat heaving with people, a freezing day, Cally walking down the steps. There I was, minding my own business, when suddenly a couple of chicken breasts and a jar of curry powder made their grand entrance by way of the bottom of Cally's shopping bag, completely giving way. Throw in a bottle of wine and tinned tomatoes, and yeah, it was funny.'

Nina laughed. 'No way. You're making this up.'

Logan held up his hands. 'I swear, it was a comedy scene. One minute, I was looking at my phone. Next, I was hit by a wayward onion and pelted with raw poultry.'

Cally smiled. It hadn't been a comedy scene to her. Movie scene more like. Or some sort of fantasy. A delicious fantasy.

Logan continued as Nina laughed. 'Anyway, we got everything sorted out in the end, and Cally was able to go on her merry way, curry ingredients intact. But I have to say, it was definitely one of the more memorable moments of my week.'

Cally felt weird. It seemed as if he might be flirting. 'Thank you again for your help that day.'

'Always happy to help someone who makes their own curry.' Logan winked.

Now she was sure. He was *definitely* flirting. She loved it.

Nina laughed. 'I'm presuming you got an invite to dinner that evening?'

Logan shook his head. 'You'd think. Shame I didn't get an invite, no.'

Nina was clearly enjoying herself. Cally couldn't quite compute what was going on. Nina widened her eyes and nodded her head in a knowing way. 'Looks like you'd better change that, our Cally. You could invite Logan here to your new abode.'

Cally felt her heart skip a beat. The feelings swirling inside her were strange and slightly terrifying. Her mind again went blank as she tried to think of something witty to say. Images flashed in front of her eyes, imagining Logan in the tiny flat. He was shirtless. Eating curry wasn't the only thing she was thinking about. Pah. There was no way he'd be thinking the same thing. Logan would never in a million years be interested in her. He was just making funny chit-chat with a couple of Lovely Manor workers. What was it they said? Keep the locals on side or something. Yup, that was totally it.

Nina continued, addressing Logan. 'Anyway, what are you up to?'

Logan rolled his eyes. 'Up to my eyes in paperwork. Boring with a side of relentless.'

'Doesn't sound like my cup of tea,' Nina said. 'I outsourced bookkeeping right away in my business. Useless springs to mind.'

'I hear you.'

'What is it that you do?'

'Short version is that I have my own business.'

Nina smiled, 'In?'

'Broadly it's tech in maritime navigation technologies. It keeps me busy for sure.'

As Logan chatted, Cally gave herself a mental shake as she checked his left hand for a ring. What was she thinking, getting all starry-eyed over a man she barely knew? She was acting like a teenager with a crush, not a grown woman with a life of her own. Maritime navigation technologies, though? Fancy.

Nina glanced in the rearview mirror. 'Oops, looks like we're holding up traffic. See you, Logan. Have a nice weekend.'

'See you later.'

Nina put the car in gear and pulled away. She shook her head. 'Well, well, well. Looks like someone's got an admirer.'

Cally felt her cheeks burn. 'Pardon. Who?'

'You! You *two*, in fact!'

'What?'

'It was like there was a bolt of golden hot light buzzing right past me, connecting the two of you.' Nina laughed.

Cally dismissed Nina's words. 'Don't be ridiculous. I don't even *know* him.'

'That may well be, but he clearly wants to get to know you. Clearly.'

'I don't think so. The Logans of the world aren't interested in people like me.'

'You can't fool me, Cal. I saw the way you two were looking at each other. I'll take his comedy routine and up it to a romance novel.'

Cally scoffed, trying to play it off. 'Oh, please. He was just being friendly. You know how charming these posh types can be.'

Nina raised an eyebrow, unconvinced. 'Friendly, my left foot. That man was practically undressing you with his eyes. He was flirting like crazy. And don't think I didn't notice the way you were with him.'

Cally shook her head. 'I wasn't any different to how I am with anyone.'

'Uh-huh, sure you weren't,' Nina teased. 'Have to say he is *unfairly* handsome. Really, really good looking. If I wasn't…'

Cally gaped. 'Nina!'

Nina laughed, waving off Cally's shock. 'I'm just saying, you could do a lot worse. And from where I'm sitting, it looks like the feeling is mutual.'

Cally shook her head. 'Nah. I don't know, Neens. Men like Logan don't go for girls like me. I'm just a nobody from the wrong side of the tracks. He probably has some posh, perfect wife or girlfriend waiting for him at home.'

'Nup, not buying it. For the record, you are not a nobody. You're a smart, gorgeous, talented woman. Remember that.'

'I work on a chatbot thing and have spent my last how many years caring…'

'So what? That means nothing. Don't even go there.'

Cally took a deep breath. Maybe Nina was right. Maybe it was time to stop putting herself down. 'Ahh, I don't know.'

'Trust me on this one.'

Cally nodded. Maybe she should. As they made their way to Lovely Bay, she decided that it was time to change her narrative. She could be who she wanted to be and do whatever she liked now she was free. Couldn't she?

19

Cally stepped carefully down the stairs to the flat, crossed over the first level and then made her way down to the back of the deli. Letting herself out the back, she walked up the alley towards the street with a bottle of wine in her hand and a smile on her face. She couldn't quite believe it, but she was doing precisely what she'd been thinking about for a long time; not only living in Lovely Bay but going to a speakeasy to boot. Her life was on the up. She might be in a small, cramped flat with not much to her name, but she was in a good place and it felt nice.

A few minutes later, she was waiting for Nancy outside The Drunken Sailor. Nina had messaged to say she was running late because of a problem with her daughter Faye and for Nancy and Cally to go ahead and she would see them there. Once Nancy arrived, Cally ambled along beside her, chatting away as they made their way to the hidden chowder speakeasy.

Cally was fascinated by these secret little spots and the weirdness around them. From what she'd heard and gathered here and there, all of them were tucked away in unexpected little nooks and odd places throughout the town. As they meandered across the road, past the lighthouse and underneath a huge old tree on the other side of Lovely, Cally made conversation. 'So, where's our destination tonight?'

Nancy frowned. 'You know the first rule of speakeasies, right? No asking about the location.'

Cally chuckled. 'Ha, Nina said the same. I thought that once you were actually invited you got to know where you were going.'

Nancy shook her head with a grin. 'Nope, not necessarily. Totally depends on who you are.'

'Will I need to wear a blindfold as I enter?' Cally joked. She loved the air of mystery and secretiveness of it all.

'Spot on. I can tell you that we will be near the legendary waters of the River Lovely and that's about it.'

Cally played along. 'Hmm, let me guess.'

'No, no guessing. You'll just have to wait and see,' Nancy teased.

As they continued their stroll, they crossed over not far from the train station, went down a back lane, and walked along by the river. Cally remarked as she looked over to the other side of the river, 'I haven't been over to this side of Lovely. There's so much I still need to explore.'

'Ahh, I love it over here. I walk here often.' Nancy pointed in the direction of the sea. 'The marshes are beautiful as the weather warms up.'

'I'll have to go for a walk over there once I'm fully settled in.'

'Yeah, it's a good spot. You'll see otters if you're lucky. It never fails to deliver.'

Cally frowned as they walked off the path and seemed as if they'd double-backed on themselves. She pulled out her phone and looked at the map app. 'I have no idea whatsoever where we're going.'

'That's the whole point.' Nancy lowered her voice. 'The

setting of this one is out of this world. It hasn't been on for a long time. You'll love it.'

Cally wrinkled her nose as they ventured behind an old building. 'Where on earth are we going? I thought we were going to that house I've heard so much about over near The Summer Hotel.'

'Nope. That's a good one, though. If you ever get invited to that one, run, don't walk.'

They walked down the side of a building, through a car park, and then Cally realised they were back near the river again. She kept quiet as Nancy checked her phone, tapped a few times and then rang an old ship's bell to the right of a rickety old not very attractive door. Inside, she wondered how good it was going to be. As far as she could see, the place wasn't very special.

She raised her eyebrows as Clive, one of the men who ran the riverboat service answered the door - the same man from the day with the lamp. He was a bit odd, obsessed with France, and spoke in a very strange faux French accent that didn't sound very attractive or French to Cally most of the time. 'Bonsoir. Password?'

Cally tried not to laugh as Nancy answered with the password. Before she knew it, her eyes were nearly dropping out of her sockets. She'd thought the setting would be fairly nice; in Lovely, that was a given. This was more than nice. So very much more. Via a sign on the wall in front of her, she realised that she was standing underneath Lovely Bay Sailing Club. The whole place was illuminated by fairy lights strung across old beams overhead. Makeshift tables set with candle-lit jam jars were squashed in and covered in striped tablecloths. Vintage bits and bobs were stacked here and there, oversized lanterns filled with flickering candles twinkled, old sailing life preservers hung on the walls. A large, rustic table stood in the centre of the room with a faded blue linen tablecloth and a collection of mismatched candlesticks on the top. Against one wall, a long, low bookshelf overflowed with dog-eared sailing books and a few hardcovers with worn spines and faded pages. A pair of plump, overstuffed armchairs with faded floral upholstery sat on either side of the shelf. Little cushions everywhere told people to sit and stay awhile.

Cally inhaled. Chowder and freshly baked bread were front and centre. Working in the chemist for Birdie, she'd smelt chowder drifting from all sorts of places many times before, but somehow, in the dimly lit old building, it smelt better. It was homey, warm, and comfy all in one. She was very glad she'd said yes.

As she made her way further into the room, glasses clinked, people chatted and French jazz drifted through the air. Lovely old rugs were scattered here and there over the weathered wooden planks. At the far end of the room, a huge wide picture window looked out over the water. Cally couldn't fathom how an ordinary little basement area space had been transformed into something extraordinary. The power of a few lights and a great community. She loved it.

She followed Nancy to a small table set for three at the back, tucked into the corner. As Nancy weaved in and out, she stopped here and there to greet people. There were lots of smiles and hellos and just a general happy, buzzy atmosphere. Cally looked around and marvelled at the ingenuity of the speakeasy's location. It was what was really a nondescript area underneath the sailing club deck. It had, however, been transformed into a little haven. She felt a rush of gratitude towards Nancy for inviting her.

Just as they'd sat down and were making themselves comfortable, Nina rushed in and navigated her way through the crowded room. She sat down with a grateful sigh. 'I'm so sorry I'm late. Faye's been fussing all evening, and I just couldn't seem to settle her. At least I'm here now. Phew.'

'The little ones always seem to know just when you've got plans, don't they?'

'They certainly do,' Nina agreed, her shoulders sagging with exhaustion. 'I swear, sometimes I feel like I'm running on fumes. What a week!'

Cally smiled. 'Let's get you a glass of wine.'

'That sounds heavenly. I've left Robby to it back in the trenches while I sink a wine. I hope I'm not up all night.'

Cally poured Nina's glass and Nina took a long, appreciative sip. 'I needed that more than I realised.'

Nancy chuckled. 'Settle in for a nice time.'

About half an hour later, the wine had been flowing. Cally was cracking up with stories about Faye and various Lovelies had been over to the table to say hello as the place began to fill with locals. As Cally listened to Nancy telling a story about a trainspotter at the station who had lost the plot because the moveable platform had not performed to the second, a group of people entering the far side of the room caught her eye. The flutter she'd felt in the car earlier that day slammed into her like a rocket. Boom. Logan was in the room. Wearing a blue shirt and jumper, Cally couldn't take her eyes off him as she watched him navigate the crowded room. Cally felt the conversation float away and Nina and Nancy fade into the background as she watched Logan settle into a seat at a table with a group of people she didn't recognise.

Cally wondered whether or not the two people with Logan were the voices she'd heard from Lovely Manor when she'd earwigged through the door. Now they'd sat down, their faces were obscured by the dim, flickering light of the candles and lanterns. Cally frowned to herself about how Logan and his friends had been invited to a speakeasy. He was clearly more of a local than she'd realised.

Suddenly, as if sensing her, he looked over. His eyes locked with hers and for Cally, for a quick moment, time seemed to stand still. The chatter and laughter faded as she found herself not looking away. Logan smiled and raised his glass in a little salute. She gulped and lifted her glass, mirroring his gesture. What in the world was she doing? She flicked her head, blinked to look away, and felt a flush creep up her neck and into her cheeks. Her heart raced, and a little thrill of excitement ran through her. Flipping heck, she was nigh-on juddering. Her skin tingled and her pulse quickened.

'Earth to Cally,' Nina's amused voice cut through the haze. 'Where did you go just then?'

Cally blushed and she wiggled her head. 'Oh, nowhere,' she said brightly, her voice unconvincing even to her own ears. 'Just lost in thought. Recovering from you working me hard at the manor.'

Nina leant forward and chuckled. 'You and me both. How nice is this? I haven't been to this one before.'

Nancy lowered her voice. 'It's only on now and then. In fact, I cannot remember the last time it was here. Don't you two forget that you're here because of your connection with me.'

'Should we be honoured?' Nina bantered.

'Indeed you should. I'll expect direct payment into my account later.'

Cally flicked her eyes over to Logan again. She wondered how she could shoehorn a question about him into the conversation. She was now intrigued to find out more about him. How had he snagged an invite to one of the speakeasies? 'So, how does one get a ticket? Am I allowed to ask that question or is that also classified information?'

Nancy sucked air in through her teeth. 'First of all, someone has to initiate you into the WhatsApp group. Gone are the days of the ledger at the library.'

'How does one do that?' Cally giggled and played along.

Nancy kept a straight face. 'Baptism in the River Lovely first.'

'I'm out.' Nina chuckled. 'I draw the line at being dunked in the river.'

'Me too. Way too cold.' Cally agreed.

'Lightweights. You'll just have to elbow your way in through me, then.'

Cally wanted more information so that she could apply it to how Logan was there. 'So can any old person get a ticket?'

'Nope, not really, but yes.' Nancy shook her head. 'Hmm, no and yes. Technically once you're in the group you can buy tickets for anyone.'

'Right.'

Nancy frowned. 'Why the sudden interest?'

'Oh, no, nothing. Just wondered how it works, you know?'

Nancy smiled. 'It's one of Lovely's funny strange things from the past.'

'Mmm. I love it. There are so many odd customs here,' Nina stated as she took a sip of her wine. 'It had me hook, line, and sinker right from the word go.'

'Same,' Cally replied as someone plonked a bowl of chowder in a sourdough roll in front of her. She waited for Nancy and Nina to be served and then dipped a spoon in and shook her head in pleasure. 'Oh, wow, yes, very nice. Really good. How is something so simple just so tasty? I need to start gathering recipes.'

'It's a good one.' Nina agreed as she tucked in.

'Nearly as good as your efforts,' Nancy laughed.

'Yes, I've heard all about them.'

Nancy rolled her eyes. 'She's very particular about them.'

'Apparently, I'm going to be getting some.'

'You'd better keep it under lock and key.'

Cally dipped her bread in. 'This is fantastic.'

'Not bad.' Nancy laughed.

'What are you on about? It's delicious.'

Nancy rolled her eyes and joked. 'Perhaps your chowder palate isn't as refined as mine just yet.'

Cally laughed. 'Apparently not. But honestly, I'm enamoured with this whole setup.'

'You get used to it when you've lived here all your life.'

'I can imagine. You must feel quite fortunate.'

'Indeed, it's a special place,' Nancy acknowledged.

Cally agreed. 'I'm beginning to see that more and more.'

As the night wore on and the chowder disappeared, the room got a bit more noisy and boisterous. Even though she told herself not to, Cally stole way too many glances over at Logan's table. She wasn't quite sure what was happening to her. She watched as he laughed and joked and a couple of times she could have sworn he looked at her too, but maybe she'd imagined it. The same as when she'd seen him on the driveway, she dismissed her thoughts as stupid and teenager-like. There was no way he would be even glancing in her direction. She needed to stop being ridiculous. She knew nothing about him, for starters, apart from the fact that he was up at the manor and worked in maritime navigation tech. Whatever that even was, but it sounded quite impressive. Trying to talk herself out of looking at him didn't work. Not even a little bit. Even if she didn't glance over, she kept wondering about him. Who was he? Where did he work? Was he single? It was as if she was being pulled towards him by an invisible force. She frowned at herself and squeezed her eyes. She must have had too much wine. She felt a tap on the side of her glass.

'Hello! Welcome back to the land of the living.'

Cally gripped her glass with a start. 'Oh, sorry. Miles away.'

Nina chuckled and lowered her voice. 'Thoughts about a certain tall, fair, and handsome stranger, perhaps?' she nodded towards Logan's table.

Cally's eyes widened and she felt herself go hot. She pretended she didn't understand. 'What?'

'Oh, come on,' Nina said, her voice low and conspiratorial.

'Sorry, I don't know what you are talking about.'

'Logan, over there.'

'What about him?'

Nina widened her eyes to saucers. 'Don't tell me you haven't noticed the way he's been looking at you all night. That man is smitten from my side of the fence. It was the same in the car, too. I *did* tell you that.'

Cally's heart leapt. She wanted Nina to be right, but there was no way in the world she was going to admit it. She tried to play it cool, shrugging nonchalantly. Her voice was neutral. 'I don't know what you're talking about. We barely know each other.' But even as the words left her mouth, Cally knew that they weren't true. The weird thing was that although it was correct that she and Logan had only had a few brief interactions, there was something about him that made her feel as if she had known him for ages. Then there was how good-looking he was on top of that. That helped, to be frank. Oh, the shoulders.

'That might be so.' Nina laughed. 'He was flirting bad in the car.'

'Get away with you. I know nothing about him.'

'What happened in the car?' Nancy asked.

Nina leaned forward, her eyes sparkling with mischief. 'We bumped into Logan on the driveway at the manor today.'

Nancy joked. 'Is that so? How convenient. And what happened, exactly?'

Nina launched into the story, her hands gesturing animatedly. 'Well, there we were, trying to leave the manor, when who should pull up but Logan in his fancy car. We chatted for a bit and let me tell you, the sparks were flying. It was good to see.'

Cally nearly choked on her wine. 'It wasn't like that at all. We just said hello, that's it. In actual fact, *you* were the one doing all the talking.'

Nina shook her head. 'Oh, please. You two couldn't take your eyes off each other. I was just a bystander.'

Nancy chuckled. 'Well, well, well. Our Cally and Logan from the manor. I never would have guessed.'

Cally shook her head vehemently, trying to downplay the whole thing at the same time as wanting to fire a million questions about Logan Nancy's way. 'Honestly, you're both reading way too much into it. We barely know each other. He was just being friendly, that's all. After the shelf toppling and everything.'

Nina snorted. 'Friendly, my foot. I'm telling you, Nance, there's something brewing between these two. You should have seen the way Logan was looking at her, like she was the only woman in the world.'

Cally wanted to crawl under the table and die of embarrassment. 'It's nothing. You're making a mountain out of a molehill. It was just a brief conversation, nothing more.'

Nancy leaned back in her chair and joked. 'The lady doth protest too much, which actually means it's true. Ha! If you ask me, it sounds like there's a bit of chemistry there, whether you want to admit it or not. Our Neens is calling it. Noted.'

Cally sighed, realising she wasn't going to win the battle. 'Look, even if there was something there – and I'm not saying there is – it doesn't matter. Men like Logan don't go for girls like me.'

Nina rolled her eyes. 'There you go again, selling yourself short. Cally, you're a catch. Any man or woman would be lucky to have you, Logan included.'

Nancy nodded in agreement. 'Yeah, don't say that. I work at the railway station so there's no hope for me, then!'

Cally felt embarrassed. 'Sorry, I didn't mean it like that.'

Nancy batted her hand. 'It's fine. Don't let your insecurities hold you back from something, though.'

Cally felt a lump form in her throat. She'd always done precisely that. Her home caring circumstances had always stopped her from doing *everything*. People didn't get it, but maybe they were right. Maybe it was time to start having a bit more faith in herself. 'You're right.'

'Just keep an open mind about Logan; see where it leads.'

Nina held up her hands. 'Yup. I'm just calling it like I see it. There's something there.'

Nancy chuckled, shaking her head. 'Exciting! Ask him out, Cal.'

Cally made a face. She whisper-hissed. 'Ask him out? I'd rather stick pins in my eyes. I'm *not* doing that.'

Nancy giggled and as the conversation shifted to other topics, Cally continued sneaking glances at Logan. Maybe it would go somewhere if she let it. Perhaps it was time to open up a bit. Stop being so closed off and stuck by what had happened to her.

About half an hour later as the evening began to wind down and the crowd started to thin, Cally pushed her chair out and made her way to the toilet. Weaving through the tables she purposely gave Logan's table a wide berth and scooted into the bathroom.

After going to the toilet, she washed her hands, whipped her makeup bag out of her bag and peered in the mirror. With Logan's appearance at the event, she'd wished she'd made a bit more of an effort. Her hair was the same as it always was, scooped up on top of her head in a messy updo. She'd put on a bit of makeup but not a lot and was in her same old uniform of skirt, tights and ballet flats. She rummaged around in the bottom of her make up bag, pulled out a round pot with some pearly cream highlighter, unscrewed the lid, dabbed her finger in and wiped it across the top of her cheekbone and blended it in. Not bad. After another root around, she ran a thick chunky eyeliner across her top lid and dabbed at it with her index finger. Smoky eye of a YouTube guru's tutorial it was not, but as ladies toilet makeup operations went, it wasn't too bad. She pulled out a lip gloss that promised to "bee sting plump", slicked it on and then took out her piece de la resistance. The celebrity Cloud perfume known by those in the know to be a dead ringer for something ten times the price. Cally had been under the power of its spell for years. She took the handbag size from the inner pocket of her bag and sprayed with abandon. She giggled as she pulled her shirt away from her chest and sprayed liberally on her bra.

Two minutes later, she re-emerged from the toilet with smoky eyes, glossy lips and expensive but actually not, scent wafting around her. At that moment, as she sucked in her non-existent tummy and flicked her head, the world came crashing down to earth with a ginormous bump. So much for Logan. He'd gone.

He and his friends were not to be seen for dust. As Cally stood by the bathroom door for a second her heart sank as she noticed the empty chairs where Logan and his friends had been sitting. The disappointment was palpable. She felt a twinge of regret for not seizing the opportunity to talk to him earlier in the evening. She also felt stupid. *Just so stupid.* Spraying her bra with Cloud? What in the name?

When she arrived back at the table Nina and Nancy were gathering their belongings, preparing to leave. Cally rested her bag on her chair. She masked the disappointment she felt inside with a huge smile. 'Ready to call it a night?'

Nina looked over as Nancy leaned under the table to get her

bag. She then sat up, leaned in close and spoke in a low, conspiratorial tone. 'So that you know, Logan left a few minutes ago.'

'Oh, really? I hadn't noticed,' Cally lied, attempting to sound nonchalant and as if she couldn't have cared less.

Nancy straightened up, shaking her head as she fussed with her bag. 'I caught him sneaking glances at you when he thought no one was looking and he watched you go to the loo.'

'Well, I guess it doesn't matter now,' Cally said, trying to brush off the disappointment. 'He's gone.'

Nancy shook her head. 'If there is one thing I do know it's that in Lovely Bay you're bound to run into him again soon.'

Cally nodded. 'Whatever.'

As they made their way out, Nina put in her two pennyworth. 'Don't worry. If it's meant to be, it'll happen. And if not, well, there are plenty of other fish in the sea. Loads of them. Swimming around everywhere.'

Cally chuckled. 'Are you counselling me in romance, Neens?'

Nina raised her eyebrows. 'From what I've seen at the manor, I really don't think you need much help at all. The two of you are already doing that, with him leading the way.'

Cally rolled her eyes. 'Nah. You're seeing things.'

But inside, Cally wanted it to be true. She hoped so; she really did. She didn't know it yet, but things, big things, were right around the corner.

20

After saying goodbye to Nina, about half an hour later, Cally watched as the riverboat she'd just disembarked with Nancy, pulled away. Lovely looked very pretty in the night air. Fairy lights twinkled all the way around the boat and on top of the jetty, the water reflected a low-in-the-sky moon and in the distance, the lighthouse towered above. As the boat chugged down the river and began to disappear, it left a trail of white churn bobbing on the water. Cally, buoyed by the nice evening she'd had, soaked up the atmosphere of Lovely Bay at night. The hum of the boat's engine faded into the distance and the water lapped against the jetty. She inhaled the briny scent mingling with the earthy smell of damp foliage from the shoreline and almost had to pinch herself that she was finally living in Lovely. She didn't own a property in Lovely but she was starting the process of making that happen. She was *adamant* that she would do it one day. Once she could show a stable income to service a mortgage, she would be able to use the money in the trust as a deposit to start looking around for a small flat of her own. Standing next to Nancy looking down into the water, both of them were silent for a bit.

Nancy turned to walk off the jetty and as they made their way along the path, a salty breeze whipped through their hair and there was a distant cry of seagulls from high above. 'Well, that was a nice night, wasn't it?' Nancy asked. 'Did you enjoy yourself?'

'Really nice. I had a great time. Thanks for including me. Appreciate it.'

'Not a problem. Now you're a Lovely...' Nancy joked. 'You're on a list you didn't even know you were on.'

'Am I officially allowed to be referred to as a Lovely from now on?'

'Ha. You'll have to ask one of the bosses.'

'I thought you were one of them.'

'Pah! You're kidding me. Our Birdie and our Colin and Clive. I hold a low-ranking position in the hierarchy of the third smallest town in the country. Though I am in charge of the trains in and out of here so there's that string to my bow.'

Cally laughed. 'Could have fooled me. You vet people as they come into the station.'

Nancy chatted as they strolled. 'So, how are you finding it in the flat? Nice spot?'

Cally smiled. It was early days but already the cosy space above the deli felt like home. She heard herself gushing. 'Oh, it's been brilliant. It was a bit of a mess when I first moved in, but I'm certainly not complaining. It didn't take much to get it tidied and now I'm just doing little bits every day. I ordered some of that stick-on vinyl stuff for the kitchen and I even used the powers of YouTube to fix one of the taps in the bathroom. Go me.'

Nancy chuckled, shaking her head. 'Yeah, I heard it was a bit of a mess up there.'

'Not too bad. To be fair, it was just clutter and suchlike. It was junked up. Once that was out, it was fine. Nothing a good clean couldn't sort.'

'How about the stairs?'

'I wouldn't want to be going up there in heels, put it that way.'

'No. That's why our Birds didn't rent it out.'

'Yeah, she said. She has been great. She's so kind.'

'She really is. She's one of those people who does things for others but keeps shtum about it, you know? I aim to be like her in my next life.'

'I don't know what I would have done without her. I was in dire straits.' Cally winced. 'I actually don't want to think about it.'

As they walked, they crossed over a road onto a cobbled pavement and went past a row of jumbled cottages with the distinctive Lovely shell roof tiles. A few Lovelies were milling about here and there and Nancy greeted a man out with his dog for an evening walk.

'So, what's next on the agenda for the flat? Any big plans?'

'Actually, yes. Now that I've cleared out most of the junk and I've moved in I'm slowly getting there. I had a luxury mattress delivered which is like a dream to sleep on. I'm going to start on some painting and decorating now.'

Nancy raised an eyebrow. 'Ambitious. I like it.'

'Well, I figured if I'm going to be living there, I might as well make it my own, you know? Put my own stamp on it as it were. The paint is all there, too – leftover stuff from the deli. Birdie said it was painted a few years ago and the remnants are there. All it will take is a bit of elbow grease.'

Nancy nodded. 'Even better.'

As they rounded a corner, the full height and scale of the towering lighthouse came properly into view. Cally paused for a moment. 'Wow. I don't think I'll ever get tired of seeing that,' she said more to herself than to Nancy. 'It's mind-blowing.'

Nancy nodded in agreement. 'It's something, isn't it? I've

lived here my whole life, and it still takes my breath away. I love that feeling. Never gets old.'

'I used to dream about living in a place like this. Somewhere with history and character, where everyone knows everyone else's name. When I first started in the chemist I couldn't believe it. It was so different to what I'd known.'

'Lovelies and folk here are the best you'll ever meet. We have a few dodgy characters like anywhere. I don't need to tell you that. It's not all unicorns and roses. You must have come across some of them in the chemist. Birdie has some stories from there.'

'I have. Not many, though. Most people are nice.'

'They are. So, back to the flat. Do you need anything at all? Furniture or anything like that? I have loads of stuff up in the loft. I'll dig a few bits out if you like.'

Cally was touched by the offer. 'That's so kind of you. But I couldn't possibly…'

Nancy waved off her protests. 'Nonsense. It's just gathering dust up there. Might as well put it to good use.'

Cally felt a bit of a lump in her throat. Everyone had been so nice and welcoming. 'Thanks.'

Nancy smiled. 'Get used to it. We look out for each other around here. Harks back to the old days when no one had much and it was very isolated.'

'I'm learning that more and more.'

As they walked on, the shops and houses of the high street came into view. Little lights glowed from windows and a few people were standing chatting outside the pub. Cally followed Nancy into the small foyer of The Drunken Sailor, a place she had walked past many times before but had really only been inside briefly. She couldn't quite remember what it was like. A lovely, cosy pub smell greeted her as she stood in the foyer by the door. Lovely Bay coats were lined up on hooks to the left, and someone coming the other way stopped and chatted to Nancy as Cally moved in further.

Nancy made her way to the bar, greeting multiple people as she did so. Cally loved the feeling of being included as Nancy introduced her to a few locals, many of whom were already aware of who she was. It felt a bit odd that everyone seemed mindful of the fact that she was living over the deli. She wasn't sure whether to be concerned or flattered or what.

In the seventies housing estate, residents typically rushed from their cars to their homes, slammed their front doors behind them and that was that. It seemed different in Lovely. People knew stuff and cared. When she'd lived on the estate, no one had ever really exchanged a word and there hadn't been much communication at all, bar the odd raised eyebrow or two if you were really lucky. Cally had always been a bit on edge there too, nothing concrete but it had constantly nipped at the side of her consciousness that she should always watch her back. Although she had never experienced any crime or even heard of any, something had always made her feel *very* uneasy. As if there had been an underlying tension that suggested that she always needed to stay alert. She'd hated how that had felt when she'd walked home in the evenings. It didn't feel like that at all in Lovely. In actual fact, she felt so safe in Lovely, it was as if the estate existed on a different planet altogether. It was a stark contrast to the openness and friendliness of the locals in the pub.

By the time they reached the bar, they'd stopped and chatted a few times and had been offered a drink from someone Cally didn't know. Far from feeling strange or creepy, it was quite the opposite. Cally felt included and soon found a glass of wine deposited in her hand and engaged in conversation with a local who lived next to The Summer Hotel – an old empty B&B which Cally had heard all about from Birdie and Nina. As she chatted with the woman called June, she was lost in conversation when the far door swung open and caught her eye. Things were looking up. Oh yes. She felt a tingle on seeing Logan walk through the door, accompanied by the same two men who had been at the speakeasy. Her heart gave a little jolt at the sight of him, and she felt a flush creep up her neck and into her cheeks.

Nancy saw the group walk in too and noticed Cally's reaction immediately. She gave Cally a nudge with her elbow. 'Look who just walked in. The evening continues. What did I say? You always bump into people in Lovely. I should have put money on the fact that they'd end up here.'

Cally felt her face grow hotter, and she let out a nervous little laugh. She tried to play it cool, but it didn't really work. She found herself stuttering a little bit. 'Oh, um, yeah. You did say that.'

Nancy chuckled and shook her head. 'Oh, come on. It's okay to be happy to see him. In fact, I'd say it's more than okay.' Nancy swore. 'How handsome is he? Ha!'

Cally glanced over and back again. 'I didn't even notice him.'

Nancy shook her head. 'Course you didn't.'

As June started chatting again, Cally looked over in Logan's direction. He was deep in conversation with his friends, but as if sensing her, he looked up. Cally felt wobbly for a second, the same as in the speakeasy, as she felt the rest of the pub fade away. Logan raised his glass, then his eyebrows, and Cally felt her heart skip a beat. As much as she wanted to play it cool, to act like Logan was just another guy in the pub, the strange flips in her heart told her otherwise. Her pulse raced, her palms felt a bit clammy, and her mind had gone blank.

A bit later, the pub began to empty out. June, the friendly local she'd been chatting with, left to get a lift with Colin from the boat. Logan's group had slowly edged around the bar and it turned out that Nancy knew one of Logan's friends. Before Cally knew it, the two groups had blended together and were chatting. Cally found herself standing next to Logan. Her heart raced as she tried to think of something clever or witty to say. Neither came out and as she opened her mouth to speak, she heard herself garbling. 'Hi, how are you? What have you been up to? How was the chowder? Did you continue with the paperwork you said about?'

'Hey, Blackcurrant,' Logan replied with a chuckle. 'How are you?'

Cally swallowed. Logan had only said five words, but they made her feel a bit ridiculous. He sounded posh and accomplished compared to her garbling. He had that easy, confident manner of those from his walk of life. She suddenly felt *very* small and *very* out of place. A rush, no, a tsunami, of self-doubt washed over her, soaking her to the skin. The Blackcurrant thing too. Was he taking the Michael? She cringed as she realised that he was. 'Hi.'

'How did you enjoy the other place? Good?'

Cally swallowed. She stammered, mentally kicking herself as she heard herself doing a strange mix of gushing and rambling. All of it spilling out in a rush. 'Really, really, good. Who would have even known it was there? Did you know it was there? I loved it. I could eat there every night. I've just moved in, actually, over the road here, meaning, you know, I can just walk home.' She flapped her hands a bit and didn't stop for air. 'I can get to go to chowder places every night of the week, if I like. How good is that? It's so nice here.' She trailed off, feeling her cheeks flush. Why couldn't she just behave normally, like everyone else in the pub? Why did she always have to feel like such a bumbling idiot around people like Logan? It always just felt as if they were cleverer, better, brighter, more accomplished than her. She'd felt the same way when she had spoken with professionals when dealing with her mum and grandma.

'Yup.' Logan smiled, his eyes crinkling at the corners. Cally's heart skipped seven hundred beats. 'I know what you mean. Lovely Bay has a way of making you feel like you belong, doesn't it? Like you've finally found your place in the world. I like it here.'

Cally nodded. 'Yes, exactly. I've never felt so at home anywhere else.'

Logan chuckled. 'I felt the same way when I first came down here.'

Cally wanted to know *all* the details. 'Oh, I assumed. You're not from Lovely Bay originally?'

Logan shook his head. 'No, I'm afraid not. I'm a city boy, born and bred. The family has a place here, of course. My mum is here on and off. My mum's brother is… it's complicated. I live here I'd say part-time but full-time right now because there are a few issues with the manor and I'm helping out. I run a business of my own but I can do that anywhere.'

Cally again felt inferior. A family place. Just a small one, then. You know, just a manor house with staff. As you do. 'Oh, I see.'

'But yeah, I love it down here. You've just moved, you say?'

'Umm, yes, it's like I've finally found my place, especially after my recent...' Cally stopped herself from talking about her grandma.

Logan repeated her words, lilting his words up at the end in question. 'Your recent?'

Cally heard herself telling Logan a few things about her predicament. He nodded here and there, interjected with things about his family, asked a few questions and offered insights and just seemed to get it. She was more than surprised that he seemed to understand. She flicked her head a couple of times and told herself to turn away from him and move back to the main conversation. She felt as if she was treading on dangerous ground, that the feelings swirling inside her were new and unfamiliar and slightly terrifying. There was something about Logan that made her feel as if she was on fire.

The wine and the evening, though, were doing their thing

and she decided to throw caution to the wind and just get lost in the moment. What did she have to lose? It was just a conversation in a pub with a posh boy from the other side of the tracks. She laughed and chatted and sipped her wine and simply let herself have a nice time. It was good to stop holding up the sky. She relaxed and let it flop down all around her. She felt herself flicking her hair and being silly. Giggling. Her eyelashes batted away. Happy.

As Logan chatted, though, she still couldn't quite shake the feeling that she wasn't as good as him and that it wouldn't be long before he found out but she tried to ignore the imposter syndrome rearing its head. She had always felt like a bit of a square peg in a world of round holes, constantly aware of the spaces she didn't quite fit in. Standing by the bar in Lovely Bay with Logan, though, something was a teeny bit different. Whatever it was, it was enough to make her stay rooted to the spot and continue to make small talk.

As she stood sipping her drink and talking to Logan, she laughed more than she had in months and months, possibly years. The sky continued to fall. She watched as it landed around her in neat little slices of blue. What she didn't know was that there was much more to come.

The group had been chatting by the bar for ages when Nancy stifled a yawn. Nancy glanced at her watch, her brows rising in surprise at the time. 'Well, I hate to be a party pooper, but I think it's time for this old girl to call it a night. It's much later than I thought it was. It's been a long day and I have to be at the station to open in the morning.'

Cally wanted to wail a big fat no. As far as she was concerned, she'd be quite happy to stand in the pub by the bar talking to Logan all night. Like all night long and into the next one. A week. Year even. She felt a pang of disappointment at the thought of the evening ending, but she knew Nancy was right. The pub had emptied out considerably, and the staff were starting to clear the bar and tuck chairs under tables. Closing time was fast approaching.

As Nancy put her glass on the bar, stood up straight and began to gather her things, she turned to Cally. 'Rightio, I'll be off. Want me to walk that way with you?'

Cally batted her hand in dismissal. 'No, no. I'm fine. It's over the road.'

'Sure?' Nancy asked.

Cally gestured out the window as she got her coat from a little hook under the bar. 'I'm fine. It's literally over there.'

'Okie dokie, send me a text when you get in.'

Nancy said goodbye to Logan and the rest of the group, chatted to the bar staff for a bit and then made her way towards the door. Cally put her bag on her shoulder. Logan turned to her. 'I'll walk you home, Blackcurrant.'

Cally felt pathetically happy that she appeared to have commandeered a nickname from Logan. She laughed, a breathy, nervous sound that made her cringe inwardly. 'Oh, I'm just spitting distance away. Honestly, don't worry about it.' She waved her hand in the general direction of her flat. 'I can walk, it's no trouble. I'm fine. Absolutely fine.'

Logan was already shaking his head before she'd finished speaking. 'Nonsense. I insist.'

Cally's heart skipped a beat. She knew that she was perfectly capable of making her own way home. She'd done it often enough and in much less desirable surroundings. But she so very much wanted him to walk her home. So much. She pretended and felt herself fluttering her eyelashes. Was she, in fact, flirting even more than she had when she'd first started chatting to him? She was. Absolutely. No doubt about it, whatsoever. 'If you insist.'

Logan put his phone in his pocket and opened the pub door. He joked, 'The night awaits.'

Cally also joked. 'Do you have a chariot?'

As they stepped out into the cool air everything was quiet and deserted, the shops dark and silent. A velvety black, studded with a million twinkling stars sky seemed to hang over the high street. Cally breathed in the peacefulness and couldn't get enough of the fact that she was not going back to the crappy house on the estate but walking along the road to a Lovely Bay flat. She let it all swirl around her and seep into her bones. It was nearly as nice as strolling along the road with Logan.

As they got to the lit alleyway between the shops that led to the back of the deli, Cally stopped. She suddenly felt awkward and weird. Was this the point where she invited him up? She thought about the empty flat with its daggy, mostly second hand cobbled together bits and pieces. Suddenly, Lovely Manor slam-dunked into her head. She remembered hearing Logan speaking through the door when she'd been at the manor on the first day. He was used to fancy houses, gardeners and people serving him lunch. He ran a business. He lived in what he called "town". There was no way she was inviting him up. She wasn't going to be letting him know that she lived over a row of shops in a shoebox rented to her for a favour. She slowed her steps. 'Right, well, this is me. Thanks. Here we are. See you then. I might bump into you at the manor at some point.'

Logan smiled. 'Safe and sound, just as promised.'

'Appreciate it. Thank you.'

'Well, thanks for, umm, tonight, Blackcurrant. It's been nice. I'm really glad we caught up in the pub. Yeah, it's been the highlight of my week. Of my month, even.'

Cally felt a flush of pleasure. 'Same. I can't remember the last time I laughed as much. It's been fun. Sorry I had a bit of verbal diarrhoea earlier.'

'Not a problem. I enjoyed it.'

Cally bit her lip, suddenly feeling the need to explain herself. 'I don't usually share much with people about, well, about the past. I normally keep it private if you know what I mean. I hope I didn't overshare.'

Logan shook his head. 'Sounds like you've been through quite a bit.'

Cally swallowed. He didn't know the *half* of it. She'd skimmed over the top of everything that had happened in her life. Logan had heard the skinnied down version. 'Haven't we all?'

'Ahh, I don't know about that.'

Cally smiled and went to turn in the direction of the flat. Logan stepped in, put his arm out and suddenly he was kissing her. Cally wasn't sure what to do as she felt the ground slip away from her and oh boy, did that sky fall. It crashed around her like nobody's business. She melted into the embrace and felt her arms winding around Logan's neck. Ding dong. It was fabulous. Before she knew it, though, it was over and she was pulling apart from him.

Logan smiled. 'Right, well, err.'

'Thank you for walking me home.'

'My pleasure.'

Suddenly, he was kissing her again. The sky left the building. She pushed his chest and pulled away. Stuff not inviting him up. Stuff what he thought about the flat. Stuff feeling inferior. Stuff everything. She didn't care. 'I think you'd better come in for a coffee.'

'Thought you'd never ask, Blackcurrant.'

21

With a trembling hand, Cally punched in the code to the back entrance of the deli, clicked the switch and the door swung open with a beep. She led Logan through the stockroom and past the shelves lined with boxes of ingredients and supplies, before starting up the stairs to the first floor, then turning and stepping up the steep, narrow stairs that led to her flat.

As they reached the second-floor landing, Cally tried to calm what was happening to her heart. She glanced at the messy shelves next to the front door crammed with their haphazard collection of paperbacks, old magazines and hardcover books. It was hardly the library at Lovely Manor or even the third office. She lifted her chin in the direction of the books. 'This all needs a tidy up. Sorry about the mess. I haven't had a chance to organise them yet.'

She felt vaguely embarrassed about the shabbiness of the shelves and hated that she felt that way. She had nothing to be embarrassed about, she told herself inside. As she fiddled with the key in the door, everything seemed shabby and she felt as if she'd made a mistake in inviting Logan into her world. The tiny flat with hardly anything in it. The time warp decor and the fact that she hadn't done much at all apart from clear, clean, and declutter. The fact that she didn't have much. The lack of luxuries. There were no horses in stables at the top of the deli.

Logan didn't seem to take any notice of any of it whatsoever. Whatever she saw he didn't. Maybe he had other things on his mind. He scanned a few of the titles as she tried to open the door. 'I love a good bookshelf. You never know what you are going to find. You can just randomly pull something out and enter a whole new world.'

Correct answer from Henry-Hicks. Well played.

As the door swung open, Cally cringed a little bit at the sight of the bare, echoing flat. The rooms were clean and clutter-free, but it was a very long way from Lovely Manor. She loved it and was happy to call it home, but it was a blank canvas waiting to be filled and suddenly felt as humble as she did. She baulked inside. She definitely shouldn't have invited him up. Mistake. As had happened a few times when she'd daydreamed about him, she chastised herself that she was making a huge error even looking in the direction of someone of Logan's calibre. But the falling sky had made her have a go and it had been worth it. She tried to gauge Logan's reaction to the flat and switched the little switch at the back of her throat and trilled. 'I'm still in the process of making it feel like home.'

'Nice.' Logan didn't seem to notice the lack of furniture, the hotchpotch of colours and tired curtains.

Cally busied herself with filling the kettle and setting out two mugs. As she waited for the water to boil, she second-guessed inviting Logan up but he chatted away seemingly without a care in the world. Her brain raced. She shouldn't have even kissed him in the first place. What had she been thinking? All of it was a mistake, a terrible idea that would only end in embarrassment and heartache. But, man, that falling sky.

The kettle boiled and clicked. She flicked the Cally-is-okay switch in her throat again and sounded bright and breezy. 'Right, I promised you coffee and believe it or not I have truffles from the chocolate shop, too. And not just any old ones, special editions that have not even been released yet.'

'You know how to treat someone, Blackcurrant.'

Henry-Hicks was on form. Score.

Cally scooped coffee into a cafetière and poured in boiling water. The smell of coffee filled the small kitchen and as she picked up the mugs, she flicked her eyes and tilted her head towards the French doors in the sitting room and in the direction of the tiny balcony. 'Come and have a look at this.'

Logan followed her out onto the small, narrow balcony. His eyes widened as he took in the view. The rooftops of Lovely Bay stretched out before them, the rows of shops, little cottages and winding streets were bathed in the glow of the moonlight. 'Wow,' Logan breathed, leaning against the railing. He swore. 'I can see why you fell in love with this place. It's magical up here. What an amazing outlook.'

Cally smiled. Maybe she shouldn't have questioned the flat after all. 'It's the best spot in the whole place. You can see for miles up here. I'm truly taken with it.'

Logan nodded. 'I bet. You need to get a telescope.'

Cally went to get the coffee and swallowed. What was happening? She was upstairs in a flat in Lovely Bay with a gorgeous man, showing him a view from her balcony. Okay, she was renting the flat. It wasn't hers, but whatever. There was no question that he was gorgeous. How her life had changed in a few months. She was a long way from the hotel on the side of the motorway. Thank goodness. And Logan? There were no words.

Cally returned with the coffee and a small plate of chocolate shop truffles, carefully balancing them as she stepped back out onto the balcony. Logan turned. 'Nice. I love that shop.'

'Who doesn't? These are special edition.'

'I'm intrigued by a special edition. What's so special about them?'

Cally put the plate down on the little table. 'Apparently, they're made with some rare Venezuelan cocoa beans. Super limited batch. Birdie managed to steal a few boxes for the deli before they're officially released. I got in on it, too. The perks of working for Birdie. There are many.'

Logan whistled. 'Blimey. Must be good then.' He picked up a truffle and popped it into his mouth and his eyes widened. 'Mmm. Oh, wow. That's incredible.'

Cally giggled. 'Right? I had the same reaction when I tried one earlier. I need a subscription to the chocolate shop. Imagine that. How good would that be?'

'I make you correct.'

They sipped their coffees in silence for a few moments, taking in the moonlit view. Cally's mind reeled from the events of the evening. She loved it all; from the chats to the kiss that had made her heart race and skin tingle. She side-eyed Logan. It was almost too good to be true.

Logan raised his mug at the view. 'Coffee's great and I've had a good time. It was nice bumping into you.'

Cally blushed. 'It's been a bit of a turn up for the books tonight.'

Logan chuckled. 'In the best possible way. I have to say, I wasn't expecting my night to end like this when I walked into the pub earlier. I'll take it for the team, though.'

Cally bit her lip. 'Me either.'

'Works for me. The best, actually.'

Henry-Hicks was on fire.

Cally could feel another kiss coming and the sky falling. She loved the falling sky so much it made her feel giddy. She leaned in closer to Logan. Her heart hammered, her skin prickled with anticipation as she waited for him to close the distance between them. This was going to be so good.

All of a sudden, there was a shrill ringing of a phone. It totally shattered the moment. Cally jumped. Logan groaned. He pulled back and fished his mobile out of his pocket. 'Sorry, I should probably get this.'

Cally nodded, trying to calm her racing heart as she watched him step back into the flat to take the call. She took a deep breath, redid her hair and tried to collect herself. What was she doing? She barely knew this man, and here she was, inviting him up to her flat. Kissing him on the balcony. Reckless, possibly dangerous, impulsive, and completely unlike her. She flipping *loved* it. She'd take reckless any day of the week. It beat holding up the sky left, right and centre that she knew for a fact.

She looked in Logan's direction as he stood talking into his phone in his left hand and with his right squeezing the back of his neck. Something weird about him felt right. Cally couldn't explain it, but she just felt as if she should just go with it and see what happened.

Logan stepped back outside, an apologetic and slightly harassed look on his face. 'I'm so sorry. I'm going to have to shoot. I need to head back to the manor.'

Cally felt her heart sink. *Of course. Of course, something would come up.* She swore over and over in her head, but plastered a smile on her face. She flicked the Cally-is-okay switch to the on position. 'Of course! No, no, it's fine.'

She sounded fine on the outside. Inside, she wasn't at all. She'd wanted to kiss him again. All the days. To do more than that. To throw every bit of caution into every bit of wind. She turned her head to the side. She didn't want to understand. She wanted to wail. Maybe stamp her feet a little bit, too. *So not fair. **** sake.*

Logan frowned. 'I don't want to leave, but yeah, I need to get back.'

Cally nodded and made light of it. 'All good. Not a problem at all. I'll see you out.'

A few minutes later, Cally was standing by the back door of the deli and Logan was on the step in the yard. She continued to pretend and sound bright and not too bothered. 'See you then.'

'I'll message you.'

'Right, how are you going to do that?'

Logan frowned. 'What?'

'You don't have my number.'

'Oh, ha, yeah.' Logan pulled his phone out of his pocket, and started to tap. 'Blackcurrant.' He looked up and raised his eyebrows, 'Number?'

Cally reeled off her number. 'Thanks for tonight.'

'Yeah, it's been fun. I'll text you. We'll go out or something, yeah?'

Cally felt awkward and a little bit embarrassed. 'Great. See you later. You don't have to text me.'

'What?'

'Don't, you know, feel as if you *have* to or anything.'

'I *want* to.'

Correct again. Well played that man. It's a score from Henry-Hicks.

Cally smiled. 'Okay, well, err thanks. See you later.'

'See you Blackcurrant. I'll be in touch.'

As she walked back up to the flat and closed the door behind her, Cally leaned back against the solid wood and smiled. She couldn't quite believe how the evening had turned out. Was it all real? Had the events of the night actually happened? The flat, Lovely, the chowder evening, the pub, Logan. All of it seemed too good to be true. Or was this just what happened in places like Lovely? Did nice things just occur as part of the regular old day to day? As if it was all totally normal. Did nice things just happen to people who didn't have to hold their hands up to keep the sky from falling down? Cally shook her head. If it was the way things happened in Lovely, she wouldn't mind finding out more. And another thing; she definitely wanted more of the tingling lips, the racing heart, the giddiness. She'd like to bottle that bit and sell it. She'd throw in instructions on how to stop holding up the sky. She'd end up super rich, hobnobbing with Elon and his gang.

She pushed off from the door and made her way to the balcony and cleared up the tiny table. After rinsing out the cups and cafetière and washing them up, she turned them upside down, left them to drain and went into the bathroom. As she scrubbed at her face with a flannel, she looked in the mirror and squinted.

Hang on, wait, who even was this person looking back at her? Did this person have a bit of a sparkle in her eye? Was this the girl who used to hold up the sky all the time? It was. And oh my, this girl actually had a pizzazz about her person. A few kisses and a man named Logan obviously did that for a girl. She watched herself smile at the woman in the mirror and realised who she was. Not Cally, the daughter, the carer, the sister or the granddaughter. Just the Cally who had not had to worry about anything for a *whole* night. Cally, who had let the sky fall down and had allowed herself to be carried away by a kiss. Now all she needed was for the pizazz to last a bit longer. For one gorgeous, long, delicious, nice day. That wasn't too much to ask for, was it?

22

Cally woke to the sound of her phone buzzing on the bedside table. She groaned, rolled over, and fumbled for it, her eyes heavy with sleep and her head feeling like a dead weight. However, when she saw Logan's name on the screen, she was suddenly wide awake. Ooh, yeah. She leant up on her elbows, her heart missed a beat, she gulped, stared at her phone screen for a very long time but didn't open the message. He was probably going to make up some excuse. Yes, he'd more than likely just be sending her a text so that it wasn't awkward if and when she next saw him at the manor. In the cold light of day he would be full of regret. She'd make a cup of tea before she opened it.

Grabbing her dressing gown, she went to the loo, washed her hands and face and shuffled to the kitchen and put the kettle on. As she stared at the coffee cups and upside down cafetière on the draining board, the kiss from the night before slammed into her head. Her mind raced as she replayed the moment over and over again and tried to recapture the spark that had coursed through her body at his touch. It had been so unlike her and unexpected, too. Now, in the harsh light of morning, she second-guessed herself. She must have had too much wine. What had she been thinking, kissing Logan like that and right in the middle of the street too? Completely inappropriate when new in Lovely Bay.

She busied herself with making the tea and as she waited for the water to boil, she leaned against the worktop and looked out the window. Lovely was shrouded in the hazy swirl of a grey, misty morning. Fog clung around the lighthouse and the tops of the buildings. The kettle clicked off, she poured steaming water over the teabag, stirred the mug, added a slosh of milk and carried the mug back to her bedroom, delaying the time before she opened the text. Popping the mug by the side of her bed, she pulled back the covers and hopped back into bed, leant against the headboard, blew on her tea and looked at her phone. She didn't want to open it and see a brush off. She was fairly sure that Logan would now be regretting the kiss. Then again what if he'd felt the same spark? She took a sip of her tea, it scalded her tongue a bit, she picked up her phone and tapped on Logan's message. It started with a string of emojis.

Henry-Hicks was very good at this game.

Cally may have grinned like an idiot.

Logan: *I hope you slept well. I just wanted to thank you again for last night. It was nice. HH.*

Cally inhaled, lifted her ribs, closed her eyes and thought for a second. Whoop-whoop. She reread the words six times over. He felt it too! A giddy, disbelieving, extremely excited and very witch-like cackle came out. *Yesssssss!*

Nice? It was more than nice in her opinion. She followed his lead.

Cally: *It was. Thanks.*

Logan's response was immediate. She waited for the little dots to finish and the message to arrive.

Logan: *Nice night, Blackcurrant. Apologies that I had to leave like that.*

Cally: *Is everything okay? With the manor?*

Logan: *Just some drama with my mum. Families, eh?*

Cally: *Yep. Tell me about it.*

Logan: *What are you up to? Doing anything tonight?*

Cally contemplated for a minute. Should she pretend she actually had a thriving social life? Play hard to get? Nup. Sod that for a game of soldiers, she was diving in head first. Wading around in a fallen sky was way too nice to try and play it cool.

Cally: *Nope, nothing planned.*

Logan: *Come to the manor tonight. Have dinner with me.*

Cally's heart pounded. She'd had worse invitations. Did she want to go to a manor and have dinner with a very handsome man? Tricky one. She couldn't type fast enough. Her thumbs flew over her screen. Stuff being too keen. She was going for gold.

Cally: *Just tell me when and where.*

Logan: *Seven o'clock. I'll pick you up.*

Cally: *Done. See you later.*

As she put her phone down and stretched out on the bed, Cally punched upwards into the air and did a funny little cheerleader shuffle rumble-dance up and down the bed. Girlfriend was going to the manor for dinner. Girlfriend was grinning like a Cheshire cat.

23

Cally was practically buzzing around the flat as she made herself a second cup of tea. Shame she had a chat shift to start, otherwise she'd totally spend the whole day romanticising everything. If she'd had time, she would have wasted hours idealising her new existence. Instead, she would spend the day controlled by a little box on her laptop, a camera would take a screenshot of her screen activity every eleven and a half minutes and she would have to placate (and pretend to be even slightly interested) in missing cashmere socks and holiday dresses made with Irish linen that had arrived with holes.

At least it would take her mind off the dinner because once the initial furore about Logan's invitation had died down, she'd begun to panic a bit about what she was going to wear. Working a long full daytime shift wouldn't give her time to stress about her outfit choice. She'd been doing the chatbot job long enough to know that it would be a busy day full of problems. She'd have at least three customers at the same time and there would be a queue as long as her arm. There would be a line of the same low-key passive-aggressive women who thought they were nice and would be sure to inform her of that very fact. The odd one here and there who would tell her that they were "furious" and would, by way of the little text box, rant on for ages. Cally would have to wrap them up in cotton wool and soothe them. Grrr. Then there would be the customers who would assume that she would be able to read their minds. The same customers would then proceed to get cranky when she didn't jump high enough to answer their questions.

She'd seen it all before. At least it was a job. The money went into a savings pot which would eventually mean that she would be able to buy a flat. She needed to keep that front and centre. With a really happy sigh, she sat on the sofa with a mug of tea, pulled out her phone, and dialled Eloise's number. Eloise picked up on the second ring.

'Hi, what's occurring?'

'What is occurring? You're probably not going to believe it. Brace, brace, brace.'

'Oh dear. Do I want to know? Not something else with David. Honestly, I want to wring his neck for him. Let me at him. I'm so over this, Cal! I thought we'd seen the back of him. We had. He hasn't reared his ugly head for ages.' Eloise ranted, referring to Cally's half-brother David.

'Yeah, no, nothing on that front. Now he knows there's no money he's scarpered.'

'What then? Actually, it can't be him because you sound happy. I didn't clock that right away. Spill the tea.'

'I have a date tonight.' Cally stated matter-of-factly.

There was a shriek. 'Oh, what the heck? With you know who? The one you told me about at the manor with the shelf?'

'Yes! With Logan.'

'I don't know what to ask first. Where?'

'At Lovely Manor itself.'

There was a moment of silence on the other end of the line, and then Eloise let out an ear-piercing squeal. 'Oh my god, Cal! At the manor! You have to be joking me!'

Cally winced, holding the phone away from her ear. 'Thanks, but now it's sunk in, I'm kind of freaking out over here. I have no idea what to wear and I have no time to sort anything out because I'm working all day.'

Eloise clicked her tongue. 'I get it, babe. It's a big deal. What are the options for a person who still basically wears their school uniform every day?'

Cally sighed. 'Precisely. *You* get it. You know how weird I am with that. I don't know. I have a couple of dresses, but they both seem too fancy or too casual. And I don't want to look like I'm trying too hard, you know? I always wear the same thing. It's just me. It is what it is. I love my tights…'

'Mmm, I see your point about being you,' Eloise mused. 'What about that black midi dress you wore to my birthday last year? Is that one of your options or did you give that to the charity shop like you always do after events?'

'Yeah, it's an option, but I don't know. Isn't that a bit much for dinner? It's quite dressy.'

'Yep, true, it is quite fancy.'

Cally bit her lip. 'I don't know. Maybe this is a mistake. I mean, Logan is so out of my league. He's rich and successful and comes from this whole other world. Dinner is at an *actual* manor. What if I make a fool of myself? Actually, now that I think about it, the dress or outfit is probably the least of my worries.' Cally swore. 'I'm second-guessing myself.'

'Who gives a stuff where he comes from or how much money he has? Don't even go there. Don't do that, Cal.'

'Too late. I already have.'

'Right.'

'I do give a stuff where he comes from and *that* is my point.'

'I get you, but you mustn't.'

Cally wasn't sure if Eloise *did* get her. The last time she'd checked, Eloise hadn't been holding up the sky for most of her life. 'Part of me wants to text him and say no. You know?'

'You are *not* doing that.' Eloise's voice softened. 'You have to go. You've waited long enough to be able to just go out like a...' Eloise stopped herself from what she was going to say.

'Like a normal person?'

'Something like that.'

Cally sighed, leaning back against the sofa cushions. 'What if I'm just setting myself up for disappointment, though? We're worlds apart. He even speaks differently to me.'

'Who cares? Ooh, a posh boy. Love it. No, this is good. I can feel it in my bones. You even *sound* happy.'

'I am, actually.'

'I know.'

'It's weird. I feel as if things might be turning.'

'They are because you didn't give up. You're a trooper.'

'You always know just what to say, don't you?'

Eloise joked. 'Ha, it's a gift. Seriously, I really think you should give this a chance. Don't let your doubts sabotage stuff before it even starts.'

'I'll just go and see what happens, shall I?'

'You're going even if I have to deliver you myself.'

'What shall I wear, though?'

'Just wear what you normally wear but put that silky shirt on with the frilly bit on it. Then you'll be comfortable. Wash your hair, put some make-up on, and chuck on a nice pair of earrings. It's not what you *look* like that's important. That's the least interesting thing about you. Worrying about what you look like is so boring, Cal.'

'Actually, yeah, I love that shirt.'

'See? Problem solved. You're going to knock Posh Boy's socks off. I just know it.'

'Yes, you're right. Just be me. Thanks. I don't know what I'd do without you sometimes.'

'That's what I'm here for. We talk each other down from the

ledges we put ourselves on when we're overthinking things. Which is almost always, by the way.'

Cally snorted. 'You're not wrong. Overthinking is my superpower.'

'True, but sometimes you need to just go with your gut or mine. And right now, my gut is telling you to feel comfortable and go out with a handsome man who clearly likes you, and enjoy the heck out of your evening. Am I right? I'm right.'

'You're right. Absolutely right. I'm going to do this. I'm going to let myself be swept off my feet by the charm of Lovely Manor and the company of a member of the fancy-schmancy Henry-Hicks family.'

'That's the spirit. I want to hear all the ins and outs of it tomorrow.'

'You'll get a full report. Okay, I'd better skedaddle. Now for a long shift of moaners.'

'That will take your mind off the dinner, then just have a bath, do your hair, and go. Don't overthink it, Cal.'

'I won't.'

'Text me later.'

'Will do.'

Cally sat for a moment, letting the conversation replay in her mind. Eloise was right. She'd put the silky shirt with the ruffle on and be done with it. Who cared what she looked like? She rummaged through the wardrobe to find the shirt, noted that it needed an iron, and held it up for inspection. It was not bad – dressy enough for a nice dinner, but still comfortable and easy to wear. She laid it out on the bed, already mentally pairing it with her skirt, tights, and ballet flats. Simple. She thought about the dinner. Maybe this was the start of something or maybe it would be a total disaster. Who knew, but she was going to go and see what Henry-Hicks had to offer. See how well he played his game.

24

Cally had been on the customer support chat portal all day and was coming to the end of her shift. It had been excruciatingly busy, which had ended up being a good thing. She'd certainly not had time to worry about what she was going to wear to dinner at the manor. She clicked on the next waiting customer and pasted her ready-formulated greeting into the box where her fake name told the customer that her name was Alex. According to research, Alex was a name that could be attributed to being genderless, and research told those in the retail game that people felt comfortable and less volatile when associating with customer retail assistants named Alex.

Customer Support Agent (Alex): *Hello. Thank you for contacting Whitley & Co. Customer Support. My name is Alex. How can I assist you today?*

Customer (Linda B): *At last! Hi, Alex. I'm really frustrated. I bought a cashmere scarf from your store, and after just one wear, I've seen pilling. This is unacceptable!*

Boo hoo. Get me a violin. Cally selected the most suitable pre-made answer, copied it and hit paste.

Alex: *I'm very sorry to hear that, Linda. I understand how disap-*

pointing it can be when a product doesn't meet your expectations. Let me assure you that we will do our best to resolve this issue for you. Could you please provide me with your order number?

Customer (Linda B): *You're joking. I'm logged in, so you can see that. I thought that was the whole point of this. Hang on. It's #98765432. I expected better quality for the price I paid.*

Alex: *Thank you for providing your order number. I'm looking up your order details right now. Please bear with me for a moment.*

Customer (Linda B): *I've already been waiting for ages. Really?????*

Alex: *I see that you purchased the cashmere scarf two years ago. I apologise for the inconvenience. Could you please describe the issue in more detail or upload a photo of the scarf?*

Customer (Linda B): *A year. No!?!??? It's pilling all over! I don't have time to send photos. I just want my money back. This is SUCH a waste of my time.*

Alex: *I apologise for the inconvenience, Linda. I understand how frustrating this must be for you. We can certainly process a return or exchange for you. Would you prefer a refund, or would you like to exchange the scarf for another item?*

Customer (Linda B): *I want a refund but I'm not sending it back. And I don't want to go through any hassle. How do I get my money back?*

Here we go. That old chestnut. Cally had seen it many times before.

Alex: *I completely understand, Linda. To process your refund, I'll need you to return the scarf to us. I can email you a prepaid return label so you won't have to pay for postage. Once we receive the scarf, we'll process your refund immediately. Does that sound acceptable?*

Customer (Linda B): *Fine, but I want my money back as soon as you get the scarf. No delays.*

Alex: *Absolutely, Linda. As soon as we receive the scarf, we will process your refund within 1-2 business days. Is there anything else I can assist you with today?*

Customer (Linda B): *Just make sure I get my money back quickly. I'm really disappointed. Honestly, I should invoice you people for my time.*

Alex: *I'm very sorry for the inconvenience, Linda. We value your feedback. Thank you for bringing this to our attention and I apologise again for the trouble.*

Customer (Linda B): *Course you do.*

Alex: *Thank you for your understanding, Linda. Have a good day.*

Cally sighed and once she'd checked her time was correct, logged out of the portal. She closed her laptop, tidied up her work area and put the busy work shift out of her mind. There was one thing for sure; it had taken her mind off the dinner and she now had little time to faff around worrying about what to wear or how the dinner would go.

She went and had a shower, got dressed, put her usual makeup on and stood in the kitchen feeling a surge of nerves about the date. As she fiddled with her earring, she realised that she felt a bit nauseous. She checked the notes on her phone she'd made in a lull in the chat portal. She'd written a short list of bullet points of things to make her sound interesting. She knew who the Prime Minister was and what was happening in the world, so that was a plus. She'd read the first few articles on the CNN website so she'd appear worldly if she had to. The antics of middle-aged politicians would give her a talking point if indeed she needed it. In case she got overwhelmed, she intended to have a sneaky glance at the notes to make herself sound up-to-date and compos mentis with what was going on in the world, intelligent even. As she scanned down, she shook her head. It was actually pointless; she would end up looking uneducated anyway.

She decided to wait on the balcony overlooking the street, pondering how her life had suddenly seemed to veer off the anticipated course she'd thought she was on. She was immensely grateful for the veering. Just a month or so before, she'd still been in her old routine, never imagining she'd be going on a date with a handsome man. Yet here she was, not just on any old date either, but being picked up by someone who would take her to a manor house—a twist in her life's narrative for sure. So twisted that it didn't feel real. She'd take the twist for Team de Pfeffer and run with it.

Opening the door to get some fresh air, she stood on the balcony and drummed her fingers against the railing as she looked out over Lovely Bay and inhaled air laced with the sea and the scent of chimney smoke or a bonfire somewhere. The distant sound of the pub on the corner drifted across the evening and the lit-up lighthouse loomed overhead. She checked her phone for what felt like the hundredth time. Every time she'd looked at her messages, she'd half expected a text from Logan telling her his invitation to dinner had been a joke. Her stomach fluttered with a mix of delicious anticipation and outright trepidation. It was still a good ten minutes before Logan was due to arrive, but she couldn't seem to settle her nerves. She considered having a swig of wine from the open bottle in the fridge. Or perhaps lug down a neat vodka or six. As if on cue, her phone buzzed with an incoming call from Eloise. She tapped to answer.

'Hey, I just wanted to check in and see how you're doing. Ready for the big date?'

Cally bit her lip. 'I'm kind of freaking out. It's like, I don't know. As if there's something different about this.'

'Ooh, exciting!'

'I know.'

'You're going on a proper grown-up date, to a blimming manor house no less! It's like something out of a Netflix show.'

'Ha, not quite.'

'Oh my goodness! I've just thought. You're in a modern-day episode of Bridgerton! There'll be a carriage to pick you up. Doormen and all sorts.'

'Ahh, don't say that. I'm nervous enough as it is.'

'Why not?'

'I'm a basket case. Thank goodness I've been sorting out customers' retail problems all day and didn't have time to over analyse this, or I would have totally cancelled.'

Eloise tutted. 'Remember what we said hours ago. You are a catch.'

'You would say that, you're my best friend.'

'It's true, though. It's my job to reiterate that to you at any given opportunity.' Eloise deadpanned.

'I don't have much luck with men,' Cally stated morosely.

'Fair point. You have had a run of particular losers without a lot between their ears.'

'Precisely. This one has lots between his ears. I'm way out of my skill set here. Actually, what is my skill set exactly? Any ideas? Being a carer and working for a call centre? I mean, really? I don't even work in a call centre – they employ remote workers pretending it's to aid in work-life balance when really it's so they don't have to provide an office or any perks and to save them money.'

'Don't even *think* about stuff like that.'

Cally sighed. 'Sometimes I can't help it. All that work to get my degree and for what?'

'Just relax, be yourself, and let the magic happen. I hate it when people say this, but you've got this.'

'Anyway, I'll be fine, I made notes.'

'What the? No! Please don't do that. Notes are a no-go. Who even are you? I've never heard you like this before about a date.'

'Too late I have been making notes all day in between customers.'

Eloise sounded disbelieving. 'What the heck do you have notes on?'

'Various topics in case I feel like I need to sound interesting or educated or something.'

'Put them away! Look, I've got to go. I was just ringing to give you a boost.'

'Thanks. Wish me luck. I'll call you tomorrow with all the gory details.'

'If you need a get-out clause, text me the password.'

'Ha. I'll send you that after I put the phone down then.'

Cally slipped her phone back into her bag, smoothed down the front of her top, and adjusted her hair in the reflection of the balcony door. She looked okay and she was comfortable, so there was that, at least. She shook her head and the little drop earrings she hadn't worn for ages tinkled happily. At least her earrings were not feeling out of their depth. They were about the only thing that wasn't.

The sound of a car pulling up behind the fence in the lane below jolted her out of her musings. She leaned over the railing and watched as the car reversed. The window wound down, Logan looked up and waved. Cally felt her stomach do a little flip as she waved back. She flew down the stairs and as she stepped out onto the street, she shivered slightly. She flicked the switch in the back of her throat and attempted to be carefree, but as she climbed into the car, she was so nervous and uptight and borderline scared all at once that she more or less fizzed from head to toe and first of all didn't really know what to say.

Logan did not sound nervous. He *did* sound gorgeous. 'Evening Blackcurrant. How are we?'

Tra la la. 'Good, thanks! You?'

'Same, yes, well, thanks.'

'How have you been? Good day?'

'Ahh, you know this and that. Went out for a ride this morning. That was pleasant.'

'Ride?'

'Horse ride. We took the horses out. What have you been up to today?'

Cally swallowed. *Took the horses out? Seriously?* She swore in her head. She knew she shouldn't have said yes. *Oh, I've actually been going by the name of customer retail support person Alex today. Talking to customers about the lack of my employer's care about the people who pay their bills. More than one person swore at me and I earn just over minimum wage for my sins.* 'Just pottering around.'

'Nice. It's good when you can just do nothing, isn't it?'

Wrong move Henry-Hicks.

Cally swallowed. She wished she knew. 'Mmm.'

As Logan drove through Lovely, Cally looked skyward at the shell roofs, beautiful bunting, and gazed up as they passed the lighthouse as Logan chatted about his day. She imagined him galloping over fields on a horse. With or without a shirt. An image of the manor flashed into her brain. She felt like a duck out of water in the fancy car with the fancy man. She contemplated escaping and wondered what would happen if she opened the door while the car was moving. Would she be able to do some sort of commando roll onto the pavement and do a runner? She watched a bus go past and told herself that she was being stupid. She did not need to feel out of her depth. There was nothing wrong with her; she was fine. She didn't have to worry about anything, but all she could think about was the fact that she was not cut out to move in the sort of circles where people took their horses out for a ride on a Saturday afternoon.

Answering one of Logan's questions brightly, she attempted to calm herself down and focused on the fact that she might not have the same circumstances as Logan, but she'd educated herself well enough. She thought about her grandma, who had always told her from an early age that books were her university – that reading books would give her everything she ever needed in life. Cally had taken that literally, reading everything from the latest romcom by the Irish writer she'd been reading for years, to autobiographies of professors, to books about the pharaohs in Egypt. She really tried to buoy herself up and tell herself that she might not have an Eton education, but she was bright. Though knowing who the Prime Minister was wasn't always top of her agenda, it changed way too often for that.

Even though her stomach was all over the show, Logan seemed perfectly at ease. She didn't have to worry too much about making small talk, as he kept up a stream of casual conversation as he drove. She found herself not having to make too much effort at all and felt herself relax a little bit. She laughed at his jokes, said all the right things in all the right places and played along as if she was right as rain.

As they turned left away from Lovely and rounded a bend in the road, Lovely Manor came fully into view. Cally felt her breath catch in her throat at the sight of it. It was massive, a sprawling estate that seemed to glow from within. Once they got closer to the gates, Logan pressed a remote button on the console in the middle of the car and the gates began to clang and open inwards just as they had when she had walked up to them in her stained blouse on the day when she'd tumbled over by the church. She gripped the side of the handle on the car door and nervously flicked the switch for the window back and forth. First, there were the horses and now electric gates with remote controls. She felt all wrong. She heard her voice change a little bit as she answered Logan's question about the weather forecast for the following week.

Logan clocked the change in her tone right away. He turned to her as the car started up the drive. 'Are you okay?'

'Yes, yes, absolutely fine.'

'Are you sure?"

'Yup. Brilliant, absolutely great. Perfect.'

With the tyres crunching on the gravel driveway, Cally tried not to be concerned about her surroundings. She told herself to instead focus on having a good time. Logan was nice and he'd invited her to dinner. It was as simple as that. It was difficult, though, not to feel nervous, considering where she was. She suddenly felt nauseous as she had visions of being in a huge dining room, having to sit and be served some fancy meal by a man in tails. Cringing, she thought about what cutlery she might have to use. An image of a gigantic lobster on a plate and those funny pincer things came into her head. What if there were oysters? How on earth would she navigate her way around an oyster shell?

She swallowed and realised that she had made the completely wrong call; she should have said no to dinner at the manor house in the first place. She smiled to herself at her funny situation as an image of a date she'd been on in the past flashed through her head. The date had been on the total other end of the stick. She'd said yes to someone who had worked at the agency that had provided relief care for her grandma. She'd chatted with the guy on the phone a few times, met him once or twice, and found herself on a date to the cinema with him. When he'd turned up in an electric blue boy racer car with a lowered suspension, fin on the back and white go-faster stripes down the side, she'd wanted the ground to swallow her up. Instead, she'd hopped in and spent an awful night regretting the whole thing, especially when he'd wanted to go halves on a box of popcorn. Now here she was in a very different car, about to enter a very different world. She hadn't fitted into either world. This one was worse, though. At least the other one was sort of funny with the go-faster stripes and cheap aftershave. Here she wasn't laughing. About to throw up, more like.

Everything felt a bit dreamlike as the car, with the house in the distance, made its way up the drive and then proceeded to go completely around the main manor and past the stables where she had been with Nina. It then turned away from the house along another, narrower gravel driveway around the back of the new wing. They approached a small, cottage-like building

Cally hadn't set eyes on before. As Logan chatted away about nothing much, Cally wondered where they were going. He pulled up outside the small cottage with a little gabled porch where shrubs sat outside the front and ivy climbed around the door. It looked as though, back in the day, it might have been perhaps a worker's cottage or something similar. Because, of course, everyone had little workers' cottages up their sleeve. Logan was completely unaware of the chatter going on inside Cally's head. She got out of the car and followed him inside.

Not saying a word as she stepped in, she felt a tiny bit easier and sighed in relief that they were not in the main manor house. The house was lovely, but not anywhere near as fancy as she'd made up in her head. Logan put his keys on a dresser in the entrance and swept his arm around the hallway.

'Welcome to the cottage. The place where I hang out when I'm in Lovely.' He chuckled. 'It's not quite as fancy as the main house.'

As Cally smiled and looked around, she noted that the place might appear at first to be a cottage, but it was still much larger than anywhere she'd ever lived. As she peered into a sitting room, she nodded. Admittedly, it was smaller and cosier than the manor, but it still screeched old money loud and clear. It was decorated in a similar style to the new wing: thick, heavy curtains, traditional furniture mixed in with modern pieces, huge, expensive-looking art, beautiful old rugs, and lovely lamps. Cally looked around, making mental notes for her flat, and laughed to herself. The flat over the shop was a long way from this so-called cottage. Old money aesthetic subtlety screamed. She loved it. No flashy designer candles anywhere in sight. The only thing doing any flashing was the monstrous manor tucked in the distance. It beat a designer candle hands down.

Once in the kitchen, a smell of comfy, normal, country cooking hit her nostrils and Cally felt her shoulders drop. There wasn't a lobster in sight. The kitchen was cosy and fairly unassuming in that old-money sort of way that made you think the place and the things in it had been there for years. She took her cardigan off and handed it to Logan. 'Mmm. Smells good. What's cooking?'

'Chicken risotto. I hope you like garlic. I thought risotto would be a safe bet. Oh, I didn't ask if you were vegetarian or had any food allergies. What an idiot. Yikes.'

Cally rolled her eyes. She didn't have the time, inclination or money for allergies. 'Nope, no food allergies. That would be a big no.'

'Oh, okay. Excellent. Do you like chicken?'

'I love chicken. It's one of my favourites.'

'Good,' Logan said as he settled her in. She felt herself relax further as she realised that Logan seemed to be completely unaware that she was feeling out of sorts. He opened the fridge and pulled out a glass bottle with a ceramic lid on the top. Inside was a pre-prepared drink. He placed it on the table and chuckled. 'So, Blackcurrant. I have done a little bit of investigation work, and I present you with a mixed blackcurrant cocktail. Have you had one before?'

Cally giggled. 'Are you kidding me?'

'I am certainly not kidding you, no. I didn't think I would find anything, but apparently, you're not the only person who likes blackcurrant. There are tribes of such people lurking in chat forums all over the place. Every day is a school day.'

Cally nodded. 'Yes, you're not telling me anything I don't know, to be honest.' She joked, 'I used to like to think I was special, but I'm not. There are a lot of people out there partial to blackcurrant. It's not just me.'

Logan shook the bottle. 'Would you like to try it? Will you be partaking?' Logan winked.

'I would. As long as it's not too strong.'

'Well, I can't vouch for that. I just followed the instructions.

However, I have had a taste, and it's delicious. It may knock your socks off a bit, though.'

'I bet. Blackcurrant cordial is not short of sugar which makes everything taste better.'

Logan took two chilled cocktail glasses out of the fridge, placed them on the kitchen table, and poured the drink from the bottle. He then added a couple of edible flowers on the top with a silly flourish. Cally swooned. He slid one of the glasses towards her. 'There you go. Have a taste.'

'Ooh, fancy,' Cally said as she took a sip. 'Yum, lovely. What's in this? This is really nice.'

'Vodka, blackcurrant, and a few other secrets I slung in for good measure. You'll have to pay me to find out.'

Cally took another sip. 'Works for me. It's delicious. Thank you.'

'Well, I can't take all the credit. The internet is a wonderful thing when it comes to finding obscure cocktail recipes. Who even knew?'

Cally laughed. 'Still, I'm impressed. Very much so.'

'You're worth the effort. Thanks for coming.'

Well played Henry-Hicks.

If anyone else had said that, Cally would have stuck two fingers down the back of her throat. Logan somehow seemed to pull things off without sounding cheesy. Or maybe it was because she was in deep already. Either way, she liked it. 'Aww. This is really sweet of you. Beats a night of Netflix and takeaway any day of the week.'

Logan chuckled and stood up to check on the progress of the dinner. 'Yeah, however, I have to admit, I do enjoy a good Netflix binge every now and then.'

It went through Cally's mind that she was currently in her own personal episode of a Netflix show. 'Mmm. Good point. Me too.'

She smiled inside as all her nerves from before slipped away via a combination of the cocktail and the easy company. Logan just chatted away and pottered around the kitchen as if he'd known her forever. She found herself not worrying and, even better, not feeling any pressure to *be* anything. It was a far cry from the stilted, awkward first dates she'd had in the past, in particular, the night at the cinema with the boy racer in the blue car.

'So, you said about the flat above the deli and how you ended up there.' Logan asked.

Cally heard herself telling Logan all about lots of things she normally didn't share with anyone. Not only that, she realised as they tucked into the risotto and she downed too many blackcurrant cocktails that she was having a surprisingly nice time. It all felt delicious and not just the food. The lack of lobsters and men in tails did her well.

Logan refilled her glass and smiled. 'Umm, yep, so last night.'

Cally held her breath for a second. The kisses. Oh my, how fab they'd been. Henry-Hicks was good. She considered pretending she didn't know what he meant. Never good to appear too keen. 'Yep.'

Logan's voice changed. 'I err, I wanted to follow up on....' He coughed. 'Well, you know, the thing that happened. It just, well, came out of nowhere.'

It hadn't been from nowhere as far as Cally was concerned. She may have fantasised about it more than a few times. In her fantasy, it had moved from the kisses to, well, lots of nice things. She narrowed her eyes. Where was he going with this?

'Right.'

Logan hesitated. 'I, err, well, I hope it wasn't. I didn't...'

Cally interrupted. 'You didn't. It was good. More than good. Thanks.' She cringed at saying thanks for being kissed.

'Sorry, just wanted to get that clear right from the beginning.'

'Yes, no, right, yes.' Cally gulped, unsure what to actually say.

As far as she was concerned, she wanted to repeat the kisses. Kissing all night long and in a bed would suit her quite nicely. She'd settle for jumping on him right there in the kitchen. The table would work. She'd kiss any part of him. Even his feet. Rather than let her thoughts spiral, she attempted to remain demure and in control on the outside. On the inside, she was running around the kitchen like a headless chicken. 'Yes, good, to, err, see that we're both on the same page as it were.'

'Yes, excellent.' Logan took the plates from the table. 'Well, that was nice.'

'Yes, lovely.'

'There's tiramisu, too. Do you like tiramisu?'

'I do, I love it.' Cally patted her stomach. 'I may need a bit of a break. I'm stuffed.'

'Yeah. How about a stroll? It's a beautiful evening. We could work off the risotto.'

'Love to.'

'We'll walk out the back there and go around to the stream and then if we stand on the hill, we'll be able to see all of Lovely Bay down below. The lighthouse looks amazing from there.'

Cally nodded. Standing with Logan looking at the sights of Lovely sounded right up her alley. 'Nice. I'd like that.'

'We might be able to work out which building is your flat.'

After popping to the loo, Logan took a blue wax Lovely coat from the back of the boot room door and held it up in front of Cally. 'Will you need one of these?'

Cally laughed. 'Ooh, I'm honoured. One of the famous Lovely coats.'

'Ha. We're overrun with them up here. My mum is constantly on the waiting list, I believe. She likes to have more than one on the go.'

'I'll need it, I think. The temperature has dipped out there, I reckon.'

Cally shrugged on the coat and followed Logan out of the

cottage. He was correct that the evening was gorgeous. As she strolled along beside him, she felt a jumble of emotions. A little bit excited at what might happen, a little bit nervous, a little bit apprehensive that she was playing with fire, but not quite as in over her head as she'd assumed. It felt good to just roll with it and not worry. The notes had not been utilised and Prime Ministers or lack thereof and the state of the world had not been mentioned.

As they got further away from the house and headed in the direction of Lovely, nature took over. The manicured lawns of the manor were replaced with a stream, a wooded area stood to the side of them, and there was a little copse of trees on the top of a hill. The air felt cool and fresh and nice and the stars were bright. Cally felt as if she wanted the evening to go on forever. There was something about all of it that felt enchanting, but mostly, it was the company that she adored.

Logan pointed at the hill. 'It might be a bit slippery. Watch your step.'

Cally looked up and then to her right where the lights of Lovely twinkled endlessly away into the distance. As they made their way up the hill, it got quieter and quieter and more still. Cally was puffing a bit when they got to the top and was glad to see an old bench under a little group of trees. She turned around and widened her eyes in surprise at the view; the sea shimmered in the distance, lights from houses glowed, the lighthouse glinted, and above it all, a blanket of black was dotted with stars. Cally sat down and shook her head. 'Goodness. You wouldn't even know this was here, would you? People would pay for this view.'

'I know, right? It's so much better than all that.' Logan waved his hand around at the manor gardens. 'All that stuff. I know it's nice, but this is amazing. Mum used to bring me up here when I was little. I loved it from the word go. Sort of calm somehow.'

Cally followed his gaze. 'It really is beautiful.'

'It's like it grounds you when you sit up here for a bit.'

Cally inhaled. 'And the smell.'

'I know.'

'Mmm, nice,' Cally replied, looking in the direction of the lighthouse. 'I didn't realise you'd be able to see the lighthouse as clearly.'

Logan chuckled. 'I guess that's what it was made for.'

'Yeah, ha. Good point.'

For a good few minutes, they just sat in silence. Cally felt as if all her problems had gone away for a bit. As if there was a small tube on the crown of her head and all the mush in her brain that had been in there for a very long time started to slowly find its way out through the top. She let out a long sigh. 'I need to take in the delights of Lovely more often now that I live here.'

'I know. It makes you realise how nice it is around here, doesn't it? Plus, it's free, which is always good in my book.'

'Yeah, there's that.'

Logan pointed. 'So the flat must be there somewhere if that's the lighthouse.'

'I need to put a beacon on the roof or something so that I can make out which one it is.'

'Yes, do that for next time you come.'

Cally swallowed. *There was going to be a next time. Hooray.* She wanted there to be many next times. Pom poms punched in her head. She pointed towards a row of lights. 'That must be Lovely Bay station.'

Logan agreed and also pointed. 'Yes, and that way is the RNLI station and then just over there is St Lovely green, if I'm not mistaken.'

'Hmm. Quite tricky to make it out in the dark.'

The conversation stopped again for a bit. Cally inhaled not just the Lovely air but the Logan smell. Something unfathomable, full, easy, happy, no stress, manor houses, really, just old-school rich. She felt as if there was an odd sort of silent buzzing around them, as if the air was electrically charged. She so wanted to repeat the happenings of the night before. As if he read her thoughts, Logan put his arm around her, inched closer along the bench, put his other hand on her leg, and kissed her. Cally kissed him back. She put her hand on his chest and felt herself get lost. It was that good that she almost felt as if she was looking down on herself from above. What in the world?

She was above the sky watching it fall down around her. Here she was, sitting on a bench on the top of a hill, kissing a man for the second night in a row. She moved closer. Bring more of it on and quickly. Do it hard. Do not ever let it stop.

25

The next morning arrived in a blur as Cally woke up in a pool of fallen slices of the sky. She felt giddy in her stomach and had a happy buzz in her head. As she came to, her mind turned over the date with Logan and what had occurred on the bench. Just so nice. A beam spread across her face as she stared up at the ceiling and recalled the evening.

The entire date had been much better than she'd hoped, from the cosy cottage on the manor grounds to the homemade dinner to the blackcurrant cocktails and evening stroll. All of it had worked for her for sure, but to be quite honest, none of that stuff had been the clincher. It had been the electric moment when Logan had kissed her that had sealed the deal.

What had happened when they'd walked up the hill and gazed down at the lights of Lovely kept playing over and over in her mind. Her heart raced as she remembered Logan pulling her close and she tried to fully relive the feeling on the bench. Not a chance, though. It was as if that moment was suspended in time. A little spot of magic lost somewhere that she couldn't quite recapture. All she knew was that she wanted it to happen again and soon. Very, very soon.

She rolled over onto her side, hugged her pillow to her chest and stared out the window as she replayed every detail of the date in her mind. In the cold light of day, she wondered if she'd been imagining the way Logan had looked at her, but unless she was very much barking up the wrong tree, there had been something there. She'd seen it on his face. On top of that the easy flow of their conversation, the nice food, the comfiness of being with him in the kitchen. The feeling of his arm around her as they'd sat on the bench, the stars twinkling overhead. Then not just the sky falling but the whole world dropping away until it had felt as if they were the only two people in the world. Just the two of them kissing on the top of a hill. Fabulous.

As she stared out over the rooftops of Lovely, she basked in the afterglow of it all. Something about her felt different, looser somehow, and a bit on the special side. As if she'd been gilded by being treated nicely. Dipped in a bath of pure shimmering gold. Along with the gilding was a flutter of excitement in her chest at the thought of what might come next. Would there be a next? When would it be? What would happen?

She wondered whether they'd see each other again. It had seemed as if Logan had been just as eager to continue what had started on the bench as she was. Who really knew, though? Would he be waking up without the giddy feeling and the sky very much intact above his head?

As Cally pondered it all, she reached over to her bedside table for her phone with a thrill of anticipation that there would be a text from Logan. The thrill didn't last long when she saw a blank screen without any notifications. After swiping up, she scrolled through her messages on various platforms. Nothing on WhatsApp, no text messages and Facebook Messenger was a no-go. Her heart sank deep down to her boots. Zilch. Not even a sniff of any communication in any shape or form. No messages from Logan, no missed calls or voicemails. Nothing whatsoever from him at all.

Cally frowned. How very disappointing. Pursing her lips, she nodded, confirming to herself that it was absolutely fine—not too much of a drama. He was probably not up yet, perhaps busy, or maybe he was playing it cool, not wanting to seem too eager or desperate. She knew one thing; she was absolutely eager and ridiculously desperate.

Disappointed, she put her phone back down and sighed. Why could there not have been a little text sitting there waiting for her to open it? She'd so wanted that. She would have relished it and replied while feeling a bit buzzy and excited. Instead, she had that horrible sinking feeling of disappointment rearing its ugly head.

With an irritated sigh, she dragged herself out of bed. Stuff that for a game of soldiers. She abhorred the whole waiting game thing. In a funny kind of way, she'd had enough of waiting when her grandma had gone into the home. It had been a tough, bittersweet time where every day had been a long round of waiting to see what was going to happen next. She was over any waiting in her life.

After concocting all manner of reasons as to why Logan hadn't yet been in touch, she made a cup of tea, took it out to the balcony and attempted to regroup. She had the day off from the chemist and had loosely planned on going for a walk to the marshes by way of the riverboat. Deciding that she wasn't prepared to waste the day standing around waiting for Logan to text, she finished her tea, got ready quickly, and after assessing the weather, sprayed on some sunscreen and decided to leave her cardigan at home.

By the time she'd stepped down the steep stairs and was on her way down the High Street going past the chocolate shop, the sun was already warm, the air heavy with the scent of warmth in a seaside town. The Lovely bunting overhead fluttered back and forth in the wind and the light reflected off the lighthouse.

Deciding not to even think about Logan, she hummed under her breath as she ambled along in the direction of the River Lovely. Despite the disappointment of the no-text situation, she felt strangely lighter in a way that she couldn't quite explain. It was as if she felt buoyed by the date and no longer had to worry quite as much as she always had.

As she approached the riverboat jetty, she spotted Colin standing by the boat, by the little ticket hut, fiddling with a coil of rope. Walking down the jetty, she called out as she quickened her pace, 'Morning! Nice day!'

Colin turned and smiled as he spotted her. 'Well, if it isn't my favourite passenger! Hey, our Cally. How are you?'

Cally laughed. 'Really good, thanks. It's such a beautiful day for a boat ride.'

Colin looked up at the clear blue sky. 'That it is. Hop on. I'm just waiting for our Nancy's lot. A train just came in a few minutes late. She's just WhatsApped me to hang on for a tic.'

Cally made her way to the front of the boat and claimed a seat by the railing at the front so that she'd be able to watch the river unfold before her. As she sat gazing at the little sparkles jumping about on the top of the water and the boat waited for the passengers coming from the train to board, she found her thoughts drifting back to Logan and to the magic of the previous night. Whipping her phone out, her heart leapt into her throat as she saw a new notification on the screen, but it dropped as quickly as it had risen. She felt wrong to be disappointed that it was just a message from Eloise, checking in to see how the date had gone. Cally sighed, trying to ignore the pang of disappointment that shot through her. She quickly typed out a reply and as she hit send and slipped her phone back into her pocket, she felt a hand on her shoulder. She turned to see Birdie and heard the Shipping Forecast quietly playing from Birdie's bag.

'Hello, hello, how are you?'

Cally blinked and flicked the voice switch. 'Morning. Fine, thanks.'

'Good, you sure about that? You were miles away.'

'Just lost in thought, I suppose.'

'Ah, I see. Thoughts of a special someone, perhaps?' Birdie cackled.

Cally felt her cheeks flush. 'Something like that.'

'It's written all over your face. I know that look!'

Cally played it down. 'Don't know what you're talking about.'

'Course you don't.'

'Where are you off to?'

'I was going to say the same thing.'

'I'm popping over to Nina's to see her about a job.'

'Oh, right. I'm going for a walk to the marshes.'

'Nice. That'll clear your head. Say hello to the otters for me.'

Cally nodded. She wasn't sure that she needed to clear her head and, at that particular moment in time, wasn't bothered about otters. Rather it was nice for her head to be full and fuddled with the scene from the bench. It was even better to bask in the afterglow of what had happened the night before. And to wait for a text.

26

It was a few days later. Cally woke up with a start and went to rush out of bed thinking that she'd heard an alarm from her grandma's bed. Then she remembered where she was and what had happened. There was no longer an alarm or bed to worry about. Not only was her grandma no longer in the land of the living, but she, Cally de Pfeffer, was residing in a totally new place. She sighed and turned over. Though she missed her grandma terribly, she had to admit that she did not miss the nights, the alarms, or the worry one iota. Or the days, for that matter. She had many conflicting feelings about how the previous few years of her grandma's life had turned out. A lot of her emotions were a jumble but one thing she knew without a doubt was that she did not miss the constant battle between the love she'd had for her grandma and the frustration that being her carer had brought to the table. It had been full of ups and downs. She'd been through the same before her mum had died, too. To be frank, she wouldn't wish it on her worst enemy. Not that she had any enemies because she hadn't had time for any.

Cally's caring role had been an all-consuming obligation and labour of love, all mixed into one. It had taken up *most* of her time and *all* of her brain space and had left little time for Cally. It had frequently meant long months with little help and often no reprieve in the constant daily, unrelenting tasks. Cally let herself think about it for a bit as she laid staring up at the ceiling. So many emotions whirled around her head, prompted by being woken by the notion that her grandma's bed alarm was going off.

She thought back to the previous few years. Now she was through them, she could clearly see how everything had affected her *all* the time. When she'd been in the thick of it, though, she'd had little choice but to put up and shut up. It was just how it had been. When she'd been caring, it had felt as if she'd been in a gigantic rotating tunnel that never let up. A tunnel with no end. She remembered desperately wanting to see light at the end of the tunnel. The light was ultimately her grandma passing away, and wanting to get to that had been accompanied by raging guilt. All of it a horrible mess of tangled emotions that had always been the accompaniment to her life. Now she was no longer in the rotating tunnel, and the jumbled emotions were gone.

Even after the end, though, Cally still felt guilty. Guilty, mostly that she was no longer constantly worried. Worried about whether she was doing the right thing, worried about what was going to happen, worried that she wasn't doing enough. As well as that, there was the frustration, the constant anxiety, and to top it all the exhausting tiredness. Cally remembered how her grandma and her mum before her had relied on her for absolutely everything. It was a relief that it wasn't like that any longer. In the flat, no one relied on her at all; it was just not part of the equation. It was simply no longer a reality of her day-to-day life. Strangely liberating. Like she was free. Guilty, but free. She'd stopped having to hold up the sky. It felt so nice.

As she got out of bed, she remembered how, before the flat, she'd had to try and balance and juggle every single little thing in her life. Working on a weekly rotating roster at the chemist and the online chat job and looking after her grandma. Then there had been the physical labour involved with having someone dependent on you. The feeling was as if, for her whole life, Cally had always been on call.

Popping on her dressing gown, putting her feet into her slippers and pulling her hair back with a hairband, she pottered around, making a cup of tea and thought about the flat and, in turn, Birdie and her kindness. It had become evident to Cally with hindsight that Birdie had supported Cally left, right and centre all along and not just with the flat. Birdie had done little things here and there, giving her bonuses if and when, slipping in extra shifts, letting Cally work more or less whenever it suited her. Birdie was worth her weight in gold.

Now Cally was in Lovely Bay she felt as if a burden had lifted off her shoulders. In the flat, she felt free. Lovely Bay was giving her so many things she hadn't seen coming. It was as if she was waking up, slowly unfurling and blossoming. Her health had improved by leaps and bounds. She looked better, felt better, and there was finally light at the end of the rotating tunnel she'd been trapped in for so long.

She stood by the window with her tea while she waited for a couple of crumpets to toast. The curtain moved back and forth from the breeze coming in off the sea and a blue sky with a few white clouds here and there was more than welcome. About twenty minutes later, she'd made another mug of tea and toasted two more crumpets and was sitting on the balcony looking over in the direction of the lighthouse. She could just make out people hustling by on their way to work and a couple of runners, who were stopped by the bottom of the lighthouse, used it to do their stretches.

Taking out her phone, she re-checked her rota for the chat portal and re-read a message from Nina regarding what days she was required to help with A Lovely Organised Life. She scanned her messages and felt down in the dumps that there was still nothing from Logan. So much for the kisses and the sitting on the top of the hill. She'd typed out messages to him more times than she'd ever admit and had promptly deleted them. She absolutely didn't want to be the one who texted first. Even though he'd made the move to invite her to dinner, she was adamant that she wasn't going to follow-up. She so wanted to be chased. A bit pathetic, really. She tried to analyse why and came to the conclusion that it was somehow something to do with the caring. After looking out for other people's needs for so long, living on pennies, having to always have her balls in the air, she was not prepared at all to chase, organise or rally around in any way for anyone ever, ever, ever in her life. If Logan Henry-Hicks wanted in on Cally's world, he very much knew where to find her.

She nodded to herself as she got showered and dressed. Logan would have to be the one to text and chase but there had been radio silence from him. She wouldn't think about it. She had more important things to think about than whether or not a posh man from a manor house was going to ask her out on another date. At least that's what she tried to tell herself.

Half an hour later, in her usual uniform of white shirt, jumper, short skirt, tights and ballet flats, she walked down the back lane heading in the direction of the River Lovely. She'd decided on a walk to clear her head via a huge loop which would take her past the lighthouse for a stroll by the river, end up at the top of the High Street where she was going to pop into the charity shop and have a rummage.

It was a gorgeous day in Lovely and the temperature was warming up. Loads of Lovelies were out and about enjoying the upturn in the weather as the sun made itself known. The river glinted and there was a smell of good things in the air. Just as Cally made her way across St Lovely green, she bumped into Nancy.

'Hello, hello, hello. How are you?' Nancy asked with a smile.

'Well, thanks. You?'

Nancy raised her eyebrows and turned her head to the side. 'I heard you're very well. More than well.'

'I am, yup.'

'How was it after the pub the other day?'

Cally frowned. 'How do you mean?'

'Did you have a little visitor to the flat?'

Cally giggled. 'Ha, how do you know about that?'

'I make it my mission to know things in Lovely.' Nancy winked. 'Plus, if you choose to live over the deli, Lovelies will be over it. You can't move without people knowing your whereabouts. Get used to it. It's part of living here. Plus, you've probably clocked that Birdie knows *everything*.'

'Ahh, I should have realised that. Good point.'

'And you actually work with our Birdie, so *nothing* you do is sacred,' Nancy noted with a laugh.

'I'm learning that.'

'So, how was Logan? A dickie bird may have told me you went out?'

Cally felt a blush creep up her cheeks. 'Umm, yes, we did.'

'And?'

Cally felt embarrassed and not really happy to share too much. 'Nice.'

Nancy's eyes widened. 'Nice! Is that all you've got for me? Come on, spill the beans! I want all the ins and outs. Dish the dirt. Spill the tea.'

Cally laughed. The dinner and what had happened after it had been more than okay. The lack of communication since was not. She didn't want to delve into it too much. Nancy was being sweet and interested, though, or just full-on nosy. 'What can I say? Very, very nice. Better than I thought it was going to be.'

'I knew it!' Nancy clapped her hands together. 'I could tell by the spring in your step and the glow in your cheeks. So, what happened? Where did he take you?'

'We didn't go anywhere as such. He cooked dinner for me at one of the cottages on the manor grounds.'

Nancy's eyebrows shot up. 'You went up there. Love it.'

'Yes, it was good.'

'And he cooked. Sounds like a keeper to me!'

Cally giggled. 'It was sweet, actually. He really went out of his way to make the night, well, as I said, nice.'

'I'll bet he did.' Nancy nudged Cally with her elbow. 'And after dinner? What happened then?'

The walk up the hill, the stars, the breathtaking view of Lovely Bay, and the magical bit at the end flashed through Cally's mind. There was no way she was telling Nancy about the end bit. She'd rather keep that little delicious morsel all to herself. 'We went for a walk up to the top of this hill overlooking Lovely. It was gorgeous up there. The lights, the stars, the sound of the sea in the distance. Yep, really good.'

Nancy sighed. 'I know exactly where you mean. That's a great spot. I love the views from there.'

'I didn't know it was there, not being from here and all that.'

Nancy shook her head. 'Ahh, no, I suppose you wouldn't. It's a known spot, even though it's part of the manor. At least officially, it is, but Lovelies go up there to the bench.'

'Yes, so it all went well.' *Shame that seems as if it's the end of it, though,* Cally added in her head. *It's a pity I've been ghosted.*

'Great to hear. I thought it might all kick off after what happened at the chowder night.'

Cally frowned. 'What do you mean?'

'There were sparks there. The whole of Lovely could see you two eyeing each other up across the tables.'

Cally cringed that it had been that obvious. She tried to play it down. 'No way. Really?'

'Pah! Don't even think about denying it. It was written all over both your faces.'

Cally chuckled. 'Don't know what you're talking about.'

'Anyway, whether or not you're going to admit it, I loved it. I'm living vicariously through you for a fix of romance and excitement. Let me tell you there's none of it happening in my actual life at the moment. My dating life is sorely non-existent. I'll have to fill you in on it one day.'

'It's been a while for me, too.' Cally agreed.

'So what's next?'

Cally laughed and then winced as she remembered that she'd heard nothing from Logan. 'Not sure anything else is going to happen…'

'No?'

She decided to come clean with Nancy. In for a penny. 'I haven't heard from him, actually.'

Nancy stepped back and gave Cally a once-over. 'Oh, right.'

'Yeah, disappointing.'

'Let's talk strategy.'

Cally shook her head. 'No, no. We didn't make any concrete plans, anyway. It was just sort of left hanging and, hmm, I'm hoping he'll call. Or text. Or something. But, whatever, it is what it is.'

Nancy tsked. 'He'd better get his finger out before someone else comes along and snaps you up.'

Cally shook her head. 'Yeah, they're not quite lining up at the door. Fat chance of that.'

'Not yet. Just you wait and see. Now things have changed for you. After what happened with your grandma, everything will open up. It's the way the universe works. You're more open to things now and you've moved and everything. Lovely will work its magic on you, too. It always does.'

'I hope so. Something or someone needs to.' Cally joked.

'Anyway, changing the subject; how's the flat?'

'Good. I'm about to get stuck in with the painting. I just need to get some more rollers and stuff. I'm using the leftovers from the deli, but I realised that some of the rollers have seen better days.'

Nancy jerked her thumb. 'Pop over to mine. I've got loads of spare ones still in the packet from when I did a refresh last year. I went a bit over the top and didn't end up needing anywhere near as many as I thought I would. So, yeah, I have loads. I wouldn't mind getting shot of them, actually. I was thinking about putting them on Marketplace but just haven't got around to it.'

'Oh, right, yes. If you're sure that would be great. It would save me a trip to B&Q and mean I can get on with it pronto.'

Nancy looked at her watch. 'I've got a shift later, but if you want to head over now you can take whatever you want.'

'Great, suits me, thanks. I was only going to the charity shop for a walk.'

As they strolled in the direction of Nancy's cottage, they chatted about all sorts but mostly about how Cally was getting on living in Lovely and the flat. Cally took her surroundings in as they proceeded over a second of Lovely's greens and made their way across a third. As they went under a vast, tall conker tree Nancy pointed to a row of cottages running along the back of the green. Cally had to stop herself from feeling *super* jealous. The cottages looked as if they'd stepped out of a brochure on British country style. A long row of exposed brick houses, each one with window boxes, hanging baskets, and timber front doors. They crossed the road and got to a cottage with a narrow cobbled front garden, a white picket fence butted up to the pavement, a name plaque sat to the right of the door and a bench under the front window. Nancy pushed open the gate and then stood on the front doormat. Small black coach lights sat on either side of the front door. A wicker love heart hung from a window and an old-fashioned doorbell with a little rope swung in the breeze.

Cally heard herself gushing as she peered up at the cottage. 'Oh wow, this is really nice. I love it. Jealous! What I wouldn't give...'

Nancy smiled. 'Thank you. It's nice and quiet over this way.'

Cally nodded. 'Yes, it seems it.' She turned back and looked in the direction of the lighthouse and the bay. 'So nice. I love the view from this perspective. Really different.'

'Yeah, you see it in another light from this side.' Nancy pointed to the bench under the window and looked at her watch. 'Time for a cup of tea before I have to get going? It'll have to be a quick one.'

'Wouldn't say no.'

'Okie dokie. I'll put the kettle on.' Nancy pushed the door open. 'Come on in.'

Cally took her ballet flats off, left them on the mat on the doorstep and stepped into a cosy but tiny hallway with a stripped and whitewashed timber floor with a small Paisley rug in the middle. Nancy hung her blue Lovely coat on a white dresser with brass hooks, put her keys into a huge white clamshell and hung her bag on the bannister. A set of stairs with brass rods and seagrass runner went up the left-hand side. As they took the few steps across the hallway, Nancy led Cally past an understairs cupboard with a tiny door and she peeked her head around to a sitting room as they went past to see the same lovely floor, another beautiful rug, and a brick fireplace. She followed Nancy to a galley kitchen with Shaker cabinetry, scalloped tiling and a little table with a vase of flowers in the centre.

Cally gushed. 'I wasn't expecting this! It's right up my street. I love it.'

'I did everything myself. I can't afford decorators or painters, which is why I am in possession of a multiple number of rollers and brushes. In fact, I have gobs of leftover paint, too, should you require it.'

'Great. Thanks for the offer.'

Nancy filled the kettle with water, made a cup of tea and then they went back through the tiny cottage to the front, where they sat on the bench and watched the world go by.

'So, what are your plans for the flat? Just painting to give it a freshen up, is it? Birdie was saying you've done a great job of clearing it out. It was on her list of things to do for a long time.'

'She's the one doing the favours,' Cally replied. 'I really was up the creek without a paddle until she helped me out. I'm so grateful.'

'She does that. Always helping people is our Birdie.'

Cally nodded. 'I've now worked that out.'

'Yep, and the best thing is that she quietly helps people, you know? Not like these sanctimonious idiots you see all over the papers with their tours to African countries or wherever. No cavorting around in fancy cars and designer clothes shaking less-fortunate people's hands with a pious look on their faces. Not our Birdie. She helps *real* people who need *real* help.'

'Yes! That's it. That is so it. She's been great to me. I really am fortunate.'

'Yup. I think she'll be pleased to see someone making the flat good, though. So I guess it's a win-win for Birdie. What are you going to do with it?'

Cally wrinkled her nose. 'Just clearing it out has made a huge difference. The paint job is next. I think that is going to be a game changer. It's lovely up there. Have you been up?'

Nancy raised her eyebrows. 'Gosh, years and years ago now. I mean like when I was a youngster. I can't think why I would have been up there. Must have been something to do with the Lings or the Hongs, I guess. It was full of clutter then, so I can imagine what it was like for you.'

'Yup. It took me a good while to get it sorted. I went up and down those stairs a trillion times. At least it felt like it, anyway. Not that I'm complaining.'

'I know, Birdie said. How long do you reckon it will take you to paint it?'

'Not sure, but not very long. It's not as if it's a big area. I reckon I'll crack on with it quickly.'

'Yeah, it won't take long.' Nancy drained her tea and looked at her watch. 'Right, speaking of cracking on, I need to get a wriggle on and get to work. Follow me out to the shed and see what you want.'

Cally pushed herself up from the bench and followed Nancy back through the house. She sort of hugged herself as she realised she was again a recipient of the Lovely community kindness. It felt good to be on the end of something nice. Great to have some help and no longer having to do everything for everyone else. So what if Henry-Hicks hadn't yet messaged? She wasn't going to get too bothered about it. In fact, Logan could take a running jump. Who exactly did he think he was?

27

Walking back across the three Lovely greens with a huge bag over each shoulder and her arms full with various DIY equipment courtesy of Nancy, Cally was feeling full of the joys. Struggling a bit, she pulled her phone out of her pocket just in case there might have been a message from a certain someone while she'd been at Nancy's cottage. There wasn't. Zilch. Stuff that for a game of soldiers. She squidged her lips up and shook her head. So, that was the end of that then. Henry-Hicks had obviously decided the dinner hadn't been that good and would leave it at that. Whatever. Cally could deal with it. Couldn't she? She'd been on her own for quite a while anyway. She didn't need the Logans of the world to take care of her, that she already knew without having anyone reiterate it for her. She would be fine. She could hold the sky up very well on her own.

She held her chin up and nodded. If he didn't want to see her again, it was his loss. Big mistake on his part. Huge. Maybe she was massively disappointed underneath but she'd be damned if she was going to let it show. No. Logan Hickory Dickory or whatever he liked to call himself could trot on. She mentally slapped herself for even giving him the time of day. She wasn't going to let him take up residence in any of her brain space. Bothered? Nup. Ahh, actually, maybe a teeny, incy-wincy, tiny bit.

Bumbling along through Lovely instead of going up the main road, she made her way to the service lane behind the shops, let herself into the back of the deli, and made two trips to get the supplies up the steep stairs. After taking out the bits and bobs Nancy had given her and collecting the tins of paint from the shed, she stood in the middle of the sitting room wondering where to start first. Painting and DIY were hardly her skills. She pressed her lips together and shook her head. How hard could painting a wall be? It had to be easier than learning the ins and outs of a bed hoist.

She read the back of a tin of white paint a few times over, examined the walls, watched a little bug crawl horizontally from left to right across the coving and decided that she would start with the sitting room wall behind the sofa, do that and that alone and go from there. Pulling her phone out of her pocket she worked out her shifts in the chemist, her scheduled work with Nina and her customer service work and ascertained that taking all that into consideration she'd have to pace herself on the painting otherwise she'd end up in a right old mess. Walking around and assessing, she made a loose plan in her head and decided to pop down to the deli for a coffee to have a look at the paint on the walls down there, before she got on with the job in hand.

Walking down the stairs she went out the back, down the alley and back in through the front door so that she could look at the paint colours in situ. If she could get the flat looking half as good as the deli, she'd be doing well. She peered around and observed how it all worked together somehow; a vast collection of glass jars holding herbs and spices, a cork noticeboard full of Lovely flyers, one wall full of vintage advertisements in frames together with old pictures of Lovely Bay, a row of antique lights over the counter, glass display cases shone and shelves held bag upon bag of coffee beans. The neutral paint colours just sat in the background showing it all off. She looked more closely at the wall full of photos. There were faded black-and-white images of Lovely's early days, with horse-drawn carriages and ladies in long, flowing dresses strolling along the cobblestone streets. Colourful Art Deco posters advertising the grand opening of the local picture palace, and sepia-toned portraits of fishermen and their families, their faces etched with the Lovely weather. Cally wrinkled her nose and tried to work out how to do the same sort of look in the flat. The deli was inadvertently soft and welcoming and a bit of a jumble all at the same time. An organised chaos of clutter and bits and bobs that all slotted together. She wanted to bottle the look and feel and translate it two floors up.

She'd loved the deli from the first moment she'd stepped into it one day in her lunch hour on one of her first shifts at the chemist. It was always busy with a welcoming atmosphere, an eclectic mix of delicacies and what somehow always seemed to feel like loads of hidden treasure or maybe she was just imagining that part. She inhaled the aroma of fresh coffee and stopped to look on the noticeboard at a haphazard collage of flyers and business cards from the Lovely Bay community. There were advertisements for all sorts; a running club by the river, art workshops in the lighthouse hall, notices about upcoming festivals, and a farmer's market. She read a message about a lost cat and the fact that drinks at the lighthouse would be missing a week. As she scanned down, she recognised a few of the names here and there and felt almost as if she belonged.

On the way to finding a table, she peered into the display counter and felt her mouth water at a little tray of pastel macarons all lined up in a nice little row. Next to it, a platter was piled high with freshly baked biscuits and next to that, a cake stand with a marble cake displaying its insides looked ready to accompany a nice cup of tea.

She smiled at one of the pensioners she knew from the chemist and went to stand by the ordering counter just as Birdie came through from the back. Cally frowned. 'Oh, hi, I thought you were having the day off.'

Birdie flicked her eyes upwards. 'I was.'

'But?'

'That changed. I can't keep away.' Birdie chuckled.

'Right.'

Birdie narrowed her eyes. 'Anyway, what are you doing coming in this way?'

'I don't really know. I just took all those paint tins upstairs and thought I would come in the front way and have a look at the paint colours in this light. See how you did it down here. Thought I'd get a nice coffee, too, before I get going. I'm going to do the painting in stages, one wall at a time.'

'Ahh, I see. What, you just lugged all that lot up the stairs from the shed?'

'Yeah. Nancy gave me some of her leftovers too, so now I'm raring to go.'

Birdie nodded. 'She said she had some when she came in for her prescription earlier.'

Cally shook her head. 'Everyone has been so kind to me since my grandma and everything.'

'Ahh, well, now you live here we *have* to be nice to you. That's the way it works.' Birdie joked, 'It's not because you're special or anything. It's just the Lovely way things happen.'

'What else do I get now I'm an apprentice Lovely?' Cally also joked with her head turned to the side and her eyes narrowed. 'Any other benefits?'

'I think that's your lot.'

'Ha.'

'So, coffee you said?

'Yes, please.'

'I'll get Alice to bring you one over.'

Cally smiled as she went to sit down. It was nice being known and feeling as if she belonged and was wanted. Shame Henry-Hicks hadn't felt the same way about wanting her. What did she care though? She tried to pretend she didn't give a hoot. In actual fact, she cared a lot and felt *monumentally* let down. Even in Lovely, disappointment did not taste nice.

28

It was the next day and despite having checked her calls, WhatsApps, text messages and even Facebook Messenger notifications every five minutes, Cally had *still* not heard from Logan. She'd spent an unhealthy amount of time considering ways he may have contacted her and, in turn, figuring out how she may have missed them. She'd even checked through her emails, just in case. Did people email after dates? Her inbox told her that in this case, they most certainly did not.

She'd been a mix of embarrassed and desperate when she'd found herself clicking on the spam button and not only looking for signs of any recent communication from him but also scanning the list of bizarre emails to see if there was anything that might have slipped down the list. Half, or most of her, was glad that he hadn't joined the desperation of her spam box. There were many versions of scams; a prince in Nigeria wanted her to be his princess – she rolled her eyes, turned her mouth upside down in contemplation and considered. Worth a go? Nah, not *that* desperate. A fictional supermarket congratulated her that she'd won a thirty-six-piece modular lunchbox set and a florist she'd once used to send flowers to Eloise told her via the subject line that "Mama Deserves More". She tutted at the "Mama" word, mumbled to herself that she actually did deserve more and closed the app. Cally de Pfeffer was not a happy bunny.

After getting up blearily early at five thirty that morning and doing a shift on the chat line sorting out problems for middle class, middle-aged women and the whereabouts of their cashmere scarves that cost more than Cally's shopping for the week, she'd then got ready for a shift in the back of the chemist. Accompanied by the Shipping Forecast in the background and with Birdie up to her eyes in the dispensary, she'd stuck her headphones on and listened to her first, and last, paranormal romance audio book and got on with the job in hand.

Now, feeling as if she'd been up since the crack of dawn, which she had and having finished off at the chemist mid-afternoon, she'd forced herself not to even glance at her phone for signs of the Henry-Hicks contingent and decided that she'd play Lovely Bay tourist for the rest of the day.

Cally tapped on the tourist information page on the Lovely council website and scrolled through. There were loads of nice coffee shops and heritage buildings featured, a historic trail around the Lovely Bay harbour area, a riverside path where you could stroll and watch the boats go past that doubled as a running track, and a free audio guided walk to download that took the listener all around the nice things to see in Lovely Bay. Considering all the options, Cally downloaded the audio guided walk to her phone. She could do with strolling around, not thinking, and having someone else lead the way.

Grabbing her favourite insulated travel cup, she popped blackcurrant cordial in the bottom, topped it up with hot water, and instead of her usual ballet flats slipped on her trainers, tied a light jacket around her waist and ensured she had her phone and earphones at the ready. The afternoon was pleasant as she stepped out, locking the door behind her. She popped in her earphones, loaded the audio guide, and started her walk. As she set off from the back of the flat, a sea breeze smelling of salt and seaweed whipped through her hair. She undid her jacket from her waist, popped it on, zipped it up, tucked her hands into her pockets, and hit play on the audio guide. A cheery female voice she felt sure she recognised greeted her through her earphones.

Welcome to Lovely Bay, the third smallest town in the British Isles. Our charming seaside town is steeped in history and natural beauty abounds every which way you turn. We'll be exploring some of the most iconic Lovely spots today and will discover the charming sights and sounds of our beautiful heritage seaside town. Our journey weaves us in and out of the historic cobblestone streets, takes us past the towering listed lighthouse, around the harbour, where you can stop for a bit and watch the boats on the water, hear the calls of seagulls overhead and take in the fresh sea air. Get ready to be Lovely-ed.

As she made her way down the street, she glanced at her phone, hoping for a notification. It remained silent. She chided herself again for being so caught up in what Logan might or might not do. Determined not to think about him, she followed the guide's instructions and made her way away from the High Street and listened as the voice told her all about when the shop buildings had been built. She paused to peer in at a window display in the chocolate shop and stopped at The Drunken Sailor as the voice in her ears told her how the pub had been notorious for smuggling back in the day. The voice took her a different way to the route she'd become accustomed to taking to and from Lovely Bay station. She found herself going down winding back streets with cobblestones like the ones outside the church when she'd tumbled with her blackcurrant. All around her, quaint little cottages and tall Victorian villas seemed to jostle for the best positions. The tour led her through the heart of the old town, past the vast townhouses that had once housed prominent Lovely Bay maritime families. She came across things she'd not seen before and others she'd never really looked twice at.

As the voice pointed things out, Cally marvelled at intricate wrought-iron balconies and stained-glass windows and crossed her fingers that one day she'd too live somewhere just as nice. Fat chance of that, to be quite honest.

The guide continued to chat away as she walked.

From the old town hall to the ancient church, each site has a story to tell. You may have now noticed the famous Lovely blue wax coat all around you. This item goes back to the heritage of the town where the coats were custom made to deal with Lovely's unique microclimate whereby the town and its surrounding area often experiences four seasons in a day. The coats are still handmade in Lovely but you'll need to be a resident in Lovely itself to get on the waiting list for one. Look out for the coats as you stroll around the third smallest town in the country.

Following the voice to the letter, Cally looked up as she approached the hall, a gorgeous building with a clock tower that dominated the skyline. The plaque outside detailed its history, from its construction in the 18th century to its role in the town's civic life. As she approached the harbour, the audio guide chimed in again.

Dating back to the 18th century, Lovely Bay's harbour was the heart of the town for generations. It was once a bustling hub of fishing and trade, with vessels coming and going from all corners of the United Kingdom.

ONE NICE DAY IN LOVELY BAY

Cally paused at the water's edge, watching the boats bob on their moorings. She tried to imagine the harbour in its heyday, alive with fishermen and the clatter of crates being loaded and unloaded. Now, it was more peaceful than bustling; a group of seagulls wheeled overhead and she watched the distant chug of a boat heading out to sea. There were still a few fishermen around here and there, and in the air, the smell of saltwater mixed with the faint scent of fish and chips from a nearby stand. The audio guide continued, describing the history of Lovely Bay's maritime industry and the significance of the harbour in its development.

You can still see the remnants of Lovely's storied past in the architecture and the old warehouses that have been converted into quaint shops and cafes.

Cally walked past a row of shops and stood for a bit looking in the windows. One had an array of handmade pottery, another displayed pretty jewellery and candles. As she ambled around taking in the third smallest town in the country she was having a whale of a time just soaking up the atmosphere. It was a tough life. The guide directed her towards an historic trail further around the harbour area.

As you follow the path, you'll encounter several blue plaques detailing the history of significant buildings and events. Take your time to read them and imagine what life was like here in centuries past.

Pausing at one of the plaques describing an old shipbuilder's yard Cally looked up and smiled. The yard, now a lovely café, displayed a menu detailing its special chowder. Continuing along the path, she found herself in a small area overlooking the sea marked off with heavy, old-fashioned black bollards. Sitting down on a bench, she sipped her now tepid blackcurrant and watched various boats glide by.

These days, the harbour is more of a leisure spot. But if you look closely, you can still see remnants of its past. The old customs house on your left, the long line of three-storey fishing huts on your far right.

Cally got up again to keep up with the voice, turned, strolled, and listened. She stopped to examine a boat that had lots of history and continued to follow the audio guide's prompts. It led her past the lifeboat station, where she was informed that volunteers had been saving lives at sea for over a century. Before she knew it, well over an hour had flown by and the audio guide was drawing to a close.

And that concludes our tour of Lovely Bay's historic harbour. We hope you've enjoyed this glimpse into the third smallest town in the country's past and your journey through Lovely Bay. Our little town is more than just a place; it's a community of stories by the Lovelies who call it home. Thank you for exploring with us. You've just been officially Lovely-ed.

Liking being Lovely-ed, Cally nodded to herself. She was now one of the people who called the third smallest town in the country home. She was well pleased with that. It had really, significantly, *absolutely* improved her life in a very small amount of time. Maybe it was a place she could put down roots and build something lasting. As she looked around, she felt as if she was right where she was meant to be. Not that long before, she'd been deep in the rotating tunnel of worry, not able to see a way out. That had changed by way of Lovely. She was never going to go back in the tunnel again. She felt pleased with herself for getting out and doing the walk. It had given her a totally different perspective on Lovely. She'd liked it in the first place, but now, it felt as if it was even better as she'd learnt all about its history and fabulous old buildings. She nodded to herself. She was in the right place. Lovely was now her home. It had been a long time coming. Shame about the Logan thing, she'd put it behind her and move right on. Or perhaps something else was going to happen on that front, too.

29

Cally felt pretty pleased with herself on the success of the audio walk. It had really given her an insight into the delights of unseen Lovely. She felt even more sure that it was the area for her to start getting on with her life. She'd read once on an estate agent's site that when you walked into a place, you just knew and something clicked. She'd chortled at that at the time. Now, in Lovely, perhaps the luxury of just knowing somewhere was right for you was indeed correct. She and Lovely Bay clickety-clicked. She continued to walk and take in Lovely as the sun began to go down and the light changed. Little glowing lights started to pop on all around her. Ooh yeah. She walked along past a small parade of shops just alongside the harbour and stopped to look in a tiny bistro restaurant with a little bow window out the front and a small low door. It displayed mostly chowder on its handwritten menu board in the front with a special deal that sounded good to her. Deciding that she didn't want to go home and sit on her own in the flat and deliberate the Logan thing to death, she figured that she'd go in and see what was what.

A little shop bell rang as she walked in and she was greeted by a tiny entrance area completely clad in timber. As she stood there, she took in vintage fishing nets hanging from above, plants and ferns spilled from woven baskets, and a long line of shelving on the left was stacked with jars of sand and sea glass, each labelled with the collection date and location. An old distressed dresser held loads of umbrellas and baskets and as Cally inhaled, she knew she was staying as a mixture of salty sea air, fresh herbs, and the aroma of garlic, fish, and chowder wafted through the space. Absolutely heavenly.

Peeling off her jacket, she wiped her feet on a doormat with an anchor printed on the top of its bristles and pushed open the inner door. She raised her eyebrows and blinked for a second at what was in front of her eyes. Gorgeous. She should have known, being Lovely, that there was no way it was going to be a typical seaside café with a load of cheap and nasty tat. There wasn't a sniff of dreadful plastic tablecloths, disposable cutlery, or generic nautical decorations that tried to tell you you were by the sea in sight. This, rather, was the Lovely version where Cally felt as if she'd stepped right into a walking talking version of the pages of a coastal living Pinterest board.

All around her, mismatched wooden chairs, each painted a deep green, were neatly set beneath tables worn smooth with age and use. Huge pots of lush green ferns and palms were tucked here and there all over the place. Though warm outside, a little fireplace crackled away in the corner, its mantelpiece crammed with a collection of antique glass floats. Against the opposite wall, a plush window seat piled with sea-blue cushions looked ready for someone to take a seat and behind it a large picture window showed off the boats bobbing in the harbour.

Cally just stood and looked around for a bit. Towards the back of the café, a long driftwood bar stretched along the wall. Huge galvanised metal tubs overflowed with bottles and a big stack of napkins looked as if they'd just been pressed. Cally couldn't get enough as little details caught her eye. Long strings of seashells hung to the sides of the picture window, vases filled with wildflowers sat atop each table, watercolour pictures of Lovely Bay lined the walls, and lamps of all shapes and sizes were shoved in wherever there was a space. The whole place was a gorgeous higgledy-piggledy, organised yet intentionally chaotic mismatch of decor. Cally took mental notes for the flat.

A friendly worker caught her eye and gestured to a small table with a wingback chair by the picture window. Cally settled in, sinking into the battered old Chesterfield armchair, and took the weight off her feet. She gazed out the window at the lights starting to turn on around the bay and decided that she might just have to partake in a little drink to go with her chowder. Life felt good. As she perused the menu handwritten on thick, textured card, she went from trying to decide on whether to have the special or not to looking up and marvelling at the place. She looked back down at the menu, considered the prices and decided that the deal chowder, which detailed freshly caught fish and herbs from the kitchen garden, sounded right up her alley.

While she deliberated and waited for the girl to come back she looked over at bookshelves lining the walls stuffed with well-thumbed books on local history, maritime lore, and coastal foraging. Baskets on the lower shelves overflowed with cosy blankets in muted hues and just along from her a shelf was loaded down with cards and board games.

The worker, with her hands full of dishes, beamed as she came back. 'Hi. Cally, isn't it?'

Cally felt taken aback and also pathetically pleased to be recognised. 'Yes, hello.'

'I know you from seeing you in the chemist with Birdie. You wouldn't know me…' the girl explained.

'Ahh, yes.'

'First time here?'

'Yes, I actually live in Lovely now, so I'm exploring a bit. It's so nice in here.'

'Ooh, you picked the right day for it. The weather's been great today, though it's nippier again now.'

Cally touched her ear. 'I just did the council audio walk. I learnt so many things about Lovely that I didn't know about. It was really good.'

'Ha, funny you should say that. My dad did it the other day and said the same thing and he's lived here all his life. Lovely Bay's got stories around every corner if you know where to look. I might have to do it one day.'

'It has! Yeah, thoroughly recommend it.'

'At least the council got something right.' The girl rolled her eyes.

'Too funny.'

'Anyway, what are you after?'

'I was going to have a bite to eat.'

'We have a lovely chowder on. The fish this morning was the best. It really makes a difference. It won't last long at this rate.'

'Just what I like to hear. Great. I'll have that. Thank you.'

'Too easy. Order up at the counter there, you'll get a paddle and I'll take it from there. I'll pop it over when it's ready.'

'Thank you.'

'So where did you move from? Local was it?'

Cally was not going to mention the awful estate she'd inhabited. She was way too embarrassed. No need for anyone to know about that. 'Actually, no, not really. I was more inland before.' Cally pointed towards the door. 'About forty-five-minutes thataway on the train.'

'Oh, right you are.'

Cally screwed her face up. 'Actually, it was quite awful, really.' She gestured out the window at the harbour. 'Now I'm here, I realise how horrible it was. You know?'

'Lovely does that to you. We're quite simple here and we all stroll around in blue coats looking weird, but we get under your skin.'

'I reckon.'

'Ahh, well, you're here now. You've been Lovely-ed.' The girl raised her chin in the direction of the counter. 'I'll make sure you get the Lovely discount.'

'Sweet. Thanks.'

'Not a bad view either this evening. Free at half the price.'

'This place is absolutely magical,' she gushed. 'I feel like I've stumbled into a little goldmine and I don't know whether to pull out a board game, get mesmerised by the harbour or read a book about the old days.'

'That's what we love to hear. Glad you found us.'

'Me too, for sure.'

A few minutes later, Cally was sitting with a glass of wine and a paddle with a number stencilled on the top, staring out at the bay getting darker and seagulls wheeling over the water. Pulling a book out she idly started to read about the wildflowers that grew in and around Lovely. She sighed a long, slow exhale after taking a gulp of wine as she decompressed from the day. The bistro was the kind of place you could lose track of time and sit in a cosy chair and do nothing, escape from swirling thoughts, work stuff, and the fact that the man you'd been on a date with had decided to ghost you because, more than likely, he'd decided that you were from the wrong side of the tracks. It was nice to feel removed from it all and just sit and look out at the sea.

When the girl came back with a steaming sourdough full of chowder, Cally's visit got better by the second as she tucked in. Blissful was the word; the chowder did not disappoint. Rich with cream and herbs, brimming with fresh fish and all-around deliciousness. She couldn't tuck in fast enough, washed it down with the wine and thoroughly enjoyed herself.

She watched the scene out the window change right in front

of her eyes as the night sky came in. The first stars started to come to life and the sea became less friendly as it turned darker and darker. Cally was in her element as the little fireplace crackled away to itself and she finished off the chowder. She heaved another contented sigh, ordered a second glass of wine and as she sat back, cradling her wine and watching the comings and goings of the harbour, she went over the conversation she'd just had and the fact the local had recognised her.

She realised that she was beginning to feel a sense of belonging settling in her bones. She really did like it in Lovely. Feeling lighter than she had in a long time, she sat back and revelled in her full tummy and nice surroundings. It felt so very good not to be constantly worrying, not to have to care. She no longer had to hold up the sky. It simply did that on its own. She only had to care for herself. The relief from not having to worry was fantastic. She didn't really even care about the lack of communication from Logan. That could wait and so could the Henry-Hicks of the world.

Cally de Pfeffer had much bigger fish to fry. Her own.

30

Cally sat for a bit longer, ordered a slice of homemade apple pie and as she waited for it to arrive, just sort of mused and pondered things in her life. Whatever she told herself about not giving a hoot, her mind kept going back to Logan. How weird was it that he hadn't contacted her? Odd. He'd seemed just as keen as her. She'd clearly read the signs all wrong. Maybe it was a game for him. Why bother doing that? She made a mental note to ask Eloise her opinion. If it was a game, she didn't like it at all. She absolutely wasn't playing ball.

She tried to reason with herself that it was not Logan's duty to message her. At the end of the day, he'd just invited her to dinner. She ruminated with herself that she was no feminist if she insisted on sitting around waiting for someone to chase her. The thing was; she still felt as if she *wanted* to be chased. It wasn't about feminism or lack thereof. It was much more than that. No one in the world had to tell her that she didn't need a man. She'd worked that out well enough on her own. What she did need was to be *wanted* and *treated*. To be wined, dined, pampered, princess-ed, chased. All of the things. All of the days.

She felt a little bit as if her head was on upside down, though, because her brain kept flicking between two things poles apart. On the one hand, she was monumentally miffed that Logan hadn't messaged her and chased her. At the same time, she quite liked it. It made it somehow exciting. Not boring. She'd had enough boredom in her life to last her a lifetime. Perhaps, she did in actual fact, *like* the game. It was quite intriguing. So very different from the regular old humdrum of how her life had been caring for her mum and then her grandma and doing two and sometimes three jobs. This was something different. Would he? Wouldn't he? Da da da.

The apple pie appeared and she decided to throw caution to the wind and ordered an Irish coffee so that it would arrive just after she'd scoffed the pie. The same girl she'd chatted with before shook her head as she put the piece of pie on the table. 'You're tucking it away. Where do you put it?'

Cally laughed. She'd always been able to eat like a horse and had remained exactly the same size, which in fact, was tiny. Sometimes, she got her tights and shirts in the children's department. She'd never understood when people talked about putting on weight. Hers had remained resolutely the same whatever she did. She'd often put it down to all the toing and froing with her grandma and lugging about all the equipment. She did know that watching her weight was not a worry. At least that was a plus. One thing that she'd never had to be concerned about. Her consumption of blackcurrant cordial and apple pie was therefore vacuumed up accordingly.

Just as she'd finished polishing off the pie and the coffee had arrived she suddenly sat up straight. She heard and smelt Henry-Hicks before she actually saw him. She leaned back into the side of the wingback chair and cringed. She didn't want to have to lamely chat to him in the restaurant. It was going to be awkward. Now what? So much for enjoying the game. She felt her stomach flip over. She hadn't heard from him and now here he was right behind her with someone else and she was Billy No Mates on her own.

She winced at another voice. One of the posh ones from the lunch, unless she was very much mistaken. Alastair or something. Straining her ears, she listened to the two voices talking to the girl who had delivered her pie. She heard them being really civil and polite. She listened to Logan order a bottle of wine. Trying not to move much, she sipped her coffee secretly and remained pinned to the back of the Chesterfield. Her brain toggled between telling herself not to listen to what was going on behind her and considering turning on the record button on her phone and popping it over the top of the back of the chair. No one would notice if she did that, would they? She'd be able to play it back later and examine Logan a bit more closely. Nuts.

Cally sat as still as a statue, fully earwigging on the conversation. The voices were talking about something that had happened at the manor. Her back pressed against the old leather of the wingback chair. She hardly dared to breathe lest she draw attention to herself. The last thing she wanted was for Logan to spot her eavesdropping. Her heart raced as she strained to catch every word, trying to piece together the fragments of dialogue floating over the chair's high back. Logan's voice sent a shiver down her spine. She cursed herself for caring. She chuckled to herself though. In an odd sort of way, she *was* having fun. Playing the game was actually quite nice. Much, much better than pushing medical buttons on the side of beds and grappling with hoists. The thrill of the chase did its thing. She tuned back into the conversation.

'Nice day out there today, wasn't it? I'm glad the horses were okay. Looks like the rain is on the way again tomorrow. Always four seasons in a day down here.'

Alastair agreed. 'Yes, rather nice. Perfect weather for tucking into a nice bottle of red, wouldn't you say?'

There was a clink of glasses, and Cally could practically feel how posh this Alastair was from behind the back of the chair. She rolled her eyes and then berated herself. She hadn't even met the man and he couldn't control where he'd been born in the world.

'Quite right,' Logan chuckled. 'A nice wine never goes amiss on a day like this. Though it's the chowder that makes this place if I'm not mistaken. We say that wherever we are in Lovely, though, don't we?'

Cally bit her lip, trying to quell a strange and very irrational surge of jealousy that had risen up in her throat. It was ridiculous but *she* wanted to be the one sharing chowder with Logan. That ship had clearly sailed. She'd obviously not lived up to expectations on the hill. What a shame. She'd tried so very hard, too.

As the conversation meandered, Cally found her mind wandering. She thought about how she'd wanted the post-dinner scenario to play out, but it just hadn't happened. Logan hadn't bothered to call or message her and that was that. She shook her head. She was being ridiculous, mooning over a man who had made it perfectly clear, by his lack of communication, that he wasn't interested. If he had wanted to see her again, he would have messaged her. It was as simple as that. Now, she was in a bit of a stitch, though. What did she do, get up to go and scoot past, hoping he didn't see her or sit there until they were finished? There was no way she was going to stop and chat with him as if nothing had happened. It was a bit off that he'd full-on ghosted her. She wasn't going to just stop and say hi and be all nice. Nup she'd ignore him and run.

Behind her, the conversation went on, Logan and Alastair's voices fading into an indistinct hum. Before she knew what she was doing, she tapped her phone pressed record, and aimed it past the side of the chair. Two glasses of wine in, she sort of knew she was being ridiculous but still went right on ahead anyway. Just after she pressed the big red button, it went through her head that it was more than likely illegal to record someone's conversation without getting their permission. She still did it, but it did not go to plan as the phone tried to adjust to the dim light and the bright torch light automatically came on. Mortified that the light was so bright, she fumbled and tapped to stop recording and get the torch to switch off. Suddenly her phone slipped and to her horror, it tumbled out of her hand and slid across the floor behind her in the direction of Logan.

Cally's heart leapt into her throat as she peered around the chair and watched her phone skitter across the floorboards. It clattered and banged and time seemed to slow to a crawl as it spun and slid making a beeline straight for Logan's table. She sat frozen in her chair not sure what to do. One swear word on repeat streamed through her mind. What had she been thinking, trying to record their conversation like some lovesick teenager? *Pathetic.* And now, thanks to her own clumsiness and poor judgement, she was about to be caught red-handed by the very man who had been occupying her thoughts for days – the same one who hadn't even bothered to call her back after their date. She'd been ghosted and now here he was about six feet away from her. Her mind raced, frantically trying to concoct some plausible excuse for having practically thrown her phone at him. But before she could even begin to formulate a plan, he'd pushed his chair back, spied the phone, picked it up, and turned around.

Logan frowned on seeing Cally behind the chair. 'Oh, hi. Hello, Blackcurrant. I didn't see you there.' He held the phone out looking confused. 'Sorry, is this yours?'

Cally felt her cheeks burn with humiliation as she reached out to take the phone. 'Thank you.' She wanted the floor to open up and swallow her whole. It was now completely obvious, at least to her, that she'd been hiding in the armchair. 'I was just trying to get my card out to go and pay and I was balancing my coffee...'

Logan's expression was unreadable. 'Looks like you got away with it not breaking.'

Cally swallowed. Little did he know that she'd actually got away with secretly filming him. 'Sorry?'

'It's not cracked or anything, is it? The screen I mean. Not that I can see. It might have a hairline one when you look at it in the daylight.'

'Oh yes, right, no, I think it's fine. Thank goodness.'

'There you go. Do you always go around throwing things at people willy-nilly?'

'Sorry?'

Logan's eyes twinkled. 'The boat. It was chicken and curry powder that day. Then the books and the shelf and now you're hurling your phone around in the middle of a restaurant.'

'Oh, yes, ha.'

Logan pointed to her table. 'Dinner for one?'

Cally felt suddenly nauseous as it flashed through her mind that Logan was mocking her. He'd not only ghosted her but he thought it was funny too. Along with feeling sick, she felt irrationally irritated. Was he actually being snide that she was having dinner on her own? Cheeky ****. 'Yes, actually, it *was* dinner for one. I quite enjoy it.'

Clocking Cally's change in body language, Logan was awkward. He ran a hand through his hair. He went in for the kill. 'Look, about the other night.'

Noooo! Now he's going to start making excuses! Cally shuddered inside but tried not to let it show. He was totally going to blow her off right there and then in the middle of the restaurant. The game was no longer thrilling. Embarrassing, more like, with a sprinkle of cringe on the top. She flipped the voice switch she used when she was pretending to be okay. She couldn't believe it! He was actually going to tell her right there and then that he wasn't keen. That he'd changed his mind or some rubbish that he wasn't in the deal for a relationship at the moment. Or that he didn't want to lead her on. Yadda yadda.

To her horror, she felt tears prick at the corners of her eyes. She blinked furiously. The game was no longer anything like fun. She'd rather operate a hoist. There was no way in the world she was going to let him see her upset over it, though. Not a chance. She wanted to skedaddle, and quickly, instead, she stayed where she was and beamed. Cally was many things; an expert at pretending she was fine was one of them. 'All good. It was a nice evening, wasn't it? I've been so busy since. Absolutely flat out. You know how it is.'

'Yes, me too. Look, I err,' Logan glanced at Alastair and then back again.

Cally interrupted him. She felt like she'd been punched in the gut. Her voice was high and sounded happy and carefree, but she was far from it inside. 'I meant to message you to say that it was lovely, but…' she wrinkled up her nose and made a funny little face. She lied through her teeth. 'You know, I'm not really in the place for, well, taking it further at the moment, so, yeah. Hope that's okay with you. Anyway, I must push off.'

Logan frowned as the realisation of what she'd just said went across his face. 'Sorry, what? Oh, right, okay then. I was going to say… right, but, yeah, whatever.'

Cally cringed as she dug herself deeper and was horrified that she'd read the room wrong. The look on Logan's face told her that taking it further had *never* been on his radar in the first place anyway. It had obviously just been a one-off dinner to him and nothing else. Sitting on the bench kissing him swam around in front of her eyes. Now she'd gone and insinuated that she'd thought something more had been on the cards when it hadn't been at all. She now looked *more* stupid. He hadn't thought it was going to go further anyway. Clearly, he just kissed people willy-nilly on benches under trees on the top of hills every day of the week and thought nothing of it.

Ahhh! Cally closed her eyes, taking a second to compose herself. Hurt and embarrassment churned in her gut. At least she knew where she stood. It was crystal clear. No more wondering, no more hoping for a call, no more stupid thoughts of chases. He was pretty nasty, though. Mean, that was it. Mean *and* nasty. He didn't seem at all perturbed either! She didn't know how to dig herself out of the hole of what she'd just said. Not trusting herself to speak, she stuttered initially. 'I'm not, well, no, sorry, look, anyway, I was just on my way out. Have a nice evening.'

Logan reached out as if to touch her arm but seemed to think better of it, letting his hand fall back to his side. 'I was going to say that I'd text you. See if you wanted to go out, but sorry, I must have got the wrong end of the stick the other night. You're not up for anything, right.' Logan swore. 'Yeah, right. Sorry, what an idiot. Not being funny, though, how about like saying that right away? Who does that? I did ask you in the kitchen. Anyway, whatever.'

Cally went from crashing down to flying back up again. What? Was he saying the opposite of what she'd thought? What a muddle. She soared up in the sky, nearly bumping into the lighthouse. So the look she'd thought she'd read had been wrong. He wasn't saying what she'd thought. She heard herself backpedalling like crazy. 'Did you? What? I err, I didn't mean...'

Logan shook his head and was abrupt. 'No, it's fine. Don't worry about it. I just thought… anyway, if you're not in a place for, well, anything, then I guess that is that, as it were. You know what? Just a note for you; next time, don't bother.'

Henry-Hicks was so hot. Absolutely on it.

Cally felt as if she was sitting in the front car of an emotional rollercoaster. Her heart leapt at Logan's words, then plummeted again as she realised the misunderstanding she'd just created.

She scrambled to find the right words to salvage the situation. She'd gone and put her foot right in it and she'd been completely and utterly wrong. 'Sorry. I didn't mean that I didn't want to see you again. I just thought maybe you weren't interested since I hadn't heard from you so I, well, you know...'

'You just said you weren't in the place for anything anyway. You should have been up front in the first place.'

Henry-Hicks took no prisoners. Cally de Pfeffer loved it.

'Ah, umm, yes, no, I didn't actually mean that. I made that up.'

'What? You're not making a lot of sense. You made it up? Really?'

'Sorry. I thought you ghosted me and you didn't want to…'

'I've been meaning to call or message, honestly. It's just been a crazy week at work, and I didn't want to bother you if you were busy and I didn't want to send a message too late because you said you got up for early shifts on the bot thingamabob.' Logan trailed off, rubbing the back of his neck awkwardly. He shook his head. 'Ghosting? Sorry, but what are you saying? I'm confused.'

Cally felt both a pang of sympathy and over the moon at the same time. She didn't know what to say. 'I shouldn't have assumed.'

'It's okay. I know how it must have looked, me not calling and then showing up here with Alastair. To be fair, I didn't see you.' He glanced back at Alastair, who was studiously examining the menu, pretending not to listen. 'I really did have a great time with you the other night. And I would love to see you again if you're still open to it. If that is what you're saying, is it?'

'I'd like that. We'd better start this again.'

Logan chuckled. He held out his hand and his eyes sparkled as he joked. 'Hi, I'm Logan. I think you might have dropped this?'

Cally laughed. 'Nice to meet you, Logan. I'm Cally. I throw

things at people when I first meet them if I think I might like the look of them.'

From the table, Alastair cleared his throat pointedly. 'Not to interrupt this moment, but err, sorry, but we need to order if I'm to be back in time.'

'Yes, right, sorry.' Logan raised his eyebrows at Cally. 'I'll message you. I really will this time.'

Cally's heart soared. 'Okay, great, look forward to it.'

'Yes, we'll go out.'

'Excellent. I'd like that.'

As she turned Cally practically jigged as she walked up to the desk near the entrance and paid her bill. What a funny state of affairs. She'd gone up and down like a yo-yo. She liked it. The ride up and down, the thrill-y, chase-y thing. It was a darn sight better than being stuck in a rotating tunnel watching and waiting for the end of someone's life that she knew for certain. And things were going to get so very much better.

31

As she left the restaurant, Cally replayed the conversation in her head and cringed. She also felt as if her whole body deflated in relief. She'd totally jumped the gun and told Logan that she wasn't interested in a relationship because she'd thought that she would get it in first. She'd been sure that was what he was going to say. Then, when she'd realised that he actually wasn't thinking that at all, she'd had to backpedal like crazy. All part of the very nice, delicious, or was it delirious, game?

She shook her head at the prospect of very nearly being caught spying on him with her phone. What in the world was happening to her? She wriggled her head and closed one eye. It was very strange. Part of her knew what was happening. Oh yes, indeed it did. She barely even knew him from Adam, but Logan was doing something to her and not just her mind. From the first time she'd clapped eyes on him when he'd handed her a packet of chicken and a pot of curry powder on the boat, she'd felt the earth slip away and herself falling. That had only intensified eighty million times over when he'd first kissed her, and then the bench had totally sealed the deal. She was no longer in a rotating tunnel. She'd now fallen into a whole other world.

She hugged the fact that Logan was going to message her. She was *so* pleased with how things had turned out that she danced down the road. If she had been able to, she would've done that funny little thing where people jump to the side and click their ankles together. She felt inordinately delighted with both what had happened and herself. He did like her, after all! He was going to message her. Woot woot. She hadn't been imagining things on the bench. He *had* enjoyed his time with her just as much as she had with him. She twirled and whirled and swirled it around her head again and again. Ding a ling ling.

As she made her way down the pavement and around the harbour, she began to think about whether or not she should get on with it and text him to get the ball rolling. She'd toyed with the idea before, but now he had been congenial and nice to her she thought that perhaps she'd take the lead. She wondered whether she should push the button and be the one to text first. She took her phone out to do just that, then suddenly changed her mind, deleted the text, and put her phone back in her pocket. She was going to stick with what she'd thought in the first place. She wouldn't be doing any of the chasing. No siree Mr President. *He* could do the running. Perhaps people like the Henry-Hicks of the world had things given to them on plates way too often in their lives. She would not be on anyone's plate. She would be the person who would not give him what he wanted unless he chased or danced or possibly both. Naked might be good.

She pushed her phone further into her pocket, her resolve firm and as she walked through Lovely Bay, wondering when he'd message and what would happen next, she felt a bit dreamy. The setting helped; old-fashioned street lights glowed illuminating the cobblestone streets, the moon hung low in the sky, and the air was full of the scent of the sea. Cally inhaled deeply, letting the air fill her lungs and clear her mind. She felt contentment and excitement and a little bit of calm all at the same time. Things were not only looking up, they were looking Henry-Hicks phenomenal.

She slowed down a bit as she approached the lighthouse. She loved how its cylindrical shape dominated Lovely Bay's nighttime landscape. It felt to her as if it was standing there tall and proud, looking after the third smallest town in the country below. Little spotlights sitting at its bottom pointed up, making its already bright white exterior gleam. She stood at the base for a second or two, craning her neck to take in the full height of it. She could see it from her flat and had walked past it many times, but lit up in the dark sky, it seemed even more imposing and somehow intrusive than it usually did. Standing there squinting with her chin raised, she felt tiny and liked how now that she actually lived in Lovely, she felt somehow as if a minuscule little piece of the lighthouse was there for her.

Continuing on, as she strolled down the main street, after what had happened with Logan, everything looked better; the twinkling fairy lights in the shop windows, the quaint street lamps, the sounds of the night, and as she walked past a pretty house, she could hear the faint tinkling of wind chimes. Approaching her flat, she noticed the little lights on in the deli below. She peered in the glass and looked at the display of glass cloches. What a place to live. On approach to the alley going down to the back of the deli, she paused for a moment, looking back at the town. The lights, the soft sounds, the enchanting smells. She smiled to herself, feeling incredibly lucky to have the flat and, more importantly, to have been the recipient of Birdie's kindness.

After heaving herself up the stairs and well-pleased at how the once untidy bookcase now looked neat and orderly, she unlocked the door and stepped inside her flat and thought about Logan. Slipping her jacket off, she hung it on the hooks by the door and stopped right where she was and did a double take. The flat had suddenly all come together. It was a far cry from the junk-filled time-warp place she'd seen on the first day with Birdie. It, in actual fact, looked nice, welcoming, cosy even. She'd put lamps and bulbs on timers and apps and set them all to come on as evening fell and they were doing their job well. The space was filled with the few favourite things that she'd kept when she'd sold her grandma's house and all of them told her she was home. Big piles of books, a few soft blankets, and an oversized four-wick candle she'd bought on a whim. A sofa she'd found on Marketplace appeared as if it was smiling up at her from its new home. An array of mismatched velvet cushions in muted blues and a patterned throw Nancy had given her looked lovely. A little coffee table she'd found in the charity shop next door to The Drunken Sailor held a stack of illustrated books about Lovely Bay she'd found on the bookcase on the landing and a vase of fresh flowers set the scene. At the windows, bamboo blinds she'd bought in B&Q in the clearance section juxtaposed beautifully against the chalky white paint from the deli. The old-fashioned fireplace with its intricately carved mantel was now white and welcomed. Even the little wood burner seemed to say hello, just needing a few flames so that she would be able to sit, stare and think about Logan, ponder what might happen next, and ruminate about how exciting it all was.

Cally was so pleased with both herself and the flat that she felt a bit emotional. She moved into the kitchen, where a coat of eggshell paint, new handles, and vinyl worktop covering all worked together to do an amazing job. She couldn't actually quite believe it. Okay, the tops were not marble, but they looked it and she'd outshone herself in how the vinyl covering had gone on. The open shelving, once deep sixties brown, now white, showcased oversized glass jars filled with pantry bits and bobs. She nodded to herself at the copper pots and pans found in another charity shop hanging from a rack above the stove. She'd be an interior designer yet.

She flicked the kettle on and as she waited for the water to boil, she leaned against the counter, her thoughts drifting back to Logan. She deliberated over what to do about messaging him and continued to hold fast. The kettle clicked off and she poured hot water into a little glass teapot she'd found in the cupboard when she'd first moved in, popped in an extra teaspoon of tea leaves and let it brew.

With the tea ready, she stood for a bit and gazed out the window at the twinkling lights of Lovely Bay. With the third smallest town in the country quiet and the streets mostly deserted, the streetlights, the lighthouse, and the occasional flicker of a passing car created an almost dreamlike quality, or maybe she felt dreamy because she was floating. Who knew? Whatever it was, she liked it and never wanted it to go away. Floating was so very much better than sky holding.

Her mind wandered back to the events of the evening. Should she really let him chase? Popping her mug down, she pulled out her phone and stared at the screen for a moment. Her fingers hovered over the keyboard and, as before, she changed her mind. She didn't need to rush anything. She would take her time and let things unfold naturally. Sleep on it and see how she felt in the morning.

Deciding to revel in how the evening had turned out and not wanting yet to go to bed, she went in to run a bath. As she walked into the bathroom, she smiled. The gauzy, sheer curtains she'd hung on the old sash window looked lovely, the once avocado green wall was now white and adorned with six little matching framed botanical prints, and a large, antique mirror with a distressed white frame balanced nicely on a small dresser that had come with the bathroom. She was a very long way from the grotty house on the estate - that she knew for free. Oasis sprang to mind. She lit a few scented lavender and vanilla candles, turned the taps on the tub, and prepared to be soothed. As the bubbles began to froth, she dimmed the light, slipped out of her clothes and eased into the water, sighing as the heat enveloped her. Leaning back against the tub, her head resting on a folded-up towel, she closed her eyes and let the warmth seep into her muscles, listened to the crackling of the candles and mused everything Logan.

She wondered what he was doing, whether he was thinking about her too. Probably not. Most likely, he was just having a normal meal with his cousin and not mooning around in a dreamlike state as she was. Just as she was thinking about messaging Eloise and telling her about what had happened, her phone pinged from its spot on the stool beside the tub. She opened her eyes, reached for it, and fist-pumped when she saw it was a message from Logan. *Boom de boom.* Her heart skipped a beat as she unlocked her phone.

Logan: *Hey Blackcurrant, how are you? So good to see you this evening. HH.*

Cally whooped and water splashed as she pumped her fist into the bubbles. She took a moment before typing a response so that she didn't look too keen. She was so flipping keen it wasn't even funny.

Cally: *Hey, yes, it was. I'm good, thanks.*

She hit send and almost immediately, her phone pinged again.

Logan: *Look, sorry it took me a while to get back to you.*

Cally felt her cheeks flush.

Cally: *No worries.*

A few moments passed. She watched as the little dots flashed, stopped for a bit, flashed again and then there was another ping.

Logan: *I was wondering if you'd like to go out. Maybe this weekend?*

Cally's heart raced. She hesitated for a moment, considering her response. Did she want to go out? Biggest understatement *ever*. She paused to create a bit of drama and waited for two full minutes to click over on her phone.

Cally: *I'd love to.*
Logan: *How about something a bit different? I'm there with bells on.*
Cally: *When and what time?*
Logan: *How about three on Saturday?*

Cally frowned. Funny time for a date. She'd go on a date with Logan at any time of the day, to be fair. She'd run around at 4 a.m. starkers if he wanted her to. She checked her shifts at the chemist and waited again for a bit so she didn't look too eager.

Cally: *Sounds great.*
Logan: *OK.*
Cally: *I'm looking forward to it.*
Logan: *Me too. I can't wait to see you again.*

Cally put her phone back down, smiled and let herself sink back into the bubbles. Just a few hours before, she'd been filled with uncertainty and doubt and had convinced herself that Logan wasn't interested. Now, it appeared he was. She stayed in exactly the same position for ages and let herself do nothing but think and as the water cooled she felt better than she had for a long time.

After she pulled the plug and watched the bubbles disappear, she dried off, caught a glimpse of herself in the mirror, frowned and pulled back away. Who was this carefree person looking back at her, no longer holding up the sky? Not Cally the Carer but Cally the Carefree. This person had glowing bits on the top of her cheekbones, her eyes sparkled a little bit, the permanent frown in the middle of this person's eyebrows had miraculously disappeared. She liked this person a lot.

Pottering around, getting ready for bed, she could barely get the smile off her face. She was safe and happy and worry-free and had something to look forward to to boot. As she plonked down the bamboo blind and pulled the curtains on Lovely Bay's twinkling lights, she shook her head. What a strange old turn up for the books. The funny little town, Birdie's kindness, the Lovelies, and she had to admit, what had happened with Logan, had changed something in her. She simply felt okay. She hadn't felt just okay, nothing more, nothing less, in a long time. It had turned out to be one very nice day.

32

It was the day of the date. Cally had absolutely no idea where she was going, but more importantly, she really didn't care. Like she *absolutely* didn't care. It felt extremely nice not to have to be the one caring and being in charge. She could get quite used to someone collecting her, taking her out, and doing nice things to, for, and with her. A first in her life. She squinted out the window as the car that had picked her up indicated to turn off the main road, zoomed along a slip road, and very quickly zipped down a narrow lane with fields and hedgerows on either side.

The car and driver, with Logan in the back, had come to pick her up. She'd wondered why Logan wasn't driving and where they were going to end up but Logan had told her that it was a surprise so she'd said nothing. She frowned as she saw a hand-painted sign for paintballing. Apparently, Die Hard Paintballing took one to the next level of immersive interactive gameplay on exclusive battlefields. Ouch.

After another five minutes, the driver slowed down and pulled into a turning with a double farm gate into a field. Cally didn't say anything as she read another sign for Die Hard Paintballing attached to the gate. She shifted in her seat and peered out the window to see nothing much really apart from a large, flat, open field. As she read the number for the paintballing company she went a little bit cold and remembered the boy racer with the go-faster stripes and his idea of conversation and a date. Surely Logan wasn't taking her paintballing? If he were, it would have to be a no from her. A big fat no. Paintballing for a second date? Just no. Not going to work. She'd have to regroup afterwards. Paintballing alone made all sorts of little red flags dance around in front of her eyes. Grown people in fields splatting paint at each other. No, thank you.

Once Cally and Logan had got out and the driver had gone, they'd strolled through the gate and Cally had still not had a clue what was going on. She pretended she was quite happy when part of her thought that she should come clean and make it known that war games and paintballing in fields weren't really her thing. Not that she'd ever tried running around shooting paint at people for fun, but still. She winced as she realised that she'd probably have to wear a stinky boiler suit thing. Disgusting. She also wasn't sure she was strong enough to carry a gun. There'd probably be people in teams with strategies and all kinds of game plans. She'd have to pretend to enjoy splattering people with paint. A little bit of the hotness of Henry-Hicks fizzled away.

They followed a path down the side of the field, turned right and then left, and walked a bit more down past a low hedge. They turned again and then she saw it. A hot air balloon.

She gasped. The balloon's silk sections in pale pink and white swayed in the wind. A gauzy mass of white and pink frothed up and appeared to take over the sky in front of them.

Cally heard a strange sound come out of her mouth. 'What in the name of goodness? What? What is that?'

'That is a hot air balloon.'

'Is that where we're going?'

'Correct.'

'I thought we were going paintballing.'

'Don't insult me, Blackcurrant.'

Good play from Henry-Hicks.

'Are we actually going up in that?' Cally pointed in the direction of the balloon. Her eyes were like saucers.

Logan nodded. 'We are. Only if you're comfortable with it. I wasn't sure, but I decided to chance it. I thought you might like it.'

Cally blinked like crazy. 'If I'm comfortable with it? Might like it?'

Logan looked pleased with himself. 'I take it you think it's a good idea. Excellent!'

Cally couldn't believe it for many reasons. She felt as if something had slammed into her as emotions came in waves. This man was pulling out all the stops for her. No one had *at any point* done anything like it for her ever. As in ever, ever, ever. So much so, in fact, that she wasn't quite sure *how* to handle it. Perhaps for the Henry-Hicks clan, a casual little weekend daytime balloon ride was a thing. In her life, not so much. She couldn't even begin to think how much it would have cost. 'I love the idea. I can't believe it.'

She stared at the pastel hot air balloon on the far side of the large open field. Grass undulated back and forth in the breeze and the muted colours of the landscape blurred around the gigantic balloon and basket. A man in a uniform stood next to the basket underneath the balloon, fiddling with some knobs. Another man supervised and a woman in the same uniform greeted them as they approached. The dome of the hot air balloon rose further above them as Cally stood listening, a bit dumbstruck at the slightly surreal scene going on around her. She was going up into the sky to ride in a balloon.

'Afternoon. Logan and Cally, it must be!' The woman said as she greeted them warmly. 'Welcome. You're in for an unforgettable experience today. The weather has played ball for us. This morning's ride was a stunner and by the looks of it, this one could perhaps be even better.'

As the woman took names, filled in forms, and briefed them on what to expect from the flight, an inflation fan hummed in the background. Cally felt a little bit overwhelmed and not quite sure how to behave. The woman smiled. 'Get ready for an amazing adventure. It's going to be a great ride over Lovely and the coast.'

'We're ready.' Logan smiled.

Cally didn't really know what to say, so she just stood, taking it all in as the burner roared and occasionally flared up to add hot air to the balloon. She whispered to Logan. 'Gosh, this is amazing.'

'It is. Prepared to be wowed.'

Once the balloon had been fully inflated, the woman beckoned them over to the wicker basket where the pilot fiddled with a few things here and there. Cally's heart raced as they approached and she stepped inside the basket to a surprisingly spacious compartment lined with soft padding and sturdy handles.

'Ready for liftoff?' the pilot asked with a grin, his hand on the burner control.

Cally gulped, a bit too stunned to speak and Logan nodded.

The woman closed the gate on the basket. 'Rightio, there we are then. Get ready to enjoy yourselves. Have a great flight.'

After a final check of the equipment, a few words with the woman in the uniform, and some keying into an iPad, the pilot pulled a burner valve. Cally gripped a handle in front of her like a vice. Much sooner than she'd anticipated the balloon began to rise slowly and gently off the ground. She'd never even thought about a balloon ride in her life. One didn't tend to think about flying atop the earth in a balloon when one was wondering how to make ends meet. Balloon flying was something for other people. Despite never having thought about it, she hadn't expected it to be smooth and almost dreamlike as the basket fully lifted away from the ground. It was as if they were being swept by a soft invisible force as they ascended up and away and the ground below seemed to shrink further and further from them.

Cally hadn't said a word since they'd stepped in and simply kept shaking her head. As the view and the countryside took her breath away her chin fell to the floor. Rolling hills and the coastline bathed in soft light stretched out in every direction. Everything looked dream-like when above the ground floating in a basket hanging from a gigantic pink and white balloon. Little copses formed blurs of green. The sky felt heavy with pastel hues and Cally leaned against the edge of the basket with her eyes wide not quite able to get enough. The view was unlike anything she had ever seen before, quieter, too, and peaceful somehow, as if they were serenely floating through a watercolour painting all around them. She could see the River Lovely winding its way through the landscape and peered at a green patchwork blur of fields, meandering streams and clusters of trees here and there.

'This is incredible,' she whispered, more to herself than to anyone else.

Logan moved closer to her and nodded. 'It really is. I thought you might like it.'

As they drifted higher and higher, things got better and better. It was so quiet, the only sounds were the occasional whoosh of the burner and the odd calls of a few birds here and there. To Cally, the tranquillity of the flight and the floating was almost otherworldly. The pilot didn't say much at all, picking up the magnitude of what Cally was feeling. He expertly guided the balloon, adjusting the burner with a whoosh every now and then. As the balloon drifted higher, Cally released her grip on the handle and couldn't believe how peaceful she felt. Like no other feeling she'd ever experienced before.

They passed over various landmarks below and floated over a small village where rooftops glinted in the light. Tiny figures could be seen going about their routines unaware of the balloon silently gliding above them, as if they were looking down on a miniature world, every detail perfectly in place. After flying slowly over Lovely Manor, the pilot brought out a bottle of champagne and two flutes and handed the glasses to Cally and Logan. Cally beamed. If this was the way the Henry-Hicks lot did things, she'd take it, thank you very much.

'Cheers to an amazing adventure,' Logan said, clinking his glass of bubbles against Cally's.

'Cheers. I can't believe how beautiful this is. Thank you so much.'

'To many more adventures together.' Logan chuckled.

Cally loved that. So much. She fizzed much more than the bubbles. She'd drink to adventures with Logan Henry-Hicks any day of the week. She sipped as they continued to drift over fields dotted with grazing sheep and inched closer to the coast. 'This is perfect. I love it up here.'

As the balloon floated, Cally was mesmerised. She pointed out the row of cottages where Nancy lived and commented on the winding cobblestone streets going towards the harbour. She leaned over the edge of the basket, her eyes wide as they passed over the High Street and she looked at the balcony on the side of her flat. From above, the distinctive shell-shaped Lovely roof tiles looked prettier than they ever had and the bunting on the shop awnings and around the pub at the end of the road fluttered in the breeze.

Logan pointed. 'Look at the lighthouse.'

'Wow, it seems so much smaller from up here.'

As they continued to drift over the bay, the pilot pointed out a few other landmarks – the quaint little church with its steeple reaching upwards where Cally had fallen with her hot blackcurrant, a weather-beaten old pier Cally had never seen before stretching out into the water and the lush greens of the marshes with their labyrinth of boardwalks.

Cally couldn't quite believe how different everything looked from the perspective of a great big basket dangling from an air-filled balloon. The everyday sights she already loved and had walked past every day on her way to work in the chemist, took on a new level of Loveliness when viewed from above. It was as if she was seeing Lovely Bay for the first time all over again, discovering things and seeing little spots she'd never noticed before.

Logan put his hand on the small of her back. 'How nice is this? Good day for it.'

'It really is,' Cally nodded. Inside, she was actually quite overwhelmed by everything. It felt so ridiculously *unusual* to be treated. She was up in the sky not underneath it holding it up. She'd said thank you to Logan lots of times but repeated herself again. 'Thank you. I'll need to give you some money.'

'Don't be ridiculous. I *wanted* to do this. You're certainly not giving me any money!'

Cally felt stupidly emotional but couldn't quite seem to fathom how to control what she was feeling or whether she actually *needed* to. She'd spent so long putting everyone else's needs before her own, always being the one to carry the weight of responsibility and care, that Logan simply treating her felt verging on wrong. To have someone look at her with what appeared to be actual, real, genuine kindness and seem happy about it, too, felt very weird. She tried to suck it up, love it and get used to the new feeling flying around her veins but it was tricky as she thought about the cost. A personal balloon ride for two was way out of her league and had been for a very long time. She couldn't get her head around how expensive it may or may not have been.

After another half an hour or so, the balloon began its descent back towards the launch field. It felt oddly bittersweet as the end of the ride neared. Cally had loved the trip much, much more than she'd thought she would have done. The pilot brought them in gently and as the basket touched down with a soft bump on the grassy field, she shook her head at it all. She could have stayed riding around in the sky all day long. She smiled at the pilot. Job goals right there. *Oh, what do you do? I'm a hot-air balloon pilot. Course you are. What about you? Yeah, I work as a customer service chatbot assistant going by the name of Alex.*

She clambered out behind Logan and felt a bit wobbly after so long in the air. The woman who had initially booked them in rushed over to help. 'How was that? It must have been a good one. Hope so.'

Cally raised her eyebrows. 'Out of this world. I *loved* it. I don't even know what to say. It was that good. I can't describe it. Surreal.'

The woman nodded. 'Aww, so pleased. I thought you'd have a nice time up there today.'

Cally frowned. 'Who wouldn't have a nice time up there? It was spectacular!'

The woman shook her head. 'You'd be surprised. I can normally tell from the moment I set eyes on someone whether or not they're going to get it. I thought you would.'

Cally wrinkled up her nose in question. 'Some people don't love it? Wow, I would never have thought that. It was one of the best things I've ever done.'

'Nope, they're not that interested. They get in and act as if it's nothing. You wouldn't believe how many people we get here who hop on and spend the whole journey on their phones, and I don't mean taking photos. Some of them don't even look up.'

'I am not one of those people.' Cally gushed, 'In fact, I think I'll be back tomorrow and every day for the foreseeable future.'

She turned to Logan. 'I don't even know how to begin to thank you. It was everything.'

Logan frowned. 'You've thanked me so many times, Cal. You really don't need to.'

'Sorry, yes, right.'

'One thank you is enough.'

Cally smiled. Henry-Hicks had played a good game. The date had started well. She couldn't quite see how it was going to get better. No, that was not true. She *absolutely* knew how to top a ride in a hot air balloon. A different sort of ride altogether. She hoped it would happen sooner rather than later.

33

After arriving back in Lovely, Logan had suggested chowder in the bistro where Cally had dropped her phone. Cally hadn't minded where she'd gone and so they'd strolled around the harbour and walked in. She cringed inside when she found herself sitting opposite him in the same chair she'd sat in when she'd tried to surreptitiously video him. Not that he knew that and never would, but she felt awkward and stupid. As she sat with a glass of wine, chatting away about the balloon ride, she suddenly went a bit cold when she spied a security camera tucked up in the corner of the room. She groaned inside and then winced. It was possible that someone had witnessed her dreadful attempt at spying. She was never going to make a good James Bond.

'Well, here we are. How nice was that balloon ride?' Logan asked.

'I could make it a weekly trip.' Cally joked.

'I'll book us in.'

'Everything looked so different from up there, didn't it?'

'Yep. It did.'

Cally sat back as Logan ordered and relaxed in her chair.

She'd had such a nice afternoon. Not a bad date. Not long after and once their chowder arrived, they chatted about all sorts and Cally found herself as she had before when she'd been with Logan at the cottage: calm, peaceful somehow, and, more importantly, just happy and not worried about anything at all.

They discussed Logan's job, talked about his mum living at Lovely Manor, and about his cousins Alastair and Jasper. As he chatted away, Cally felt a huge gap in their respective starts in the world as if she'd had such a different life to him, almost to the extent that she was embarrassed to say too much about hers. As he talked, her mind started to whirl. She didn't really have a lot to say and nothing interesting to contribute. She had no small business, though she'd always been vaguely interested in having one. She'd worked on the customer service portal for years because it suited her and had meant that she'd been able to look after her grandma and she helped out in the back of a chemist. Not exactly a groundbreaking or particularly interesting career.

Despite her misgivings, she listened with interest taking it all in. Shame there wasn't too much for her to say on her end. Logan didn't seem to notice, though, so she just went with the flow. He started chatting about where he'd gone to university in Scotland. St Andrew's, to be exact. Cally thought about how she'd done her degree on her laptop in her grandma's spare room wedged on an old table behind the door. Truth be told, her degree had been done on the same secondhand laptop she'd used to help people whose fancy clothes had got lost in the post. She flinched inside as an image of Logan flying around Scotland doing all the student things flashed in front of her eyes.

Logan flicked his head. 'What about you? Where did you do your degree? What was it in again? Sorry, you did say when you came up for dinner but it's completely gone out of my head.'

'English.'

'And where was it you went again? Mind like a sieve, or maybe you didn't say.'

'I didn't go anywhere.'

Logan appeared keen to hear more, at the same time as looking confused. 'Pardon. I don't get you. You didn't go anywhere?'

'I did it online.'

'Oh, right, okay. Any reason for that in particular?'

'It, err, well you know...'

'Were you overseas or something? Combining it with travelling the world?'

'Umm, no, not quite like that.'

'How was it doing it online? Did you still manage to do all the student things? I had a riot up there. Absolute riot. Those were the days, eh? Nothing to worry about in those days, was there? I was so poor in those days.'

Oh, dear Henry-Hicks. Your game plan is failing.

Cally's eyes rolled so far back in her head she was looking into the rear of her skull. Henry-Hicks had the luxury of being *able* to be poor. He knew *nothing*. She went to flick the switch in the back of her throat to its "I'm Okay" position. It would notch her voice up a little bit and slot nicely together with a happy look she would put on her face. She'd blink a little bit faster, too and then she'd start to lie. Easy enough, she'd done it enough times before. Something, though, made her stop herself from doing it. Instead, she went for the jugular. My goodness, she was actually going to tell the truth. The world stopped turning for a millisecond. 'Yeah, not great, actually. It wasn't the best time for me.'

Logan looked a bit taken aback at both her words and her very obvious change in body language. 'Oh dear. Why was that then?'

Cally inhaled. Logan was nice, but he had *no* idea. Not a clue. Not even an inkling about a life less fortunate than his had clearly been. She'd never really told anyone about how she'd been a carer all her life. Eloise knew some of it, but not the down-and-dirty nitty gritty of what it had really been like. Yeah, people knew she'd looked after her grandma, but no one had known about how she'd mostly done the same for her mum because of her mum's debilitating mental health problems and so then, in turn, her half-brother. While her mum had solved her mental health crises with various things from drink to counselling, Cally had cared for herself and then her brother from around the age she'd first been able to think. Basically, she'd been caring since the day dot. It hadn't got much better since. If she was truly honest, which she mostly *never* was, she'd been on what felt like an uphill struggle since she'd been able to walk and talk. Her mum passing away and her grandma getting sick had sealed the deal. Cally took a deep breath in. She couldn't believe what was coming out of her mouth. 'Look, Logan, I err, look, I might as well come clean right from the start here. I don't know why, but it feels important.'

'Oh, right, sounds a bit terrifying. Are you a serial killer?' Logan joked. 'Should I back away now? Do I need to run fast?'

Wrong move Henry-Hicks.

Cally didn't laugh. 'I haven't had the sort of life you have had, to be quite honest.'

'The life I've had? Sorry?'

'I think it could be a sticking point.'

Logan leant forward. 'I have no idea what you're talking about. What does that mean? What sort of a life have I had? Sticking point?'

Cally went to backpedal and fluff over it and had second thoughts. For once in her life, she was going to say how she felt and what had happened to her. No jollies around university towns for Cally de Pfeffer. Student poor? A world for other people who hadn't a scooby doo about a life like hers. Pah.

'I know I said I cared for my grandma, but it wasn't just her.

My mum had very bad mental health episodes, and well, I've always done everything for myself all my life. When I wanted to go to uni, there wasn't any money because Mum was really bad at that stage so I did it online. I was really, really lucky because I got a partially funded bursary via a charity who were involved with my mum. I don't think that exists anymore. It was pretty hard going trying to do that and work and care. I used to work through the night sometimes...'

'I'm sorry. I see. I think.'

'I haven't had the sort of life where I could shoot off and go to uni for fun. There was no floating around in balloons for the afternoon in my life.' Cally wrinkled her nose at how bitter she sounded. For once, she didn't care.

Logan swore. 'Sorry, I just rambled on for ages, dominating the conversation about how amazing it was at St. Andrews. What an idiot. I should have picked up on your body language. I should have realised.'

'No, no. All good. You couldn't have known.'

'No, it sounds awful. I should have made myself aware.'

Cally went to say it didn't matter and then started to blurt out loads more. Loads and loads more. She felt as if she was sitting on the top of a train which was racing along. As the train zoomed, she chucked off bits of emotional baggage she'd never shared with anyone before: about her half-brother, about her grandma's last few years, about dealing with solicitors, about the debts on her grandma's house, about the funeral, about bed hoists and prescriptions. Off it flew from the train, flying out in one big long jumble of laden tumbling words.

Logan didn't say much. 'Wow, that's not pleasant. I don't know what to say apart from I'm sorry.'

'I know.'

'So, how did you end up in Lovely if your grandma's place wasn't here?'

The train continued to trundle on. 'I got a job at the chemist.

There's a very long story about how I got that, but it suited me because it was flexible with my other job. Birdie's family has a lot of shops and one of the ones near where my grandma lived knew me because I always went there to pick up her scripts. They put me in touch with Birdie. It worked because we got on right away.'

'Right.'

'From the word go, I wanted to live here, but, obviously, I couldn't afford to.' As soon as the word "obviously" was out of Cally's mouth it was clear that things were not obvious to Logan. He wouldn't know things such as how much it might cost to rent a place in Lovely. He didn't have a clue. At least she assumed he didn't.

'So, how did you get the flat?'

Cally again went to tell a half-truth and then found herself explaining what had really happened. 'I was on the brink of being homeless.'

Logan looked horrified. 'What? No way! How? What do you mean?'

Cally sighed. She was telling Logan, this stupidly attractive man, all the crappy, ugly things about her life. The things about who and what she really was. She might as well give up on the relationship now. He would run a country mile. 'You know when people say they can't understand how people become homeless? Well, that was actually me. I took my eye off the ball. The rent kept on going up and it just snowballed from there.' Cally shuddered. 'I wasn't far away from it. I mean, it would have worked out in the end, I guess. I have some money in a trust I could have used in an emergency.'

'So, the flat?'

'It's Birdie's from the chemist. She helped me out.'

Logan leaned back in his chair. He looked both surprised and concerned. 'Blimey, Blackcurrant. I had no idea you'd been through so much. I feel like a right idiot, going on about my cushy uni days when you were dealing with all that.'

Right answer Henry-Hicks.

Cally shook her head. 'Don't be daft. How could you have known? It's not exactly something I advertise about myself. I can't believe I just blurted all that out to you, actually. You're probably going to run a mile now. I don't know, though, it needed to be said.'

'Nup, not going to run a mile.'

'Yeah, I've had a few ups and downs. All good, though.' The switch flicked. 'I'm fine.'

'No. Not good,' Logan insisted, 'I'm sorry you had to go through all that alone. It must have been incredibly tough. Not good and not fine. Awful.'

Ding dong, correct answer again from Henry-Hicks. He was doing well.

Cally felt a shiver go down her spine. 'It was,' she admitted, her voice rough. 'I got through it. I didn't have much choice, really. It was either sink or swim.'

'You're a lot stronger than you give yourself credit for. Most people would have crumbled under that kind of pressure.'

Cally sort of shuddered at the praise but belittled it. 'I just did what I had to do. Anyone would have done the same in my shoes.'

'I'm not so sure about that. You should be proud of yourself.'

'Nah.'

'I'm just calling it as I see it.'

'Thanks.'

Logan broke the tension with a joke. 'I mean, I already fancied you a lot. It just tripled.'

Henry-Hicks reached the top of the leaderboard.

'Right back at you.'

Logan grinned. 'So, tell me more about this job at the chemist. How did that come about?'

'It's a bit of a funny story, actually. I was picking up my grandma's prescriptions one day, and I got to chatting with the pharmacist. Lovely woman, been working there for donkey's years.'

Logan nodded.

'Anyway, we got to talking about my situation and how I was struggling to find work that would fit around my caring responsibilities. And out of the blue, she told me about Birdie.'

'That's quite a stroke of luck.'

'Turns out, as I said, that chemist is one of Birdie's family's other businesses. She put in a good word for me, and the next thing I knew, I was in the back of the Lovely Bay chemist, accompanied by the delights of the Shipping Forecast. She's been really good to me.'

'Sounds like fate intervened.'

Cally agreed. 'All I know is that that job was a lifeline. It gave me the flexibility I needed to be there for my grandma and still earn a living. I'll always be grateful for that.'

'You were lucky to have her in your corner.'

'Birdie has gone above and beyond for me. First with the job and now with the flat. I don't know how I'll ever repay her kindness.'

'Something tells me she doesn't expect you to,' Logan replied. 'From what I've heard, that's just the kind of person Birdie is.'

'She's one in a million, that's for sure.'

Cally couldn't believe she'd told Logan the actual no-fluff truth about her circumstances. She'd shared parts of herself she usually kept well hidden away. She'd let down her guard and simply been herself. It one-third thrilled her and two-thirds (six hundred) terrified her. After so many years of keeping people at arm's length and never letting anyone get too close, she totally just opened up and put it out there. She couldn't quite believe it herself that she might quite like to let Logan in and see her as she really was. Allow him to get to know her without the switch in place. 'Anyway, enough about me and all that. Sort of boring and depressing.'

'No, thanks for sharing. It's made me see you differently. Better. Much better.'

'Flatterer.'

'Guilty as charged. But I mean it. I'm glad you told me that stuff.'

Henry-Hicks was flying out in the lead.

'Me too.'

Logan glanced at his watch, blowing out a low whistle. 'Blimey, is that the time? I hadn't realised how long we've been nattering on.'

The bistro had emptied out around them, and only a few stragglers remained as the staff began their closing routine.

'I suppose we should let them shut up shop,' Cally said reluctantly, not wanting the evening to end.

Ten or so minutes later, they'd settled the bill and gathered their things. As they stepped out into the street, Logan slipped his hand into Cally's and they strolled along in the direction of Cally's flat.

'Beautiful evening.' Cally noted. 'Look at the stars.'

'A nice end to a very nice day.'

Cally hoped it wasn't the end of the day. Since the balloon had landed she'd been scheming how she could extend it. How she could fly again but in a very different way. She wanted the day to go on forever, right through late into the night. Her dreams were about to come true.

34

Cally had fully committed to spending the morning after the date with a huge lie-in, schlepping around in her pyjamas and drinking lots and lots of tea or hot blackcurrant if the date had not gone well. She'd lined everything up perfectly before the date in preparation; she'd changed her chat shift to later so she wouldn't have to get up, she'd put clean (and ironed) linen on the bed, bought croissants ready to be warmed, and had not one but two boxes of truffles from the chocolate shop just in case she'd needed their healing post-date-blues properties. Eloise was also lined up to come around for dinner that evening for a full-on post-date debrief.

She hadn't needed to be healed and she definitely didn't have any sort of blues whatsoever. She *had* stayed in bed for ages, drunk lots of tea and stuffed croissants, all the while reliving what had happened after she and Logan had strolled back home to her flat. The ironed sheets had been put to good use and not just by Cally. The end of the night had been nothing other than brilliant, glorious, amazing. Oh how she had flown. She'd wanted just one nice day for a long time. Boy, did our Cally get it. Not only had she received a nice day, it had gone on into the early hours of the morning.

Henry-Hicks had been on fire.

After finally getting up and having a shower, she'd spent a few hours tidying and cleaning the flat in preparation for Eloise coming to the flat for dinner for the first time. Cally wanted everything to be just right. She'd vacuumed the floor and mopped with Dettol, added a few extra fairy lights around the top of the mantelpiece, and dusted every single inch of space everywhere she could. Candles were ready to be lit, cushions were plumped, and she had her fingers crossed that the weather was going to be warm enough for them to sit out on the balcony so that Eloise would get the full scope of how amazing it was to be up on the top of the deli looking out over Lovely Bay.

Putting a little pot onto the hob, she tapped the Notes app on her phone and navigated to the chowder recipe forwarded to her by Nina. Nina had given Cally her version of chowder, telling her that it was not only tasty but also simple and easy to make. Nina had joked and laughed and told Cally to guard the recipe with her life as she had taken bits of it from seeing what went on in Birdie's version at the back of the deli. Nina reckoned that the secret was fresh fish from the stall on the harbour. Cally had followed instructions, strolled over and bought herself the requisite fish mix, and was now set to go.

She scanned Nina's notes and took in the section where Nina had twice underlined that proper butter and various fresh herbs were what sealed the deal. As luck would have it, they were the same herbs Cally had bought as plants from B&Q and were now taking pride of place in little pots on the balcony. She went outside, snipped rosemary and parsley, then went back in and dropped what she thought was a rather large dollop of butter into the pan. It sizzled and melted, she scooped in a chopped-up onion and, unsure about whether or not it was too much garlic, plonked it in anyway and hoped for the best. After adding the rest of Nina's ingredients, the little flat smelt of delicious home cooked things. She chuckled to herself at the fact that she'd successfully made a chowder; before she knew it, she would be calling herself a bona fide Lovely. She might even get a chance to wear one of the famous Lovely coats if she was lucky. Life really was on the up.

∽

Later on that afternoon, Cally had had a lovely bath, conditioned her skin with a luxurious body cream, sprayed herself with perfume, and blow-dried her hair. She put on her usual outfit of short skirt, ballet flats, and a shirt and pottered around lighting candles and foofing with the flat to make it welcoming. She added an embroidered white tablecloth on the little dining table, placed two candles on it, and laughed to herself as she took a chilled glass bottle out of the fridge, stuffed in loads of fresh herbs, added a generous amount of vodka, some blackcurrant cordial, and sloshed in lemonade.

'Anyone for a blackcurrant cordial?' she said to herself. She knew that Eloise would roll her eyes at the fact that she had made the cocktail Logan had presented her with but she loved it at the same time.

The whole time she'd been preparing for Eloise she'd been reliving the day with Logan. By the time she'd gone down to let Eloise in and the pair of them had climbed the steep stairs she'd barely been able to contain herself with the details about the night before.

As they stepped into the flat, Eloise got in first as her eyes swept around the sitting room. Eloise swore. 'Cal! It's amazing in here. What a difference.'

Cally looked around. 'Is it? Yes, I suppose it is from when you last saw it.'

'You've come on in leaps and bounds. I thought you said you've been working all the time.'

'I have. I just did it in spurts here and there. I painted one wall at a time. It's hardly a large area to have to deal with.'

'What even is that wall colour? Wow, it looks fantastic!'

Cally shook her head, 'I don't actually know the name of it. It was just castoff paint from the deli. I just slapped it on and hoped for the best.'

'Not bad for a hand me down. Gosh, it all looks fabulous. Well done you.'

'I didn't pay a penny for anything really, only the sofa and that was from Marketplace. I found loads of things in the charity shop…' Cally trailed off. 'I just cobbled it all together, really.'

'You've outdone yourself.'

As the two of them stood there, Cally saw the flat with different eyes. It did look *very* different from the first day she'd walked in with Birdie. The space had been transformed from a dusty, cluttered area into a cosy little spot with a gorgeous view. The grubby walls, now painted in a soft white hue, made the whole area feel light and airy. The sea breeze helped – it wafted through the open door, making everything feel better. The vibe was cosy and calm from the sofa with its pile of assorted pillows, to little stacks of books here and there, to a vase of fresh flowers, and a scattering of seashells displayed on a little wicker tray.

Eloise ran her hand along the back of the sofa. 'It's great. Really sort of casual and coastal. I half expect a woman clad in white linen and bare feet with a side plait scooped over her shoulder to come waltzing out of the bedroom any second now.'

Cally laughed. 'Well, I don't know about that. But I have to admit, I'm pretty chuffed with how it's all come together. It beats that last hell hole I was in.'

Eloise followed Cally to the kitchen where the stock pot

bubbled on the hob with the chowder and all Cally's decorative touches were on show. 'I can't believe you found all of this at the charity shop. You've got a real eye for treasure hunting.'

Cally smiled to herself. She *was* good at charity shop hunting because it had always been a case of having to be. 'It's amazing what people give away, isn't it? One man's junk and all that.'

'Yeah. I never seem to find anything nice.'

Cally didn't say anything. Eloise had had the luxury of never *having* to find anything in charity shops. She didn't need to acknowledge that and so opened the fridge and took out the bottle of blackcurrant cocktail she'd made that afternoon. She gave it a shake and laughed. 'Fancy a tipple?'

'What in the world?'

'I know. It's the one Logan made me. Remember I told you about it?'

'Yep. Ooh, what are we celebrating? How fabulously the date went yesterday?'

'You could say that, but no, no occasion, really. Just thought it would be nice to have you here now that the flat has come together. And to catch up properly, of course.'

She handed Eloise a glass. Eloise raised it. 'To new beginnings and old friends.

Wow, this is delicious. So how was the date? Where'd you go?'

Cally raised her eyebrows. 'You'll never guess. It almost doesn't feel real now.'

'Ooh. I like the sound of this. Spill all the tea.'

Cally slipped out her phone as they walked into the sitting room. 'I'll show you.'

Eloise sat down, tucked her feet up under her, cradling her drink in both hands. 'I want to hear all about this date. Don't leave out a single detail.'

'I don't know what to say other than that it was perfect. Better than perfect.' Cally tapped on her phone screen and then turned it around to show Eloise a picture of the hot air balloon.

Eloise leaned forward and squinted. 'Sorry. What?'

'That was the first part of the date.'

'Blimey! Did you actually go up in that?'

'Yes!'

'Goodness. He's good.' Eloise nodded and giggled.

'It was dreamy. Honestly, you have to do a balloon ride. Yeah, so that was good and then it just got better.'

'I need specifics. Where did it end? Did he kiss you goodnight?'

Cally laughed. 'We went to that little bistro with the chowder where I eavesdropped.'

Eloise shook her head. 'I can't believe you went on a balloon ride on your first date.'

'Technically, our second date, but yeah, I know, right?'

'He's got it bad to have done that right out of the gate.'

'I hope so. I just really like him.'

'Cal! You never say that.'

'I know. I even told him stuff.'

'Like what?'

'About mum.'

Eloise let her chin drop and she blinked multiple times. 'That's *massive*.'

'I know.'

'What, you didn't do the voice thing all the time?'

Cally frowned. 'The what thing?'

'The voice thing you do you think no one knows about.'

'I didn't realise…'

'Come on. I'm your best friend. You don't think I know when you're pretending that you're okay when you're so very much not? You don't think I haven't heard you lie to people? Yeah, right. When you pitch your voice a bit higher and widen your eyes and do that thing with your head.'

'Right, I thought...'

'So, anyway, you didn't *do* that. You actually told him some of the truth. That is *monumental*. I'm actually a bit flabbergasted.'

Cally decided not to pursue the rest of the thing about the voice. 'I told him loads of stuff. I am so happy.'

'You're happy? I'm happy too!'

'It's a bit surprising after everything I told him that he didn't run for the hills.'

'No way. You deserve this. More than anyone I know. I have a feeling this is just the beginning.'

'I really, really hope so.'

'Don't think you're going to leave it there and not give me the juicy stuff. Did you invite him up for a nightcap?'

'I did.'

'What sort of nightcap was it?'

Cally nearly choked on her cocktail. 'Ha. I cannot possibly divulge that. It may have involved ironed sheets.'

Eloise leant forward and squealed. 'I knew it!'

'I can't believe I'm talking about this with you. It's so surreal.'

Eloise flopped back against the cushions. 'It is. I mean, look at you, Cal. Look at this place. You've come so far in such a short time.'

Cally glanced around. Eloise was right – it was a far cry from the dingy, cramped house on the estate she'd had to leave. She felt tears prick. Eloise scooted closer and put an arm around Cally's shoulders. 'You okay?'

Cally laughed. 'Happy tears. I just can't believe this is my life now, you know? I keep waiting to wake up and find out it's all been a dream or for my luck to change or something. One minute I was viewing a hovel of a hotel and now I am on the up.'

'It's not luck and it won't change.'

'I'm not so sure.'

'No, not having that. You've worked tooth and nail to get

here. You deserve every bit of happiness that comes your way. Don't you forget it.'

'You make out as if I've climbed mountains or something.'

'No, you did more. You cared for everyone else but you Cal.'

'Thanks for noticing.'

'It's my job as Chief Best Friend.'

Cally laughed. 'Thank goodness I have one.'

As Eloise continued to fire off questions about Logan and the date, Cally felt happier, more relaxed and more comfortable than she had possibly ever felt. Everything felt right. She had a funny little feeling that she was exactly where she was meant to be; in a little flat overlooking the third smallest town in the country sipping blackcurrant cocktails with her best friend talking about the man who'd been in her bed. All. Night. Long. And what had been one very nice day. She hoped that things were only going to get better.

35

A good few months had gone by since what Cally had come to refer to as Balloon Day. Since then, there had been lots and lots and *lots* of nice days. To be frank, it was very simple; she was loving the thing with Logan. In fact, she was so into it she couldn't quite see the wood for the trees. She just waded around up to her eyes in Logan and doing nice things. Henry-Hicks had been on form and then some. If he had indeed been partaking in playing any kind of game, he'd won hands down. She'd work with that.

Not only had Logan been playing well he'd been at the top of his game, too. He'd whirled her and twirled her, wined her and dined her, and ticked every box six times over. Cally and Logan were most definitely an item. Or at least that's what Cally liked to tell herself.

Despite initial inklings that Henry-Hicks was out of her league, Cally had actually turned that on its head. As he'd wined and dined she'd told herself on repeat that actually *she* was the one who was premier league. Her little attitude change had worked wonders and Henry-Hicks had upped the ante. In turn, Cally had experienced how those with ancestral homes and money under their belt did dating. They did not disappoint in any shape or form.

It had to be said that Cally was living it up with Logan and she had loved every little aspect of it. There had simply been *nothing* to worry about on her part. He'd taken the reins and she had sat back and enjoyed the ride. They'd been on days out and had lots of dinners at the manor. There had been an occasion on the bench where she'd seen stars, and not the ones in the sky, and he'd become quite the clandestine visitor to the little flat overlooking Lovely.

The best thing about it had been that Cally had maxed out at being chased and treated and simply being *loved*. It was almost as if Logan had somehow clocked, after she'd blurted out the grimness of her upbringing, that she needed someone to care *for* and *about* her. He had come along, swooped on in, taken her by the scruff of the neck and smoothed out all her stressy bits. He'd turn up out of the blue with a bag of food and cook her dinner, he'd paid for her to go on a spa day all by herself, he'd run her baths with fancy-pants oils, undone the knots in her neck after a day on the customer service chatbot and one day when she'd done a double shift at the chemist to help get orders out for Birdie she'd come home to a top to bottom cleaned flat complete with Diptyque candles lit on the side and bleach down the loo. Was Henry-Hicks, in fact, too good to be true? At this particular stage of the game, Cally de Pfeffer didn't really care.

It was early evening, the sun was beginning to set and Cally and Logan were on their way to a chowder evening. Hand in hand with him as they walked past the railway station and over St Lovely green, Cally couldn't quite wrap her head around the fact that she was in a relationship at all, let alone with Logan. Things like easy relationships just simply didn't ever happen to her. It had been the happy, loved girls at school who'd had the relationships. The ones with the trendy bags, good hair, mums who cared, lashes, dads with jobs and all the right gear who had bagged the what she had thought were nice boys. Cally hadn't ever been one of those girls. Not that she'd *wanted* to be, but she'd never had the chance. Now, she felt as if she was one of those girls. A happy, happy girl, and it felt so good, good, good.

'Where are we going, then?' Logan asked.

Cally laughed. 'Don't you know that you're not allowed to know that? I thought you were the one who knew about how Lovely works.'

'Ha, I thought I'd catch you out. Anyway, us lot at the manor are barely ever allowed to go to these things. That time I saw you when you were with Nancy and Nina was via scrounged tickets. They think we're too up ourselves.'

'Have to agree. You are.'

'Very funny.'

'I like it, though.'

'Good. Do you have a password?'

Cally nodded. 'I certainly do.'

'How come? I thought you hadn't been initiated into the clan yet?'

'I'm in because of my association with Birdie and Nancy.'

'Are you in the elusive WhatsApp group then?'

Cally giggled. 'I cannot possibly divulge any information to anyone in the Henry-Hicks family.'

Logan laughed. 'Too funny.'

A few minutes later, they approached Lovely lighthouse. Cally whipped out her phone and looked down. 'Here we go. Around the back of the old hall.'

As they walked around, the place was quiet. Logan squinted at the lighthouse, 'Are you sure it's in the hall? The whole place feels as if it's deserted.'

'Maybe we just go in this way. It says not to go near the front door on these instructions. Wonder why?'

As they rounded the corner of the old hall, the sound of their footsteps echoed in the evening air. The lighthouse building

ONE NICE DAY IN LOVELY BAY

itself loomed above them, its gleaming white façade glinting in the fading light. Cally double-checked her phone, squinting at the cryptic instructions. 'It definitely says to go around back,' she confirmed. 'And to knock three times on the blue door.'

Logan laughed. 'You're joking? Very cloak and dagger. I feel like we're in a spy movie.'

'You'd better brush up on your covert ops skills then, Henry-Hicks. Wouldn't want to blow our cover.'

They approached the rear of the hall as gravel crunched underneath their feet. A heavy wooden door painted in a weathered old sea blue and pockmarked by the elements, with sun bleached paint peeling here and there was set into a wall. Cally glanced at Logan, giggled, raised her fist and knocked three times. She whispered, 'This is ridiculous. I kind of love it, though. It's so weird and very Lovely.'

For a long moment, nothing happened. Cally was just about to knock again when the door swung open abruptly. Cally whisper-squealed at a familiar figure silhouetted in the dim light. 'Nance!'

'Password?' Nancy demanded.

Cally kept her voice low, 'Third smallest.'

Nancy's face split into a grin. She stepped aside to usher them in. 'Welcome, welcome! Come on in, you two. You're in for a right treat tonight, even if I do say so myself.'

As they walked in, Cally felt as if she'd stepped into another world. The hallway was lit by flickering lanterns and somewhere in the distance, the faint strains of old-fashioned French Piaf-style music floated in the air.

'Stunning.' Cally gushed.

Nancy laughed. 'Consider yourselves very lucky. The seats on this one were limited.' She winked at Logan. 'We even have one of your manor lot slumming it with us commoners this evening. Gold. That's going in the town ledger.'

Logan chuckled as he placed his hand on the small of Cally's back. He played along with the banter. Cally swooned. 'I consider myself well and truly honoured.'

Nancy fired back. 'You'd better be on your best behaviour, Hicks.'

'Don't you worry.'

Cally loved how Logan just seemed to fit into her world. Despite their vastly different backgrounds, he could go anywhere. If anything, *she* was the problem. He just sucked it up and got on with it. Cally loved that. He was teaching her so many things, many of which she spent too much time over-thinking.

As they rounded a corner, Nancy came to a stop in front of a spiral staircase twisting up into the dimness above. 'This is it. Up you go. Watch your step, it's a bit of a climb. But trust me, it's worth it. Remember Neens, though, our Cal? That night was one to remember. We don't want anyone giving birth up there this evening. My nerves couldn't take that again.'

Getting closer to the top, the music grew louder and they could hear conversation and the sound of dishes clattering. The circular room mesmerised as they emerged at the very top of the lighthouse. Cally gasped and her eyes widened as she took in the scene before her. The space had been transformed into a cosy, intimate speakeasy with low lights and the view doing all the talking. A makeshift bar had been set up along one curved wall, its surface crowded with glass jugs and glasses. Candles flickered on every surface, but mostly, it was the Lovely Bay sunset through the glass that was the main attraction. The view took Cally's breath away. The entire outer wall of the room was made up of panorama windows showcasing the Lovely Bay coastline. The sun was just beginning to fully set over the water, painting the sky in streaks of orange and pink. The sky a canvas of colours with splashes of orange and deep pink blending with little ripples here and there of lavender, periwinkle, and gold. An ethereal light swirled around the room as people stood looking out the windows. Cally traced the colours of the sunset with her eyes as they gradually deepened and the sun dipped down low. For a minute or two, a burnt sienna set the sky ablaze, dots of pink deepened to magenta and the colours shifted and blended across the horizon.

Logan smiled. 'The sunset has outdone itself this evening. Who needs anything else?'

Cally had been around Lovely Bay for a while and thought she'd seen most of what it had to offer, but she'd never witnessed the colours in the sky quite as they were. 'I certainly don't!'

As they stood marvelling at the view, Nancy bustled over. 'It's do it yourself on drinks over there. Chowder will be up in a while. Seats are labelled.'

Logan went over and got two glasses of drink. He held his up after he'd passed Cally one. He bantered. 'To new friends and old haunts.'

Cally clinked her glass to his, took a sip, and gazed around the room. She noticed the woman from the post office and recognised a few customers from the chemist. She waved to Millie from the chocolate shop and saluted Birdie, who was on the far side talking to Colin from the riverboat. She felt a bit emotional as she took in the motley crew of Lovelies standing chatting all around her. All of them a mishmash of ages, backgrounds, personalities, and circumstances, but everyone chatting, laughing and simply being part of a community. As far as Cally was concerned it was really nice to be Lovely-ed.

As if sensing her thoughts, Logan slipped an arm around her waist. 'How nice is it to be included in this? Having fun?'

'If I'm truly honest, more than I ever thought possible.'

'Same. Nowhere else I'd rather be. Hope you know that.'

Well played Henry-Hicks.

'Ditto.'

Despite what he'd said, however, Cally didn't absolutely

know how Logan really felt and whether or not it was true. How could she really? It didn't *feel* real to her. From her side of the fence, it felt as if she was counting her lucky stars one after the other. As if she'd been plucked from her old world and dropped into another one entirely. Sure, Logan had twirled and whirled her until the cows had come home, but he hadn't actually sealed the deal with the three little words. Would they indeed be part of this strange new world?

Mostly, the previous few months had been a lovely, long lot of happy confusion for our Cally. To her, it was as if her heart had always been a bit of a puzzle. She'd sometimes wondered if there was actually something wrong with her and her heart. Like *it* and *she* had been damaged or something, which, if you analysed it, wasn't that far from the truth. The thing that had happened since the bag episode on the riverboat was that Henry-Hicks may have just gone and nudged the healing of her heart. As if he'd come along and fitted the last jigsaw piece precisely into the gap right in the centre. There was no way on earth she was going to tell him that, though. She was still enjoying the chase far too much. Let him want a little bit, eh? Who needed the last puzzle piece when one was still so very much enjoying working out how it all went together?

After the chowder and, in Cally's case, possibly a few too many drinks, most people had trotted off home. Nancy made the rounds with a tray of tea for the last few stragglers. Cally and Logan took a mug each and then stood watching the now inky black water of the bay and the glints of silver from the moon dancing on the top.

'I could stay here forever. What a little bubble of perfection.' Cally noted as she gazed out.

'Yep. Really nice. What a fab night.' Logan lowered his voice. 'The best bit was that funny password thing and me being allowed in.'

'Agreed.'

'And then the company.'

'Oh yeah?' Cally raised her eyebrows in question.

'Yeah. There's this gorgeous girl I know. She likes her fair share of blackcurrant as it goes. I'm partial to her short skirts and when I go out with her, we always have such a laugh.'

'That so? I like the sound of her.' Cally giggled as she sipped her tea.

'Totally besotted myself. It's quite disgusting, really.'

Cally laughed, but inside, she was not laughing. Oh, no, no, no, she certainly wasn't laughing in there. Inside, she was sort of a cross between wailing in happiness and full-on snotty-nosed crying because even though he might have been jesting she *was* not. She was more than totally besotted.

She felt herself flick the switch in her throat. However, instead of using it to cover things up and say that she was "fine", she just used it because she was *actually* happy. It felt strange and nice and so good to just use it for that. No lies. 'Well, I happen to know she's just as gone on you, Henry-Hicks. Has been from the start, even if she didn't want to admit it at the time.'

Henry-Hicks squeezed her hand as he tapped the missing puzzle piece nicely into place. As he did so, Cally de Pfeffer stood stock still as she felt a hundred thousand tiny clicks all over her body. On her skin, in her legs, inside her brain, deep down in her stomach, right at the ends of her hair, every little fibre in every little dark, hidden place. She loved the clicks, absolutely a million per cent adored them. They were so much more than good. She was absolutely blooming terrified to admit that they were everything. Not because Henry-Hicks had fixed things or treated her or that she needed a man. So not that. She'd never needed anyone, not on the outside anyway. It wasn't that. It was because the clicks had made Cally realise that she had backed herself and man did it feel good.

36

Morning sunlight filtered through the bamboo blind and gauze curtains of Cally's bedroom. Little blobs of soft, dappled light made a pattern across the rumpled bedsheets. Unlike in her previous existence when she'd often been jolted awake to sort out someone else's problems, she stirred slowly and luxuriated in the fact that for the early part of the morning, she had nowhere to go and nothing to do. Glorious. She smiled at the memories of the previous night's speakeasy at the lighthouse.

Rolling over, she reached her hand out to be met by an empty space. It seemed Henry-Hicks had gone. Frowning, she sat up, blinking the sleep from her eyes and squinting at the bed. She couldn't remember whether or not Logan had said he had to go and do the horses at the manor. Obviously, he'd done just that.

She revelled in a lovely long stretch, swung her legs over the side of the bed and padded to the kitchen to put the kettle on. As she waited for the water to boil, she leaned against the worktop to see a folded slip of paper on the table in front of her. Her name was scrawled across the front in Logan's slanting handwriting. Cally picked it up and frowned as she unfolded the note.

Morning.
Didn't want to wake you - you looked too peaceful. Had to dash off to a thing at the manor. I couldn't remember if I'd told you that or not. Anyway, I'll be back. Want to go out later - dinner or something? Only if you're up for it.
Wear something nice. I'm feeling fancy. I'll text you anyway.
HH.

Cally beamed. She was well up for a nice outing. To be frank, she was getting quite used to nice dinners and nice things all around. The activities of the Henry-Hicks of the world were not bad ones. Nice things and activities were the least of it, though. What was happening to her was way more than money and niceties. It was much simpler than that. Not that she'd told him, but she loved Logan. It was so obvious to her that it frightened her a little bit. The way he had fit so seamlessly into her life, as if he'd always been there, boggled her mind and pickled her heart.

She reread his note and wondered what "feeling fancy" meant. Perhaps it was time to crack out one of her two dresses? She winced a little bit. If they were going somewhere hoity-toity, which didn't faze her as much as it had when she'd first gone out with him, she had some preparation to do. She wanted to up the ante a little bit. She finally felt she was worth it. Cared enough about herself.

As she sipped her tea, she mentally rifled through her non-existent wardrobe, considering and discarding options. She thought about a dress she'd bought on a whim in the charity shop along the road. She'd been in there buying things for the flat and had seen it in the window. Something about it had caught her eye which considering she rarely, if ever, swayed from her skirt and tights uniform, had been a thing in itself. The dress was a plain black shift dress with a slash neck at the front and a deep scoop at the back. She'd never ever worn anything like it before in her life. Not had the opportunity. Perhaps that had just arrived.

She finished her tea and headed for the shower, mentally going through options of things she could wear if Logan was "feeling fancy" as he had put it. She didn't have too much time to worry about it, though. She'd been lucky enough to have the easy, slow start, but she had a full day ahead of her - a shift at the chemist's, a meeting with Nina about a decluttering job, and she was covering for someone on the customer service portal in the afternoon. She also had a mountain of laundry to tackle that had been getting out of hand. Deep life joys in Cally's world.

Nothing could dampen her spirit, though, not even the premise of women complaining about their cashmere scarves. She felt happy, lighter than air, buoyed by just being herself and letting go. As she lathered her hair with shampoo, her mind drifted to the conversation she'd had with Birdie at the speakeasy. They'd been standing by the window looking out at the water.

'You know what?' Birdie had said. 'I've been around the block a time or two. Seen my fair share of stuff. And let me tell you, Logan and how he is with you. It's the real deal. Nice to watch, to be fair.'

Cally had made a funny face. She'd brushed it off at the same time as loving it. 'Don't be silly. How do you know?'

Birdie had nodded sagely. 'Oh, I know. The way he looks at you. That's not something that comes along every day. You hold on to that, my girl. Hold on tight and don't let go. Listen to someone with a bit of experience under her belt.'

Standing under the hot water in the shower, Cally rumbled Birdie's words around her head and hoped that she was right. Maybe Birdie was correct. Cally had felt it, too, in her bones, but wasn't sure if she'd been imagining it or not. As she stepped out of the shower, wrapped herself in a towel and padded back to the bedroom to start getting ready for her day, she let her mind wander about where she'd be going that night. Since the balloon ride date, it had become a thing between Cally and Logan that they went places Cally had no clue about. He'd not said anything, but she'd ascertained that he'd picked up on the fact that she'd not exactly done much or been many places. Logan had seemingly made it his mission to change that and she'd enjoyed the ride. She'd been to more places with him than she'd ever been. He had spent more money than she'd thought possible. All around, he just made her feel special. She couldn't put into words how much she adored it and or him.

As she slipped into her work clothes and grabbed her bag, her phone buzzed with an incoming text.

Logan: *Did u get my msg?*
Cally: *Yes. Thx.*
Logan: *Sound good?*
Cally: *Yes.*
Logan: *Great. Dress up. We're going uptown. I'm looking forward to it. x*

Cally felt a giddy little flip in her chest. She typed quickly as she hurried out the door and down the steep stairs.

Cally: *Me too. Can't wait for tonight.*
Logan: *See you later. Xxx*

~

After loads of problems with drug deliveries in the chemist, coffee with Nina, and a customer complaining that a delivery man had been rude to her dog, Cally closed the lid of her laptop and walked into her bedroom. Tired from her day, she undressed and then went and had a shower.

Half an hour after that, after blow drying her hair and putting on some makeup, she pulled on the black dress with the scoop back and stood in front of the mirror, critically turning this way and that. Scooping her hair up with little clips into an updo, she pulled bits out at the side, decided to let the dress do the work and not add any jewellery and fluffed highlighter across the top of her cheeks. Once she had her shoes on, she wasn't sure what to think about the person in the mirror. The person who had always just worn the same old thing was now in a dress and looked quite nice. This person's hair shone, and unless she was imagining it, there was now a lot of sparkle in her eyes. She liked this person a lot.

After dousing herself in Cloud perfume, tidying up the bedroom and putting a blackcurrant carton in her bag, she heard Logan at the door. She grabbed her bag and walked out into the sitting room as he stepped in. He'd scrubbed up well and by the look on his face, he clearly thought the same thing about her. He raised his eyebrows.

'Flipping heck, Blackcurrant. You look stunning. Absolutely stunning.'

Cally blushed. 'You don't look so bad yourself, Henry-Hicks.'

'Where did you get that dress? You look fantastic!'

Cally giggled and tapped her nose. 'No can tell.'

Logan grinned. 'Ready to paint the town red?'

'I most certainly am.'

Cally smoothed her hands over the silky fabric of her dress and marvelled at how transformed she felt. Not that long before she'd actually seriously considered the fact that she might be homeless and living in a hotel for a bit while she got her act together. The notion of that now seemed strange to her. Not that she was ever going to forget it. She'd remember that feeling in the hotel for the rest of her life. It had rocked her to her core. Squirrelling away money from her three jobs as much

ONE NICE DAY IN LOVELY BAY

as she could was a testament to how bad she'd felt. She would never let herself get into that situation again. It was her mission to be secure. As soon as she had enough to add to the money from her grandma, she'd be getting a mortgage and buying a flat.

Considering her situation when she'd gone to look at the hotel, she would never have imagined herself dolled up for a posh night out on the town with a man like Logan. Yet here she was doing just that. Not only was she dolled up, but she actually felt so radiant and glowing with happiness, it was practically oozing out of her pores.

Logan shook his head as they waited for the train they were on to slow down as it approached its destination. He lowered his voice. 'You look amazing, Blackcurrant. Stunning.'

'You keep saying that.' Cally giggled and held onto the handle as the train rumbled over the last few sleepers and pulled into the platform of an old Victorian London train station. 'Do I?'

'You do.'

With her bag in her hand, she took a few steps closer to the door and stood behind another couple who were just as dressed up and obviously on their way to somewhere nice. Cally ran her eyes up and down the woman and took in everything about her. She admired the woman's beautiful shouting-it-was-oh-so-very-expensive dress and hoped that she looked even half as good. As the train juddered to a stop, the doors opened, and she stepped out onto the platform. She watched the heels of the woman in the nice dress and suddenly got hit by a massive case of comparison-itis. It slap banged her right in the middle of her chest.

Cally attempted to ignore it and looked up at the roof. The station was massive. She'd never been in anything like it before or surrounded by as many bustling people. She felt as if the enormous, ornate roof and gaggle of hustling passengers were swallowing her whole. Busy, accomplished, big job, in the know, fancy people swarmed around her, hurrying to their destinations. She turned her head slightly to her left and stole a look at Logan. Handsome, also accomplished, also with a busy life. She suddenly felt way, way, way out of her depth and so very wrong. Horrid, nagging doubt swarmed her in a huge revolting, nauseating swirl. As if it was going to gobble her whole. Her silly charity shop dress, her sticking-up baby hair piled high in cheap clips, her past their best ballet flats. Everything felt wrong. Everyone else felt right. Doomed.

Logan squeezed her hand. 'All good?'

She switched on the switch. Up went the voice. Let the pretending begin. 'Yep.'

'Looking good to me, Blackcurrant.'

'Where are we going?'

'I told you. Somewhere fancy. You're being treated. Just suck it up and enjoy. I love going out with you. Absolutely love it. Get ready to be spoilt.'

Cally's doubts multiplied by the dozen. She did not feel good as the comparison thief robbed her of her joy and cackled away to itself. She felt stupid and poor and ugly and out of her element. She followed along, staring at the woman from the train's shoes, where a little gold tag hanging on the back of the heel displayed a label. Cally had no idea what the brand was. The gold disc swung back and forth just above the concrete platform. Wherever the shoes were from, Cally knew she wouldn't be able to afford them. 'Thanks.'

Logan picked up on her body language instantly. 'Sorry. Are you not feeling quite the ticket? Bit of motion sickness from the train or something?'

'Nope. I'm fine.'

'You don't seem it.'

'I just...' She frowned. 'The dress and everything. Am I going to be okay? I should have asked you when you arrived. You didn't say what to wear.'

Logan frowned. 'What? Of course, you look okay! Trust me, Blackcurrant. You look fabulous.'

Cally didn't feel fabulous. She felt like the word beginning with 'S' and ending with 'T'. She tried to remember how she'd looked bright and sparkly in the mirror in the flat. As people swarmed and buzzed around her in the manic station on their way to the ticket machines, she swallowed. The woman in the dress and the heels with the little dangly label had taken the wind out of our Cally's sails. Oh, how those sails had drooped. They sagged and flapped around her. Inside, she felt dreadful.

As they stepped out of the station, the street heaved with people hustling this way and that. Cally felt her doubts intensify a trillion-fold. The city pulsed with energy and money and she didn't know what it was but it knocked her for six. She did not pulse. Shrivelled, more like. Everywhere she looked, she saw people who seemed to belong in a world she just wasn't in, never had been, and knew little about.

Logan sensed her tense at the sight of the street. 'It's busy for sure! You okay? We can hop in a taxi if you like.'

As you do. Cally pretended, forced a smile and tried to push down the nagging feeling that she was an imposter. She felt like a fish out of water in her charity shop dress. Not that anyone was looking at her anyway. People were way too important with their big, full, happy lives to be even glancing in her direction. All of it was in her head. All of it was foul. Debilitating. 'Are you sure this is a good idea?'

Logan frowned. 'Yeah, sorry, I thought it would be fine to walk, but it is really busy. Shall I try to hail a cab?'

Cally hadn't meant about walking. She'd spent her life walking. She'd meant was it a good idea that she was there with him. She shook her head in quick little movements and blinked. She had to pull herself together and get a grip or she'd ruin the night. She pretended the street being busy was her problem.

The switch flicked again. 'No, it's fine. I'll just keep hold of your hand.'

About ten minutes later, they turned a corner to see even more people milling around outside a beautiful old theatre. Cally gasped at the building. It was fancy and posh and something out of her league. She wasn't sure what to think. She'd thought she loved being treated, but it had turned on its head. It just felt wrong, as if she wasn't worth it.

Horrible self-doubt swarmed around her. Logan was clearly used to doing things like trotting off to the theatre every day of the week. In his expensive clothes and general all-around well-brought-up confidence, education and all that rigamarole he just took it in his stride. He was simply not fazed at all and in his element. Leading Cally by the hand and without much fuss at all, he strode across the concourse, up the steps, under the theatre sign and into the foyer. Cally looked up at the ceiling, took in the beautiful people in their gorgeous attire, peered at the swirling carpet, and at the glass display cases full of fancy things.

Logan took two programs from a woman cradling a pile of them, paid for two and handed one to Cally. Cally was astonished by how much the programs had cost and flicked through the thick, glossy pages as Logan checked his phone for the tickets. She drank in the sights and sounds going on around her. The grandeur of the Victorian building and its architecture took her breath away. Intricate carvings, large, arched windows, tall, polished columns. Red carpet, velvet ropes, glamour, occasion, elegance. All of it everywhere she looked. Charity shop dress.

An usher in an old-fashioned gold and red suit jacket and white gloves beamed as she greeted guests by an opulent door. Huge chandeliers hanging from an ornately decorated ceiling glowed above and rich, dark wood panelling showed off large mirrors in gilded frames. Plush, crimson velvet drapes framed the windows and doorways. Women were dressed to the nines:

hairdresser hair, strong perfume, filler, heavy dresses, injectables, designer handbags by the dozen, all of the things. Cally hesitated for a moment, insecurities enveloping her. The woman in the jacket by the door smiled warmly. 'Welcome to St Thompson's Theatre. If you head over to the far side, there's not as much of a queue for the bar that way.'

'Thank you,' Logan replied as he rested his hand on the small of Cally's back and guided her through a throng of people queuing for a long, polished bar.

There was no doubt about the fact that Cally de Pfeffer was out of her depth. She felt overawed and underdressed as she watched people mill about chatting animatedly and sipping champagne from delicate flutes.

'Right, drink? What do you fancy? I don't think I'll be able to rustle up a blackcurrant cocktail here.'

'Oh, I don't know. Whatever you're having.'

'What?' Logan wrinkled his nose. 'I'm having a beer. You want a beer?'

'Yeah, I don't care.'

Logan touched Cally's elbow. 'A beer? You never have that. Sorry, are you okay?'

Cally flicked the switch. 'I'm fine. It's a lot to take in.'

'What is?'

Cally gesticulated in front of her and then up at the ornate ceiling. 'All of this.'

Logan sounded surprised. 'Sorry, have you never been to the theatre before? Really?'

Wrong question Henry-Hicks. So very wrong in every way.

'No.'

Logan stumbled a little bit but regained himself well. 'I knew you'd love it. It's a beautiful place, isn't it? I wanted to make this something you'd remember.'

'You've definitely succeeded.'

'Stay right where you are. I'll be back.'

Cally stood in an alcove and people watched. A woman in an emerald dress passed by, her perfume trailing behind her. A man she was sure she recognised from the telly smiled and raised his eyebrows. Cally had to stop herself from turning around to see if he was smiling at someone else. She smiled back. The sound of laughter, clinking glasses and successful people being happy tinkled in the air. Logan came back with two drinks and as they stood and sipped, chatted and observed, Cally felt a teeny bit more comfortable. After a bell went they made their way out of the bar area and in the direction of the main theatre doors. An usher in a red and gold uniform with a little stand-up collar greeted them with a polite nod. 'Good evening. May I see your tickets, please?' He held out a gadget in front of him.

Logan tapped his phone and placed it under the gadget. The usher frowned as he examined the screen. 'Sorry, no, you're at the completely wrong door for those tickets.'

'Oh, right, okay, sorry mate, what door is it?' Logan asked.

The usher put the gadget in his pocket, turned to his colleagues, said something, and indicated for them to follow him. 'I'll escort you up there for those tickets,' he said.

They walked back over the foyer and up a set of majestic stairs. A few minutes later, after a walk over heavy carpet down a wide corridor, the usher opened a small door. 'There you go for the Royal box.'

Cally gulped and flicked at the hem of her dress. Inside were four seats. She faltered, not sure of the protocol. Logan didn't even notice her reaction. He turned to the usher after stepping in. 'Thanks, mate. I would have been lost getting up here.'

'Not a problem. Enjoy the performance. It's drinks to your seat service here. QR code on the panel in front of you. Order via that and someone will be with you in a jiffy.'

'Yeah, yeah, sweet, cheers,' Logan said as the usher turned to leave.

ONE NICE DAY IN LOVELY BAY

Cally didn't know where to look first as she squeezed around the seat and made to sit down. The interior of the theatre was even more stunning than the foyer. Row upon row of plush, red velvet seats stretched out before them facing a grand stage framed by heavy, ornate curtains. Fancy walls adorned with intricate gold leaf detailing, and a grand ceiling painted with a beautiful fresco surrounded them. Cally gaped at enormous crystal chandeliers hanging from above and squinted at the thick gold tassels on the balcony in front of her. She was mesmerised by the seats and theatre below filling up with people dressed to impress and the buzzy anticipation in the air.

Cally smoothed the underside of her dress and sat down. Logan leaned in close to her and whispered, 'I hope you like the show. I've heard it's fantastic. Plus, you look stunning, Blackcurrant. Love being here with you.'

Cally smiled and nodded as her whole being swirled with emotion. 'Hope so.'

As the lights dimmed, everything hushed. Cally loved the anticipation and as the curtain rose she felt as if she'd been transported to another world. She threw all her doubts out the window as Logan leaned over and put his hand on her leg. He'd done well. Despite her initial discomfort she was beginning to have a nice time.

She loved Henry-Hicks. So much.

~

'That was amazing,' Cally whispered.
    Logan smiled, clearly pleased. 'I'm glad you enjoyed it. I knew you would.'
'Thank you.'
'No need to say thank you.'
'I feel like I owe you.'
'What?'

'The tickets and everything.'

'Don't be ridiculous!'

As they made their way out of the theatre, Cally no longer felt quite as overwhelmed – the show had done its job well and taken her away from all that.

Logan nodded over to a pub on a corner. 'Quick one for the road before we head off?'

'Love to.'

Logan took her hand and they found a table near the window, where they watched the world go by as they enjoyed their drinks.

Cally sipped her drink. 'Thank you for tonight.'

'It was really good, wasn't it?'

'Yeah. I loved the costumes and the music. It really took me away. Sort of bewitching or something.'

'Ha. Like you.'

'What?'

Logan laughed. 'You've bewitched me, Cally de Pfeffer.'

Cally heard herself do a funny, tinkly little out-of-character giggle laugh thing. She didn't say anything back. *Let him chase.* Inside, though, she very much knew she'd been caught. So captured. She didn't say anything but made a funny face. A little voice in her head answered him back.

I'm mad about you, Henry-Hicks. I have been more than bewitched.

37

Cally chuckled to herself regarding what was now her commute to work. It involved coming out of her flat, down the stairs, out the back, along the service lane, and into the chemist. If she wanted to go the long way around, she went via the High Street. It was a whole world away from the days when she'd had to walk through the housing estate to the train station and then sit on the train for forty-five-minutes. Now, she strolled a few steps through Lovely. Things had been a lot worse.

She stopped and chatted for a bit to Millie, who was winding down the awning outside the chocolate shop.

Millie beamed. 'Morning, our Cally. How are you? Nice day for it. Bring on the good weather. I'll have my bikini on yet.'

Cally looked up at the blue sky and the sunshine landing in puddles all the way along the High Street. 'I'm good, thanks. Yes, hope it stays nice for the weekend. Ahh, thank goodness for sunshine.'

'I was just listening to the forecast. They're saying it's going to be a warm one. The first of the season. It seems to have been a long time coming this year. We've had every season in a day as usual. Hopefully today will just be sunny!'

'Great. Just what I like to hear.'

'Any plans for the weekend, then?'

'Nope, not if the weather is nice. No plans other than to amble down to the beach, put up my umbrella and stay there all day long.'

Millie chuckled. 'I might have to join you. You're easy to please.'

Cally played along. 'That's what I like to tell myself.'

Millie smiled warmly. 'So, tell me, how are things going with you and Logan? You two seem like quite the item these days.'

Cally glanced down at her feet. She attempted to sound nonchalant. 'It's going well, I suppose. We're just taking things slow, seeing where it goes.'

Millie raised an eyebrow and bantered. 'Taking things slow, eh? That's not what it looked like to me when I bumped into you in the Sailor the other night.'

'Really?'

'I saw the way he was looking at you. I'd say he's smitten.'

'Ha. You think so? We've only been seeing each other for a little while.'

'Trust me, he's got it bad for you. Love it. You two are the talk of the third smallest town in the country.'

That might have been true, but since the theatre date, Cally'd had major doubts about the whole thing and its longevity. How could someone like him and her really be together in the long run? She'd fallen hard for Logan but she wasn't sure how it was going to go. Hearing someone else's view on it made it all the more real. 'Ahh, we'll see.'

Millie grinned. 'Well, I say enjoy it. Young love and all that. You two make a lovely couple. Make the most of it when you're gallivanting around the place with your beau. Birdie said you've been here, there, and everywhere these past few months. Shows, hot air balloons, the lot.'

Cally laughed, shaking her head. 'Yes, I have, for sure.'

'Better than withering away from boredom and doing nothing with your life, eh?'

'It is.' Cally absolutely knew how a withering away life felt.

'But seriously, I'm happy for you, our Cal. It's nice to see. Lovely is working its magic on you. I love it when it happens.'

Cally felt a lump in her throat. She'd moved into the flat in Lovely Bay with not a whole lot of other options on her plate. It wasn't as if she'd been looking for a fresh start as such. She'd not had the luxury of that. She'd been *desperate* to find somewhere to recalibrate and take a breather from holding up the sky. A roof over her head had been the goal, security the end destination. She'd found so much more than that. Somewhere that had softened her landing. Logan was part of it. 'Thanks, yeah, it is.'

'Anytime. Right, I'd better get a move on or we won't have any chocolate today. Can't have that, can we?'

Cally chuckled. 'No, we certainly can't. I'll see you later. Have a good day.'

'You too. Don't work too hard for our Birdie and don't forget to enjoy this sunshine. I might have a little stroll down to the beach at lunch if it carries on at this rate.'

'Good idea, enjoy. See you.'

Cally continued down the High Street towards the chemist, a spring in her step and a smile on her face. Lovely was showing off in the sunshine; the colours of the shop fronts popped, the bunting fluttered, and the lighthouse looked as if it had had a fresh coat of brilliant white paint overnight as it stood out against the blue sky. She thought about the weekend and a whole lazy day on the beach. She was really looking forward to it. It was going to be one nice day.

The Shipping Forecast blared from the back of the chemist as Cally made her way in through the gate down the alley. The back door was open to the fresh air as Cally strolled in, took her bag from her shoulder and hung it on the coat hooks in the corridor. She poked her head around into the pharmacy area where Birdie, in her white pharmacist's tunic, stood looking at a huge pile of white drug boxes piled nearly up to the ceiling alongside the counter. *Biscay Northwest 2 or 3, smooth, fair, good.*

'Morning.' Cally sing-songed. 'Gorgeous day out there.'

Birdie turned around and smiled. 'Morning, our Cally. It is, yes. Thank goodness you're here.'

Cally lifted her chin towards the white boxes. 'Not looking good on that front. What time did they arrive?'

'They didn't arrive on time. Hence, why they are now in here in that state.'

Cally looked at her watch. 'Ouch.'

'I know.'

Cally leant around the door and craned her neck to look in the adjacent room where stacks of cardboard cartons held more deliveries. 'That lot has arrived, at least.'

'Yep, but I don't know how I'm going to get through this.' Birdie swung her arm around the room.

'How about I stay later to do that other lot and start on these?' Cally said, pointing to the white boxes. 'At least if I start going through them, it will save you a bit of time.'

'I wasn't sure if you'd be going out or working later.'

'I'm doing neither. I had it earmarked to get some ironing done.'

'So you can stay late?'

'I can.'

Birdie let out a huge sigh. 'Lifesaver.'

Cally smiled. 'Looks like you are in need of a coffee or tea.'

Birdie nodded. 'I am. You know me too well. You might have to run me an IV straight into my veins. So much for me getting out and enjoying a bit of the weather. Actually, I'll have tea.'

Cally chuckled as she made her way to the tiny kitchen at the back of the chemist. The space was barely big enough for a few people to stand in, but it had become a bit of a ritual for her and Birdie to have a pre-work coffee and moan, nearly always accompanied by Lovely chocolate and the Shipping Forecast.

She filled the kettle, flicked its switch, and then rummaged through the cupboards for their favourite mugs and popped in a couple of tea bags. The kettle clicked, and she poured steaming water over the tea bags, letting them steep for a minute. She added milk and put them on the small table as Birdie walked in.

'Thanks,' Birdie said gratefully, wrapping her hands around a mug. 'I needed this. What a morning already. It's a good job I love this place!'

Cally smiled. 'I know the feeling. It's been a bit of a busy week. I'm looking forward to the weekend.'

Birdie sighed. 'That's an understatement. I don't know what we'd do without you. Thank goodness you can help out later.'

'Happy to help out where I can after all you've done for me.'

'Get away with you.'

'I mean it.'

Birdie flicked her hand in dismissal. 'You're the one doing me the favours.'

Both of them knew it wasn't true, but neither of them said anything else. 'Anyway, what's been going on with you? How's the fair Henry-Hicks?'

Cally hesitated and fidgeted with the handle of her mug. She flicked the voice switch. 'Yeah, fine. Great.'

Birdie picked up on the change instantly, despite Cally thinking she'd hidden how she really felt. 'You sure?'

'Aww, I don't know. Things are going really well between us, but sometimes I feel like we're from two completely different worlds. Do you get what I mean?'

Birdie nodded. 'Hmm. Tricky one. I can understand that. It's not easy being with someone who comes from a different background.'

'Exactly. I mean, he lives in this grand manor house and has a fancy education and all that. And then there's me, living in a tiny flat. I'm not exactly trying to make ends meet these days, but I'm saving and well, you know all that…'

Birdie patted Cally's hand. 'I know it can be tough. But at the end of the day, none of that stuff really matters. What matters is how you *feel* about each other, I guess.'

'I know, I know. It's just hard not to feel a bit intimidated sometimes, you know? Like I'm not good enough for him. No matter how much I talk myself up, it's just the cold hard truth of the matter at the end of the day.'

Birdie deliberated. 'It must be intimidating, but there's no doubt he adores you. I thought that the other night when he came to pick you up. He just loves you, Cal.'

Cally spun at Birdie's words. She felt tears prick at the corners of her eyes. She downplayed it. 'Pah. I don't think we're at that stage yet.'

'Whatever. He's head over heels, and it's not because of where you live or what you do for a living. It's because of who you are. It's as clear as day.'

Cally nodded. 'I guess you're right. I just need to stop overthinking things and enjoy what we have. There have been a few occasions, though, where I've just felt so out of my depth.'

'Like when?'

'In a box at the opera comes to mind.' Cally laughed and rolled her eyes. 'A hot air balloon floating in the sky…'

'Ooh, look at you! Going on fancy dates with your posh boyfriend. You should not be complaining about that!'

'Yeah, tell me about it.'

'Seriously, life's too short to spend it worrying about things you can't change. Just take each day as it comes. Worry about all that stuff in the future another day. For now, enjoy the finer things in life. Grab 'em by the balls.'

Cally grinned. 'I guess I can't argue with that.'

'Nope. Own it.'

Cally drained her tea. 'I suppose I'll mull it over while I tackle those boxes.'

'The power of drug unpacking. Much cheaper than therapy.'

As they shuffled into the pharmacy area accompanied by the Shipping Forecast, Birdie's words rang in Cally's ears. She smiled to herself as she started sorting through the first pile of boxes. Maybe Birdie was right – maybe it was time to stop worrying as much and just enjoy the moment. Life was too short to spend it fretting over things that didn't really matter. She needed to get a grip. But something niggled at the back of her mind.

The rest of the morning passed in a blur of activity as Cally waded one by one through the piles of boxes and got the dispensary back in order. Birdie stood on the other side, preparing scripts and Cally got her head down to get through the backlog, and by lunchtime, the pharmacy section looked much more organised and tidy.

Just after lunch, Birdie was dealing with a pensioner's insulin order problem, and Cally was spraying down the pharmacy counter with disinfectant cleaner when her ears pricked up as the bell on the main door tinkled. She heard a voice she recognised and moved behind a row of overhead cabinets so that she couldn't be seen from the shop floor. Logan's cousin Alastair stood with someone she didn't know as he waited for

Birdie to finish dealing with the pensioner. Alastair chatted away, sounding just as well-spoken as he usually did.

Cally busied herself with the disinfectant, spraying it liberally on the pharmacy counter as she listened to Alastair's conversation drift over from the shop floor. His posh accent carried easily. It grated on her a bit.

'I'm off to the villa in the Maldives next month. Two weeks of pure paradise. Join me if you like.'

His friend chuckled. 'Tempting, very tempting. But I'm afraid I've got loads on. Father's keen on me taking a more active role. I haven't been to the Maldives for ages.'

'Ah, the burdens of responsibility,' Alastair sighed dramatically. 'Well, you'll just have to live vicariously through my Instagram feed then.'

They both laughed. Cally felt a pang of inadequacy, knowing she could never afford to even look in the Maldives direction or sniff its exotic air. The closest she'd come to paradise was a weekend in Rye with Eloise, but that hadn't happened because she'd had to look after her grandma.

As she moved to walk out the back, not wanting to hear anything else, Alastair spotted her. He beamed. 'Hi Cal! How are you? I wondered if you were working today.'

Cally forced a smile. Alastair had done nothing wrong. It wasn't his fault where he was born. He'd always been more than nice to her but he grated on her most of the time. 'Hello. Nice to see you. Lovely weather.'

Alastair's eyes flicked her up and down. 'Likewise. We're popping to the pub for a pint. Has to be done when the weather's so nice.'

'Lucky you.'

'Want to join us?'

'Ah, no, sorry, I've got loads to do.'

'Right, yes. Can you skive off?'

Cally jerked her thumb towards Birdie. 'No, my err...'

ONE NICE DAY IN LOVELY BAY

'Right.' Alastair gestured around and made a funny laughing snort sound. 'It's so quaint in here. Love it. Nice and simple. Good to have a little job in here to pass the time, eh?'

Cally bristled. He wasn't even being knowingly condescending which made it so much worse. She flicked the switch to neutral. 'Yup.'

'Next time, maybe. Anyway, what have you been up to? As you know, I've been away here and there while you've been gallivanting all over the place, I hear.' Alastair smiled kindly. 'I needed to have a bit of a break. Logan was telling me about the show you two went to. I'd really like to see that one. I imagine it must have been quite a new experience for you. Did you understand much of it?' Alastair squinted.

Cally felt her cheeks flush with a mix of embarrassment and indignation at his question assuming she might not have appreciated the show. Did she understand it? 'I err, I did. The performance was incredible.'

'Ah, yes, good, glad to hear it. Logan said it was fabulous but that it was very busy in town.'

Birdie finished with her customer and approached the counter as Cally replied. 'It was very busy, yes.'

Birdie held up a little box and wiggled it in Alastair's direction. 'Prescription?'

Alastair turned his attention to Birdie and smiled. 'Afternoon Birdie. You're looking well.'

'I am. Busy!'

As Birdie handled Alastair's prescription, Cally slipped back into the pharmacy area and out the back, her heart pounding and her mind reeling. Alastair's words had struck a nerve, multiplying the doubts that had been plaguing her about Logan and her feelings that he was from a different world to her. She busied herself with boxes, trying to push away the nagging feelings of inferiority and irritation by Alastair's assumptions.

Alastair's face kept floating through her thoughts. His

comments about the "quaint" chemist niggled her no end. An image of the box at the show with its red plush seats burned in her brain. She slammed a few things around and sighed repeatedly. Alastair's little visit had left her thoroughly deflated. She was not in a good place at all. The worst was yet to come.

38

Oh my, how spectacular the crash was when Cally de Pfeffer came hurtling back to earth after months of being in the honeymoon period of dating Logan. There was no balloon basket softly gliding onto land, that was for sure, as she hit the ground and slammed back down with an almighty bang.

It was a couple of weeks after Cally had chatted to Alastair in the chemist. Cally had continued to see Logan and he hadn't put a foot wrong. She loved being with him, but she'd pulled back a little bit emotionally. She'd spent nearly all her spare time with Logan and they'd been on more dates of a similar ilk to that of the show. She'd stayed at the cottage at the manor, he'd been at her little flat lots and overall they'd been in and out of each other's pockets all the time. Despite that, inside, Cally had found herself doing way too much overthinking. She'd overanalysed the fact they were from the opposite sides of the tracks so much that she was not in a very good place.

In her head, not that she thought Logan had realised, she had come to the conclusion that it would never work out between them in the long run. Her insecurities and self-doubt had swallowed her whole, chewed her up a bit and spat her back out. She felt as if she was somehow back in the rotating tunnel. This time, though, the tunnel wasn't just turning; it was spinning and turning at high speed. Inside the tunnel she was falling, falling, falling. The ground wasn't even close.

Despite how she felt about Logan, as time marched on, it was getting more and more obvious that they were from two very different places. As weeks passed it became more and more evident, if only to her, that that would never change. As she'd sat in the cottage at the manor one evening, she'd looked around and felt out of her depth and hadn't been able to stop obsessing that she wasn't good enough. She realised that in Logan's world she mostly felt discombobulated nearly all of the time. At first, she'd loved it when it had been new and exciting when he'd introduced her to things. Things like the hot air balloon, posh restaurants, dinner at the manor, shows… but as the weeks had gone on, the glaring differences between their two sides of the fence felt as if they were screaming at her twenty-four-seven.

The discrepancies to her seemed stark but rather than the big fancy outings it was actually more the tiny little things that accentuated their differences further. Things like the way he'd paid so much for two programs in the theatre. She'd thought to herself at the time that she would never have bought one program, let alone two. The same thing had happened when he'd ordered drinks in the box. To Cally, the drinks had seemed vastly overpriced. Then, there was the whole box itself. Who even pays for a four-seat box for two? She couldn't quite get her head around *any* of it. She'd kept going over the cost of the seats in the box and the programs and how she could have squirrelled that sort of money away for her fund to get herself a flat of her own. Buying her own property was the crux of her life. Everything else felt frivolous and when Logan, in her opinion, appeared to fritter money away, to her if felt borderline obscene.

The more she thought about it, the worse she felt. Was she

ever going to be able to keep up? Not that she needed to, and it didn't appear as if Logan cared or even noticed, but for her, it was an issue. She'd looked up the price of the box on the theatre website and had nearly fallen off her chair. At the time, she'd been on a break from the customer service retail job where she earned not much more than minimum wage. The box had been many, many minimum wage hours. She hadn't liked how that made her feel at all.

She'd realised at that moment that the gap between him and her was huge. It had slapped her in the face and made her question what in the world she thought she was up to.

Cally was on her way to a drink with Eloise and, as she waited for the train to pull into the station at her destination, her mind swirled with doubts and insecurities about herself. The more she thought about her relationship with Logan, the more she felt like she was drowning in a sea of uncertainty. She just couldn't shake the feeling that she was utterly out of her depth. She nodded to herself. There was only one thing to do; she was going to have to call it off. She downed the rest of a carton of blackcurrant and dumped it in the bin by the train door, certain that it was the only thing she could do. As she walked out of the station and headed for the wine bar she'd arranged to meet Eloise in, she decided she'd break up with Logan before it went much further. Better to call it off now and hedge her bets. No need to cry over spilt milk in the future. In the long run, she'd be better off on her own.

Arriving at the bar, Eloise was sitting with a glass of wine when Cally pushed open the door and walked in. Eloise slipped off her stool and kissed Cally on the cheek. 'How are you?' Eloise was cheerful.

Cally was relieved to see her. 'Good. Great.' Cally didn't sound good or great.

Eloise signalled to the waiter for another glass of wine. Cally waited for him to pour it and then took a massive swig. Eloise raised her eyebrows. 'That good, eh?'

'I'm fine.'

'You seem stressed.'

'How did you pick that up so quickly?'

Eloise rolled her eyes. 'The voice thing, duh.'

'I thought I was so clever with that, too.'

'What's up?'

'I think I need to talk.'

Eloise's tone shifted to one of concern. 'You never say that. You always soldier on. What's going on? Is everything alright?'

Cally sighed, unsure of where to begin. 'It's Logan. No, it's not. It's me. Me and Logan. Me mostly.'

'Ahh, has the honeymoon shimmer started to wear off?'

Cally shook her head. *If only.* 'No, not quite. I just don't know if I can do it. I feel like I'm constantly out of my depth, and I'm starting to wonder if we're just too different. I have imposter syndrome like *all* the time.'

'You said that before.' Eloise acknowledged.

'It's getting to me.'

There was a pause. 'You can't keep comparing yourself to Logan. You're two different people with different backgrounds and experiences. That doesn't mean you're not good enough for him.'

'I can't help myself.'

'What's triggering this?'

'So many things. For example, remember ages ago when we went to the theatre? You should have seen the way he was spending money. The box alone cost a fortune, and he didn't even bat an eyelid. And then there were the programs and the drinks. I just can't imagine ever being able to afford something like that. I've watched the pennies *all* my life. It feels all wrong to me.'

'That's not his fault. I think you're being really unfair.'

'I know. I am well aware of that.'

'He likes you for who you are, not for how much money you have or don't have. If he wanted to be with someone who could match him pound for pound, he would be.'

Cally tried to let Eloise's words sink in, but it was as if she couldn't see what was what. 'I know, but I can't help feeling as if it will go wrong. Like he's going to wake up one day and realise that I'm not good enough for him, so I might as well put an end to it now.'

'I think you have a money block,' Eloise stated matter-of-factly.

'A what block?'

'I was reading about it the other day. We all have these blocks and stuff that keep us in our little boxes. Yours is obviously around money. You have a money block. It starts in your childhood.'

'Oh.'

'Yeah, and when they get triggered, they block you left, right and centre. You can't get over it because it is a block that was formed in your early days.'

'Tell me more.'

'I listened to a podcast about it. So, if you were always told money was scarce or that you couldn't afford anything, if and when you do have money or are around money, you'll have huge problems about it. I reckon that is precisely what you are feeling right now.'

Cally computed what Eloise had said. 'That is *exactly* what it feels like. As if it is a gigantic block.'

'Maybe your brain is blocked around the money and so you're projecting that onto Logan himself.'

'You're sounding very knowledgeable,' Cally joked.

'It just makes sense. He has done nothing wrong and you have no reason to feel like this about anything to do with him, so it makes sense that it's coming from somewhere else.'

The nagging voice continued to whine in Cally's ear. She shook her head. 'I keep finding myself thinking about the price of everything. Even little things, like when he came around with that huge bag of treats that week when I worked every day from 5 a.m. I couldn't help but think about how much it cost. He bought all the fancy stuff. I'm always own-brand. It's ridiculous how much I'm noticing the little things...'

Eloise was quiet for a moment. 'You have to remember two things: one, that Logan is *choosing* to spend money on you because he wants to share nice things with you, and two, he is *allowed* to have money. It's not a bad thing. I reckon you have a block about that, too. You're getting yourself all het up about things that just don't matter.'

'Since when did you become a money counsellor?' Cally laughed.

'Dunno.'

'I'd just convinced myself that I'm going to call it off with him.'

'For god's sake! From what you've told me, and how I've seen him with you, Logan is crazy about you. What is your problem?' Eloise was blunt. 'Sorry, not sorry, you're being really immature.'

'Am I?'

'Yes! Listen to yourself. You're going to dump a bloke who has not put a foot wrong because you think he wastes money. Come on, Cal, take a look at the writing on the wall.'

'It's not just the *actual* money.'

'What then?'

'Everything. His whole lifestyle.'

'Get over yourself.'

'Easier said than done.'

Eloise reassured her. 'You don't have to have it all figured out right away.'

Cally sighed, taking another sip of her wine as she mulled over Eloise's words. Doubt had taken root in her mind. 'It's so weird. I've never had this before. I just feel like I'm constantly second-guessing myself. Like I'm waiting for the other shoe to drop, for Logan to realise that I'm not the right fit for his world.'

Eloise swore. 'That's a load of old codswallop.'

Cally chewed her lip. 'I guess I'm just scared. Scared of getting hurt, of investing too much of myself in something that might not last.'

'Suck it up, buttercup. Just enjoy the ride.'

'Yeah, I guess I should.'

'Stop overthinking and I don't want to hear you say anything about the money again. I mean, really? You're complaining that the man who's walked into your life and is treating you like a queen has too much money! Said no one ever. Ever, ever, ever!'

Cally giggled. 'It's so weird.'

'No, you are being bloody weird. Get over it, Cal. I'm sorry, but just no.'

Cally nodded. She pushed the doubt down and thought about the way she felt when she was with Logan. The way everything else seemed to fade away when she was with him. How when she was with him she didn't have to worry about holding up the sky. How she just loved him.

39

Cally sat with a cup of hot blackcurrant and looked out over the little boats in Lovely Bay harbour. She was at Nina's place helping Nina organise some supplies that had arrived for Nina's business, A Lovely Organised Life.

As she sat staring at the water and the little ripples on the surface, she thought about Logan. If she was honest with herself, from her side of the fence, things had not been right since the date at the show. Although the show had been amazing and had opened her up to another world, there was no denying that she had been totally and utterly rattled by it right from the word go. From the moment she'd stood behind the woman with the designer shoes on the train to when she'd sat looking over the rows and rows of velvet chairs, observing people who clearly led a different life to hers, she'd felt a shift inside. She'd realised as she'd sat in her charity shop dress that, in the long run, it was never going to work between someone like Logan and someone like her.

Part of her also wondered why Logan liked her in the first place. In a strange, backward sort of thinking way, she wondered if there was something wrong with him that she didn't know about. Her self-esteem was low enough that self-doubt changed her thoughts and made her dream up ridiculous things.

She sighed and took a sip of her blackcurrant and watched as a few seagulls swooped down, skimming the surface of the water. Nina came out with a cup of tea in her hand and sat down on the bench. 'Yep, we needed a breath of fresh air. How nice is it out here?'

'Mmm.'

'Everything alright with you?'

Cally forced a smile and flicked the switch. 'Yes, just enjoying the view. It's beautiful here. I love where you live.'

Nina nodded. 'Me too. The harbour is one of the reasons I like this place so much.'

'Yeah, it's so nice.'

'You've seemed a bit lost in thought today. How are things? You've been working long hours the last few months, what with helping me at the manor and the chemist, etcetera. Tired?'

'Ahh, no.' Cally put her head to the side. 'Actually, yes, I am a bit.'

'Burning the candle at both ends.'

'I suppose I am. I'm focused on my savings plan as my main goal. Tiredness can wait.'

'Right, I get it.'

Cally made a non-committal noise. She very much doubted that Nina, with her large house on the harbour, small business, husband, and baby, got it or anywhere near it.

'Anything else up?'

Cally hesitated. 'Nothing, really. Just thinking about things.'

'Logan?'

Cally's eyes widened in surprise. 'How did you know?'

'Call it intuition. You've been a bit off. I noticed it when we were at the manor yesterday and he popped in to see you. Your vibe was off. Did something happen?'

Cally sighed again. 'No, nothing's happened. I don't think it's going to work between us. He's, I don't know, out of my league, I guess. It's as black and white as that. You know what it's like at the manor.'

Nina frowned. 'Don't say that. What makes you think that?'

Cally looked down at her hands. 'Everything, really.'

'Well, I didn't see that coming. I didn't get that impression at all from him.'

Cally nodded. 'I don't want to get hurt.'

'Fair enough.'

'I went out with Eloise. She told me to suck it up.'

'Right. Easier said than done.'

'She said most people would not be complaining.'

Nina sucked air in through her teeth. 'She has a point there.'

'Yup. She's known me for a very long time. She says it how it is.'

Nina nodded and took a sip of her tea. 'Does he know how you feel?'

'I don't think so. It's all in my head.'

'We do like to overthink things. My first husband used to say I might think my own head off one day.'

Cally pressed her lips together. 'Do you miss him?'

Nina nodded. 'Oh yes. Every single day. I think I *always* will.'

'Aww. Sorry.'

'It's fine. I'm better now.'

'Better?'

'Yeah. I used to miss him so much that it made me ill and I was constantly sad. Now I miss him, but I'm happy. I don't mean happy he's not here. It's tricky to explain. I talk to him sometimes and it helps. Don't tell anyone that, though. I don't want to get carted off.'

Cally chuckled. 'Your secret's safe with me.'

'Thing is Cal. Not being funny, but yesterday when Logan popped in it reminded me of Andrew, well, Andrew and I.

Obviously, I wasn't going to say anything. I'm sure you don't want to know that your new love interest reminded me about my dead husband.' Nina smiled.

Cally wrinkled her nose up in question. 'Really? How?'

'You see, when Logan came in, it threw me a bit. I was suddenly right back standing beside Andrew. Andrew was looking at me with that same look Logan had on his face. Andrew used to look at me *exactly* the way I've seen Logan look at you. If I'm honest, it spooked me a bit.'

'Right.'

'I'd be holding onto that.'

40

Cally was up very early and cradling her hands around a mug of milky coffee. She'd sat on the balcony and watched the sun come up just behind the lighthouse and had enjoyed the calm of a Lovely Bay sunrise. With a whole day off, she'd intended to start her morning with a long walk to the marshes to try and clear her head and decide what she was going to do about the Logan situation. She'd thought that the marshes might work some magic on her ridiculously fuddled brain. Something needed to. Nancy had told her that seeing otters would most probably be part of the equation if she stopped for a bit on one of the labyrinth of boardwalks in the marshes. She wondered if otters would be able to talk some sense into her head. Worth a go and free at half the price.

She looked out over Lovely to assess the weather. The sky was blue, not really a cloud to be seen and a warm day with high temperatures had been predicted by the weather forecasters. The south coast of England had bikinis and factor 30 at the ready. Still, there was a tiny tad of an early morning chill lingering in the air. After closing the balcony door and making a warm blackcurrant in a travel cup, Cally popped on her trainers, grabbed Logan's jumper that had been hanging on the back of the door, and popped it over her head. In cut-off denim shorts, the jumper skimmed down to the top of her legs as she made her way down the steep stairs and out onto the High Street. Grabbing a handful of Logan's jumper, she inhaled the Logan smell and wondered what she was going to do about the conundrum between him and her. Not that he knew that there was one, but to her, it was all too evident.

With hardly a soul about and the sun shining, she decided not to bother with the marshes and headed for the bay itself. As she arrived, she stood on the promenade for a bit, looking down over the sand. There weren't many people around at all, just one solitary stripy umbrella right in the middle of the beach with a couple of towels underneath it, ready for a warm sunny day. Cally was surprised there weren't more locals up and about, but things were quiet and still – so still that it even seemed as if the sea itself was quiet, with no boats and not many seagulls. Even they were still asleep. Cally inhaled the fresh air, revelled in the downtime and continued to think about her problem.

She mulled over fate, sliding doors, and any other thing it happened to be called and wondered about Logan and her and if fate had played a hand. Had it all been meant to be? Had someone up there looked down on her and said that he and she were supposed to meet? She went through all the occasions. It seemed that way perhaps: the bag bottom episode on the boat, Nina asking her to work at the manor, Nina indeed getting the job at the manor in the first place, the speakeasy, the pub when she'd dropped her phone. Was it all perhaps a sliding door of happenstance or something of a similar ilk? And if it had been fate that had worked its hand and pushed the two of them together, why was Cally wondering and questioning it so much?

Why was she making such a mountain out of a molehill? She

knew why – it was the little nagging voice of self-doubt that had always lived in her head. Sometimes in her life, the nagging voice had been dormant, lying in a corner of her brain. When she'd been doing her degree or fully in the midst of caring, it hadn't had the time or energy to be up and about. But it had always been there, lurking in the shadows. Now, with a bit more time on its hands, it was more than evident. In fact, it was enjoying itself way too much. It had decided to dance around and jig in front of her, telling her that someone like her didn't deserve someone like Logan. She hated it, but for some reason, she couldn't get it to stop. The little dancing, jigging character was a pain in the proverbial. Asking her just quite who she thought she was. That there was no way she and Logan could ever make it long-term – someone like Logan just wouldn't stay with someone like her. Why would Cally even bother wasting her time? She really should just leave it, keep in her lane, put her head down, stay in the same place and go back to holding up the sky.

As she passed an ice cream kiosk completely clad in pale pink and white stripes, her brain continued to whirl. That in itself was part of the problem—the old spinning of the noddle that wouldn't let it go. There were just too many thoughts, too much of the time. As if they were connected to a tight, raw knot right in the centre of her chest that simply wouldn't give up and unravel. The knot clung on wanting to continue with bothering to hold up the sky.

Cally ambled along in a world of her own, not really sure about where she was going, just strolling along by the sea, watching here and there as Lovely Bay began to wake up to a beautiful day. She pulled the neck of Logan's jumper over her mouth and nose and cuffed the sleeves over her wrists. She loved how it felt on her – heavy, thick, and expensive – as it scraped underneath her shorts. And safe, that was it, yes, that too. She took a swig of her blackcurrant cordial, spotted a couple with a dog who was chasing a ball on the beach in the very far distance, and followed the path along the shore. Lovely was showing off and basking in the early morning sun. All around her felt calm and easy; she wished she felt the same.

She strolled along for ages, looking up at a huge blue sky stretching away as far as the eye could see. Just as she was walking in the direction of a row of benches adjacent to what she realised was the old pier she'd seen on the balloon flight, she did a double-take as she saw someone who looked similar to Logan further down on the other side of the walkway. Squinting and looking closer, she realised that it was indeed him. She shook her head as her heart hammered. Another sliding door? Could the whole of Lovely Bay hear the sound of her heart exploding as he came further into view?

She went to turn around, not sure whether she actually wanted to bump into him, with her head jumbled with emotions. Maybe she'd just stay where she was. She watched him cross the road and stand by the pier for a few minutes. He chatted to the couple she'd seen with the dog who'd just come up from the beach. Her heart jumped as he ran his fingers through his hair. All sorts of memories flushed through her brain – how she'd felt when she was standing in the street when he'd first kissed her, under the trees on the bench on top of the hill overlooking Lovely Bay, all the times he'd stayed the night. How she'd loved waking up next to him instead of being woken up by the alarm on her grandma's bed. How she'd loved hearing him in the shower in the mornings before he went off to work, how he'd made her a cup of tea when she'd stayed in bed.

She kept walking, and before she knew it, she was standing beside him. He turned, frowned, beamed, slipped his hand in hers, and nodded out in the direction of the sea. 'Hey! I didn't think you'd be up yet.'

'Hi.'

'I was up early for the horses and thought it would be nice down here.'

Cally smiled and flicked the switch. He had no idea what she was feeling inside. 'Me too. My body clock always wakes for the shifts and I found myself wide awake.'

'I'm actually on my way to you, but I didn't want to wake you if you'd slept in, seeing as you've got the day off. I thought we could go for breakfast. What a gorgeous day. That looks nice.' Logan pointed to the same lone beach umbrella Cally had seen when she'd first passed it going the other way.

'It does.'

For a few seconds, both of them stood looking out at the waves. Logan squeezed Cally's hand. She wished they could just stay there forever, just him and her, their hands holding, watching the waves and the huge sky on a loop that never came to an end.

'Nice jumper, by the way.' Logan gestured to the travel cup. 'Blackcurrant cordial?'

'Yep.'

'How about we get an umbrella and set up down there like that? Spend the day on the beach.'

Cally didn't say anything.

'Cal?'

'Sorry, yes.'

'I'll phone the deli, get them to make up a picnic for us. We can pick it up in a bit.'

Cally squirmed as the little voice yelled in her ear. *Phoning the deli to get them to make up a picnic! Really???* 'You see, there's something I need to tell you. You and me.'

Logan frowned and went to speak. Cally held her hand up and didn't let him speak. 'We need to talk about us.'

'Us?'

'Yeah. We're from completely different worlds'

'And?'

'I just don't think it will work.'

'Work? Sorry, what? What are you going on about?'

'You, me, the manor, horses, shows, tickets and the picnic thing. It's just...'

'What?'

'All of it. Hot air balloons, fancy restaurants, cottages on estates, big gates...'

'Blackcurrant, you're not making any sense.'

Cally looked at Logan looking at her, clearly not having a clue what she was harping on about. 'I'm not like you, Logan, and your family with the manor and your staff. Get it?'

'Really? I didn't notice that when I was clambering up the steepest stairs ever to a tiny flat with a ceiling beam I always bump my head on in the bedroom. Or when I had to squeeze around the bathroom door as it knocked against the bath. Or when I watched my girlfriend drag herself out of bed at 5 a.m. to go work on her laptop.'

Henry-Hicks was doing well.

'My point exactly.'

'What are you saying?'

'I'm saying we're from different sides of the tracks.' There it was out there. Cally turned to face Logan fully, her heart pounding as she met his confused, concerned gaze. She continued blurting out words. 'I care about you a lot. Like, really, a lot. More than I ever thought possible. But I can't shake this feeling that we're just *too* different, that our worlds are too far apart for this to work in the long run.'

Logan shook his head. 'Shut up, Cal. None of that stuff matters to me. I don't care about your flat or your job or any of that. I care about *you*.'

Well done, Henry-Hicks. Nicely played.

Cally shook her head. 'But it *does* matter, Logan. It matters to your family, to the people in your world. I see the way they look at me, like I'm not good enough, like I don't belong.'

'Well, that's easy then. If that's your problem.'

'What? Easy? How is that easy?'

'They don't get a say in this. This is about you and me, nobody else. And as far as I'm concerned, you're the best thing that's ever happened to me.'

'Oh, right. Okay.'

Logan put his arm around Cally. She breathed in the Logan smell. She watched the sky crash around her in big fat slices of Lovely blue. 'What if we're just too different, too far apart in our experiences and our expectations?'

'It's not a drama. We'll figure it out. That's what you do when you love someone.'

'You love me?'

Logan nodded. 'Duh. Of course, I do.'

'Oh, right, I thought…'

'Do you really think I mess about with hot air balloons, blackcurrant cocktails and seeing ridiculous shows I don't give a stuff about for any old one?'

Cally coughed and frowned. 'I thought, you err, you just did things like that.'

'Right, okay then. Of course, I do. I ride balloons and sit in Royal boxes all the time just for fun. Every day of the week.

Cally giggled. 'Ha.'

'So, are you in then or not, Blackcurrant? Because, to be quite honest, if you're not, I'll jog on right now. It might save me a few bob in balloons.'

Cally beamed and raised her eyebrows. 'I'm in. Henry-Hicks I am so very much in.'

'Good and if you don't mind can you stop doing that weird voice now?'

Cally smiled as Logan squeezed her hand. She closed her eyes for a second and as she opened them revelled in looking around at the fallen sky. She gazed out at the bay and looked forward to the picnic and Logan and simply loving him. It had finally arrived. She'd got it in the bag. It was right there laid out in front of her. One nice day.

Order Cally's next part.
ONE SWEET DAY IN LOVELY BAY

ONE SWEET DAY IN LOVELY BAY

Welcome to LOVELY BAY - a heartwarming, feel-good, small-town story with romance, community and friendship set in a to-die-for British seaside town perched just off the English south coast. Sweet, small-town romantic women's fiction you'll adore.

Cally has settled down quite nicely after her gorgeous ride in Lovely Bay. She's feeling all the life feels, and that old sky she'd been holding up for like ever is no longer there (at least she hopes it isn't). Everything is swoon-worthy as she plans to take a few new paths here and there —that is until she discovers something she hadn't seen coming, and it knocks our Cally for six.

Full of Polly's amazing setting descriptions that will whisk you off to your happy place, settle in as Polly weaves her magic romance wand and the ups and downs in Cally's world keep on coming.

An utterly gorgeous romantic comedy that will make you laugh, cry and definitely continue to fall completely in love… and not just with the romance but with Cally and with life in a small town tucked down on the British coast.

READ MORE BY POLLY BABBINGTON

(Reading Order available at AuthorPollyBabbington.com)

One Nice Day in Lovely Bay
    One Sweet Day in Lovely Bay

The Summer Hotel Lovely Bay
    Wildflowers at The Summer Hotel Lovely Bay
    Seashells at The Summer Hotel Lovely Bay

The Old Ticket Office Darling Island
    Secrets at The Old Ticket Office Darling Island
    Surprises at The Old Ticket Office Darling Island

Spring in the Pretty Beach Hills
    Summer in the Pretty Beach Hills

The Pretty Beach Thing
    The Pretty Beach Way
    The Pretty Beach Life

READ MORE BY POLLY BABBINGTON

Something About Darling Island
   Just About Darling Island
   All About Christmas on Darling Island

The Coastguard's House Darling Island
   Summer on Darling Island
   Bliss on Darling Island

The Boat House Pretty Beach
   Summer Weddings at Pretty Beach
   Winter at Pretty Beach

A Pretty Beach Christmas
   A Pretty Beach Dream
   A Pretty Beach Wish

Secret Evenings in Pretty Beach
   Secret Places in Pretty Beach
   Secret Days in Pretty Beach

Lovely Little Things in Pretty Beach
   Beautiful Little Things in Pretty Beach
   Darling Little Things

The Old Sugar Wharf Pretty Beach
   Love at the Old Sugar Wharf Pretty Beach
   Snow Days at the Old Sugar Wharf Pretty Beach

Pretty Beach Posies
   Pretty Beach Blooms
   Pretty Beach Petals

OH SO POLLY

Words, quilts, tea and old houses...

My words began many moons ago in a corner of England, in a tiny bedroom in an even tinier little house. There was a very distinct lack of scribbling, but rather beautifully formed writing and many, many lists recorded in pretty fabric-covered notebooks stacked up under a bed.

A few years went by, babies were born, university joined, white dresses worn, a lovely fluffy little dog, tears rolled down cheeks, house moves were made, big fat smiles up to ears, a trillion cups of tea, a decanter or six full of pink gin, many a long walk. All those little things called life neatly logged in those beautiful little books tucked up neatly under the bed.

And then, as the babies toddled off to school, as if by magic, along came an opportunity and the little stories flew out of the books, found themselves a home online, where they've been growing sweetly ever since.

I write all my books from start to finish tucked up in our lovely old Edwardian house by the sea. Surrounded by pretty bits and bobs, whimsical fabrics, umpteen stacks of books, a plethora of lovely old things, gingham linen, great big fat white sofas, and a big old helping of nostalgia. There I spend my days spinning stories and drinking rather a lot of tea.

From the days of the floral notebooks, and an old cottage locked away from my small children in a minuscule study logging onto the world wide web, I've now moved house and those stories have evolved and also found a new home.

There is now an itty-bitty team of gorgeous gals who help me with my graphics and editing. They scheme and plan from their laptops, in far-flung corners of the land, to get those words from those notebooks onto the page, creating the magic of a Polly Bee book.

I really hope you enjoy getting lost in my world.

Love

Polly x

AUTHOR

Polly Babbington

In a little white Summer House at the back of the garden, under the shade of a huge old tree, Polly Babbington creates romantic feel-good stories, including The PRETTY BEACH series.

Polly went to college in the Garden of England and her writing career began by creating articles for magazines and publishing books online.

Polly loves to read in the cool of lazing in a hammock under an old fruit tree on a summertime morning or cosying up in the winter under a quilt by the fire.

She lives in delightful countryside near the sea, in a sweet little village complete with a gorgeous old cricket pitch, village green with a few lovely old pubs and writes cosy romance books about women whose life you sometimes wished was yours.

Follow Polly on Instagram, Facebook and TikTok
@PollyBabbingtonWrites

AUTHOR

AuthorPollyBabbington.com

Want more on Polly's world? Subscribe to Babbington Letters

Printed in Dunstable, United Kingdom

70168804R00185